Trees

Sam Smith

WORDCATCHERpublishing

Trees

© 2020 Sam Smith
Source images supplied by Adobe Stock
Cover design © David Norrington

The Author asserts the moral right to be identified as the author of this work. All rights reserved. This book is protected under the copyright laws of the United Kingdom. No part of this book may be reproduced, stored in a retrieval system, or transmitted in any form or by any means, electronic, electrostatic, magnetic tape, mechanical, photocopying, recording or otherwise, without the written permission of the Publisher.

This is a work of fiction and any similarity to real people (living or deceased) or events is entirely coincidental.

British Library Cataloguing in Publication Data.
A catalogue record for this book is available from the British Library.

Published in the United Kingdom by Wordcatcher Publishing Group Ltd
www.wordcatcher.com, Tel: 02921 888321
Facebook.com/WordcatcherPublishing

First Edition: 2020
Print edition ISBN: 97817894222054
Ebook edition ISBN: 97817894223167

Category: Fiction / Eco-Fiction

Versions of some of the haiku were published in the following magazines: At Last, The Frogmore Papers, Moonstone, New Hope International, Northwords, Purple Patch, TIME HAIKU and Weyfarers.

My thanks too to Sir Tony Cunningham, MP, for keeping me up to date on changes to forestry legislation.

One

Her eyes were round and of such a dark brown that they seemed to have no definable centre. He hadn't known where to focus. Not knowing exactly where to focus had made him feel shifty-eyed and so, by association, he had felt somehow guilty and feeling guilty he had wanted to make recompense, to please her.

But he couldn't please her, had to force himself to say, "Six months. Yes."

He said this sitting at his desk, black keyboard and lit screen before him.

The young woman, whose gaze he was doing his best to meet and to avoid was sitting on the edge of the chair to the side of his desk.

He looked away from the screen, braved her eyes again, and said to please her, "It's only the roughest of estimates though."

From her records he knew that he was only three years older than her.

"I wanted to know, safely," she explained the purpose of her visit, "near enough how much longer I have."

"Safely?"

"While I'm still me."

"You mean physically well?"

The woman gave the slightest of nods and, as if instructing him, glanced towards the screen.

"Ah, yes." He turned gratefully back to the screen. "I see what you mean. Yes, you should be you for another six months. Quite possibly a year."

"That's what she reckoned." The eyes were again locked on his. "Nothing else there?"

On the screen was the latest letter from the hospital consultant. He slowly scrolled to its end, knew that the consultant would have sent the patient a lay version of the letter.

Before opening his door and calling her name down the

corridor he had looked back through her medical records. She wasn't registered as his patient. He was but one of several GPs in this practice, a large polyclinic in town, this suburban annexe a newly built one-storey block. Her GP was on long-term sick leave prior to retirement.

The consultant's letter had been sent two weeks back. The patient had made this appointment only yesterday, had said that she didn't mind which doctor she saw, whoever happened to be available. "In practice these days," an older colleague had told him, "you're deluded if you think the individual GP matters to the patient. To be seen straightaway and leave with a prescription is all that most patients want."

Just once before he had seen this young woman – for a scald gone septic. She had left the routine timed-session with a prescription for antibiotics and a salve. For this appointment, having been warned by the receptionist and having read the consultant's letter, he had allowed more time.

He didn't remember her eyes from the scald. Maybe last time he had the injury to examine, this time only her face to look at. Even so, apart from the eyes, hers was an unremarkable face. Possibly if she had been tall and slim the eyes would have made her round face conventionally beautiful. As it was she was short and she could, without insult, although she would not have welcomed the description, be described as, if not fat, stout. Indeed she herself, when dissatisfied with her changing room reflection, called herself 'dumpy', her legs 'stumpy'.

He swivelled around from the screen.

"That's all there is," he said with an almost apologetic shrug.

She was quiet a moment, then, "Thank you," she said.

If she had been going to weep now was the time. But there was no sign of tears: all that she had wanted from him had been last ditch confirmation. Pulling her peppery-green jacket around her she started to stand.

"Anything we can do…" The doctor attempted a smile. "At any time. We're only a phone call away."

By this time she had reached the door handle, nodded to him – she was not a person given to easy expression – and she left the room.

* * *

The corridor wasn't that long, was painted beige, the carpet a tough brown. In the waiting room, also beige, the carpet was a tough blue. Hard chairs lined three of the walls, a reception desk inset into the fourth. In the middle of the waiting room were two back-to-back short rows of chairs.

From this room all that was visible outside – through the high strip of window – was the top of a winter-battered palm between two cropped leylandi. Both of the leylandii, having once been allowed unrestricted growth, had been severely cut back to mostly dead underwood.

The young woman came to a stop before the plump knees of an older woman sitting alone in the middle row. Looking up the older woman said, "That it?" and she laid a magazine on the chair beside her. In the corner play area a toddler was talking to himself as he put plastic bricks into the back of a plastic lorry. A pale tired father looked on.

As she stood the older woman glanced over to the reception desk: "Another appointment?"

The young woman gave a sharp shake of the head, and waited while the older woman gathered up her coat and handbag. Both women called out 'Goodbye' to the receptionist as they left. The receptionist was on the phone, didn't hear them.

Two

Cupresscyparis leylandii is a spontaneous hybrid of the Monterey and Nootka cypress, the most popular variety of which – in the UK – is Haggerston Grey, renowned for its vigorous growth. That vigorous growth, reaching two storeys high in as many years and thus becoming the frequent cause of neighbourly disputes – theft of sunlight principally – has seen the planting of leylandii forbidden in some house deeds and covenants and banned retrospectively by quite a few housing associations. If kept trimmed and topped, however, leylandii can make a near solid and most effective hedge. Too often, though, one forgetful year and it is let go.

My own dislike of leylandii is their stick-dry interiors, as dead and deserted as an unvisited mausoleum. Pulling aside their branches I get the feeling that, despite their waxy evergreen exteriors, and along with many other of the cypress family, they are dying from the inside out. These days of course leylandii hedges could indeed be dying, the dead parts being due to the leylandii aphid.

* * *

The palm, *cordyline australis*, is of New Zealand origin where it is known, because of its evergreen lanceolate foliage, as the Majestic Cabbage Tree.

The *cordyline* comes from the Latin *Kordyle*, club, that name coming from the shape of the palm's root.

Sold by nurseries as frost-hardy, with claims that the palm can withstand temperatures as low as -8°C even in the soft winters of southern counties, the Majestic Cabbage Tree does still fall victim to heavy snow falls, the crown suffering damage. Not necessarily fatal: come spring the palm may well put out fresh shoots from base or trunk. That is if the Majestic Cabbage Tree is let live that long. Because, come spring, one does occasionally catch sight of a suburban front garden with a palm that has all the appearance of being wholly dead. From khaki bottom to top the bedraggled palm looks like nothing more than a thick-handled and very dead mop.

Those sheltered palms that do survive English winters with full foliage come summer can produce a spray of cream florets which yfair burst from just below the crown, their fulsome scent as drenched sweet as a mouthful of Arab pastries.

Three

I'm writing all this down by way of an explanation. To explain to myself as much as to anyone else.

And I have a lot to explain, all muddled up inside my head and body, image atop memory with thoughts, suspicions, stomach lurches, trembling hands, sudden deep breaths, doubts recurring, frowned at and puzzled on. And I'm not sure what order all this should be in.

When I sat down to start this ordering I saw it taking the form of my explaining the ins and outs of the past few years as if to a close friend. A kitchen table tête-à-tête over a fine china tea set. Except that I don't have a fine china tea set nor any friends that close. Certainly none that I'd go to the bother of explaining myself to.

The writing was easy enough to think of doing. The only way I could get started though was as if I saw myself as somebody else writing about two other people. Not that I've written that much, but already it seems that just that small amount needs me to explain it further.

Why, for instance, did I start with that particular visit to that particular Health Centre/Polyclinic/what you will? It certainly wasn't Hazel's first visit there. Nor was it by a long chalk the first waiting room I'd been left sitting in, flicking through magazines and avoiding eye contact.

So why did I start in that Health Centre?

Was it because Hazel had been pale that day, her face rigid, a determined look about her? Like when she was eight in that gym competition she had no chance of winning, knew she'd look a fool but had been determined to see it through.

Or is that one doctor visit at the forefront because in the beige ordinariness of that Health Centre the unwilling repetition of the prognosis put Hazel's premature death beyond question?

* * *

Hazel's first visits to the medical profession had begun anywhere between a year and eighteen months before. Those early appointments had been for flu-like symptoms that wouldn't go away. Then came the persistent stomach cramps and debilitating headaches. Got so that Hazel felt that the doctors didn't believe her and had her down as a hypochondriac.

Which was when she came to me: beyond miserable, wretched and with hardly the energy to be tearful. I knew my daughter. Her pain, her distress, did not have imaginary causes. One locum had even suggested that she 'seek counselling.'

I went with her to her doctor's, not mine. And this doctor, all-wise, all-knowing, had Hazel and I look angrily to one another.

Smiling sweetly at mother and daughter, this 'family doctor' had said that possibly, at Hazel's age, these complaints might be something that I, her mother, had gone through.

"Hardly," I told that smug female GP, "I'm her adopted mother."

Which sounded odd every time I said it. As if baby Hazel had filled in all the forms, had been put through the interviews, that she had cleaned the house top to bottom before every remotely connected official had come to assess her eligibility to adopt Ian and me.

I probably overreacted that day in the surgery, maybe saw my chance, having wrong-footed the doctor, to strike home. I'm not, even when unprovoked, in the habit of suffering fools. And that doctor was the type anyway who got me on the aggressive-defensive. There she was all tall and blue-eyed, serene and unrummaged. While I know myself to be a flustered and red-cheeked frump. On our way in, looking for a parking space, Hazel had pointed out this doctor's hardtop sports car. Mine was a secondhand hatchback.

I was more than pumped up for a fight. And my mother-hen hostility certainly had that over-tailored GP taking heed. Bloods were taken, even a DNA swab; and I delivered urine and stool samples to the surgery the following day.

A week or so later the test results led to Hazel being referred to a specialist. Which was when Hazel got told that she had a rare genetic condition. That specialist said that, so far as he had been able to find out, there was no known cure, as yet. Probably because it was such a rare condition.

He told Hazel that not every female child inherited the full condition from their mother. Not every mother with that DNA died from the condition, some were just carriers. Did Hazel have any sisters? A sister big-hearted enough to undergo surgery on her behalf? If so a bone marrow transplant might – such a treatment had worked with similar genetic conditions – might allow her to live to a 'happy old age'.

I knew as part of the adoption process the name of Hazel's birth mother, but not whether Hazel had any birth-siblings. Ian and I had been told at the time of the adoption that Hazel had been an only child. What I didn't know was if her birth mother had subsequently produced any sisters.

Hazel hadn't wanted me to go with her on that first visit to see the hospital specialist. At that time, despite my having accompanied her as Rottweiler to her GP, Hazel had seen herself as an independent adult perfectly capable of dealing with grown-up affairs. And I had long got over the feeling of being shut out of her life, was happy to let her decide the ground rules for how often we met as adults. She called in on us pretty near every other Sunday, Christmases she always spent with us, summer holidays sometimes with Kevin's family, sometimes a package holiday just the two of them. I had my own life, problems and plans of my own, wasn't living through her.

Until this of course.

Hazel didn't even come to me straight from the hospital, phoned me the evening of the following day, which must have been a Friday because it was the Saturday afternoon that she came over. I'd had to hurriedly get one of the girls to fill in for me at the café. Although Hazel hadn't been alarmist – she had a distrust of melodrama – she had said that it was important, that she wanted to see both Ian and I together. Insisting on us being a pair, I had expected her to come with Kevin. Yet she arrived on her own.

Ian had been tetchily put out, having had to cancel a ride with a friend to be there. And then, as if contradicting his grumpiness, he wept when Hazel told us the prognosis.

"Oh, Dad, don't," Hazel said, and it was she who had to comfort him. Which had me clamping my mouth shut: my tearing into Ian then would not have helped Hazel.

Because by that time Ian and I were no longer living together. He had only been in the house on sufferance, at Hazel's request (she had phoned him); and then he had been wondering beforehand if – Ian could only think within the parameters of convention, and despite knowing of her many visits of late to the doctor – if her 'announcement' was to have been news of pregnancy or 'wedding bells'.

Paradoxically Hazel had that day seemed, she had certainly looked when she arrived, healthier than she had for months. Which in hindsight was probably down to her knowing that the illness wasn't all in her imagination, that she definitely did have something wrong with her. Add to that the specialist having started her on painkillers appropriate to the pain and not just feeding herself Paracetamol.

But it was through that first visit to her GP how I became

involved in all that was to follow. Ian was obviously going to be of no help. And it was I who had to go searching through all the old paperwork and initialise the search for Hazel's birth mother.

"Who quite likely," the specialist said, "will have a one in four chance of having had this same condition and of not being any longer with us."

* * *

Almost straightaway I discovered that Hazel's birth mother, Moira, was dead, had died years before when Hazel was eight. According to the Social Services preliminary reports Moira had fallen victim to an abusive relationship, not to an inherited condition. Actual cause of death was listed as accidental drugs overdose, a mix of morphine and amphetamines. Even so, the specialist later told Hazel and I, Moira could have been just a carrier.

It took a couple more weeks of phone calls and visits to Social Services plate glass offices before we could be sure that Hazel had no birth-sisters at all, let alone one compatible with her blood type and capable of donating bone marrow. I spent two more weeks, possibly longer – it's hard to give up hope – looking to see if Hazel's birth mother had any sisters who might have had daughters still alive. I extended that search for birth-aunties. Found none.

At that time neither Hazel nor Ian shared my interest regards her birth mother. I wondered then if Hazel's birth mother, Moira, had only gone so wild so young because her own mother had died from the condition during Moira's early teens, and Moira had been left at home – I guessed – with a dodgy stepfather. According to Social Services' records Moira had certainly left home at fifteen to set up house with the first of her many boyfriends.

And there had been Ian and I, when offered baby Hazel for adoption, concerned over possible damage done to the foetus by the mother's – then only suspected – history of addiction. Consequences of maternal drug abuse we had been prepared for, had read books on; and we spent years on the lookout for signs – failure to thrive, intellectual incapacity, compulsive behaviours…

A genetic time bomb hadn't entered our considerations.

Meanwhile Hazel went for more examinations, agreed to student doctors studying her rare condition. I was present, hand-holding, a couple of times when doctors said, 'the character of the illness', as if 'the condition' was a person in its own right, as if my daughter had another person inhabiting her. She didn't. Made her out to be next best thing to a schizophrenic. She wasn't. She was a whole person, had her own history. The failing was mechanical, bits of her had gone wrong. Built-in obsolescence was kicking in early.

"The patient…" the hospital's pinstriped consultant said.

"My daughter's name is Hazel," I said from my chair beside her bed.

"Hazel…" the pinstripe smarmed across Hazel's smoothed covers at me.

Hazel wasn't as prickly defensive as me, and for the sake of rare others agreed to submit herself to various tests and treatments. Some of those treatments were painful, none to any good effect. The researchers were happy, nay relieved – they couldn't be held responsible – to admit to the limits of their knowledge. Hazel and I wished they knew more.

A medical science student researching his PhD and keen to relay his learning, told Hazel, "In times gone by the majority of working people died by the time they were forty. That is if they survived infancy. Mothers, young mothers, frequently died in childbirth. Female ancestors of yours who died in their early thirties would have been unremarkable. It is only now, with everyone living so much longer, that genetic conditions such as yours are being exposed."

By which time I had, the permanent visitor, become an expert on hospital people – receptionists, nurses, doctors, porters and patients. And I knew that among all those hurrying by professionals the parent – mother or father – with the child held on their lap, or numb and small beside them – that parent saw the whole child, knew where that child had come from, had hopes for what that child might become... Doctors looked for fresh symptoms, named 'the condition'.

* * *

One of Hazel's trial treatments had her throwing up, while a course of steroids made her so water retentive that she damn near sloshed as she walked. Waddled I should say. It all became so disfiguring and uncomfortable, and with no assurance that any of the treatments would cure her.

Which led Hazel to grab hold of the consultant's more accessible registrar. She only ever saw the consultant on his weekly rounds, and then only if there had been a change in her treatment regime. Holding onto the registrar's white sleeve she demanded to be taken off all medication.

"I don't want to die in this state."

The nervous registrar – I was scowling across the bed at him – although reluctant to lose the opportunity to test how Hazel's condition would respond to other as yet untried treatments, did sympathise. As did the consultant when fetched along to the ward. Leastwise the consultant started talking about Hazel's 'quality of life' as if it was his own bright idea. As another doctor, equally impotent, will later talk about giving my daughter 'a good death'.

Theirs wasn't a quick decision. A staff nurse was called over and the three talked for a good hour, considerations going round and about. Boiled down to the consultant having no option but to admit that what they had so far tried hadn't had any beneficial effects. When Hazel couldn't be persuaded to try any other treatments she was talked into taking medication to steady her occasional loss of balance, and was given a store of painkillers to keep by her. The pain at that time was mostly headaches.

The consultant wrote to Hazel's tailored GP. That GP, if

GPs do ever admit to being wrong (is that why so many doctors become politicians?) invited Hazel in to offer help howsoever she might need it.

That, however, was Hazel's last visit to that doctor. Because shortly afterwards Hazel moved in with me and transferred back to our 'family health practice', but where the chances of seeing the same GP twice in a row is now about the same as anywhere else in England.

Four

Ian hadn't been at all pleased when the garage's only available courtesy car had turned out to be a three-door hatchback. He had expressed his displeasure, but hadn't wanted to hang around the garage while they had transferred his bike carrier to the hatchback. Not that they had offered. Nor had he insisted: with his carrier being customised to his estate he doubted anyway that they would have been able to fit it.

Fortunately it was late summer, a warm Friday evening. Because, even with the rear seats folded down and the bike's front wheel removed, he still couldn't fully close the hatchback's rear door. He had to tie the door down with a stretch strap through the back wheel's spokes. Unfortunately the strap's elasticity meant that it gave just enough to have every bump and pothole banging and rattling the rear door.

For the first five miles at least he muttered on about the distracting rattle and about his having to have the side windows and the vents fully open so that the exhaust fumes didn't, caught in the airstream vortex, come swirling back into the car and have him falling asleep at the wheel.

If the garage didn't fix the electrical fault in his own car this time, or even if they did, he would certainly be making known his thoughts about this wholly inadequate courtesy car. Luckily his own car, if luck it was, was still under warranty.

Even so the garage had still been acting as if it had been doing him a favour.

For the past eight months he'd had this problem – indicate left and sometimes, only sometimes, the headlights came on and a dashboard warning flashed up saying gearbox failure. Or, just for a change, the warning was for engine overheating. But it didn't happen every time that he indicated left. In the garage they switched on the indicator and nothing happened. Four times they told him that there was no fault.

"We've run it through our diagnostics," he was told. "There is no fault."

"Yes there is," Ian puffed himself up to say, "and the fault is with your diagnostics."

Then one of the young mechanics had taken his estate out for a test drive and, lo and behold, when one time the young mechanic indicated left the headlights had come on and the dashboard had warned of the engine overheating.

The garage had only then got in touch with the manufacturer and had discovered – the chatty showroom receptionist had let slip to Ian – that quite a few of his model had this software problem. Going online Ian discovered that a batch of components were to blame and were being slowly replaced. But not by the original component manufacturer, who had gone bust. While the new supplier had encountered compatibility problems.

Ian was told by the garage that, now that they were aware of the cause, they wanted to thoroughly test his car before handing it back. They had made a big deal out of arranging this courtesy car for him.

This inappropriate courtesy car.

* * *

When Ian left the motorway, heading west, the sun was setting. He pulled both of the hatchback's visors down.

The bike track he was going to was in a steep wood. As there were going to be heats all of the Saturday, an early start was required. The semis and final were on Sunday.

Ian was aiming for a pre-booked Bed and Breakfast on the far side of the woods. And that had been a lucky last minute reservation. Racing weekends like this he usually unrolled a sleeping bag in the back of the estate: he told Hazel that sleeping in the car reminded him of those rained-through tents on camping holidays. The hatchback though was too short to sleep in: he would either have been uncomfortably curled up or had his legs hanging out the back.

He had been to this woodland track before, didn't need his satnav.

The road, in this countryside of water meadows and low hills, has several straight stretches and, where meandering streams ran under, some tight bends. On an early straight Ian changed down to swing out around a slow grain lorry. The hatchback's acceleration thrust him back in his seat, came as a surprise.

"Nippy little beast." Ian lifted his right eyebrow.

In his rear-view mirror Ian saw two cars also overtake the big metal box of the grain lorry. He thought he recognised a fellow biker in a maroon Ford, second car back, a mountain bike standing on its roof.

"C'mon beast," Ian said, and speeded up. The back door being open the exhaust gave a satisfying roar.

The car behind the car behind overtook it.

"You're on," Ian said, changed down into a bend by a small copse, came up behind a slow silver Fiat, and followed it out of that wooded bend to between fields again. He glanced across the top of the clipped hedgerows, took a chance and swung past the Fiat on a right hand bend and into a left. That would slow the maroon Ford.

Ian, leaning forward in his seat, came out of the long left hand bend and, as he accelerated away into the next straight, two cars came in the other direction. They would hold his pursuer behind the Fiat.

Just before Ian drove into the next long bend he saw the

silver Fiat way back emerging from the last bend, with the maroon Ford pulling out around it.

* * *

Winter water had damaged the roadside. Ian's glance to the rear-view mirror had steered the car closer towards the road verge. The hatchback's front wheel dropped into a soft ditch. Ian wrenched at the steering to free the wheel. The long ragged-edged pit pulled the tyre off. With the tyre gone the courtesy car shot across the road turning onto its side as it went. The thorn hedge on the far side tipped the car right over. Upside down, roof crumpling as it slid along the ground on the other side of the hedge, windscreen pieces spraying back inside the car, the weight of the engine tilting the car forwards, small bushes being torn aside, at 80 mph the car piled into a stand of Scots pine.

When car met tree, Ian was squashed and killed.

Five

Hawthorn, *crataegus monogyna*, also known as 'May' and 'Quickthorn', can be distinguished from its occasional hedgerow neighbour, Blackthorn, *prunus spinoza*, in that the hawthorn's blossom comes after its small lobed leaves. This creamy may blossom can lay heavy as snow along hawthorn's full-grown boughs. Blackthorn blossom on the other hand comes much earlier in the spring – in dotted sprays of white on its otherwise bare black branches.

Although the spines on the blackthorn are longer and more fearsome-looking it is the less prickly hawthorn that is mostly used in the making of hedgerows. Even though after a few years the hawthorn bushes do become leggy and leave gaps, the hawthorn can be cropped back to the base and, having been thus drastically lopped, a hawthorn hedge will become dense again within a couple of years. It has to be said, however, that such drastic and labour-intensive lopping rarely happens nowadays. Hydraulic flails being used to keep all hedges square and trimmed a hawthorn hedge very soon becomes all top growth, and from a distance looks like so many one-legged tables laid end to end.

Come autumn the hawthorn produces clusters of maroon berries, readily distinguished from the singularly spaced scarlet of rosehips. Both berries and hips provide winter sustenance for migrants such as fieldfares and redwings. And not only for the thrush family; those same berries and hips can be made into jellies and jams for human consumption. And there's plenty of them: older untrimmed hedgerows that time of year can be as florid as a boozer's jowls.

The winter fruit of the often straggly blackthorn, the blue-black sloes, have a more specialised application. They are used, along with almonds and sugar, in the making of sloe gin.

Where regular maintenance of hawthorn hedges has been abandoned, several fields merged into one say, those individual hawthorn trees that have survived browsing sheep will grow to about twenty feet high, their trunks usually twisted, and often with tufts of sheep's wool caught in their bark. Their shape and height will depend on the prevailing weather and how exposed their situation.

Prior to the Acts of Enclosure in the 1800s, when most pasture was common land, single hawthorns – their ancient trunks moss and lichen-coated – often marked the sites of local moots. After the Acts of Enclosure the easily rooted hawthorns were used to make mile upon mile of new hedgerows.

* * *

Scots pine, *pinus sylvestris,* is the slim cousin of the Lebanese cedar, *cedrus libani*.

Scots pine, as a native conifer, can be readily identified by its scaly lower bark, ovoid cones and blue-green foliage rising in near horizontal clouds around its newer pink bark towards its crown. A survivor of the Great Caledonian Forest, although the timber of the Scots pine is durable – it contains a natural preservative – and continues to be traded as 'redwood', most of its plantings in southern England during the last two centuries have been for decorative purposes only, creating romantic landscapes in the Walter Scott mode.

Six

Any death connected to you, no matter how remote the connection, how unlikely the cause of that death related to you, can nonetheless have you finding reasons to feel guilty, seem to have your mouth saying of its own accord, "If only I had done this, said that…"

I'm feeling my way into this explanation.

I knew Ian so well, have sat beside him in so many cars on so many journeys that it wasn't difficult to imagine the circumstances preceding the crash. It was guilt though that had me getting hold of the coroner's full report and so carefully weighing the evidence of the other drivers, deciphering the shorthand in the pathologist's report and the Traffic Officer's Road Traffic Accident Assessment.

Guilt even had me checking out the tree, who had planted it, and why there.

The Scots pine that brought Ian's life up short was one of several stands of Scots pine within a cotton king's long since disbanded estate. Planted for ornamental purposes on the short tongue of land between road and stream, the dozen trees where Ian crashed had also served to hide the grand house from the road.

I didn't tell Hazel but I drove out to the crash site one Tuesday. (Before the inquest that is: chronology is the very devil.) I thought I'd do the decent thing and leave a bunch of flowers. I took along string and scissors.

And that's not the real reason I went. The flowers were just, should anyone ask, my excuse for being there. Truth be told I didn't know why I was there. Seeking to be absolved? To find the evidence that would tell me that I'd had no part in his death?

I parked in a field gateway beyond the crash site and, ready to leap into the hedge if a car came, walked back to the bend. The fence hadn't been repaired, only a stretch of orange plastic webbing for me to step over – where it sagged between stakes. I noticed that the older broken branches in the hedge had been oxidised yellow, while the fresh breaks from Ian's crash were a clean white.

One upside-down wing of Ian's car had ploughed a single dark furrow to the tree, wilted leaves and twigs from the hedge scattered to either side. Where the car had hit the grey tree trunk it had gouged a deep gash – red-brown, unlike the hedge's white splintered branches. Above the wound, in among the trunk's alligator scales, were darker scars from previous crashes. These, taken with the older broken branches in the hedge, made this one dangerous corner. Which is what the signs on the approach to the bend had said.

These other wounds to the tree trunk had the bark edges rounding off and growing in to cover the exposed pith. On a neighbouring tree one ancient scar had become a prominent callus.

An arc of paint flakes around the mossy base of the tree were, I suddenly realised, the wrong colour for Ian's car. A puzzle instantly resolved by my remembering the courtesy car, recalling the messages left on his landline, the garage wanting to know when he was going to collect his car, fault repaired, if they could have their courtesy car back, needed it for another customer…

Another surprise was a wilted bunch of yellow-going-brown chrysanthemums already by the tree. Couldn't make out the message of the card, the ink had formed one large blue blob. My guess was that the bouquet had been for one of the previous crash victims.

I found myself, flowers lain beside the others, running

my fingertips over the neighbouring tree's callus and thinking back to Ian's driving. He had always driven fast and erratically, provoked to silliness by what he perceived as other drivers' breaches of road etiquette.

"Can we just get safely from A to B?" I used to, I confess, shout shrewishly at him. But I would be shouting because I had just been frightened by yet another near miss. And, even with Hazel in the car, still Ian would drive hunched over the steering wheel, always looking to overtake...

It was as if he cared what other drivers might think of his driving. Drivers never likely to be seen again. Yet still he would get drawn into motorway games of overtaking and cutting up. To prove what? To whom? And frightening himself in the process.

As passenger, to fill the travel void, I'd turn the radio on. He'd turn it off.

"Too distracting. Need to concentrate." Everyone and everything outside the car was an enemy, a threat to him.

When I drove, radio on, Ian slept.

* * *

I can't recall my exact states of mind as I drive. In fact I find it easier to think myself into other people's shoes than I do to relate what's been going on in my own size fives. Often I don't know why I do what I do, what I've done, can't say until years afterwards. If then. I overhear café customers say, "You know what I'm like..." I was fifty-seven the year that I wrote this and I still didn't know what I was like. Hence these attempts here to explain to myself what has happened.

Let's get the chronology straight.

Ian and I separated prior to Hazel's diagnosis. We called it a trial separation. Well that's what I called it when I first suggested it. But I had long before decided to live apart from Ian.

Once we got to live apart I hadn't had any specific plans, other than to go on as I was. I had just wanted shot of him.

I suppose that this is where the bulk of my guilt over Ian's death comes from. I had always been able to manipulate him, to bend him to my will. I talked him into marrying me, manoeuvred him into adopting Hazel, persuaded him that I needed a life outside the home, engineered him into getting me a loan for the café.

Did I love him? I don't know. Not now. All those years, those decades of marriage don't allow for such easy answers. I think that any fondness I had for him, gratitude for saving me from singleness and for giving me Hazel, had long been offset by irritation with him verging on contempt.

I had needed a man. Ian had been there for the taking. He had let himself be taken. Too easily. I quickly became dissatisfied. He didn't understand my dissatisfaction, tried to please me. By then it had already been too late: everything he did was wrong.

"What do you want me to do?" he asked. And all I could reply was, "Something! Anything!"

At weekends, so formless was Ian, a lump of unmoulded clay, that he would follow me around the house saying, "What shall we do?", "Where do you fancy going?", "Want to go anywhere?". I know that I deliberately opted to cover weekends in the café just so that I wouldn't have to be around him.

Two words that come to mind when I think of Ian are 'weak' and 'pathetic'. As when Hazel told us of her prognosis and he couldn't control himself enough to comfort her. No, she had to comfort him.

But I'm not here to build, to rebuild, a case against Ian. That's done, no need for that now. What's needed now is explanations. And it's beyond denying that Ian was a good and caring father.

Once Hazel was beyond toddlerhood, however, and she didn't need entertaining by him, by him finding things for her to do, once she could occupy herself, he was lost. Both Hazel and I used to send him off to mow the lawns, trim the hedge or, if wet, to find some telly sport. And once Hazel had left home and didn't need fetching or taking, so aimless was he that some Sundays he even turned up in the café.

Hazel was altogether more indulgent, more accepting of his formlessness than I.

Guilt comes again, catches me unawares with that deadness in the heart feeling, because it was I who bought Ian his first mountain bike, and I did it just to get him out of the house at weekends. I told him that the bike was to help him get rid of his office paunch, he could go off-road and burn off his fat.

At first embarrassed among some young riders, once Ian had made some friends closer to his own age he became an enthusiast. While for Hazel and I the buying of Christmas and birthday presents became that much easier. All that we had to do was go on mountain bike websites and search out arcane pieces of equipment... And no more of, "Shall we go back to so-and-so again this year?" Holidays now took care of themselves. While he was off sweating up some track, skidding down one (and proudly showing me the scratches and grazes later), I'd find a shady spot with a book.

All of which meant, when I broached the possibility of a trial separation, I was able to say, "This is no marriage. We hardly see each other. I'm working. You're working. Weekends you're off biking. I'm stuck in the café. And we're so tired when we're home together we nod off in front of the telly."

That Ian accepted my suggestion so readily was, I suspect, because he had his eye on one of the young woman cyclists – all that lycra wobbling about in front of him. Once separated he would be able to see his way clear to approaching her. Possibly already had. I didn't mind: conjugal relations so to speak not having been the core of our marriage.

It had all seemed so very important back then. Hazel had long left home, and I had come to see my purposeless life just going on. Alone. Outside the café I had no friends to speak of. And inside the café they were more colleagues and acquaintances than friends.

Within the peculiar loneliness of our marriage the decision had been built frown upon sigh. It had been then that I had decided that we are all exiles in our middle age – no childhood home to go back to, no fantasy place pulling us forwards. We find ourselves trapped by responsibilities of our own making (café & marriage) in places we don't want to be (marriage & café). Not that we have any great yearning to be anywhere else in particular, are just aware of our being trapped, of being unable to move. So we set about freeing ourselves, solely for the unpredictability of freedom.

Or not.

* * *

Ian, despite his love of adrenaline rushes, was not a brave man. Ian could only be reckless in prescribed situations – as with hurtling downhill on a mountain bike, or macho behind a steering wheel. But he was fundamentally a timid man, anything for a quiet life. Should anything out of the ordinary overtake him he was lost.

For instance he was sitting on a park bench by a town's war memorial when, out of nowhere, three young men – usual type, all shoulders and tattoos – came up to him, said, "Your bike?" as one of them looked it over. Ian nodded.

"Mine now," the one examining it said, and rode off.

One moment Ian was sitting there, legs stretched out before him, pumped up from an hour's ride, his faithful steed of a bike leaning against the end of the bench, the next he was left powerless and afraid in his lycra and heel-less bike shoes. The weeks that followed saw him being prescribed medication to alleviate his anxiety attacks.

He never got that bike back.

To be fair to me – it is me I'm judging here – there was pity mixed in with my contempt. Ian was timid certainly, but not a bad man. He had once told me that although he often imagined himself in fights, beating his antagonist to a pulp, he knew all the fantasising-while that should he actually find himself in a threatening situation – as with the bike being stolen from him – he would do all that he could, even pleading cowardice, to avoid violence.

And I had begun to appreciate his steadfastness again in the months before the crash – after Hazel had let us become involved in her illness. His distress over Hazel's diagnosis was so obvious, and – it has to be said again – his helplessness so irritating.

His being upset wasn't helping Hazel. So once again I became exasperated by his lumpishness, resentful of the space he occupied when in the house, his very lack – lack of drive, lack of insight, lack of initiative…

I have to consider, being charitable, that just prior to the crash Ian might well have been thinking of Hazel, possibly even crying, and those tears could have been what caused him to crash.

Sense and memory however tell me to doubt any such scenario. Ian was after all a single-minded man, one idea at a time. It was hard to distract him.

Guilt nevertheless comes again, and I feel myself rising to my defence.

* * *

Maybe I only feel so guilty because Ian's death has left me so much better off.

As it was a 'trial' separation we hadn't done anything about the house. We had only a small mortgage remaining, and Ian had taken a short-term contract on a rented flat near his office. He had quite enjoyed, so Hazel told me, setting up home on his own. She had helped him choose a fridge-freezer and some rugs.

The café income had been taking care of the mortgage, and Ian had been happy still to do the café's books. He had said, so he must have been anticipating it too, "Even after the divorce."

These explanations, this getting it all down, is not easy.

How much have I written so far? How many pages? And here I am saying for the very first time that Ian was an accountant, had been an accountant all his working life.

Like every other accountant I met Ian too disliked being an accountant; but not enough to pack it in, to even move to another firm. He said that wherever he went he would still be an accountant, and an accountant was what he didn't want to be. There was no other work though that he had wanted to do.

As an accountant the most excitement in his working life, aside from office gossip about the reckless domestic lives of others, had been when he had signed off accounts. "Signed off so-and-so today," he would announce on his homecoming, pride lifting his still-knotted tie.

Truth is Ian had practically no imagination. He even had to be told where he wanted to go on holiday. He was a man adverts were made for.

Hazel and I liked to read, novels mostly, all genres. Evenings, wet weekends, we would each find our corner and curl ourselves around a book. Ian didn't even read biographies.

"Most of them are made up," he said. He picked holes, "Implausible," in films on the telly, watched only sport and nature documentaries. And if there was none on he came looking for Hazel or I.

When Ian died in that crash we weren't divorced, hadn't even started divorce proceedings. And because we weren't divorced, because Ian hadn't changed his will, because his life insurance still had me as primary beneficiary, the insurer paid off what was left of the mortgage, I got a lump sum payment, and the house became mine. His firm even offered to keep on looking after the cafe's books.

Because of, or despite, the guilt, when some time after Ian's death Hazel said that she wanted to move in with me, I said, "Please."

Seven

I've been sitting here half a day looking down at a blank sheet of paper. Looking away from it. Losing myself... The trouble is I have all this seemingly unconnected crap going round and around in my head, no sense, small sense, to be made of it.

It's like a building has exploded inside my brain, all shattered bits and pieces suspended mid-air, and I've been sitting here wondering how I can put it all back together. As a building. The house of myself. Impossible. Then I look across the dining table to last night's bedtime book, the tasselled bookmark where I stopped…

I read stories. So I have told myself to tell of myself like a story.

Right. Let's put some order into this period.

First came the separation, Ian and I living apart.

Next came Hazel's diagnosis, and all those early and useless treatments.

In the middle of those came Ian's death. And it was shortly after that – possibly to keep me company, but I can only guess at her real motives – that Hazel left Kevin and moved back in with me. Whatever her motives she was there to support me as I dealt with all that went with Ian's death – the funeral, the solicitors, the will, and his family's anger at both Hazel and I.

I could understand their being pissed off with me ending up with Ian's life insurance and the house. Although why they should be when Ian and I had been equally separated, when all that was yet to be done was the divorce itself and the dividing up of the marital home… And even if the divorce had been finalised his parents wouldn't have got anything from it.

Truth is their anger, their anger at Hazel and I, had nothing to do with Ian's death and his unchanged will. His death was but a peg they could hang their hatred of us on. Unless Ian had gone out of his way to tell them of Hazel's illness, and I very much doubt that he would, they couldn't have known of her condition. Their anger including her – I'm guessing – was based on the presumption that if I had predeceased Ian then all of his wherewithal would have gone to Hazel.

* * *

I'm finding enough problems explaining myself to myself. Explaining their thinking, their emotional make-up, is beyond me.

Should there be a natural disaster, or just a couple getting divorced, his mother wouldn't say, "Oh that's sad." No, she had to find someone to blame, she had to straightaway take sides.

She will blame me. And I am in part to blame for the distance between us. But I don't blame myself. From the very beginning I loathed them and their every smug, self-righteous, dirty-minded pretension. Ian's father has a store of nudge-nudge wisecracks and unfunny jokes that verge at times on the racist. As soon as he senses a social occasion in the offing out come those jokes.

"Keep those to the locker room and not the drawing room," she will smirk conspiratorially at him. And she will proceed to tell of their latest acquisition, be it car, sofa or holiday. Should anyone present dare pass comment on her husband's poor taste wisecracks she will twitter on about 'political correctness'.

Quiet Ian knew himself to be a disappointment to them:

"I could become Prime Minster and I still wouldn't be wearing the right tie."

Alone with me Ian could give up trying to impress. With them, when she told of what new she'd got, how Ian's sister's husband had again been promoted, the grandaughter got a pony, Ian and I would share a glance. Which doubtless didn't go unnoticed.

His parents were of a self-fulfilled, self-congratulatory type I came to recognise in the café; and who I served through my very best rictus of a smile.

It is a type who are also excessively proud of themselves as parents.

"Worked damn hard to put Ian through public school," he declared. Always combatively.

"Was only a lesser public school," Ian had dared say once.

Hazel went with her school friends through the state school system. Which Ian championed, even to becoming a school governor. As a boy he had hated coming back to a friendless house end of term, the ennui of those holidays. Even if he had made a friend one holiday the new friend wasn't guaranteed to be there the next – their school holidays didn't often coincide. And with his parents climbing the property ladder, always on the lookout to move elsewhere, a letter mid-term would notify him of their change of address.

Ian was no rebel, but he did have his stubborn side.

I digress. Which is the problem with explanations. Mention of anything new requires its own explanation.

I've read books by the pound, by the kilo. This is the first I've put together. I won't say written: written assumes one word has followed another onto the page and doesn't take into account all the crossings out, asterisk inserts, circles and arrows. Even the pages ripped apart and the parts placed elsewhere.

Bear with me while I stumble on…

* * *

The legal stuff around Ian's death was still being settled when Hazel decided to give up on the experimental cures. Which we had discovered – a wonderful research tool the internet – weren't experiments at all, but had been tried before and had all been found to be ineffective. It appeared that they were called 'experimental' solely on the basis of their not having been proven. Which still seems to me a peculiar use of the English language.

But, again, I digress.

It was when Hazel came off the steroids, and was returning to her previous size and shape, that she looked at her circumstances – the small one-bedroom flat that she was sharing with Kevin, who was out at work all day – and she decided that that wasn't where she wanted to waste away the last few months of her one time on this planet. At least that's what she initially told me.

What I did have in common with Ian's parents was that I too had not been pleased with my child's choice of partner. Except that I was more disappointed for Hazel than I found Kevin himself a disappointment. Although he definitely was a disappointment.

Unlike Ian's parents, with their dismissive remarks and downturned mouths, I did my damnedest to hide my disappointment. And most certainly from Hazel and Kevin.

What I found most disappointing about Kevin, and couldn't then confide in any family member, was that he was so like Ian. Quiet and unambitious, happy to spend his free time playing computer games when not going out to play or to watch football.

I don't know what more I wanted for Hazel. I only know that Kevin wasn't it.

Kevin was, is, generally a pleasant, trying-to-please man, offend no-one. If the world was full of Kevins there'd be no wars. I doubt though that there'd be anything much done. No drive. No great aspirations. Which was why I suspect, following my example, Hazel had landed herself with him.

On second thoughts, if all men were like Kevin there would still be wars. Although he's a techie and not an accountant, Kevin is still a counter. He counts the things he's done for other people, and he notches up every omission of kindness towards himself. These accounts Kevin stores in a clamp, until rage trips the lock and the years-long-festering bile comes gushing out.

I've been present twice when this has happened. Both

times over phone calls. Once when a workmate wouldn't, couldn't, repay the favour of providing holiday cover, and once at a team-mate who let him down on a promise of tickets.

Generally though Kevin comes across as soft. So soft that the few times that Ian's father has met him he has made the assumption that Kevin is probably a secret homosexual. Whenever Ian's father has unsubtly hinted as much I have found myself hoping that his much-admired, his go-getting son-in-law turns out to be a cottager. The daughter spent the whole of one Christmas weeping because she suspected – rightly – that her enterprising husband was being unfaithful. Although I did my duty in the bathroom being sympathetic I did so want the extramarital lover to be a man. She wasn't.

* * *

If I was the type to take the world's many faults onto my shoulders then no doubt I would have berated myself for Hazel having followed my lead in having chosen a safe man like her father. As I have said though, Kevin did have his spiky side, was quick to leap to his own defence. Not Ian.

Ian was a sponge. Ian was a man who soaked up condescension. At office functions I've seen clients yawn into Ian's face as he was talking and walk away from him mid-sentence. If someone had done that to Kevin he would, I'm sure, at the very least have passed comment.

Whenever I challenged Ian on his passivity, if only to say how very rude that client had just been to him, Ian would trot out one of his little defensive sayings. "Gotta keep the customers satisfied", or "That's what pays the bills". Ad nauseam.

At which point I too probably walked away. And that would have Ian coming out with something along the lines of "That time of you-know-what?" Or, "Must be a feminist issue."

Kevin's rapport was, is, most likely as limited. But it

belongs to another generation, is all acronyms and abbreviations, from techie-speak to texting. His therefore didn't have the capacity to irritate me quite as much.

I did go through a phase, prior to the separation and probably redirecting my dissatisfaction with Ian, of being angry with 'that lump of a young man' because he didn't 'get off his fat arse, get a decent salary and a bigger flat' so that Hazel could get pregnant and I could have a grandchild.

Come the diagnosis I was relieved that hadn't happened.

And come the diagnosis poor Kevin had no idea what to do. Nothing had prepared him for this – none of his car-chase films, none of his alien invasion computer games. His live-in girlfriend was going to stop living and he didn't know what to do, how to please her.

To be fair to that 'lump of a young man' he did what he thought best, bought Hazel flowers and grapes. But thereafter convention left him at a loss – you don't give a Get Well Soon card to someone who's been told they're soon to die.

Hazel said that a couple of times when they were in bed he just sobbed, saying over and over, "I don't know what to do." While the rest of the time he just looked at her 'like a doleful dog'.

And when she was throwing up from one of her treatments... "Poor Kevin," she told me the next day, "was hovering about me not knowing what to do for the best. 'For fucksake,' I told him, 'go play one of your games. Save the world.'"

With the treatments stopped, on painkillers only, weekends and evenings Hazel still had Kevin trailing helplessly around behind her. While he was at work she spent the days at home with me or in the café.

* * *

By this time the visits from her friends had dropped off. Like her illness the tailing off frequency had been a slow process, the visits becoming less when nothing much more had seemed about to happen other than a disfiguring bloating from the steroids, and then – we discovered later they were sedatives prescribed to alleviate the inevitable distress over the bloating – falling asleep while her friends were sitting uncomfortably opposite.

And her friends' lives were going on; and it's socially difficult being around the dying, especially when it does drag on so; and one can reason that we're all of us dying, just that the majority of us don't have an early expiry date. There they were trying not to tell of their new boyfriends, and of their tripping off to weddings and of their getting pregnant. How to chat to Hazel of their ongoing future-full lives without their every word being loaded with the taunting knowledge that by the time that future came to pass in all likelihood Hazel would not be alive?

So, purely for company's sake, Hazel spent more and more time with me. She said one day that she delayed going home, with seeing Kevin put on his sad face, "...And he leans forwards slightly, like he's a waiter, asks, Can he do anything..."

There has been a hardness to Hazel in her dealings with people that has sometimes shocked even me. The way she cut schoolfriends who had upset her in the slightest way. They were simply dropped from her life, regardless of their feelings. And that's what she did with Kevin.

"I don't want to spend my last days here with you," she told him. "I want my death to mean something, and you're not important enough to be there when I die."

And that was how she came to move back in with me.

Eight

Although as a young mother I had involved myself in mother and toddler activities, playgroups and the like, I suspect that by the time Hazel started school proper she was glad to get out from under my fussing presence. While, if I'm honest, I was as relieved – to not have my increasing redundancy as playmate-mother made daily, made hourly, so obvious.

While Hazel had been at playschool I had already started casting about for some kind of paid employment. I hadn't though wanted to simply return to dogsbody office work. But, with no other experience, office work had seemed my only realistic option.

Prior to Hazel's arrival I had worked here and there as a personal assistant. An accurate job description however would have said that in that subordinate position I spent my working days covering up for the incompetence of others – others who were mostly paid double my salary.

With Hazel's imminent school attendance about to cast me back onto the job market, being otherwise unqualified my only alternatives to office work had been as cleaner, teaching assistant or nursing assistant, shopworker or supermarket checkout. And with every one of those jobs I knew that I'd have to negotiate with unsympathetic jobsworth managers for time off in the school holidays and for the inevitable childhood sicknesses.

Credit where credit's due, it was Ian who suggested I start my own café.

All those years, pre-Hazel, of aimless weekend driving with always a break – pit-stops, Ian called them – for tea and cake in a country tea room or roadside café, had made me an authority on them – service, food, decor, ambience…

When I demurred, said that I wouldn't know how to go about setting up my own business, Ian said that he'd handle the accounts, would help me with the legal side. He had all the contacts.

So it was, with Hazel at school all day, that I started looking for premises.

* * *

When first I had imagined my own café it had been set in the countryside, with plenty of discreet parking, rustic furniture, cloth napkins… From within our suburban acreage, however, that would have meant at least an hour's drive from our then estate before ever I reached meaningful countryside.

As it happened a premises conveniently became available in our own High Street. There was already one café in town, but it was a long strange affair, all Formica and chrome, with the menus on laminated card and resentful flatfooted service. The naked plate glass windows made it almost a burger bar. Its steam-moist atmosphere not conducive to relaxation it wouldn't have looked out of place in a bus station.

We checked with the council that we could change the use of what had last been a shop. Fortunately it already had plumbing for washbasins from when it had one time been a hairdressers; and it had a lavatory. The bonus was that it had lovely arched windows.

In that older stretch of the High Street the traffic divided and in the centre was a narrow park with flowerbeds and benches, shaded by one large oak tree. So, in raised wooden letters above the wooden arches, ours became the Oak Tree Café. (Ian and I had hesitated over what might, given what I intended, been the more appropriate Oak Tree Tea Rooms. But I hadn't liked the almost tongue-twisting alliteration; and Ian had said that 'Rooms' was inaccurate as 'to all intents and purposes' there was only the one, albeit large, room.)

I am writing this primarily for myself, to try and clarify for me all that has happened. Occasionally, however, I find myself imagining what another may make of what I have said, am saying, and then I write for them. But be clear I am not writing to apologise, or as self-justification. Most certainly not self-justification. I don't like myself. There's not much about me to like.

If I have thus far seemed only to disparage Ian, and that I may now seem ungrateful for his major contribution to this enterprise, let me say that back then ours had been a working partnership, and in our going-forwards life both of us had contracted to help one another and raise Hazel to the best of our abilities. It was when Ian and I had only a past that I had decided that we should go our separate ways.

* * *

It had been easier to decide what I hadn't wanted in the café than what I had wanted. I hadn't wanted the stink of chipshop fat. So there was to be no cooking on the premises. Nor had I wanted one of those frothy coffee machines that hiss and gurgle at such a volume that couples sitting either side of a table have to talk to each other one hand cupped to an ear. Nor, for the same ear-cupping reason, had I wanted a speaker grille blasting out the inanities of some chirpy DJ from a local radio station.

A café does, however, need some background noise in order that the one couple alone in the café that moment aren't made self-consciously aware of the silence squatting on the table between them. But I hadn't known what noise to place there. I hadn't wanted muzak so bland and inoffensive that it caused offence.

As to furnishings… The customers' comfort being the key I didn't want the place to be overly fussy, like a spinster's boudoir all lace doilies and spindly chairs. Nor did I want cold to the touch easy wipe-clean plastic and mock-chrome.

Touring the antique marts and auction rooms, picking up mismatched pine tables and chairs (stripped white-grey pine, not the chunky lacquered orange variety) I chanced upon six Bakelite cake stands. My intention, the moment I saw them was not for the display of fancy cakes, but as static table centre pieces. No wilting flowers to be daily replaced and easily knocked over.

I also picked up a retro radio, which looked as if it came from the Bakelite era, but was actually a CD player. I toyed with the idea of using light music, big band favourites from pre-WW2, but thought – for us staff as much as the customers – such tunes would become irritatingly repetitive. So I opted for collections of string quartets, which filled the café nicely without becoming overbearing.

The cake stands and repro radio led later to regular customers bringing in various Bakelite items – ashtrays (from our opening we had been a non-smoking establishment) and vases mostly – which I used as a windowsill display. Along with several genuine old valve radios – with Bakelite knobs. This again dispensed with the need for having flowers – even if silk – in the window.

Within a couple of years this Bakelite theme led to customers referring to the café as The Bakelite. Ian even thought that it might be a good idea, the advertising contained in the name, to rename the Oak Tree the Bakelite Café. I said that it would only need one batch of cakes to sink and the café would become known as the Bake Heavy.

* * *

Presentation being nine parts of the business I made sure that there were always fresh baked cakes in the display cabinet. Anything left over I let the staff take home, that was if the cakes hadn't all been sold half-price between five and six. We had some regular customers then.

I also tried to make sure that there were no nasty surprises for new customers. In my tea room travels I'd found nothing more infuriating than being presented with a bill for three times the going rate for some very ordinary tea and scones. So every week I had a freshly typed price list put up in the frame on the door above the open/closed sign. The same price list – on heavy paper – was leant up against the cake stands on the tables as well as being chalked up on a blackboard at the back of the café.

All my efforts still didn't stop people wandering in and asking for fried egg/bacon butties and burgers. With us poor staff having to once again explain that we didn't cook on the premises.

"We do baguettes, sandwiches and cakes," indicating the blackboard price list behind us.

To which the response of these unobservant souls would be, "Oh." And, invariably, as if we hadn't spoken and the blackboard had ceased to exist, they would run through a list of other things we didn't cook.

Ah, the sons and daughters of the Great British Public.

But more of them later. (You will find them referred to as the GBP, which is how staff referred to their bad manners in the café.)

The staff first. I say staff plural, but most times there were just the two of us. Often just the one. Weekends we usually had a schoolgirl waitress for the busy times. In effect though I had one regular staff who had keys, could open and close when I was elsewhere looking after Hazel. If Hazel needed looking after for longer I got in temporary staff.

But that's all decided later, becomes a working pattern. That first year, what with setup costs, we made a loss. Year two, to Ian's delight, we made a profit. And after a few false starts my mainstay staff became Franny. Chosen in the first place because she was an older woman with no childcare commitments.

As a woman one can feel that one is betraying one's own sex when deciding thus. With two working mothers, however, and with both of us trying to cope with school holidays the staffing would have been a recipe for disaster. No, single Franny was the rock on which the Oak Tree Café was built.

My principal day-by-day contribution was the baking, which I preferred to the serving of customers unable to make up their minds and with no thought to my flattening feet. Those that say that there are few class divisions left in the UK today have not recently waited table. Waiting being the word.

Ah, the Great British Public, the GBP.

To begin with I did the baking mostly in the evenings. Which Ian liked as, with Hazel tucked in bed, he was the one got to lick out the bowls. He also, when he came upon me baking – red and bustling with flour smears always somewhere about my person – would say, "I love seeing you in your element." Variations of. Every time.

Hazel preferred the café to cooking. From primary school onwards she came in at weekends and during school holidays, and was petted by the customers and Franny. Later on she waited table and earned herself some pocket money and tips. All as anticipated. But she surprised me when a full-blooded teenager. I had assumed that she and her friends when in town would sneak by on the other side of the mid-street park. Not so: Hazel brought them into the café.

When I had been that age I had employed myriad underhand stratagems to avoid the company, the sight, the thought of my parents. I had supposed that such deceptions were a natural and universal rite of passage. With my Hazel, apparently not.

Once inside the café, again to my surprise, Hazel fiercely made sure that her teenage friends were polite and well-behaved. Although by that time Hazel had met with her share of rude customers. That snob-bound, ill-mannered Great British Public…

"Ignorant," Hazel called them. I remember her once, chip off the old block, after a customer had grumped on and on at her because she had served someone before him. He had wanted a sandwich made, the other customer only a pastry.

"He had one of those mouths," Hazel said afterwards. "So set in misery you know that as a child no-one taught him how to smile. So, no-one since has smiled back at him. So, he has never smiled back at them. Result, self-perpetuating misery. Grrrrrr."

Customers, some of them members of the Great British Public, populated my working life. Fuss-arsing, mind-changing women for a start…

Some of them older women with creased faces like slowly deflating balloons, and who called everyone "Dear". Over-heavy on the powder and perfume they stank out the café.

And smart young saleswomen with their backsides

wider than their shoulders, their hair gelled to a shine, and their perfume as pungent as the old women's; and who offhandedly condescended to the, not so nattily groomed, graduate waitress.

Then there were the scruffy and over-courteous, some inappropriately solicitous, "If it's no trouble…" Wizened monkey faces who reeked of a century's cigarette smoke on the table next to the tidy, twice-showered and imperious…

The Great British Public…

The pointed women, their round faces ending in noses pointed like pink pencils, and which pointed from cake to cake, and back again before choosing. They might even go off to consult with friends, then change their minds again. They're always in two minds. And if tall these pointed women are bent like bows towards their pointedness.

Then there are the couples…

Childless couples mostly. Or couples with children elsewhere and long ago. Young or middle-aged these couples with unreal lives, weird priorities, voiced concerns and enthusiasms disproportionate to even their own circumstances, and which certainly had no grounding in mine or the staff's 10-6 reality.

Whatever the weather the male half of one type of couple wore a misshapen jacket, sports or linen, and he would come clumping into the café emanating disdain and disapproval, lips twisted in semi-permanent exasperation. She would creep behind, and get told off for getting the wrong cake. It will always be the wrong cake.

Then there were the couples who had been on holiday in the US of A. They said, very loudly, "Over There Service Means Service," and that before they had even sat at a table. Quick to grumble, to find the tiniest fault, and slow to tip, yet they expected us to want them to Have A Nice Day. We found ourselves swayed between wishing them an obviously ironical, "Have a nice dayeee!" and between telling them in the good olde English manner to fuck off and not come back.

Then there were the couples, whole families even, who

were physically familiar with one another in public. Touching touching touching. Demonstrating their right to be familiar? Mine, the kiss, the fondle, seems to be saying; only I can touch you here.

"Yes, but not in here." I had to hold down the urge to come between them like a boxing referee.

Who we did ask to leave was anyone, male or female, who was mildewed and rancid. Especially rancid. Weathering the abuse, or ignoring the tears, we told them to not come back until they'd had a good wash.

Smokers however, their clothes leaking a pernicious carbon monoxide, but with their otherwise being socially acceptable, we endeavoured to make them unwelcome by dint of small frowns, face-pulled looks to one another, and by leaning backwards away from their chemical reek. And once they left we talked to the other customers about their smell. Committed smokers rarely returned.

Out-and-out skanks, can in hand, didn't even attempt to come into the café. They did though sometimes sit on one of the benches opposite. Until I took myself outside, stood and stared at them. Unnerved them that staring. I did get shouted at, but they did move on. And the café windows did get broken a couple of times. No need to ask by who.

The café was my life, and I worked hard to make it a success. One success was my speciality days. The second Thursday macaroons in particular had sweet-toothed cognosenci coming in from far and wide.

I was the boss, had no excuses, no alibis.

* * *

The Oak Tree Café was an escape from the boredom of my marriage, and it became as much a burden, a rut, as my marriage. Yet, for want of anything other, I kept the café going through Hazel's college years, and the nothing much years beyond. The hinterland lives of customers and staff kept me just about interested in life outside of Ian and between Hazel's occasional visits home.

How much of this do I need to explain? Because these aren't so much the entwining strands of my life and, so to speak, difficult to untangle. That infers a separateness to them. They weren't separate. My life has been more like layer upon layer of transparent ply, year on year repeated. (The glaziers used five-ply board to temporarily stop-up the café's broken windows.) I suppose the resin between each of my transparent layers would have had to be an opaque layer in itself. It was only when this board of transparencies got chipped by a new event, splintering back, that I had been able to see what may have formed that event. And then I only got to see a partial and imperfect view of the causation. Always something remained unseen.

How does anyone learn about themselves? If I hadn't been working with all sorts of people in the café, as opposed to my being alone at home baking, following the strict choreography of cooking, I doubt that I would have realised that I am definitely a task-oriented person. For instance while chatting to a customer I would be almost painfully aware, side of mind, that there were plates and dishes yet to be washed and returned to their cabinet places.

One of the staff robbed me. A tenner a day. Which was how Ian came to be suspicious – the regularity. To stop her I had to catch her in the act – she was Franny's replacement after Franny retired – and then I had to nervously confront her. And straightaway sack her. Then find a replacement and restore some of my little faith in humanity. The thief was a grandmother herself, shouted and wept over the sacking. I didn't have proof enough to involve the police, said that I had just wanted shot of her.

"Bad 'un her," Old Bob said next day.

"Could've told me before," I said.

"Would you have believed me? Got to find out for yourself sometimes. Experience the best teacher."

After a couple more false starts – but the women just unsuitable, no more thieving – Nyrene became my mainstay.

Nyrene is a thin harsh woman. Abrupt. She jerks alert, rushes to every new task. Dealing with customers she could sometimes seem fierce. No sooner challenged, however, than hers was seen to be a misleading assertiveness, covered her state of constant anxiety.

* * *

Such was my life, the people in my life. Such were, within that café, all the secondhand lives that formed mine, that informed mine. Which is probably why I had no illusions about marriage, no reverence for it as an institution: I had listened to far too many sad and bitter histories – of staff and customers.

The café was still going when Ian was killed and when Hazel moved back in with me. Like my marriage I was unsure of the worth of the café. Unlike my marriage I was undecided regards its future, being unable then to see no alternative day-by-day activity to fill my time.

Nine

Widespread throughout the British Isles are two kinds of oak. These are the sessile oak and the pedunculate oak. The principal difference between the two is that on the pedunculate oak, *quercus robur,* the stem on the acorn is longer than on the sessile, *quercus petrae.* Otherwise there's not that much difference between the two. Generally, although it does all depend on where each tree finds itself growing, the trunk of the sessile oak tends to be straighter and cleaner of limb. While the pedunculate, again generally, tends to a stouter trunk and for its boughs to look like arms bent in the beginning of a yawn.

But even here, in this self-testing of my knowledge, an explanation requires an explanation. Because over the centuries a degree of hybridisation has taken place and, as with all British crossbreeding, the difference between the two oak species is now often not that remarkable. The local environment has a more marked effect on growth than any genetic inheritance. Pollarding too can foil ready identification.

I have come to think of oaks, both kinds, as reluctant growers. Their branches don't reach straight up or out to the light, as do most other trees. No, oak boughs bend back on themselves as if unsure, their reluctance becoming all thick elbows and knees.

The oak opposite the café was an ancient and much-contemplated, many times pollarded, pedunculate. Our busy summers it sat in its own shade, trunk and limbs unseen within its green canopy. Idle winter afternoons I made patterns of its zigzagging branch ends. Early autumns window customers got excited having caught sight of a white-rumped jay collecting acorns. Late autumns we swept its dark-spotted leaves from the café door. Spring we sneezed its pollen.

Being the most widespread tree in the British Isles – spruce plantations aside – many myths and legends have been attached to the oak. In old Celtic mythology the oak was known as the tree of doors. When King Charles II was defeated in battle he escaped his parliamentary pursuers by hiding in the crown of an oak. Oak's hardwood was used in the building of Nelson's conquering fleet.

Nor have the British been alone in adopting the oak as a political symbol. Long before Nelson, for instance, the Viking longboats were famously made of oak. Indeed the word 'acorn' comes from the Danish 'eg korn', oak seed. Nor were the Vikings alone in their reverence for the tree: throughout the northern hemisphere the lobed leaves of the oak have been used to signify strength and endurance.

The Strength and Endurance Café? I think not.

Ten

It was not long after that visit to the GP that Hazel sent me back to the café.

As usual I had been doing the baking at home and taking it in first thing. But, leaving Nyrene to run the café, I had then been hurrying back home to be with Hazel. While, for something to do in the evenings, Hazel had been helping me with the baking. Which had been how she had come to scald herself.

I usually resented anyone being in the kitchen with me. In my moving from worktop to cooker to sink I would find myself tripping over, bumping into the interloper. But how now to deny Hazel, having been told she had only so long to live, the least of her whims? And with Hazel working on one mix while I did another the baking was soon over and done with. Which left us with nothing but telly, housework or books.

Neither of us had ever bothered with housework for its own sake, enough that it got done to a passable standard. We both regarded telly as something we sometimes sat in front of in the evenings, not for it to be talking to itself daytimes in a corner of the living room. No real prejudice against daytime telly, just that in both our busy lives it had seemed a wasteful irrelevance.

But our lives now weren't busy, and each our current books could hold our attention only for so long. The weather didn't always favour our being out in the garden. And neither of us had been what you might call eager shoppers. Aside from a penchant for antique marts, regards shoes and clothes both Hazel and I bought what we needed when we needed it.

We did take a few trips out. Even went to put fresh flowers on Ian's grave, made a deal of commissioning a headstone. Aside from name and dates 'Loved father' was the only inscription.

No lies there. Ian had doted on Hazel; and Hazel,

naturally, had loved her father. Ian had never been anything but kind to her. Why wouldn't she have loved him? Just because he had come to irritate the socks off me didn't mean that she had to share my daily displeasure with him. Nor had he always displeased me.

Hazel had been there when I had been fond of him. At least acting as if I had been fond of him. Which is both true and not true. Ian and I must once have been in love. I think. But after a lifetime together, of near constant companionship, of knowing practically all there is to know about someone other than one's own unesteemed self – we knew each other's lavatory smells, had avoided each other's night breath, and I had been driven to jaw-clenched rage by the very predictability of when and where he would trot out his trite little utterances... Hard then to recall the cause of love.

What Hazel had loved about Ian, his rock steadiness, his fatherly constancy, was precisely what had come to drive me nuts – his unrelenting, oh-here-we-go-again-with-that-old-chestnut predictability.

How to reconcile all these conflicts and contradictions is what has got me writing this. But no easy reconciliation here: as soon as I try give the whole picture the less simple and straightforward it all seems.

With the grave refreshed, weekly shopping done, weather too wet for even tinkering in the garden, the two of us were soon back indoors. Where my solicitous questions, even the innocuous morning greeting, "And how're you today?" if answered at all was with a grumpy, "Fine!"

Hazel was obviously far from fine, would not – according to the medical profession – ever be fine again. Which is what had sent me looking at 'alternative' treatments. Desire fogging my normally pretty sharp acuity, because each one I enthused about to Hazel she very quickly pointed out what wasn't being said in their promotional material. I think she got fed up with me cutting pieces out of the paper, in my being bowed over my laptop, hunting down the next link, possibly a Uruguayan 'cure'…

She told me to stop looking.

"When I go," she said, "I want it to be with some dignity. Not covered in Nepalese yoghurt, with some bullshitter chanting over me, and needles stuck in my 'median loci'."

"Sorry," I said. "Only trying to help."

She wasn't having any of it: "We're going to drive each other mad if we go on like this. The doc said I could be here for another year yet. I don't need looking after. I don't need watching over. Go back to the caff." Her use of the word 'caff', a word she knew I hated, signified her displeasure, her growing impatience with me.

* * *

Truth be told, and truth on these pages is paramount, I had felt a bit smug when Hazel had decided to leave Kevin and to spend her remaining time with me. I was sad of course because of the reason, but still cannot deny a certain satisfaction. Has to be said too, to unmix all these emotions, that when her condition had been confirmed I had found myself glad, relieved anyway, that she hadn't had children, hadn't had the grandchildren that I had thought I had longed for.

It is this constant, this recurring mix of overlapping, cancelling out regrets, that has got me trying to explain all of what has happened. I have to get it sorted out somewhere outside of my head.

And I was sort of relieved getting kicked out of the house, being told to go back to the café. It was a return to almost normality. I was even pleased to find that the café needed a good clean. Oh Nyrene had managed all the rostered cleans, but it was the pulling out and the cleaning behind that hadn't been done, a touch of polish here and there, the greasy fingermarks on the inside of the door needing some hot soapy water on them. All the Bakelite in the window also needed collecting up and given a hot wash, not just a dusting over. And when we were slack I also ran the hosepipe outside and sprayed it over the sign – black street specks tended to gather in the raised letters.

It was on the third evening of this new regime that I came home to find Hazel, my laptop open on the dining room table, delving into all the adoption papers, notelets stuck to several.

Hazel had spent that afternoon researching her birth mother's family; and she continued into that evening while I baked. She came into the kitchen only to ask if I'd mind her signing up – in my name on my credit card – for 'free trials' on a couple of 'find your ancestors' websites.

Hands full I said, "'Course not. Go ahead."

"Only when the free trials end," she said, "I might not be around. It might leave unnecessary complications for you. It's your laptop." (Theirs had stayed with tech-speak Kevin.) "And I don't want you getting charged with fraud because of me."

"Fine," I busily said. "Won't happen. Go ahead."

I had avoided looking at her, knew that the candour of her eyes would have had me either defensively angry or blubbing. And neither sharp words nor tears would have been of benefit to either of us.

We, Hazel and I, prided ourselves on speaking our mind, on our being down to earth; and nothing could be more down to our earth now than death. But she, the one speaking of her own death, she was the one enduring love of my life. I held myself in contempt, Ian in contempt, the Great British Public in contempt: Hazel was my life's one good deed. So to hear her make so casual a reference to what little life she had left had my insides lurch.

Not only was it the implicit mention of her death that had me swallow down my pain. Left on my own again, holding onto the kitchen worktop, I told myself that what she was doing was perfectly understandable, didn't matter to me, that we had gone way beyond that... That I had always known that she might one day want to explore her biological past, and that with this inherited illness it was only natural that she should want to know.

Although Ian and I had never hidden the down-to-earth fact of her adoption from her, that I had always spoken of it to her in a robust matter-of-fact manner, Hazel must have sensed my hurt hiding away in the kitchen, because when I went through to watch the news Hazel followed me into the living room with the laptop and, as if concentrating on the screen on her knees, she said, "What I'm trying to find out is what became of my birth grandmother. If my birth mother had any brothers or sisters. If I have any birth half-brothers or half-sisters. If the half-sisters know of their genetic inheritance. If the half-cousins don't know maybe I can warn them."

"How would that help?"

"Maybe not them themselves. Be too late for them. But if they haven't yet had children I could let them know the consequences."

All very laudable. My hurt however suspected that I had been sent back to the café just so she could, without her having to tell me what she was doing as she was doing it – look into her past.

* * *

Later that evening – I had stayed watching a film on telly while she had twizzled the mouse pad – she said, "You see Mum, all I have is a past now. That's all that's mine. And I don't know the half of it."

I nodded, as if more interested in the film. Hazel continued scrolling down websites, occasionally tapping keys. I sensed her shift of posture as she paused again.

"What else do I do?" she said. "Am I just going to hang about here until I die? I have to do something that has meaning to my life. To what life I have left."

Again I nodded a half-interested acceptance. And I did accept, accepted the rightness of what she was doing. I had long before learnt to trust my daughter, her sensibleness. She had never disappointed me, had never let me down. She has been my measure for all other women her age – like her, not like her. Even so... I still felt in some way betrayed.

* * *

Next evening I came home to papers stuck together across the dining room table and Hazel explaining who was who.

Eleven

Every explanation here seems to require another explanation. And I don't feel as if I've even started.

Trying to explain my state of mind when Hazel began her research, my emotional flux then, has had me realise anew that no life comes singly, and has made me aware of telling absences here. Because, although I'd very much like to, I cannot ignore the family from which I came. My own parents and sister, that is. Always another door to be opened.

While Hazel was sat at the dining room table researching her biological family I was sunk in the settee next door mulling over mine. That mulling, that scowling at the past, might go some way to explaining my having been less than encouraging to Hazel's researching her uncertain past.

I have a hostile attitude to the very concept of family. That hostility began in childhood and went on to become an almost involuntary sneer at any mention of 'family'. Even so it was an attitude that I didn't become aware of in myself until my teenage years.

Once seen for what it was all that has happened since, even hindsight, has served to confirm me in that attitude.

I am the second-best daughter. My older sister is pert, blonde and pretty. My sister is called Lorna. Lorna knows how to make herself pretty.

If she wasn't my sister, daughter of my parents, I suspect that I might have quite liked Lorna. Lorna knows how to make herself liked.

My slim mother and my slim father dote on her, have always doted on her; and that I suspect was, if not the direct cause of my sibling resentment, then their unabashed preference for her company certainly fed it. I saw myself as the dumpy cuckoo in their svelte nest.

On the surface their treatment of my sister and I was in no way different. They helped Lorna through college true, and I didn't go. But that had been my contrary choice. By then I hadn't wanted their money, their 'sacrifice'. I had needed to be beyond their control.

'Sacrifice… ' That would have been my mother. Who made none. Where does disillusion begin? When what your parents tell you stops being true? I don't know, but as soon as I reached eighteen I moved out and into a shared flat, took a typing course. Although I was never to be more than a personal assistant. To become a secretary it seemed that I needed to be taller, to wear short skirts and thin heels. (Ian and I paid for Hazel to go to college. She still ended up working as a PA. I put it down to our very similar build. Although, truth be told, Hazel hadn't seemed to want to be any more than a PA. Not prepared to fetch coffee and lickspittle some ego in a rumpled suit or some shoulder-padded virago?)

Hazel set up house with easygoing Kevin. I married Ian. I got Ian to marry me. Sister Lorna was pursued by big car Martin, who built success upon success and became the kind of man who made use of people like Ian and who had PAs like Hazel and I sneering behind his back.

Lorna and Martin have two children, a boy and a girl. Our parents go on holiday with them to their timeshare villa in Portugal. I used to get shown photos of them around their blue swimming pool.

My parents also spent every Christmas with Lorna and Martin. Which was 'only natural', their house being bigger. Their trees were bigger too – but still occupying only a corner of their conservatory. Ian, Hazel and I joined them on Boxing Days.

Hazel used to enjoy those Boxing Day visits, played well with her new toys and her two cousins. Ian too did his pleasant best. Even I tried to show some polite enthusiasm for my extended family. But, simply told, Ian and I weren't their kind of people. More than once on the way home Ian said, "You OK? You've said hardly a word all day." Had been no need: they had chattered away for all of us.

I suppose that, seeing how easily my sister won praise and try as I might, even to copying her, I didn't; instead I became a watchful child, analytical and not easy to like. But I did still play the second daughter role expected of me. I did begin as an accepting child: that's the way things were – I wasn't pretty and I had a pretty sister.

I have seen versions of our family in the café. The mother and father chattering away to the vivacious daughter, while the not so pretty daughter concentrates on her cake and picks up crumbs with the wet end of her finger. Until told to stop. Often by the older sister. My sister wanted to be more of a mother to me than my mother. My permanent disgruntlement was a disappointment to them both. I wouldn't be saved. Not rescued to their charming world that is.

When grown that café child will continue to feel that she has to protect herself against her parents, rather than feel protective towards their out of date old selves.

* * *

My parents' absence in this my later life (to be accurate the absences have to be explained as well) came about the final Boxing Day.

My mother and Lorna had obviously been discussing my alleged sulking. At least that's how my mother had referred to my having been quiet. She was – in her way of speaking and how she would report back to Lorna – taking the bull by the horns...

As we stacked dinner plates in Lorna's washer my

mother said – in a backed-up voice which I knew meant that she and Lorna had been chewing it over all Christmas Day (again I had been excluded from the conversation even though I had been its subject): "I really do find great difficulty connecting with you."

Connecting? That was a word new to her vocabulary. Was more like Lorna's magazine-speak.

Blow for blow I came straight back with, "That why you've said hardly a word to Hazel? But you've been all over Lorna's two?"

"Partly." She didn't deny it. "Although I think it's because Hazel's not actually ours. If you know what I mean? She didn't come from us. Both your dad and I have said how difficult we find it. We can't see anything of us in there… "

And on she prattled, regardless of my simply standing there, plate in hand, and staring at her.

I have always assumed that any brains I have I had to have inherited from my father. Although he could be as emotionally blind as my mother – she the white-coated laboratory assistant, he the up-and-coming research assistant – which had him not see the effect of his blatant preference for Lorna's company. Not that he could be blamed for the preference: Lorna was cute, intelligent and a nice person. While I was the two years behind younger sister, a second thought, silent and secretive, only to be brought into conversations once started.

I wore Lorna's hand-me-downs, until I got stouter than her. On family walks I lagged behind, my now professor father occasionally remembering to point out to me as well the scientific name for a type of rock, the Latin name for a poisonous plant. My mother would tut and tell me to hurry up. By the time I was twelve I had long given up trying to be pleased by his belated inclusion.

I did go through a phase of wishing that my father would divorce the stupid woman with her newspaper opinions, her magazine fads, which changed and contradicted one another day-to-day, sometimes hour to hour. Even my father laughed at her, and yet continued to indulge her.

"Why?" I asked him once, when it happened to be just him and I. It was my seventeenth birthday. We were waiting outside a restaurant. Lorna and my mother were queuing for the loo. "She doesn't try, doesn't even try, to rise above her prejudices."

"Superficial those prejudices," he said. Prejudices against immigrants, against trade unionists, against a neighbour not quite as clean as her, against another who dressed differently, against one old woman she said was ugly. Or she took up the outrageous opinions of others which she thought made her interesting: "Oh you know me!" Too well.

"At heart she's not a bad woman," my father said outside that restaurant. "She's just easily misled." And he went to put a jolly-evening-out arm around me. I moved away, hadn't wanted to be contained in any embrace that included her.

Hazel was my own. Mine alone. I had fought for her. And that stupid stupid woman had made as if to disinherit her, to make her of less value than Lorna's pair.

But there was no major row. I simply didn't bother seeing them again after that Christmas. They continued to do the dutiful things, to send birthday cards, invite us over; and I overheard Ian on the phone once attempting to mollify them, "You know what she's like…"

Ian though had been told what my mother had said about second-best Hazel, daughter of second-best daughter; and Ian had a refined sense of what was right and proper. He also didn't much like bullish Martin, or to make a fuss. So from then on we closed the café early Christmas week and booked holidays away. And when Ian and I moved (From this distance what's telling is that we had moved from a starter home in a Close to a small Victorian villa in a cul-de-sac, back to an upmarket Close. A shut off life going nowhere?) I didn't let my family have our new address. The house probably wouldn't have met with their approval: though newly built like theirs not nearly glass-and-brass stylish enough.

Possibly, just possibly, if my father had come looking for me I might have relented. Might have. But word from him came there none.

I know that my mother phoned Ian at work. And when he said to her that I had told him not to give them our new address, she said, "What kind of son-in-law are you?"

Obviously, in family matters, one loyal to his wife.

Ian even held out against my sister weeping down the phone. Although he told me that had been particularly hard as he had always got on well with Lorna. But I had no longer needed her pity, her condescension. And if I let her through the door would the parents follow...? Could she withstand pressure from Mrs Prejudice?

I did once almost give in – when Fran told me that Lorna had been asking for me in the café. Lorna had sat at a corner table and had wept, a pile of wet tissues growing before her. Feeling sorry for her, and wanting her out of the café, Fran had ended up giving her my mobile number.

Forewarned by Fran I almost gave in when Lorna phoned, held the 'caller unrecognised' in my hand. By then though I hadn't wanted to open doors to the past. Not then. Now it's what I spend my every unfilled hour doing.

Twelve

I got a text in the café saying that Hazel had uncovered a possible half-sister. I subsequently spent the rest of that day wondering how I could have missed that half-sister on my many trips to the Social Services' offices.

I know that Social Services have often been criticised – in child abuse cases – for their incomplete record keeping, but how – I almost stamped my foot – how could they have missed a whole half-sister? On the other hand there I was daring to hope that Hazel had indeed found in a half-sister a possible donor. At the same time I was puzzled as to when exactly in her short hectic life Moira could have produced this other child.

I arrived home to find that it wasn't a half-sister at all, but a stepsister. One brought briefly to another of Moira's brief relationships by the briefest of partners.

Such half-hopes – mine more than Hazel's – peppered Hazel's search into her ancestry. A female cousin was born premature, died a month after birth.

"Another dead end." Hazel came into the kitchen to tell me, her choice of words deliberate.

Long before the doctors had decided on her own end date Hazel had had no false reverence for death. So many of her old classmates had already died – in car crashes, from cancer, boy soldiers getting blown up in little wars; with some left maimed, but their old lives as good as gone. Hazel had already been to more funerals than I had, had seemed more accepting of life's nasty little tricks than I, more accepting of death's finality. Had her friends' deaths trained her to be fatalistic when it had come to her own?

Hazel was continually surprising me in the way she looked directly at everything. Ian had reckoned that she got that directness from me. She hadn't. Hazel's was an open and honest look at was what before her. My 'speaking my mind' was just challenging, hostile even, my being on guard against the world. Hazel's approach was candid and accepting. She was the better person.

I came home another evening to our dining table covered in pieces of paper taped together. Hazel had by this time managed to trace her female ancestry as far back as Moira's great-great-grandmother, who had died in her mid-twenties, which early death Hazel had come to expect. But before she had died – in childbirth – Hazel's great-great-great-grandmother had managed to produce three daughters, who Hazel had started to trace back down, she hoped, to the present day.

Took her five days.

And it took her so long because the one recurring hurdle she encountered in tracing her female ancestry was that every time one of them got married she changed her name, and if they remarried they sometimes changed the surname of the children from their previous marriage[s] as well. And the further back Hazel searched she found that the spellings were often different as well. One whimsical ancestor changed her daughter's forename as well as her surname when she remarried: we figured that the divorced birth father must have chosen the girl's first name.

"Or not been the birth father," I said.

Some of Hazel's great-great-great-grandmother's daughters died without issue. Two died in their early thirties, one (coincidentally?) in the Spanish flu epidemic after the First World War. One granddaughter emigrated, first to Canada, but left Toronto within two years, possibly remarrying and possibly moving to America.

Chasing that daughter down took Hazel a further two days. That granddaughter's seven-year-old daughter tripped while skipping, banged her head and died. Hazel printed off the cutting that told of 'the tragic accident' from the local Jamesville, Michigan, newspaper.

Thirteen

Again I was in the café when I got another text from Hazel. This one just said, 'Wait til u c wot I found.'

"Now what," I said to Nyrene, and showed her the phone. Nyrene squinted at the screen, pulled a face, and between serving went on to mutter about the misuse of the English language, again bemoaning the way her nieces and nephews spoke, their acronyms and abbreviations.

If this doesn't sound like any waitresses you may have encountered that's down to Fran who, way back, had got me and the other staff filling our slack hours helping her with crosswords. It got so that I had the Telegraph and Guardian delivered daily to the café, ostensibly for our customers' benefit.

Because all of the staff back then had not been up to Fran's Guardian standard, thereafter 'Do you do crosswords?' was a question I asked even when interviewing temporary staff.

I'd once complained to teenage Hazel of her generation's textspeak.

"But we do understand one another?" She had turned her luminaries on me.

"I don't. Not always."

"Could be that's why we do it."

So wise my daughter, set me that time to realising just why slang gets invented, its purpose both to exclude and to include.

That Hazel was now including me in her genealogical research, in that she chose to send me excited text messages, was both pleasing and… well, upsetting. I suppose I was resentful. I was her mother, she didn't need to know who all these others were. I had grown her: they had just sown the seed. And a flawed seed at that.

But research into her biological past was what Hazel wanted to do, and I certainly wasn't going to pick arguments with her during this last year of her life. Not that she and I had ever really argued. Hazel had told me when any of my forthright views were wrong.

"I think you're wrong," she'd say.

"And why's that?" I'd ask her. And so the debate would begin.

As it would whenever I questioned any plans of hers, she would tell me the reasoning behind them. We discussed, we debated, we disagreed, we searched for the words that would explain, the phrases that could summarise… and we did it while I was baking, over the dishes after dinner, during dinner, in the car on the way to school, sat on her bed… Anything not rightaway agreed upon Ian said, "This'll be another lengthy conflab I suppose."

I never believe a woman who says that she is best friends with her daughter. Always I wonder if that is what the daughter thinks, that her mother is her 'best friend'? I was pleased that Hazel liked, or at least tolerated my company, that we could talk into the night; and I was sorry that her friends now – those who lived close – couldn't cope with the imminence of her death. I was sorry too that her other friends had dispersed to the far reaches. Phone calls, emails, texts, cards even arriving from them, but no-one for her to spend an evening with. Just me. And I knew myself to be no friend substitute. I didn't know the slang, the key, the code words, the acronyms and the abbreviations, the one boy's name that could have them shrieking, memories unlocked... "And what about that...?"

No sooner did I close the front door that evening than I had an excited Hazel pulling me through to my laptop on the dining room table.

"Why didn't I know this?"

"What?"

"My famous ancestry."

"What ancestry?"

"My biological father."

That nonplussed me.

"Look." Hazel pulled over a chair beside hers. "He's even on Wikipedia."

"You got the right one?"

"Yup. Gustaf Eriksson. Man of the Woods." And there was the Wikipedia entry: Gustaf Eriksson. A name I hadn't seen for years. Or if I had then only in passing, while looking into Hazel's female ancestry.

The famous Gustaf Eriksson she had found, Man of the Woods, had apparently made his millions by selling his record company to EMI. With the proceeds from that sale he had subsequently set up a charitable trust whose one stated aim was to buy up and preserve English woodlands. Although the Wikipedia entry said that he had also been criticised, by environmental groups, for also owning shares in board and paper mills, and for taking on spruce plantations.

"This is the right Gustaf Eriksson?"

"Certainly is. The Gustaf Eriksson," she relished the words.

"But is this true? It is Wikipedia."

Hazel gave a happy laugh, "I've checked his other websites, woodland and haiku, interviews with him. Everything tallies. The spelling, year he was born. Everything. He gets a lot of stick for planting sitka spruce."

I looked over the screen, not so much disbelieving as unable to take it in. I hadn't come home expecting this. If anything I'd expected a one time long ago paternal connection to minor royalty. Not this.

"Haiku?"

"Japanese poetry. He's got books of it. I've been on Amazon to check. There's loads by him. Remember we did some at school? That visiting poet?"

I remembered only the rude limerick she once wrote, and for which we had to tell her off, Ian and I secretly laughing later.

"Didn't you know?" But she didn't let me answer, changed the screen.

Unable to find what she wanted she turned to me: "According to this one interview he first made his money managing rock bands. *The Purple Peas*?" Meant nothing to me. "But that was just the one band, and… What was it he said?" She hunts for the website. "Oh yes. He got so good at getting gigs for his friends' band that another band asked him to do the same for them. And it grew. Soon he was managing four bands. But try as he might he couldn't get a record company to sign any of them. So he started his own record company, got a distributor… His bands had a few in the top twenty. *Yellow Black Records* it was called. EMI bought it off him."

While she had been telling me that I had taken over the

laptop, had scrolled through the interview, gone back to Wikipedia, and followed a link to his own website, which was headed by a quote from Herman Hesse. 'It is we men of spirit, we poets, seers, fools and dreamers, who plant trees for later. Many of our trees will not thrive, many of our seeds will be sterile, many of our dreams will turn out to be mistakes, delusions and false hopes. Where is the harm in that?'

"But all this was years after you'd been born."

"The record company, yes. Didn't you honestly know that my biological father was a millionaire?"

"No." I looked at her. "Well he wasn't. Not then. We didn't pay him much attention. We thought he was a Norwegian sailor."

We were sitting side by side staring round-eyed at one another. Then we fell on each other laughing.

Fourteen

Sitka spruce, *picea sitchensis*, is the dark green conifer seen stepping up hillsides in close-planted rank upon rank. Of all the trees grown in Britain sitka spruce is the one most obviously used as crop, harvested – winter hillsides left as brown and battered as a war zone – and resown in regiments of plastic tubes.

Grown mostly in wet uplands, thriving even in poor soil, its sharp-ended needles make sitka spruce unpalatable to browsing deer. Those same sharp needles also act as deterrent to Christmas tree thieves.

Like its cousin cypress leylandii, sitka spruce grows very quickly and, packed together as they usually are, very straight. Which make a sitka spruce plantation easy to cut, trim and stack. One man in a machine can methodically rip through an entire plantation.

Some spruce timber goes for woodchip board, but most is used for paper, the molecular structure of spruce rendering it especially suitable for paper. Despite all the electronic media, or because of electronic media increasing otherwise recordless communication, the demand for paper is ever increasing. Which accounts for quite so many of Britain's uplands being darkened by spruce plantations.

Very little else thrives within these commercial forests, the evergreen canopy being so dense. Some kinds of fungus do survive in the lightless needle mass, the glowing red of agaric being the most obvious.

The land is not lost to natural regeneration. First spring after any spruce harvest the exposed ground will be covered in ferns and foxgloves.

Fifteen

"One question," I said to Hazel that first evening of her finding her birth father. "If he'd been a Norwegian sailor would you now be so excited about contacting him?"

"How can I answer that?" said my eminently sensible daughter. "He's not a Norwegian sailor." And she set about another attempt at an introductory email. I returned to my baking.

She got no response from that email the next day. She had sent it care of his woodland charity, The Tree Prospectus. So, in case he didn't regularly check those emails, she sent a copy of the same email to the publishers of his latest haiku collection, asked them to forward the email to him.

That email didn't get a response either. I arrived home two evenings later to Hazel asking me what I thought. Could her emails have scared him off? She showed me a copy.

'Dear Gustaf Eriksson, I have recently discovered that you are registered on my birth certificate as my biological father. Although, strictly speaking, that's not true – it's not a recent discovery. I've known for as long as I can remember that a Gustaf Eriksson was my biological father. It's only recently, when I became caught up in researching my past, that I found out more about you.

'Please do not be alarmed. I don't want anything from you other than to know more about you. And, if possible, to come and meet you. Please let me know how this could be arranged… '

"Final part's a bit abrupt," I said. "He could still think you're after his millions."

"What if I sent another email – saying I'm not the least interested in his money?"

"He could think thou doth protest overmuch. But up to you."

I went off to do my café baking. Hazel went back to the laptop.

To say that I was uneasy with Hazel contacting her birth father, that I was stomach-queasy uncomfortable, doesn't come close to explaining how I felt. How I physically felt – as if I was carrying a granite lump of regret in my chest.

Betrayals were everywhere. I felt that Hazel was not only betraying Ian and I, but her entire childhood, that this one act was devaluing the life we had made for her. And I felt, irrationally I know, but I felt that I had betrayed her by not having protected her, by not having saved her from this genetic disorder. And now, in my helping her, even if passively, to make contact with her birth father I felt that I was betraying Ian. Despite my years of irritation with him there was no arguing that he had been a good father. He had come along with me to all the pre-adoption parenting classes. (We had mutually decided that our own parents, both sets, would have benefited from such classes.) And Ian and I had once, we must have, yes we had, had to have once been in love. A kind of love. Ian had certainly loved Hazel.

Wiping my hands I came into the dining room. She was still looking into the laptop.

"You do realise," I said, "that so far as this Gustaf and Moira were concerned they had a pleasant weekend bonking. You were an unexpected result." (I was trying to say that it had been Ian and I who had wanted her.)

Hazel was a young woman who often dwelt so far, and

so quietly inside herself that my bitterest words could provoke but a wondering glance in my direction.

"Surprised," she smiled slow at me, "they didn't have me christened 'Pleasant Weekend'."

* * *

Next day in the café I listened to customers worrying over the downturn, the cuts in public spending, the fall in house prices, rise in the price of petrol, need to bring the troops home, outrage at a new traffic scheme… All worries about the future. My daughter had no place in that future. So why in my head was I picking quarrels with her?

I came home that evening to further developments.

Still not having received any reply to her emails Hazel had started on telephone directories. Which is by no means as easy as it used to be, people these days often having only a mobile phone, and no directories exist for mobile phones. Fortunately, as well as his mobile, Gustaf Eriksson had a landline – for his PC – and he wasn't ex-directory.

Hazel had talked to him.

"He was really cagey," she said. "Got a deep voice. I told him that I wanted nothing from him. No money, nothing. 'You wouldn't get any anyway,' he said. It's all in trust apparently. I said that I just wanted to meet him. Out of curiosity. 'What good do you think it'll do?' he said. 'No idea,' I told him. Said that I wasn't looking for a dad, that I already had one. Said I just wanted to meet. 'How well did you know my birth mother?' I asked him. 'Hardly at all,' he said. 'Didn't even know she was pregnant. Didn't know she'd had a baby. Not until the adoption agency contacted me to ask my permission.' He said that he'd given it, had never even asked for blood tests to be done, that I could quite easily, despite what it said on my birth certificate, not be his daughter. I asked if he'd do a DNA test. He said that he'd been going to make the same suggestion. 'But even if it turns out that I am your biological father,' he said, 'it'll still do you no good. All my money is tied up in Prospectus.'"

"So you're going to meet him?"

"I was hoping you'd drive me."

"Not sure I want to be there."

"You don't have to be there. If you don't mind though, I'd like you nearby."

How to refuse a daughter in the last year of her life?

"Look what came today," she said. When she had first discovered his background on the net she had ordered a recent collection of Gustaf Eriksson haiku. A limited edition hardback, the dustjacket had a pen and ink drawing of a woodland scene, a stylised sun shining down through leafless branches. Opening its soft cream pages I expected the haiku, as it had said in the rules for haiku I'd read, to be in three lines – of five syllables, seven syllables and five syllables. Instead several here were on one long line.

"His speciality apparently," Hazel said picking up on my frown. "According to the foreword that is. Some though, look, have a couple words on the second line."

Although Hazel and I were both regular, bedtime readers of novels, at least one a week, passing them on to one another, or advising against, neither of us had bothered with poetry.

I read one of the long lines aloud, "Sun circles of gold on the forest floor: woodsmen bend to logs."

"What's it mean?" Hazel asked. I shrugged.

Sixteen

Hazel's calm and unthreatening manner overcame Gustaf Eriksson's reluctance and he agreed to meet her. But not at his house, in a wood.

"He doesn't want you to know where he lives," I told her.

"Fair enough," Hazel said. "If I was him I'd be that cautious. For all he knows I could be a stalker, be harbouring all sorts of delusions about him."

Since she had started enthusiastically relating to me snippets of Gustaf Eriksson's varied career I had heard my own every comment sounding as if it contained withheld criticism of absent biological father Gustaf Eriksson. And Hazel, reacting as much to my mother-known tone as to what I was saying, was taking up the position of defender of all things Gustaf Eriksson. Lest it drive her further towards him I made myself pause and consider my every response.

He emailed Hazel the map reference for the wood, told her there was a carpark just off the road and for her to follow the one footpath into the wood.

Hazel and I set about working out how to enter a map reference into her satnav. She knew how to enter postcodes for where she wanted to go. I didn't then have a satnav: had hardly needed one to get to the café and back.

Once we'd entered the grid co-ordinates we still weren't confident, so we went on the net and looked up the nearest town to the map reference, and Hazel popped down to the garage shop to buy a road map. And that's how we set off the next morning – with the satnav woman's voice telling me which turning, which roundabout exit to take, and Hazel beside me, road map on her knees, saying, "Yes, that makes sense." Or, turning pages, "I'm not sure. Oh yes. Not the way I'd have chosen, but this road'll get us there."

And it did.

Four hours after leaving home – we had shut the front door behind us before seven, stopped off to drop last evening's baking into the café – we pulled off a narrow country road into a lane arched by green-black rhododendrons. That grey-chip and grass lane ended in a square carpark enclosed on three of its sides by more rhododendrons in purple flower.

"There's the path," Hazel said. "Wish me luck."

And before I had turned off the engine, undone my seatbelt, let out my breath, Hazel had disappeared down a dark path between the rhododendrons. We had arranged to keep in touch by mobile.

I got out to stretch my legs, read a new noticeboard by the entrance to the path. The child-height laminated noticeboard told me, helped along by bright coloured pictures, what trees made up the woodland and what creatures lived there. Apparently a green woodpecker and a greater-spotted woodpecker could both be heard and sometimes seen, as well as toads, dragonflies, badgers and foxes. In small print, bottom right hand corner, it said that the woods were maintained by The Tree Prospectus, a registered charity, and it gave the charity's number.

Although I was tempted to go under the rhododendron arch and wander a little way into the wood I had promised, been made to promise, not to go anywhere near the meeting – in case my being there made Gustaf Eriksson nervous, or my having to be introduced just complicated the meeting and took the focus away from him and her.

I wandered along the grit and grass lane back out to the road, looked up and down it. We were miles from anywhere, not a house or a tea room in sight. So back I went to the car and to the flask I'd wisely packed.

I made that walk around the carpark twice – read the noticeboard, dawdled out into the road, sniffed at the sprays of purple flowers, poured myself a coffee – before I got a text from Hazel saying simply, 'All OK. Am staying to help. Meet me carpark @ 4'.

I wasn't pleased. That wasn't according to the plan, meant that even if we left promptly at four we wouldn't get home much before eight, and she knew that I still had baking to do for the café next day. Or, I checked myself, was my being peeved nothing more than jealousy pure and simple? Because I always kept a few 'contingency cakes' in the freezer for unforeseen circumstances such as these.

I was hurting though. I was her mother. She had known me all her life. Which probably made me a boring old fart. While he, the birth father, the now famous Gustaf Eriksson, was there in the woods to be chatted to and 'discovered' . So hard to keep from sneering…

Grumpily I looked up the nearest town on the road map and slowly drove myself there, along the way shouting at the satnav to shut up. At every turning she told me that I was going the wrong way and that she was recalculating. I didn't though want to turn her off and mess up Hazel's return settings.

The town's one café, a franchise, was all chrome and plastic with the local radio station niggling away at the customers' brains. But I was able to use their lavatory, had a baguette lunch, and I had bought a paper, half-finished the crossword. When I got back to the rhododendron carpark I crawled onto the back seat of the car and curled up for a snooze.

That killed at most half an hour. I read the noticeboard again, and escaped the three walls of rhododendron to take another walk down the lane to the road. I thought I heard voices far off in the wood, but couldn't make out a word, or satisfy myself that one of the voices was Hazel's. I sighed, wandered back and sat in the car.

One of those square cars arrived while I was having a second go at the crossword. I half expected a wheelchair to be fetched from the back, but it was only a tall thin man with white hair who got out and who led a fluffy white dog into the dark path.

That square car was still there when, just before four, Hazel appeared, her trainers covered in black mud and with dried grey circles on both her knees. Her hair, which she'd had tightly scrunched back that morning, now had strands loose down about her face and wisping out about her head like a dark halo.

Cheeks flushed, eyes shining, "I told him you'd be worried," she said as she got in, lifting the bottom of her muddy jeans away from the front edge of the car seat. "And we've got a fair way to go. You OK to drive?"

She was buckled in before I'd turned on the ignition.

"Any of that coffee left?" She reached around to the back seat. "He let me have some of his tea. His very stewed tea.

And one of his sandwiches. Sure you don't want me to drive?"

Waiting for her to pour her coffee I hadn't put the car in gear, had been a little taken aback by her animation. I hadn't seen her looking so well for... years? Not only were her cheeks flushed she seemed full of bounce, her every movement quick and decisive. None of that aimless flopping about we'd had for the last few weeks. And before that, in the years living with Kevin, there had been a slowness to her, an overweight reluctance to move.

"No. No, I'm fine to drive," I said as I reversed, then waited for her to screw the lid back on the thermos and to get both her hands around the cup.

"Tell me what happened," I said as I drove into the lane. "How'd you get on?" As we emerged into the road the satnav told me again that I was going the wrong way. "And for chrissake shut her up. Put the new settings in."

Seventeen

Rhododendron ponticum has lance shaped leaves, can grow to a height of eight metres, its blooms excessive. Some books say that rhododendrons were introduced to the British Isles for the romanticking of ferny landscapes, and some say that rhododendron were first planted by the landed rich and gun-toting to provide cover for pheasants. Whichever the case rhododendron has now become, insofar as woodland management goes, a pernicious weed. Not so much a garden escapee as a hangover from grandiose Victoriana.

Liking peat, perfectly suited therefore to the loam of a woodland floor, rhododendron spreads like mangrove, leaf-heavy boughs being brought to ground and, touching, taking root. Being easily seeded and root-suckering too, once spread and covering acres, little else will grow within rhododendron's low evergreen canopy.

To find yourself within rhododendron's overgrowth can induce panic. Its dipping boughs and slim black-green trunks twisting about one another, the black soil sucking at your feet, arm-thick branches worming all around, tripping you, banging into your face, too slimy and slippery to grip, other branches curling down to thump your head, bar your way... A longing for light, for sight of sky, can have your eyes opened wide, while haste has you scrambling to be free... and being tripped, stumbling, slipping, bumping your head...

Eighteen

I'll try and condense here all that Hazel told me as best I remember. As I think I remember.

The conversation began on the four-hour drive home, and continued on and off into the evening and over the next couple of days.

Soon as she was on the path she heard the buzzsaw growling away deeper in the woods. When she eventually closed on the sound she found Gustaf Eriksson on his own – laying waste to an acre of rhododendrons.

"He calls it rhodie-bashing," she said.

"What's he like?"

"Much like his photos." On The Prospectus website. "But bigger if you know what I mean. Not taller. Of course taller than you and me. But bigger all over. And louder. Definitely louder. Confidently loud. I don't think you'll like him." ('Very self-confident' was our café euphemism for a loudmouth.)

He had on a protective visor when first she came up to him. Hazel stood off, away from the flying woodchips. When he became aware of her presence he turned off the buzzsaw and...

Her pause had me take my eyes off the motorway to look around at her.

"He just sort of stared at me. Looking for evidence of his paternity I guessed."

"You Hazel?" was all he eventually said, laid down his

saw and took off his work gauntlets. Hazel had thought he was about to shake hands, so she began to pick her way over the leaf debris and the almost black rhododendron stems. Instead of shaking hands, however, he went to his lunch satchel and pulled out two plastic swab tubes.

Hazel found this funny – that the very first thing she and her putative birth father did together was to each rub a long cotton bud inside each their cheeks.

"Other parents and their grown children, when they meet, they give each other a mwah! peck on the cheek. But there we were with two cotton-tipped swabs on the insides of ours."

That awkwardness out of the way she asked him why he was cutting down the rhododendrons. He explained that as far as woodland management is concerned rhododendron has become an invasive weed. Hazel offered to help.

"You sure?" he said looking down at her still clean trainers. "Won't gain you any brownie points. Can always use another volunteer though."

He told her to gather up all the already cut down rhododendron into a heap.

Hazel said to me later that the black-green boughs and branches had white disc ends where they'd been sawn through.

"Quite pretty really."

"I'll bring the trailer up close later," he said. "Take them where we can burn them."

He tugged on the cord to start his chainsaw again, and Hazel set to dragging the branches he had already cut down into more orderly heaps. When his engine idled she shouted to ask him to cut the branches into smaller, more manageable sections. He nodded, and cut in half the limb he had just lopped.

While he was beginning his attack on the next thicket, that was when Hazel texted me.

They didn't talk again until he stopped for lunch.

Having slapped and flapped the worst of the woodchips off his front he offered Hazel half his shop-bought baguette. They took turns with his flask tea cup.

"How well did you know my birth mother?" she asked him.

"Birth mother?" He looked at the word, said, "Hardly at all. Not that she was a one-night stand. More a series of one-night stands. If she is who I think she was. Moira? Right?"

He went on to tell Hazel that he hadn't even known that Moira was pregnant.

"I could as easily have been a sperm donor."

As I wrote those words 'sperm donor' I imagined them being said aloud in the café and the discomfort there that might well have arisen from their having been said. I knew though that mention of her father's sperm would not have shocked Hazel. She has never flinched from fact. "That so?" seemed her questioning of anything that didn't straightaway make sense.

As for her putative father couching his paternity in 'sperm donor' terms... she would have seen it, given her birth parents relationship, as a fair analogy, probably too as him attempting to shock, and Hazel of course declining to be shocked, removing from him the power to shock.

When he was 'seeing' Moira, he told Hazel, was when he had been managing his first three bands, getting them gigs, and often having to act as their roadie.

"They were odd times. Hectic times. Moira wasn't even what you'd call a regular girlfriend. As I said, was more like a series of one-night stands. While I was running around all over the place looking after my bands. If I knew I was going to be in her neck of the woods – always woods, even then – I'd give her a call, invite her along to the gig, stay over somewhere with her."

He went over to Germany with two of his bands, then across to the US.

"First I knew of your existence was when the adoption

people got hold of me, asked if I had any objections to you being adopted. They'd been trying to trace my whereabouts for months. That's how it was then."

As this was way before DNA testing, when even having the same blood groups weren't taken to be conclusive proof, and as Hazel was to be adopted it meant that Moira wouldn't be chasing him for child maintenance, so with his going to be freed of all responsibility he readily signed the adoption papers.

"Whether or not I was your father. Simply to save Moira problems. No skin off my nose. And you certainly don't have my nose. Don't look a bit like me. Nor what I used to look like. And, from what I recall, you don't look much like Moira either."

"What did she look like?"

"Young. Lots of long hair. Skinny."

"Not like me."

"You're not seventeen."

He asked Hazel, "Why now?" Why at this late stage was she looking into her past?

"You pregnant?"

"No," Hazel said. "Just curious."

"An eight hour round trip just to satisfy your curiosity?"

Gustaf went for a pee behind a tree and when he came back stood over her to say that whatever she was hoping to get out of him all of it was a dead end. He had no accessible money. And if what she wanted was to find her ancestors, then that too was a dead end. He was adopted himself. Well, long-term fostered.

"If I am your father," he said as he busied himself packing away his flask and baguette wrapping, "and if you're stuck for money…"

"I'm not," Hazel said.

"… then it's only right that I pay what I can. But if I turn out not to be your father, then for wasting my time I think it's only fair that you make a donation to Prospectus."

"OK if I volunteer occasionally?"

"That'll do."

They went back to cutting down and heaping up the last of the rhododendrons in that part of the wood. Then Gustaf – Hazel called him Gustaf – fetched his pickup.

"Four wheel drive. One of those monster pickups. But bright yellow. Front-heavy. All engine and cab. And the cab's got seats behind the driver. Number plate is HA11 IKU."

"Did you ask him about the haiku?

"Didn't get a chance. This time."

"You going back?"

"Said I'd volunteer."

"Bright yellow?" I said.

"Very bright. But battered and dented. Bit like him. Big and loud all round. You won't like him. He's one of those full of himself types. Don't think he knows how to be quiet."

She told of how he sang shanties as they used the winch on the front of the pickup to pull out some rhododendron roots. Which had been how, to avoid the whipped back broken roots, tripping and stumbling over the uneven ground, she had got herself so muddy.

"He is full of himself," Hazel said at home later, "but not full of himself. If you know what I mean. The truck's name, the model, is Excalibur. I asked if he thought he was King Arthur."

"Truck's more a rusty dagger." He had patted its tinny side. "And I'm certainly no prince."

"And you're going back?" I asked her.

"Not necessarily to that wood. Hopefully somewhere closer. I'll drive."

I nodded, but I had already made up my mind to take her. Especially as I'd seen her eyelids drooping, blinking awake as I had turned in the car to ask another question, and we hadn't then long left the wood. She had fallen sound asleep when we'd still been two hours from home.

Nineteen

Hazel took two days off to recover from the unaccustomed physical labour.

I was concerned then, naturally, for her health. But, although she moved stiffly about the house, groaned when getting out of the armchair, she laughing told of the muscles aching in her back and buttocks, and even seemed proud of a burst blister on her thumb.

On the second day she phoned Gustaf Eriksson to ask if she could come again – as a helper. He said to meet her in the same wood.

Hazel was all for driving herself. My worry though was that after a hard day's physical work she could so easily fall asleep at the wheel and drive through a hedge – like her father. I didn't have to mention her father, just reminded her that she had twice nodded off on her way home last time.

So I doubled up the baking that evening – one lot for the freezer. Hazel helped, and we dropped the cakes into the café on our way through town early next morning.

I had gone along with this second – I thought self-indulgent – trip because I wanted to avoid, in light of her prognosis, all pointless disagreements. It wasn't like when she had been a child at home and I had been training her to be an adult – not in my image, not even as someone I could be proud of, just giving her the necessary weaponry to negotiate life's many pratfalls. And I had failed: here she was with a terminal condition.

Add into that failure as a mother her own delicate relationship with her recently late father and her new-found birth father, and I was leading the both of us warily through an emotional minefield.

Even so, on the long drive back to the rhododendron wood, I did find myself asking, "Just why are we going back? You won't know for sure whether he's your birth father yet, not for a week or more."

"I liked being there." She had had to think of her answer. And it was a mile more or so of motorway before she said, "The work too. Feels like I'm doing something worthwhile with my time. Not just scratching around indoors looking for things to do."

"OK," I said. And drove on.

Just by what she was wearing – an old jumper, baggy brown trousers tucked into a pair of pink polka-dot wellies, mac-in-a-sack and packed lunch – Hazel had obviously given much thought to this second visit.

During the last two days, talking over again Hazel's first woodland meeting with Gustaf Eriksson, Hazel had told me that, because of his outspoken opinions and more particularly his loudness, I wouldn't like Gustaf Eriksson. Which certainly tempted me, of course, to the emotional opposite.

Hazel was probably half right in what types I dislike. I do judge, and I don't judge, by appearances. And anyone loud in the café does put off other customers. On the other hand we tolerated Old Bill, who was loud – from shouting over his machines, he said. What machines I never found out. But was kindness itself. So kind that me, Franny, and any of the other staff had to be careful what we said in front of him. A student waitress said how difficult it was in her shared house with a broken fridge. Bill turned up next day with one on a trailer.

I suppose Hazel had heard me make so many scathing comments on the Great British Public that she assumed that I judged everyone on surface appearances. Wasn't so. In the café we've had tattooed punks, pierced freaks, white-faced goths, gypsies, even Hells Angels, who have all been the epitome of politeness, of consideration for others. While some of the twin-set and pearls brigade have been selfish, foul-mouthed bitches.

We arrived at the woodland to find, along one side of the lane to the carpark, almost all the rhododendrons gone.

As I steered this way and that to negotiate the lane's potholes I glimpsed two men working behind a big pile of cut down bushes. One man was young and slim with tied back dreadlocks. The shorter older man was wearing a plastic visor and gauntlets, and was wielding a chainsaw. Behind them I saw part of the side of a bright yellow pickup and what looked like a tall oven cowl.

The carpark itself was still enclosed by walls of rhododendron. Soon as I stopped Hazel tripped off in her pink polka-dot wellies to join the two men.

Again not wanting to intrude on Hazel's meeting with her putative birth father, and possibly take the focus of attention away from her, I got out of the car to stretch my legs, walked in circles around the carpark, rolled the ache out of my shoulders and bent some life back into my knees. Then, as I had planned, I got into the car's back seat with my book, crossword and lunch. I think I slept most of that morning.

No-one else came to the carpark that day. Deterred I should imagine by the whine and grind of machines in the wood. Just to straighten out my body I stood by the car to eat my sandwich lunch, then plucked up nerve enough to push into the rhododendrons – in the opposite direction to the machine noises – to squat for a pee. Nor was I the first to leave a white tissue part-buried in the black soil.

The rest of the afternoon I read, returned to the unfinished crossword a few times, and read some more. Around four I became aware that the machines had stopped. Half hour or so later Hazel returned smiling to the car.

"Sounded noisy today," I said as we drove back down the half-lit track.

"My ears are still ringing." Hazel shook her head as if to clear water from her ears and, as we left the woods behind, she told of what they had been doing that day.

The rhododendrons' arm-thick black boughs they had stacked in the trailer and the back of the truck – to be taken off later and burnt. The rest – leaves, twigs, thinner branches – they put through the shredder, which was the tall cowl-like machine I'd seen.

"That all comes out as chippings," Hazel told me. And it had been her job this day, when not stacking branches, to rake and shovel up the shredder chippings into a wheelbarrow and spread them around the other trees. The men had come armed with goggles and ear-protectors, hadn't thought to bring any for Hazel. I wondered, mother-defensively, if they had been trying to put her off coming again. But I decided it was more likely, their having been rhodie-bashing for the last two days, and not being certain that Hazel would turn up, they had got in the way of looking out for just for the two of them.

"What Gustaf's hoping," Hazel said; and I was pleased that she called him by his name and not 'my birth father' or somesuch, "is that the chippings will mulch down and provide a fertile base for other woodland plants. "What we're after here is bio-diversity now," he said to me. "If we leave the rhodies nothing else will grow and the soil'll become acid." Dez though said..."

"Who?"

"I know," Hazel said. "The zed seems to go with the blond dreadlocks."

"He call you Haz?"

"No." Hazel gave a quick laugh. "But he's all right." She was certain of that. "Anyway they argued. Dez reckoned that laying the chippings is counterproductive, that the only thing that will grow out of them is rhodies again. Gustaf said it's worth a try, and they'll be back next spring anyway to pull up any rhodie seedlings. He said they can kick out any chips that may have rooted themselves then. One thing and another they kept on all through their lunch."

"About rhodies?" I was already picking up the lingua franca. Not that I then had any concerns one way or the other: trees were trees and woods were woods, with some of them pretty in autumn.

"Not just rhodies," Hazel said. During lunch apparently Dez had taken Gustaf to task over Prospectus's increasing ownership, and what Dez said was exploitation, of spruce and larch plantations. While Gustaf asked if Dez was about to sign up to the 'broadleaved fascists'.

"All trees in this country, outside of gardens and parks, are crops. Are grown for a purpose," Gustaf said; and he told Dez to get real, that they had to start from where they were now, that the work of Prospectus had to be funded somehow, couldn't rely solely on charity and government grants."

Dez called Gustaf a 'commercial apologist'.

"What next," Dez said, "biomass forestry?"

"Why not?" Gustaf said.

When Dez had gone off to find a tree to have a pee behind, Gustaf had said to Hazel, "It's all in the mind, these sylvan values based on an idealised past. Though Dez is by no means alone. Today's is a world where everyone deceives themselves to its worth and their worth in it."

"You deceived as well?" Hazel asked him. Sharp my daughter.

"Probably. Yea, probably. My excuse is that I ran out of things to do. This is what's been left for me to do."

Not wanting Hazel to find herself in the middle of an ongoing woodland row, I asked her if Dez had been that angry.

"No. Neither of them were. It was more like a ritual debate. Aspects of. New names they came up with to call each other – had both of them laughing. I had the feeling that I was a fresh audience and they were rehashing salient points for my benefit."

And having told me all that, and having said that there was no need for me to drive her when she came back tomorrow, Hazel sank into sleep beside me.

Twenty

Larch being the only deciduous conifer widespread in England it is readily identifiable in spring by the tender green of its new needles, and in autumn by those same needles changing from umber through to gold before dropping.

There are three kinds of larch, European larch (*larix decidua*), Japanese larch (*larix kaempferi*), and their hybrid (*larix eurolepsis*). The hybrid, disease resistant, is also known as the Dunkeld larch and, as fast-growing as spruce, is the variety most used in British plantations.

In summer a larch plantation feels strange – in that there are pine needles above, but grass underfoot and with drifts of golden needles along the edges of any footpaths. One gets a sense of being welcome in a larch plantation. I certainly prefer them to the damp, crowded and the frankly hostile darkness of evergreen spruce.

Commercial plantations exclusively of larch will be found at high rocky altitudes, where evergreen conifers such as spruce would suffer from winter (ice-lock) drought. At lower altitudes larch will most often be found in long strips within spruce plantations, used there as a firebreak. This is because growing larch has a tendency to smoulder rather than to flame. Although, paradoxically, larch trunks once dried do make excellent logs for domestic stoves.

Logs aside what larch timber is used for is furniture and fittings, in particular these days for stairs. In older houses any thin exposed beams will most likely be of larch. In pre-industrial Scotland larch was the preferred timber for fishing boats.

These post-industrial days the Dunkeld larch being such a hardy tree it is often first to be planted on old landfill and slag heap sites as part of the initial process of land reclamation, as well as anywhere environmental groups are trying to reintroduce the red squirrel. The native red squirrel feeds on Scots pine and larch seed.

Twenty-one

For the next few days I ferried Hazel back and forth to various woodlands. Then it rained overnight and she got an early morning phone call telling her not to come, the work detail had been cancelled.

I went to the café and caught up with Nyrene. Hazel took herself to town and got herself some sturdy wet weather gear, camouflage cargo pants and a pair of steel-capped working boots.

When Hazel, attired thus, turned up in the woods the next day Gustaf said to her, "Mean business then."

Hazel wasn't sure what he had meant by 'mean business'. Whether it was self-evidently that she was now equipped for work in the woods, or that she was intent on pursuing him as father? As later that day he seemed, by small gestures such as asking her to fetch a handsaw from the pickup, to be more accepting of her as a worker, she decided to be pleased.

Within that first couple of weeks she had few direct exchanges with Gustaf. She related to me more what she had overheard him saying to others, such as when arguing with Dez, or when in discussion with members of the groups who came along for their 'woodland experience'.

Charity-run groups of mentally handicapped or of the mentally ill, or of recovering alcoholics and addicts, all had been brought to the woods apparently to be spiritually nourished by being among greenery. Hazel happily reported back to me her surprise at how patient her loudmouth birth father had been with them.

I said nothing, but I did wonder if Gustaf's patience was only company policy. I know that we dreaded the 'odd ones', which was how we side-of-the-mouth warned each other, being brought into the café. Often they made a mess not only of the table but the surrounding floor as well. A few even made themselves deliberately sick. Of course we had to pretend (like Gustaf?) to be understanding and tolerant of the 'poor souls'.

Even if his patience was policy Gustaf did – unwittingly? – cause consternation to one mental health group by telling them, "This world is one creature, has its own lifespan." Which had one member of the group wandering off through the trees, beating himself about the head and crying, "We're all death-bound. Death-bound!"

I was still at this time, at my insistence, only the taxi. I dropped Hazel off at rendezvous points and, if close enough, made my way back to the café. If further away I sat out the day in the carpark, read a book, listened to the radio and fed crumbs to the carpark chaffinches. Often, both book and radio ignored and sighing into my circular thoughts – where been, where going – I looked unseeing at the carpark's bushes and trees.

If there was one big enough within driving distance I took myself along to the local town, pottered about the antique shops, sussed out the local cafés.

In the car on the way home I'd deliver my café critiques and Hazel would tell me of what they had been doing in the woods that day, what Gustaf might have said to someone.

"The brontosaurus weighed tons," he told a party of primary schoolchildren. "Was bigger than the coach that brought you here. And the tyrannosaurus, been dead millions of years, continues to terrify little children. But what of those big beasts survives intact? Just a few bones here and there. What does survive, complete in every part, is a gnat in amber." He showed them a stone. "See? Small is what we like," he told them. "Small is what we do."

"Did he mean the haiku?"

"Didn't say. But did you know conifers were here before the dinosaurs?"

I hadn't; and the warmth and drone of the car soon had Hazel nodding off. Then, while I baked that evening, she loitered about the kitchen telling me more. I hadn't known her to be so enthusiastic about anything since she'd come home chattering from school.

"Why all these different places?" I asked as I reset the satnav next morning.

"Dez reckons," (which was how many of her responses began) or "Gustaf said…" or "…what we plant depends on the soil and the microclimate."

"But why don't they concentrate on the one place? Get that right?"

"Gustaf says he wants to reforest England. So we go to what land is available where."

We went that day to an old landfill site in East Anglia. It was barely grassed over. I could see the yellow pickup away in the distance, small figures around it, big squares of a black and silver power station beyond.

"Why here?" I asked Hazel as she gathered up her lunch bag and waterproofs. "Got to be nicer places."

"Trees improve the soil and the climate." She gave me her how-could-you-not-know-that frown, a brief crease between the eyebrows.

* * *

On the way back from another fresh site Hazel said, "I think you'll get on well with him. Know what I heard him say today? Could've been you speaking. He said that soaps are a celebration of stupidity."

When Hazel had been living at home, before going to college that is, I had actively discouraged her from watching soaps, hadn't wanted her to be corrupted by the Great British Public dramatised.

I was apparently like Gustaf Eriksson in other ways too. My lack of respect for tradition, for the way things are done, my various stances and refusals always an upset for Ian.

"Gustaf says he doesn't trust the past: it gave us this."
"What's this?"
"According to him a very unsatisfactory state of affairs."
With all our talk about him Hazel and I were almost (I

say almost because I was conscious of it being so) but acting almost as if we had a schoolgirl crush on this one boy in our class. "What did Gustaf Eriksson say, do, today?" Part of that was, I suppose, the two men in our life having been dismissed Hazel and I had but this one man to concentrate on. With myself, during that early period, at secondhand.

One of her attempts to make Gustaf acceptable to me, and not just a careless sower of semen, albeit that his semen had given me Hazel, had been to tell me of Gustaf tearing into one of a mental health group who had started making racist jibes. Hazel had heard me often enough ranting against the silly Daily Mail prejudices of my racist mother to be confident that I'd sympathise with Gustaf.

"This nonsense of race and creeds," Gustaf had said to the man. "These found differences. Not one of these contrived differences makes you better than anyone else. Know what makes you exactly the same as one of their bigots? No? You are made alike by your seeking of differences."

Gustaf apparently agreed with me too about supermarkets.

"Supermarkets serve only their shareholders; and, by their monopoly, destroy the very communities they allege they serve."

When the nearest supermarket opened an instore café it had taken away some of my customers and had completely closed the town's other café.

I did nonetheless try to argue, out of pure jealousy, against myself and this new influence on Hazel by questioning the charity status of Prospectus. I said that for charities to be supported someone had to be making a living, making a profit, providing real jobs, growth...

"Wrong mindset," Hazel told me. Although this could have been later. "You're talking of the conservation of destruction. Which is," she hastened under my raised eyebrows: this wasn't her language, "current industrial and agricultural practices. I think Gustaf calls such people dangerous stick-in-the-muds. They bring the same solutions, economic fixes, to the same problems, which safe solutions only add to the problems. We, the Greens, he says, are the new risk-takers, the real adventurers."

Same theme, a different time of retelling: "Gustaf said science and technology have become a working against the natural, not with the natural."

This was the man with the bright yellow pickup and the noisy shredder? "Has he said yet why, really why, he became a 'man of the woods'?"

"He said that making money in itself, that being a successful businessman, had no longer been enough. He wanted more. Not things. A purpose. Something worth doing."

Acknowledging his fatherhood might have been something worth doing. But I said nothing, didn't that time get a chance. Hazel seemed to have set herself to defend Gustaf against any anticipated criticisms from me.

"He uses all the latest forestry equipment in his plantations, is not opposed to technology as such. He said to Dez today, 'Consider the difference in our civilisation if glass had never been invented. Of course we need innovation.'"

Gustaf had again been arguing with Dez, who had been saying that reforesting bits of England was all very well but they should be out on the streets, and Gustaf had said, "Protest is the failure of democracy."

I didn't know what to make of that. I did though see that poor dreadlocked Dez seemed to be getting it in the neck a lot from Gustaf. Another time with reference to his dreds: "Fashion is the camouflage of conformity."

"Their relationship seems very close," I spoke the thought. "You don't suppose Dez could be another of Gustaf's wild oats?"

By Hazel's silence I assumed that the same thought had occurred to her.

Twenty-two

Hazel and Gustaf's relationship changed with the swabs' confirmation of Gustaf's paternity.

They were putting up a deer fence around what was to be a new plantation. When they broke for lunch Hazel made a seat for herself on a fallen trunk. Gustaf came over to her.

"Mind if I sit next to my daughter?"

Gustaf had not called her 'daughter' before. On previous lunch and tea breaks he had kept his distance, either hanging about with others of the work group or retreating to his yellow pickup, head tilted to his mobile.

"So Moira was right?"

"Seems so." He opened his lunch pack. "Though I'm still not sure what you want from me. Or if it's mine to give."

"Just to be here," Hazel told him. "Like this. Helping where I can. Being a part of it." I can see her frowning as she tried to explain. "I think what you're doing is really worthwhile."

"Worthwhile?" He wasn't convinced. "You do know that all my money is bound up in Prospectus? Which pays me a wage. The money itself can't be touched."

"I don't want your money," Hazel told him. "Don't need your money." She didn't: I was keeping her. And I was happy so to do.

What Hazel didn't tell him was her diagnosis. And at that stage it would have been hard for him to even guess at her real state of health. The unaccustomed outdoor work had brought a flush to her cheeks and a shine to her eyes. Even her hair seemed to have acquired a gloss and a bounce. And she had already lost a little weight, seemed to have acquired energy.

When in the woods with him that is. What Gustaf didn't see was her drop asleep within minutes of the homeward journey. Although seeing how full of her new life she was, despite her nodding off in the car, I had dared wonder if she could be in remission…

That lunchbreak however Gustaf was still unsure of her motives, uncomfortable too on his lunchtime perch. He studied her as he ate, stopped when Hazel said, "So now tell me about Moira."

Theirs, as he had said before, had been a casual relationship. Studiedly casual. Of their age, of its time. She had been but one of Gustaf's stopover girlfriends, as he had assumed that he had been but one of Moira's stopping over boyfriends.

"No broken hearts," Gustaf said. "We suited each other's view of ourselves. No demands, no expectations. This is not to belittle you, but I was far more interested in my business then than in any girlfriend. Which is... getting a bit ahead of myself. When I was seeing Moira I was as much a roadie as a manager. I had no money then. All was before me. By the time I got to be running the record company I'd long lost touch with Moira."

Hazel told me that he frowned a lot telling her just this, was looking down at the ground, dragging the toe of his boot through a thick clump of moss, hesitant, not his usual forthright delivery.

"Truth is, when the adoption papers came," he said, "I had a job remembering who Moira was. I hadn't even known her surname. And so much had happened since I'd last seen her. And after the adoption, last I heard of her, she was shacked up with some junkie. Which is also what seemed to be happening a lot around about that time."

"What are we protecting from the deer?" Hazel asked him. And for the rest of that lunchtime he told of his long-term plans for the cleared enclosure, to make it an arboretum. At least to see if it was feasible.

Twenty-three

From that day onwards Hazel and Gustaf grew closer. Which was a worry to me.

I had read in Sunday supplements of adopted children having sought out their birth parents and having found someone so like them in almost every respect that they became physically attractive to one another. Like can be drawn to mirror-like with as much a pull as polar opposites attract: how many married couples have I served in the café who looked like brother and sister?

It doesn't take much imagination to see a new-found father and daughter, their tastes uncannily alike, same dress sense even; and for the child having been adopted their always having felt the odd one out, and suddenly here was someone to whom they had to explain nothing. While for the new-found parent, without any of the prohibitions that come from the years of having reared the child, suddenly here, adult to adult, was such a powerful attraction that it could be mistaken for sexual love.

Gustaf Eriksson was seven years younger than me, that's seven years closer in age to Hazel. And while I knew that my Hazel wasn't manipulative, well not maliciously so, she certainly did know how to exercise her dimples to her advantage, how to make herself big-eyed attractive... And here was this new-found father known for his promiscuity... She even told me that she couldn't think of him as 'father' only as Gustaf. Ian was Dad. But she already knew Ian's part in the making of her, had now to be looking for parts of herself in Gustaf... Such an overwhelming interest could so easily be mistaken for love.

Her glee the day that she discovered that Gustaf too had once been put up for adoption.

He told her that their two histories made a nonsense of genealogy. "Do trees know their parents?" he asked her. "Does knowing matter? All we can do for our careless progenitors, for all our ancestors even, is forgive them. Forgive them their ignorance of us and our ways. They were not us, did not have our understanding. And yet... we exist because of them, these strangers."

That evening Hazel informed me that genes provided no ready-made character, no off-the-shelf identity, that any ancestry had to be of intellectual interest only. "Possibly it offers us an alibi for what we most dislike about ourselves."

Had she been quoting him? I didn't care. Because what she went on to tell me was that Ian and I had been of greater importance in her life, that she loved me. And I got a hug.

Even so there was no denying that Hazel was besotted. All that she talked about in the car and at home was Gustaf said this, Gustaf did that. And her eyes actually sparkled when she told of their day's doings. The day for instance the pickup had got stuck and in pushing it out they had all got covered in mud, except Gustaf who turned the hose on them, and then they turned it on him. All innocent, silly even, and she was happier than I'd seen her in years. Yet...

"Hazel," he said to her. "What a doubly apt name. You even have Hazel eyes. And so fitting that Moira gave you a tree's name. Are you nut bearing?"

"Don't have any nuts. If that's what you mean."

Many of their reported conversations seemed to be banter.

"A shade-bearing species," he said. "Don't like the limelight."

"Part of your underwood," Hazel said. "A species whose importance is not immediately obvious." Hazel had been reading up on forests and woodlands.

Was I jealous? Without doubt. Although I have never been possessive, have always wanted Hazel to have her own full life. Not mine. Not a shadow of mine. And not for me to live my life through her.

Was I jealous? Yes, I was. And hurt too.

I was driving her one morning when she said, "I just love

this going to work with Gustaf and Dez." For the previous two nights it had rained, only for the forecast to predict five fine days.

"Today," she said, "there I'll be looking up through the trees to a mist hanging about the canopy. The younger beech trees – you know the thin low down ones? – they'll have old leaves still that'll look slices of amber, floating there in the forest dark. And the mud will be working its way up the insides of my trouser legs, and I'll be filled with happiness. How weird is that?"

I didn't answer, concentrated on my driving, and blinked to stop my eyes filling. How weird was that? Provoked to tears because my terminally ill – although she wasn't actually ill in that she was sickly – but tearful because my grown daughter was happier spending time with her new-found father and new-found friends than she was at home with me.

When they worked close together Gustaf told Hazel stories of his past, the bands he had managed, musicians he had met, places he had been, love affairs he'd had. And I was jealous of her time in his company every day, envious of his life. I have never known love's heights and despairs, even its small headlong adventures. All of my premarital affairs had contained a goodly chunk of calculation; while for the greater part of my life I had known one man, a steady man.

"Just me and him today," Hazel said. "We were supposed to be meeting somebody who's going to sell him some land. He wants me to see the business side."

It had come on to rain just after I had got back home. I had been expecting Hazel to call, wanting to be picked up earlier. But…

"We sat in the gateway to this field looking out at the rain. Eventually he gives the guy a ring. Wrong day. It's tomorrow. 'Would you really have wanted me as a regular father?' he said. 'Rich then maybe. But as chaotic as any addict.'"

All the years, all the concern I had spent on Hazel, and there she was infatuated by a man who couldn't with any certainty recall the woman with whom he had fathered her.

"They were wild times," he told Hazel. "Too wild for the likes of Moira."

Twenty-four

Hazel (*corylus avellana*) is more of a bush than a single-stemmed tree and has been one of the most consistently useful of English woodland trees. Surviving happily in the shade of taller trees, when well-coppiced hazel's new shoots – reaching for the light – grow as straight as bamboo canes. Being so straight these hazel sticks will still get cut for bean poles, pea sticks, even for weaving into baskets of the sturdier kind. And just the other day I came across woven table mats, such as the rural French use for the taking of hot-bottomed dishes, being made here in England albeit in a variety of new shapes.

Similarly – while everything changes, must change – there is a satisfying continuity in the thicker hazel poles still being made into hurdles. These hurdles were once used for the temporary penning of sheep, nowadays they get put up as 'rustic' garden fencing.

In times past hazel – cut every seventh year – was also used as wattles in 'wattle and daub' walls; and for thatching spars, for fish traps and for barrel hoops. Indeed so generally useful was hazel that at one time there were 500,000 acres of hazel grown throughout the UK. Although now, many of its uses having been taken over by other materials, the hazel is mostly a hedgerow survivor.

Where hazel does grow within broadleaved woodland it will delight the eye in spring with its long catkins glowing golden among the fresh green; and come October the hazel's slim branches will be weighed down with cob nuts. When not harvested by human agency these nuts provide winter fodder for birds, particularly great tits with their sergeant's chevron on their backs. Dormice and grey squirrels will also take their share.

In deepest winter, should all its other characteristics be in doubt, hazel can be identified by its hairy twigs.

* * *

Although these days the smooth silver-grey of their thick trunks often form stately avenues the beech tree (*fagius sylvatica*) used to be known as the tree of the poor, so essential was it to their pre-industrial way of life.

Beech mast provided fodder – pannage – for their pigs. While beech timber, being so easy to work, got used in the making of all sorts of furniture and tools, mostly indoor tools, such as box planes. If used outdoors untreated beech timber very soon rots away.

Its being so amenable to the chisel beech timber continues to be a favourite of lathe turners. While name-graffiti and out of doors declarations of love continue to be carved into the living beech's smooth pewter-grey bark.

In spring beech buds are a slender and pointed brown, the twigs a favourite of the more artistic flower arranger. By full summer the oval leaves have become a glossy dark above, paler green below, and they form such a dense canopy that exclusive beech woodland can be readily recognised by its lack of undergrowth, the undulating woodland floor owning shades of copper from last autumn's fall.

Where used as a garden hedge beech will, if trimmed in early autumn, keep its copper leaves right through winter into spring.

With both squirrels and pigeons having a taste for beech nuts, and carrying them off, a single beech tree can produce hundreds of seedlings. Even without the assistance of pigeons and squirrels, beech is a species that does readily regenerate. Which is just as well because beech, despite its often huge girth and stately spread, is a delicate tree. Being thin the bark is readily sun-scorched and cracked, which allows damaging fungi and bacteria access to the tree's core. Cruel weather can also easily split a beech tree from the crown.

Twenty-five

While I continued to ferry Hazel back and forth to various of the woodlands – although to be fair Hazel had started to drive herself to the nearer ones – while all her and Gustaf's getting-to-know-you lovey-dovey was going on among the trees and bushes, I was trying to offload the café. Since Ian's death I'd had no real need of the income.

I had already asked Nyrene if she had wanted to take over the café. I'd let her have a trial run at managing. She had lasted two weeks, said that it had given her no time to herself.

It didn't. Days I served, evenings I baked. That had been my working life. Rolling on, unquestioned. My life unquestioned. Until one day I had looked at my life with Ian and had seen it as no longer good enough. So had I begun to belatedly question all of my life, all ways of life, and had asked Ian to leave.

Then Hazel had fallen ill.

From Hazel's arrival as a baby to her leaving home to go to college Hazel had been my life – what had passed for my life in those days that had followed one after the other. Now Hazel had been told that she was to die sooner rather than later and I wasn't going to miss any of what little life she had left in trotting back and forth to a café that I had been running for the past twenty plus years.

So, carrying on baking evenings and with Nyrene holding the fort most days, I put the Oak Tree Café up for sale as a going concern. And preoccupied with seeing estate agents, valuers, chatting up prospective purchasers, I didn't dwell overmuch on the growing relationship between

Gustaf and Hazel. Until the day I came home to find Kevin's green car in our Close.

"What did I do that was so wrong?" he kept asking as he spent a good two hours sitting at our dining table blubbing. "Why is she shutting me out like this? What did I do…?"

I made tea, offered cake. Kevin blew his nose, and ate. And he burst, literally burst, into tears again, crumbs blasting out over the table and over me.

"Sorry," he managed to say. His face was all red and broken up and I noticed that he was going bald, felt sorry for him.

To distract him I asked what his parents made of it all.

"Think it's sad," Kevin said. "That's all they say. So sad. She's so young. Poor both of you."

As he was telling me that, and I was thinking 'What good people', I also had in mind what Hazel had said about them. "Yes. They're nice enough people. Really nice. But their house smells of brussel sprouts."

Looking at Kevin's woebegone visage was when I began to wonder if Hazel, by ditching Kevin, had been giving herself free rein for a final fling. The only candidate I could think of that moment was the denser thatched Gustaf Eriksson. And I couldn't be sure that she wouldn't. Hazel might have been the person I knew best in the world, but sometimes – by what she did – I felt that I hardly knew her at all.

No, I chided my dirty-minded self, when Hazel had dumped Kevin her birth father Gustaf Eriksson had not even been on the horizon. Nonetheless when I collected Hazel that afternoon and I told her that I'd had Kevin weeping on my shoulder most of the day (he hadn't gone near my shoulder with all that snot and crumbs) she didn't seem that interested. She just gave a grimace of distaste – the past over and done with – and she started to talk about her doings with Gustaf that day.

"You're not thinking of having sex with him?" I asked her.

"Ugh!" she said. Her whole body's expression of disgust was unrehearsed. "Ugh!" she said again. "How could you even think that?"

"You wouldn't have been the first to commit incest with a new-found father."

"No. No. That's just too horrible. Ugh! No."

And thus, that phase came to a close.

Twenty-six

Hazel took a day off from her woodland work to accompany me to the inquest. This was the adjourned inquest. The solicitor had told me not to bother going to the first, that the coroner would just open proceedings and straightaway adjourn to await reports.

Back then, from when the police car pulled into my drive and the two uniformed police officers had first rung my doorbell, from when my initial fears had been for Hazel, and then relief and anger when the 'bad news' had turned out to be about Ian – the address on Ian's driving licence had still been our house, not his new flat – I had been in a daze.

Even when the pathologist had reported back to the coroner, the death certificate signed, the assumption had been that Ian and I had still been married, and the body had been released to me. Still in a daze I had sent out notifications and organised the body's delivery to the crematorium. Come the service I had been more concerned about Hazel than with any funereal proprieties.

Hazel had been quite poorly at that point with one of her 'treatments'. Water, loss of balance, grief-stricken, she had literally been all over the place. Occupied with her I had been aware – a frosty day, red noses, Ian's mother in copious swathes of black – that someone made a joke about a crematorium being the place to be on a cold day. I think it had been Kevin who had nervously laughed.

Hazel, in a much better physical and mental state now,

knew that her grandparents would also be attending this inquest proper and, whether they meant to or not, they would give me a hard time. She was frowning certain too that she had to be there: "Pay my dues."

For this trip Hazel drove. Halfway there it occurred to me to ask if she had told Gustaf and Dez where she was going this day.

"Told Gustaf about Dad's crash," she said.

I found myself pleased that she called Ian 'Dad' when talking to Gustaf. I didn't want her new relationship with Gustaf to lessen all the day-by-day affection she had shared with Ian, her stalwart father.

"What'd Gustaf say?"

"He said, 'Whenever car meets tree, tree always wins.'"

That bald assessment had me seeing again the scene of Ian's crash – the wounded Scots pine, the torn up roots of the hawthorn, the long dark gouge through the moss and grass. Those were the images I carried with me across the concrete paving and through the plate glass front of the municipal building and into the coroner's court.

The courtroom was one of those modern ones done up to look old, wood veneer panels on every vertical surface, but the clerk's desk all subtle electronics.

The coroner himself was a man with wispy fair hair in a side parting. He kept moving his small-framed spectacles up and down his nose, and throughout the proceedings he would lean forward as if he was about to say something to the clerk below him, and he didn't.

The clerk, head bent behind her machines, was a young woman with dark hair – hint of a reddish streak along one side – pulled back into a complicated plait.

Proceedings seemed to begin just as soon as Hazel and I got there. Shown down to the front I never got a chance to look around the public gallery. Silence was called for and a witness called. That is the coroner leant forward and said to the clerk, "Please could we have...?" The clerk made no attempt to look up to him but cast about the unseen seating below us, and she nodded to a face she knew, who came out from underneath us and stood in a squared off space, gave her name and rattled through the oath. No lawyers like on TV to interrogate, only the coroner delivering prompts.

* * *

Technical evidence was heard first. Medical report, time of death and probable cause – concussive impact. In layman's terms, brain damage. Then came the police report – the car leaving the road, skid and scratch marks measured, the car as it turned getting tipped onto its side, as it hit the hedge rolling over onto its roof, and crashing upside down into the tree.

When asked by the coroner – who sat back (almost as if he was about to put his feet up on the desk) to ask some questions, leant forward to ask others – the very bald police officer said that the skid marks indicated a speed in excess of 80 mph. When the coroner sat back without speaking the bald police officer went on to say that the fresh damage to the long ditch on the left hand side of the road, along with the shredded pieces of nearside tyre, and supported by damage to the chassis on that side, suggested that the nearside front wheel had become caught going forwards and, combined with the speed, had rendered the car uncontrollable.

The police officer was asked about the roadworthiness of the garage's courtesy car. So far as he could tell, he said, prior to the accident it would appear to have been roadworthy.

The coroner leant back to ask if both visors being down could have impaired Ian's vision, have led him to steer too close to the left hand side of the road and so into the ditch. The police officer thought not. At that time of day, that time of year, that section of the road would have been shadowed by the stand of trees on the bend.

Before the coroner could ask another question the police officer, hardening his voice, said that he did have concerns about the hatchback's rear door looking to have been held 'incompletely closed' with an elastic strap. There had to be the suspicion, he said, that despite all the front vents and side windows having been open exhaust fumes could have eddied back into the car and affected the driver.

The pathologist, a solemn woman with straight grey hair and pointed spectacles, was recalled. We were reminded that an absence of alcohol or other narcotic substances in Ian's bloodstream had already been established. The pathologist was asked if traces of carbon monoxide had been found.

"Certainly not enough," she said, "to impair his decision-making capabilities." Having been apprised of the hatchback's rear door being partially open – she emphasised the 'partially' – she had specifically made a search for any such evidence. She and the police officer would have appeared to have conferred, and disagreed, about the effect of the open rear door prior to the inquest. With the pathologist now carrying the day one could almost hear, those many miles away, the garage owners, their having failed to supply Ian with a replacement estate car, sighing their relief.

In his evidence the policeman had referred to the statement of a witness, who turned out to be the driver of the silver Fiat. Having been first on the crash scene it had been he who had called the emergency services. His having been first meant that the driver of the maroon car had driven on past.

The coroner adjusted his spectacles to read aloud parts of the statement from the driver of the silver Fiat.

"...both cars were driving recklessly fast... I could only assume that the driver of the maroon car was going so very fast that he didn't see the crashed car... it was slightly below the level of the road... I saw steam and dust rising from the upside-down car..."

Without recalling the bald police officer to the witness box the coroner asked across the court if the police had managed to trace the driver of the maroon car. The police officer said that they had, but that he had recently moved abroad. However he had written a letter…

The coroner again searched through his papers, said, "I see that he denies, as alleged, racing against the deceased… claims that so far as he knew he had never met him…"

"And he wouldn't have known the car," the coroner took a minute's more reading to decide.

The coroner rustled once more through his paperwork, and delivered what sounded like his usual spiel about the dangers of driving at excessive speeds on poorly maintained country roads. He 'was persuaded' to record a verdict of accidental death.

Neither Hazel nor I got a mention. I wondered if the coroner had been told of mine and Ian's estrangement beforehand.

Ian's mother, who had been sniffing behind us at the back of the public gallery – either I hadn't seen her when we had been ushered to the front or she had arrived after the inquest had started – was stood outside with a big white hankie to her face. Not a tissue: she had come prepared.

They were stood by a pair of square concrete flower tubs. When Hazel waved to them neither of her grandparents responded in kind. Instead Ian's mother turned aside into her hankie. While Ian's father chose to give the both of us a grim-mouthed stare, until she tugged at his sleeve. He glared a moment longer, then turned about and followed her.

If their grief and anger had been genuine, not a premeditated display, I might have had some sympathy for them at the loss of their son. But no, in their small-minded world they had only wanted someone to blame and they had decided that Ian's death was mine and Hazel's fault.

I doubted that Ian would have told his parents of Hazel's terminal condition. But he had been so upset that he might well have done. He had been more tolerant of them than I. Whether they knew or not, I don't forgive.

Twenty-seven

As we neared home late that evening, Hazel driving, she told me that when she had mentioned to Gustaf about her having to take me to her father's inquest it had led him to ask about Ian and I.

I had a long day's tiredness squatting in me, head full of pillow, had to make myself pay attention. That was the first time, Hazel said, that she and Gustaf had talked about her home life.

"Oh, right," I said; and I wondered if that was because he had felt uncomfortable, guilty even, in daring to even speak of those who had raised his child.

"What'd you tell him?"

That Ian and I had separated several months before Ian's crash; and she told him about the café, how I was now thinking of giving it up. Especially as, while she was helping him in the woods, I spent my days hanging about carparks waiting for her.

Gustaf had asked why didn't I come into the wood, if only to watch. To which Hazel had said, "Oh, Mum won't watch. She'll get stuck in."

"In that case," Gustaf had said, "definitely bring her along."

Seemed, without Hazel meaning to, I had been volunteered.

Thinking back on it now most of that conversation had to have been continued at home while I rescued the next day's café food from the freezer and made up packed lunches for the two of us in the woods.

Before collapsing to bed I looked out my baggy gardening trousers and green wellies, and at the café in the morning I left a note for Nyrene telling her to make sure, before putting any of the cakes on display, that all had completely defrosted. It's too weird a sensation biting into a soft cake and the teeth coming up against hard ice crystals.

Once fully en route – this day I was driving – it didn't take me long to sense Hazel's discomfort. As she had before her exams she was unable to settle, wriggling this way and that in the passenger seat. I didn't have to look over to know that her face would also be squirming, as if it too couldn't decide which expression would best confront the coming ordeal. Mouth twitching, sudden deep frowns, eyes and lips narrowed… and most definitely avoiding eye contact. Hazel well knew that her big anxious eyes would invite question, and she had not yet, twisting and turning, formulated an answer.

At one time, pre-teenage, her grimacing had become so extreme that I had feared she'd been developing some form of Turette's. She hadn't been. For Hazel this physical corkscrewing and gurning was but a manifestation of self-doubt. Once a decision was reached she would be still.

"It's just," she eventually twisted around to say, "that I haven't yet told Gustaf about my… about my 'condition'. The circumstances have never seemed right. And I want to tell him time and place of my choosing."

So he wouldn't feel blamed?

Or was that just me? And I wondered if Gustaf was wondering if, now that he knew Ian was dead, Hazel had sought him out as a replacement father? Albeit that he was the natural father.

"Fair enough," I said.

"Promise you won't say? Not to Gustaf? Not to Dez? To any of them?" We had a family rule about spoken promises never to be broken.

"I promise."

Hazel slowly nodded for what seemed a whole minute, then sat back satisfied, stopped her squirming.

Twenty-eight

Set either side of a deep valley in a countryside of rolling hills the woodland, although long established, was new to Prospectus. Generations of previous owners having done little or no maintenance it was one of those woodlands where it always seemed to be squelchy underfoot.

Prospectus had acquired the wood with the help of a grant, one of the grant stipulations being that it was to be amenity woodland, with wheelchair access. There also had to be a wildlife corridor through the flat top of the wood. Which, as we parked on a new carpark clearing – "Dez and Gustaf levelled it yesterday." – was to be our job that day.

We could hear the hornet buzz of Dez and Gustaf's chainsaws some way off as we started to pick our way along the 'corridor' of water-filled tyre tracks – sunk black into the flattened grass – and past felled trees, fresh logs stacked, small pyramids of chunky sawdust... Hazel in her laced work boots and combat trews, me in my calf-slapping green wellies and baggy gardening pants, the uneven ground making us both stumble and grab hold of one another's sleeves, with in between gasps and grunts Hazel explaining to me about 'rides', which I had thought were for horses.

"More for butterflies. And moths. Smaller insects too. A channel for them to move along. And for bats to hunt in. Serves as a firebreak too." In a wood that was that dripping damp its catching fire seemed an unlikely prospect.

Hazel had told me to bring my long-handled secateurs. Dez had left a pair for Hazel leant against a tree with a piece of orange warning tape tied to a branch above. We stopped to listen to the slow crash of a felled tree some distance ahead of us.

My legs, more used to trotting around café and kitchen, were glad of the pause. We'd had to step over broken branch ends and there had been holes hidden under tyre-squashed ferns, which had twice had me on my knees, now wet through.

Hazel began dragging some of the bigger branches to the side. The secateurs had been left for Hazel where Gustaf and Dez had stopped work the day before.

"What's to be planted here, once we've got it clear," Hazel happily informed me, "is flowering bushes. Along both sides. To attract the insects. Because of the dense canopy all that grew down here before were brambles and ferns. No insects, no birds."

Hazel had also made sure that I had brought with me a pair of gardening gloves. Our other job was to chop back the brambles. They too were pulled to the side.

"Will this be levelled for walkers?" I said.

"No Mum, this is just a ride." She was almost exasperated at having to explain it twice. "We'll... They'll come back every so often and clear it. Cut down any self-sown saplings. Chop back these brambles again. The pathway," she beckoned me over to between two beech trees and pointed down into the valley, "will go at a diagonal down to the stream. The footpath will go around trees. They'll only fell a tree for that if absolutely necessary. But this has to be cleared."

"What'll happen when they get down to the stream?" A thread of cobalt-silver was occasionally visible between the trees.

"A bridge'll be put across. Then the path will go on up the other side. At a diagonal. A slight slope for wheelchairs. It'll join up with the path coming round the edge of the wood from the carpark. Dez'll start all the paths off with the little digger."

The red digger had been left just inside the wood from the carpark. Its perspex cab perched up between its caterpillar tracks looked hardly large enough for a grown man, made it seem, with its equally miniature shovel, toylike. Which fed a suspicion of mine that Prospectus might just be a rich man's hobby, a game, a playing at, not real need-to-earn-a-living work. What Hazel said next didn't disabuse me of that notion.

"The volunteers will come in at the weekend and finish off levelling the paths. Put in support for the banks."

"Who makes the bridge?" I was still thinking in terms of profit and loss, wanted to know who paid for the bridge.

"I think," Hazel said, "they wait until the path gets down to the stream, then they measure up. They were talking of bringing the mixer over."

I had known that Hazel had enjoyed being in the woods with Gustaf and Dez, what I hadn't realised was quite how much she had got involved with the planning.

That was the thought I took back to our attacking of brambles and our dragging of the bigger branches to the side of the ride.

Both our jackets came off. Mine first. I wasn't as used as even unwell Hazel to this kind of heavy work.

The only light relief that morning came when I heaved at what I thought was a thick bough, but which turned out to be a small branch under the larger, and I sat back on my arse in a waterlogged patch. Amused Hazel, and left me with a wet backside, which I kept unpicking for the rest of the day.

We came to where some newly cut logs, about six foot long, had been trimmed and stacked.

"These for firewood?" I asked, acquisitiveness in my raised eyebrows. This stack of logs was not.

"We leave log piles," Hazel teacherly informed me, "for the invertebrates. A safe dwelling place for insects, for reptiles and small animals. All those creatures play their part in breaking down the leaf litter. Nature the more efficient recycler."

"I see," I said, trying not to mock her quoting her mentors. The newly cut logs had that clean sap smell. "So why did Gustaf take away the rhodie logs to be burnt?" I asked, not to score a point but to show that I had been taking notice.

"Dez said that if rhodies are stacked there's a danger they might root again within the stack."

We didn't talk much more. Not of any consequence, nor that my questions had led to discord between us. The task occupied us. And even if Hazel was apprehensive about my being about to meet Gustaf I noticed that whenever I glanced across she was wearing her small smile of satisfaction. And that had me pleased, made my sticky bum and damp knees worthwhile.

* * *

My ears became aware of the absence of the buzzsaw at about the same time that my stomach told me it needed lunch. Although some of that hunger-queasiness could have been nervousness at my having to meet Gustaf.

I had also been given to wondering of late if I had only allowed Hazel to put up barriers to me meeting Gustaf in order to stop me going with her into the woods, because going into the woods with her was so much what I wanted to do, and we learn to resist our desires as we get older? Such strong desires having led us to make so many of our mistakes when young?

I was about to go back along the ride for our jackets and our lunch bag when I saw, and knew straightaway because of the dreadlocks, Dez coming towards us through the trees.

The sun-blonded dreadlocks were tied back in a thick ponytail and he had on a loose blue shirt and denim – not jeans – working trousers. The closer he came I realised he was much taller than I had imagined. Much better looking too. His complexion was summer brown outdoors, a straight nose with tiny nostrils, and those kind of eyelids that never seem to go all the way up over the round of the eyes. Made him look relaxed. Cool I suppose.

"Hi Dez," Hazel happily greeted him. "This is my mum."

"Pleased to meet you," he gave me a slow head forward bow.

"Me you," I said, and turned to pick my way over the uneven ride back to our jackets. I heard him tell Hazel that we were doing 'very' well. Then he asked how yesterday had gone. Hazel said that it had been horrid for me.

"Yea, I bet," Dez said. His voice was deep and matched his looks. But that was the last I heard. He was gone when I got back.

Hazel had found us a lunch seat on one of the newly felled trunks. We sat side by side with our feet dangling, like a couple of wood elves. Balanced thus pouring hot coffee into plastic flask cups was not easy.

"Now I see the attraction," I said.

"Peaceful isn't it," Hazel smiled at me, daughter pleased to win mother's approval.

"Definitely now the sawing's stopped," I said. But I was thinking more of…" I copied her greeting, "Hi Dez."

"Shut up mother," Hazel said. "He's with Jay. They've got a lovely little boy."

"Of course," I said. "Hi Dez."

"I'm serious mother." Hazel did her stern face, "Shut up."

"OK," I said, took a bite of my sandwich. "Hi Dez," I said, and she laughed.

I didn't though persist with the teasing; and when the buzzsaw started up we slid down off the trunk and went back to chopping brambles and dragging branches into the side. At three Hazel said,

"I'm knackered. Let's call it a day."

Unused to the work, to all that bending and pulling, I was more than happy to agree. While she started back along the ride I picked a tree to tie the piece of orange tape to, left Dez and Gustaf's long-handled secateurs standing under it. When I caught up with Hazel I took the lunch bag and my jacket off her, slowed to her pace.

She was pale, almost yellow. Earlier that afternoon, looking again to see if she was smiling, I'd been pleased to note instead her ruddy outdoors complexion. That was gone.

"You OK?"

"Just tired," she said. Extra stress of the day, I guessed,

her anxieties over my meeting with Dez and Gustaf.

We had no sooner driven out of the new carpark than Hazel was asleep. And it wasn't until we were a good hour down the road that I allowed myself to be relieved at the colour creeping back up her cheeks. It was then, thinking back on the day, that I realised that, after all my mental preparations for the birth father encounter, I had yet to meet Gustaf Eriksson. My guess was that he had sent Dez up to check me out, report back to him.

Twenty-nine

It was on that drive home – glancing across to watch the colour creep back into Hazel's cheeks – that I made up my mind to close the café. I'd had not one expression of interest from anyone wanting to take it on as a going concern.

While baking that evening, in bed that night, I firmed up my plans. Hazel had slumped blank-faced looking at the telly all evening. The day's work had exhausted her. She had not only worked harder showing me what was to be done, but with me not in the back of her mind – hanging about in a carpark waiting to take her home – we had worked on longer than had been usual for her.

Seeing the colour go from her of a sudden had brought home to me her frailty, and had got me to wondering if that was how she would die. Her skin yellowing, a stumble, and on some wet pathway, out of sight, she crumpled to the ground? Where would I be? What would I be doing…?

The café was unimportant. How much time did I have left with my only daughter? But I couldn't, didn't dare, dwell on that. I was already bothered by this new way of life – the sheer wastage, profligacy, involved in driving all over the country. Of course I was taking pleasure in the unexpected company of my daughter – while waiting for her to die.

So why had I been scurrying about the kitchen again that evening? Baking the same cakes that I had baked for years. Didn't even have to look at the recipes anymore.

Hamster in my wheel there I'd been baking for the café, going to the café, baking for the café... And there had been my daughter sitting alone in front of the uncaring telly when I could have been cuddled up beside her. The weather decided the next day for us: the rain had begun in the night. Hazel was woken by a text from Gustaf telling her not to bother coming. She got up to tell me, dozily took herself back to bed. I took myself along to the café.

"This afternoon we're closing for good," I told Nyrene.

Only because I knew her so well was I aware that the deepening set of her mouth meant that she was upset by the news. But she only said that she'd guessed as much. I asked if she'd mind working out her month's notice giving the place a good clean, and dealing with anyone who came to buy furniture and fittings, possibly to look at taking over the premises. I had already phoned the estate agents to tell them that I had given up trying to sell the café as a café. My one hope now was to offload the remainder of the lease.

"Once the place is clean you'll just have to be available. No need to be here all the time. Just make sure your mobile's on, and I'll give you a ring if there's anyone coming to the café to look things over. I'll be here and there running Hazel about. That OK?"

Nyrene knew of Hazel's diagnosis: she'd been holding the fort ever since I'd started taking Hazel to hospital. She didn't know about Hazel's now spending her days with her birth father.

"'Course it is," Nyrene said. "Been expecting as much." What I wasn't expecting from that severe-looking stick of a woman was being pressed against her in a long hug.

"Careful," I twitched myself loose, "Have me in tears next." I gathered up my bag and brolly. "Any food left at four give it away. Earlier if you like."

Acts of altruism always make one feel good. Which is why I'd long ago decided was why the Great British Public give so much to charity: it's their one guarantee of self-worth. And if it hadn't been for my concerns over Hazel I too would have had my share of self-worth, having been nice this once to Nyrene. But what I found myself thinking, a bet with myself, that even though it was her last working day, Nyrene being Nyrene wouldn't close up until six on the dot.

While in town I bought myself a pair of sturdy, lace-up work boots and two pairs of cargo pants, cotton, not the absorbent fleecy fabric of my maroon gardening trousers. If Hazel was determined to go on labouring in the woods then I was as determined to lighten her workload.

She laughed when she saw my purchases: "So I've got you for permanent company?"

I didn't pass comment on the 'permanent'. "I've closed the café," I told her.

"Good," she said. "It was a rut."

Which – put so bluntly and in an offhand manner – I almost took umbrage at. But a reflective pause had me see the truth of it. More than a single truth. Had Ian and I been a well-matched pair? The pair of us unadventurous, each of us hiding behind each our routines?

Those were the thoughts I took to the phone with me to organise the placing of adverts in the local papers and trade magazines for café fittings and furniture.

While I was working through my task list Hazel came and sat at the dining table beside me.

"Feel out of sorts today." She leant shoulder to shoulder against me. "Nothing to worry about though." Straightening she turned her head as if to read my tick list. "I did too much yesterday. Showing off to you. The work is not usually so full on. We pause for chats. Swap jobs around. I'll be OK by the morning." The rain had stopped.

I asked if she fancied a pastie for lunch tomorrow. "Should I make enough for Gustaf and Dez?"

"Can't give up baking just yet then?" she laughed at me.

"Should I make enough for them?"

"Just me and you," she got up from the table. "One step at a time mother dear."

Thirty

I told myself that I wasn't nervous about meeting Gustaf. Why should I have been? A minor celebrity, absent biological father... Truth be told I approached him with the usual awe of reader for author, poor for rich, had to talk myself into regarding the meeting as nothing out of the ordinary, just another café customer. Maybe an awkward one.

I think Hazel must have been as nervous about my meeting Gustaf. Conversation in the car that morning, if not stilted, had certainly seen the both of us studiously avoiding mention of the day ahead.

Wanting to get the meeting over and done with I was relieved to see – as we walked down the squelching grass and mud ride – a shorter, squarer figure just beyond Dez's dreadlocks.

"Morning!" Hazel sang out, warning of our approach.

Dez paused in his stooped labours to raise a gloved hand. Gustaf looked around him, recognised us and went back to heaving a full-leafed bough into the side of the ride.

"Hello Gustaf," Hazel said when we reached them. "This is my mum."

My identity, my status established with that blushed introduction, my anxieties about the meeting all but evaporated. Gustaf, once straightened up, looked less like a blond Viking than a thickset wrestler. He smiled a welcome: "See Hazel's got you kitted out."

"Learnt my lesson last time," I said. "We doing the same again?"

"The same, but don't knacker yourselves. Dez said you both looked done in last time."

Dez, by including me in his summary, straightaway earned my maternal affection. And, with the introductions made, Hazel and I pulled on our gloves and set to picking up sawn-off branches and dragging the larger to the sides of the ride, then walking past whoever was ahead of us to find more branches to collect and carry aside. With the four of us working steadily we seemed to be moving along the new ride at double the speed that Hazel and I had the day before last, were soon around the bend and heading towards the next.

* * *

When I bent to one of the larger boughs Gustaf told me to hang on, he'd give me a hand. I waited until he'd thrown his armful of ends into the side. Gave me a chance to size him up again. I decided that he wasn't so much squat as rectangular and heavy. There was a solidity to him
 "So," he said, "What do you want to know about me?"
 "Hazel's pretty much told me all I need to know." I gave him my of-no-account smile, and we carried the rough-barked bough to the side.
 "There is one thing," I said as we followed the tall and short of Dez and Hazel, "why haiku?"
 "Aside from their being conveniently short?" He bent to pull at a bramble, its white and purple roots slipping easily out of the wet soil. I had by this time collected an armful of branch ends.
 "It is their being short." I was surprised to see him frowning, stood still and thinking seriously on what I hadn't meant to be that serious a question. But basic manners dictated that I also had to stop, waiting on him.
 "I'll tell you what," he said, "and I don't know if you'll get this, but haiku has its roots in Zen. Moreover in Zen's mathematical contradictions of thought." His tone of voice, with a suggestion of self-mockery, told me that he wasn't taking himself that seriously. "For instance," he said, "Think This plus Think That equals Nothingness. While Think That plus Think This equals Somethingness. Yes?"
 "No," I said, and laughing went back to picking up branches.
 "I thought haiku were all about syllable counts?" I said when we came close again.

"Those numbers are for those who love the rules and don't see the poetry."

"But one line?"

"In their simplicity haiku are as beautiful as the spring song of the dunnock."

"Yea right," I said: it was my turn to let loose a laugh. And I saw Hazel smiling over at us.

My first (intuitive?) thought on seeing that small pleased smile was, 'Is she matchmaking?' She had said that she wanted us to get on. But no, she was just pleased, relieved that we weren't to start out as forsworn enemies.

"What it is with my one-line haiku," Gustaf caught up with me again, "is more my refusal to follow bogus traditions. Like folk music. Like rhymed poetry…"

"Tried and tested forestry practices," Dez said.

"You can shut up," Gustaf said, but good-humouredly, to him. "Now see what you've started," to me.

And that was the end of any further one-to-one conversations that day. Voices behind us announced the arrival of a local gang of volunteers. Which gave my cheeks rest from polite smiling and me a chance to watch Gustaf and Dez in action. Hazel too, greeting a couple of the newcomers like old friends.

**

Gustaf's voice seemed to grow with the size of the group. He set some of them to making the new path down into the valley.

In this division of labour, having come along to lighten her workload, I had sidled over to be next to Hazel. So long as she paced herself she would continue to look the very picture of outdoors health.

Dez went off with the path-makers. Gustaf kept us in his ride-clearing group, but as a subset, Hazel his second-in-command.

As Gustaf joshed everyone along, shouted regular encouragement to a nervous skinny old woman, I saw why

Hazel might have thought that I wouldn't take to him. But he was no café bigmouth making all the other customers uncomfortable with his careless loudness. Yes, Gustaf's being loud was in part him showing off, but it was also his so obviously trying to put people at their ease by his being the group's lightning conductor, taking attention to himself.

* * *

As that day wore on I had to revise many of my preconceptions built on the snippets that Hazel had fed me of her Gustaf Eriksson. For instance when Hazel had said a couple of times that Gustaf was no fool with money I had put him in a bluff businessman box alongside brother-in-law Martin. Martin had been full of his own certainties, of how other people should act, how they should be like him. But when a young lad that day said that he hadn't heard back after a job interview, Gustaf told him, "Their loss, our gain. But keep plugging away, one of 'em will see sense soon."

If that had been Martin he would straightaway have questioned the lad's interview skills, so making it the lad's fault, with Martin having gone on to tell how well he had done at interviews.

This glum boy though was handed Gustaf's flask – he hadn't brought one, said he had forgotten it – and was given the sum of Gustaf's pat-on-the-back wisdom: "Listen, in any life the disappointments will outnumber the successes. Just early days for you yet."

The boy mumbled something to the effect it being all right for Gustaf, he was a success.

"To you maybe. You don't know though what I wanted to be. Most people don't think of themselves as successes. Unless they're simple. Neither do they think of themselves as disappointments."

"My teachers said I was a disappointment."

"To them? They were a bunch of pratts then."

Towards the end of that day, or the end of mine and Hazel's day, I decided that – in his acceptance of Hazel, in how he had treated the volunteers, in his not taking himself that seriously… On the theme carried over from the lad, and harking back to our earlier conversation about haiku, he had later said, "All my finest works will end up torn into strips and lining a rat's nest. Which in itself will be a work of art."

"No posterity for you then?" I couldn't help myself chip in.

"What was it the man said?" He adapted a theatrical pose to address the nearest trees, "Only by artifice are we remembered, if at all. And never as we truly were. Anyone who strives for a place in posterity has to be seriously deluded."

I had no reason to dislike Gustaf Eriksson. I may have been at times uncomfortable hearing some of my own views coming from the mouth, via Hazel, of a man I felt I should have instinctively disliked, suspected, disapproved of. But he wasn't in himself unlikeable. I just knew that I wasn't like him. I am cautious, careful, private.

At 14:55 my wristwatch alarm beeped and the mobile in my cargo-pants pocket trilled. I told Hazel that we had to be heading home. She didn't argue.

* * *

under skies of pearl
smoke-grey poplars drift along
a darkening hillside

Thirty-one

On the Monday it was just Gustaf and Dez, Hazel and I. Gustaf and Dez were going to build the piers for the bridge across the valley-bottom stream.

We met up in the carpark, all arriving at the same time. The red mini-digger was balanced in the back of the yellow pickup.

Keeping our distance Hazel and I followed the pickup on foot as, with noise and difficulty, it negotiated the new ride, the tall digger swaying about as the pickup, wheels spinning, slewed across the track. Small wonder, I thought, that the yellow sides of the pickup were so dented and rusty, wasn't just for macho show.

Parked finally at the top of the new footpath, Hazel and I stood to one side, as with more noise and difficulty, the mini-digger was unloaded via two clanging and squealing metal gangplanks.

Sitting comically in the perspex cabin atop the mini-digger's caterpillar tracks, dreadlocked Dez guided it slowly down the footpath, followed by Gustaf with a cement-crusted wheelbarrow full of tools. Then came Hazel and I empty-handed.

I was beginning to wonder what we were doing there, if we were actually wanted or our presence was being tolerated. Although our idleness didn't seem to be bothering Hazel. Then we came to a section of the path that had crumbled away under the weight of the mini-digger, and Hazel and I were dispatched back up the path to collect sledgehammer, saw and spade; our task that day to shore up those sides of the path that had subsided.

Having watched volunteers elsewhere shoring up footpaths Hazel had the two of us searching out straightish branches from those we had pulled away from the ride. Tidying off side growths we then sawed the poles to manageable lengths. Hazel used an axe to hack the shorter ones to a point. I was appointed wielder of the sledgehammer, and I thumped the stakes into the hillside's soft earth. Hazel and I then laid other branches along the gap and backfilled them with the fallen away earth.

The work took more exertion than did gardening, where the heaviest job was forking over the herbaceous border. This day though I was swinging a sledgehammer, and enjoying the weighty thump of it atop the stake, taking satisfaction from each inch it was driven down. Breathing deep from the exertion I inhaled peaty scents rising from the disturbed soil, the sapsweet scent of newsawn wood, was aware of muscles being stretched taut, with my hot skin feeling every cool breeze that came searching through that woodland valley.

I was happy, and mostly happy to be there doing it with Hazel, pleased now that I had insinuated myself into her company. Not knowing what she had been up to during her days alone at home had been a worry. Back before the search into her biological past had begun, in that drawn-out period of "you could be with us for another year or more," she had been talking one evening in desultory fashion of her own death and she had said, "The best thing for me is just to disappear." I hadn't wanted that – not knowing where, when.

* * *

Dez came up the path pushing the empty wheelbarrow just as we were finishing the backfilling, shovelling the spilled soil and stones up from below the footpath.

"You've done a really good job," Dez sounded surprised. "Tell you what though, with that other collapse, lower down, don't bother throwing the soil up from down below. When I bring the digger back up I'll pull some earth down from above, pack it down."

When he and his wheelbarrow, all approving smiles, came back down laden with bags of sand and cement, Hazel and I had made a start on the second small landslide. This one didn't require as much timber as the first and, as we didn't have to backfill the gap, we soon wandered on down to join Gustaf and Dez.

They were both ankle deep in red mud in the sections the digger had cut out of either side of the stream bank. Dez asked Hazel and I if we'd mind going to look for more rocks from the stream and add them to the piles they already had and were starting to pack down into the mud.

"Most times," Gustaf informed us two volunteers, "we fill bags with sand and cement for these small piers. The locals here though wanted the piers to be 'natural.' We said

OK because there seemed to be a lot of stones around."

"Now we're not so sure," Dez said.

Hazel and I went upstream to search for more, made trips back with what we could carry. Once they had got a base to work from Gustaf decided to have a lunch break before they started mixing up any more mortar. The first lot had been a practically dry mix. "Slow to go off," Gustaf said.

For their lunch break Gustaf and Dez took themselves up to the yellow pickup. Gustaf had to make calls and hadn't been able to get a signal down in the valley. Dez's lunch was up there. I'd had ours with me in my rucksack. Hazel and I found a mossy bank, made ourselves comfortable on our coats, and cracked open our tupperware.

Lunch didn't seem to last long, and the rest of that day saw Gustaf laying rocks one side of the stream, Dez the other, with Hazel and I fetching and passing rocks to them. One wet rock I was about to hand to Gustaf slipped from my grasp and had him jerking his feet back out of the way. The bottom of the pier being uneven he caught his heel and sat with a bump in the mud of the bank.

Both Hazel's and Dez's exclaimed laughter was almost involuntary.

"Mind my famous father," Hazel said.

"Famous my arse," Gustaf grumbled at her. "Which arse is now soaking wet thank you." But his grumble was aired, as he picked the wet fabric away from his backside, not with genuine ill humour.

He carried on laying the rocks that, with both hands now, I passed to him. Across the way Dez and Hazel were nattering on, something about Dez's little boy. The silence my side felt unnatural, unbalanced; and as this was the first time I'd been close enough to Gustaf for any real kind of conversation, I asked him, "So what's it like being famous?"

"Don't know that I am," he said as he sized up an uneven rock, put it aside and pointed to another on the pile.

"I haven't got a Wikipedia entry." I handed him the rock.

Taking it from me he said, "I'm famous only to those

who've heard of me. Hardly universal fame. You only heard of me because of Hazel. Bet you hadn't before that."

True. "But what about your band now? Hazel said you've got another band."

"They let me on stage with them. And only occasionally. We're none of us exactly exciting new bloods." He laid a couple more stones. "Plus we have to compete for gigs these days with the strange nostalgia of tribute bands. Truth is," another stone, "me and my haiku to musical accompaniment is a tad too original for most live audiences. And," he slapped some mortar down, "so far as the general public's concerned the actual new is scary. Punters prefer the safe secondhand. Even if a poor copy."

"His band," Dez said, "call the pickup the Haiku Banana."

I misunderstood: "That the name of the band?"

"'Issa's Lot', we're called."

"Thought the public were keener on the new," I said a few stones later.

"The unthinking are keen on novelty, not the new, not anything that requires them to change their point of view. They're by and large sensation-seekers. But we play mostly in pubs. Real ale pubs. And they're traditionalists to a man. Anoraks all. And Issa's Lot don't conform to type. While formalists like them prefer the bogus traditions. Like Hitler's synthetic Volk."

Which little discourse had me thinking that Hazel had been right, Gustaf was, if delivering with more certainty and a larger vocabulary, as opinionated as me. And louder. Not though as a show off, rather that he gave unrestrained voice to his beliefs. Unlike Ian for instance. Not wanting to cause offence Ian had prefaced his every opinion with "I hope you don't mind but... I could be wrong but... No offence but... I know it's not everyone's cup of tea but..." He never straightaway said what he thought. Gustaf did.

Gustaf however was by no means precious, did not hold either himself or his beliefs above others. He had taken the laughter at his fall in good part; and, if he was opinionated, I had already seen with the day-before's volunteers, that he was no judgemental bigot.

"If you had all that money, why this?" I gestured to the mud and cement splashes all over him.

"Had to do something."

"You could have stayed home and concentrated on your writing. You written anything longer than a haiku?"

"Some. Didn't work though. What I wanted were nature poems, but nature poems that were more than a litany of flower names. Haiku are moments in themselves."

"Have you stopped writing?"

"Not completely. But there's only so much one can write poetically about trees. About grass. About birds, animals. Greylag goose, now there's a poem in a name."

I could understand, sympathise with his liking for haiku. If not then as a reader, certainly now that I'm writing this. As a reader I like a story that draws me in and keeps me there. But I too dislike waste. Which was why towards day's end in the café I always dropped the price of cakes. Rather than drop the cakes in the bin. Same with words. I hate having to say the same thing twice, would be useless around the deaf.

"What I didn't want, as a writer of haiku," he said, "was to measure my life out in small publications."

"Did you want to be famous?"

"My fame, such as it was, was a necessary part of what I've done. It was never fame for fame's sake. Like this trowel, fame has been a tool."

"Being called a tool is considered rude these days."

Gustaf ignored that (didn't merit a response?) and spread mortar along a flat-topped rock, placed a round-ended rock atop it and pressed it down, scooping up the squeezed out mortar.

"I saw," he said, "what happened to the kids in my first bands. They thought being famous was the absolute. They were famous. Bits on the telly, names in the papers. They'd made it. And they very quickly found they hadn't. Or they had, but it wasn't them. It was some media construct, some publicity creation with their haircut and name. And what they went on to discover was that the fans all wanted to project their own non-famous selves onto them. For the members of the band to be them, to be their avatars. And those fans gave them characteristics, virtues even that those young band members didn't, couldn't possess. They were bound to disappoint. And when they did they became hated."

Two rocks later he said, "People want something from the famous that the famous cannot give them. Even had they the power."

"That how you see yourself, a reluctant celebrity? A reluctant minor celebrity?"

"I see myself as an obstinate idealist. Now pass me that rock woman. No. By your left foot."

Thirty-two

Loyalty wants me to say that it was Hazel who got me interested in trees. Hazel it most certainly was who inveigled me into woodland, but it was Dez who had me share his enthusiasm for trees.

I'm not sure why it should be but the first time I saw Dez as more than Gustaf's workaday foil was when Hazel and I arrived at a wetland site to find Gustaf and Dez with a large group of twelve to thirteen-year-olds. That awkward between age anyway. The group being so big Gustaf had split it into two. The site leant itself to such a division, a wide swampy area below with a to-be-forested hill above.

The day was overcast, a covering of cloud like thin grey skin. Gustaf's group, plus Hazel and the teacher, were to go up the hill to plant holly seedlings around the oak and beech seedlings they had put in the day before. (Can't recall the reason Hazel and I hadn't been there.)

"Don't want plastic tubes sticking up everywhere." Gustaf's voice easily carried across to our reluctantly gathering together group. "We still have to, though, protect the new seedlings from browsing deer. So this is by way of an experiment. Do what Hazel's doing and grab a couple of holly seedlings each."

As Gustaf led them off he started to tell them about the New Forest – a tale I was to hear many times – how holly trees were still growing in circles around oak trees planted over a century before.

"Stories, not statistics," Gustaf was to tell me again and again, "impress children more."

By which time Dez had made a start at explaining to our half of the group what The Tree Prospectus was hoping to do with the wetland half of the site. Even those boys who were paying attention, however, looked resentful at being talked to by a dreadlocked scruff not of their clipped scalp kind. While a few of the girls, less tribal, had gone gooey-giggling over every word good-looking Dez was saying.

There had already been some willows growing in among the yellow sedges of the swamp, recently pollarded stumps leaning like malformed penises. Although Gustaf and Dez intended making the swamp into an osier bed they were at that time undecided whether to use the crop as biomass of for basket making. Today's activity was to help them decide.

Dez, unlike Gustaf, was no performer. He was not being listened to. Which this day was not due wholly to Dez's lack. His charges were adolescents and to adolescents all adults appear ridiculous. It has to be said mind you that at the same time the concerns of adolescents appear as ridiculous to adults. This gulf of incompatible ridiculousness stays between them until the adolescents succumb to adulthood.

While Dez had been talking one subgroup of boys had found something to snigger over, three of the girls to whisper.

"What we're going to do today," Dez gave up on the theory behind the planned activity, "is use these willow whips from the pollarding to make baskets. I'm going to show Hazel's mum what to do and then she can help you. Gather round and watch."

Dez picked up four of the willow wands and, squatting, laid them one across the other.

"Now we have a grid," he said.

"Do that again. Slower." I bent to watch.

Within a circle of the pupils' thin legs, one wand across one, over and under, Dez showed me again how the base was made. Then he held up the sides and began to weave a wand in and around.

"Got it," I said.

"Right." He divided the group up into pairs, doled out batches of willow wands, and we set about instructing our reluctant charges. Four of the boys had to be told not to use the wands as whips – unfortunate choice of words on Dez's part – while the girls competed in sweetly calling Dez over to ask if they were "… doing it right." Emphasis on the smirked 'it'.

Hard to isolate now all that I didn't know then. But I'm sure that I'd divined straightaway that Dez knew the effect that he had on women. I have never once though seen him respond to it. What I was to later see were middle-aged women like myself go weak at the knees when in workshops, like that basket making, when Dez leaned in breathing close to them.

What had me occasionally all aquiver wasn't Dez's face, conventionally straight-nosed and clean-jawed handsome though he was, it was his forearms. Sleeves rolled up even in winter his forearms were surprisingly hairless and such a lovely shape. Round up by the elbow they tapered down to the wrist, sinews radiating out into the hand, ending in long, strong brown fingers.

I've smiled to note the hip twitch of those women working close to Dez, some even daring to lay, if briefly, their fingertips on Dez's bare forearm. For myself I've gone so far as to say to him, "Show me again." Just to see the long fingers at work, the movement of the long muscles in his arms.

But that particular day I was Dez's classroom dolt, my beginner's basket to be held up to light ridicule: 'See what Hazel's mum has done here…', 'Now don't do as Hazel's mum has done here…'

While everyone was busy, pairs helping one another, some griping back and forth between themselves, Dez said loudly to me, "What do you know about trees?"

"They're made of wood," I said.

"An outsider's view. As soon as you work with trees you respect them, respect them for what they are. When you look at a full-grown tree you are looking beyond your own time." As Dez talked he was walking slowly from pair to pair. "I've had to fell trees that were seedlings – like they're up there planting – before my, or your, great-grandparents were born. Even trees planted now as crops won't be harvested for fifty years or more. Every tree deserves our respect. Just for being here. Most trees planted now are for a future you yourself probably won't see. Trees are the oldest living things on planet Earth. Some of them are centuries old."

"I thought the oldest living thing was a fungus," one boy said.

"You're right," Dez said. "And it probably began life in a symbiotic relationship with a tree. We must never undervalue fungi in a forest."

"Hear that boys and girls?" I said. "Never undervalue fungi."

Thirty-three

Because of how they propagate the many varieties of willow, *salix*, would seem as adult trees to grow only in watery environments. This is due to willow's male and female trees being separate, their fertilising pollen being wind-borne, as are their short-lived seeds; and being only those seeds that alight on moist soil, inaccessible to browsing beasts, that survive and take root. Indeed Goat Willow, *salix caprea*, got its name because its seedlings were once most likely, I kid you not, to be eaten by goats.

Goat Willow is probably the one true willow. Found among streamside alders its wood, the stem being so low as to make it almost a bush, renders it of little use to us humans. Other names for Goat Willow are 'common sallow' and in Scotland 'saugh'.

In England the willow most often seen pollarded along ditch and stream banks is White Willow, *salix alba;* but more commonly known as 'pussy willow', its name taken from the downy covering of its plump seed buds in spring.

The timber of White Willow is both light and tough, which is what made it a prime contender for rendering into cricket bats. So versatile is White Willow that it was bred into a variety, *salix alba coerulea,* and for years got made into dairymaid yokes and gardeners' trugs. At craft fairs these days many of the lathe turners' bowls will often be of the easily shaped White Willow.

Along with a shrub variety, *salix viminalis,* and a purple-stemmed variety, *salix purpurea,* willow also lends itself, when stripped of its bark, to weaving. In those marshy areas where basket making has become a local industry willows, in this instance called osiers, will be cropped so low and so regularly that their massed wands, with their long lanceolate leaves, can look like an extension of a reed bed.

The ornamental weeping willow, *salix babylonica*, seen in parks and large gardens is, as its Latin name suggests, an import. Although there is a White Willow variety, *salix alba tristis*, that also weeps.

Indigenous and of distinctly damp places is crack willow, *salix fragilis*, so-called because as well as by blown seeds it propagates itself by its easily broken off branches getting carried downstream, cast up on mudbanks and there taking root. A survivor tree crack willow's waving about pink roots actually draw sustenance from flowing water, while its bankside roots help to stabilise river and stream courses. (Not to be confused with Bay Willow, *salix pentandra*, also found on riversides, but which has dark green glossy leaves.)

* * *

When telling of wetland trees I couldn't not mention alder, *alnus glutinosa*. There's no way though that alder can be confused with any of the willow varieties. Not only does alder have round leaves and darker bark it is also festooned with long maroon catkins and small groups of what look like dark balls, known as 'nutlets', though they aren't nuts.

One previous and sinister use of alder was, in its lending itself to the making of charcoal, as a constituent of gunpowder. These days though, when explosives are made from other substances, alder is seen as another wood good for turning, but darker and of more functional use than cricket bat willow. Tool handles are often made of alder.

Alder roots, like crack willow's, are used for checking the erosion of riverbanks. While in low damp land alder has the added benefit of fixing nitrogen in the soil. This is due to the bacteria, *schinzia alai*, that dwells in alder root nodules.

* * *

Dez, with his penchant for old-fashioned ways, loves holly, *ilex aquifolium*. Every chance he gets he collects up holly berries and stores them in trays of damp sand. It takes eighteen months for a holly berry to sprout. In Dez's polytunnels are row upon row of holly seedlings with, out the back, the bigger spikier plants.

It is this evergreen spikiness of holly's lower leaves that makes holly so useful to foresters. If placed around saplings at risk from browsing deer holly's prickly leaves are as good a deterrent as electrified barbed wire. And if planted close in line, and kept trimmed, the very density of their spiked leaves, will stop even large livestock pushing through a hedge of holly.

Holly's one drawback, as Gustaf is happy to point out, is that, because of holly's waxy leaves and its lack of water content, it very easily catches fire. Nonetheless the one tree left standing in tractor-flailed hedgerows will often be the pale grey trunk of the holly. Left standing not out of fear of its flammable properties, but due to a superstition persisting since Roman times which says that it's unlucky to cut down the slow-growing holly.

A latter-day word of warning regards holly, and not based on superstition, concerns its appearance on the woodturner's stall. The wood's density, and if dyed black, can be passed off and priced as ebony, *diospyros tessoloria*. Buyer beware!

* * *

Second brood blackbird
at a run, stops on a lawn
tail cocked like a gun.

Thirty-four

Mine and Hazel's woodland role, when not fetching and carrying, seemed to be that of teaching assistants, or stooges. Mostly this was under Dez's tutelage, on occasion Gustaf's.

Like Hazel I found myself enjoying these late summer, early autumn days. To pause and look about the wood; and in those still moments, bathing in the green light, I too began to believe in the spirit-enhancing properties of massed trees.

On the downside I did occasionally have the GBP, the Great British Public to deal with again.

This though wasn't the Great British Consuming-and-all-critical Public. Here we had none of those grumpy, middle-aged, middle-class women who know the price of everything and still can't buy themselves happiness. These woodland volunteers were women who wanted to give, to contribute, and who had actually considered the consequences of their actions.

Nor were the volunteer men those of the cuckold English – with their willingness to be gulled. Of all the woodland volunteers the one criticism that I could level at them was their sometime excessive self-righteousness, or of their being all too quick to take offence on behalf of someone not present.

In a quiet hour in the woods these contentious souls seemed to invite incident and controversy. Although it could simply have been their love of debate. I very quickly learnt to identify those volunteers who hesitantly – to start with – dared disagree with whatever Dez or Gustaf was saying regards silviculture; and, if only by their soft reverent tones, that the disagreeable were – and were usually male – snobs. The kind of snobs who try to impress the help. The help in this instance being quiet unimpressed Hazel and I.

Even so being volunteers they had given thought to what they were doing and, rebels in each their own small way, they were prepared to disagree with anything said with authority, and therefore by authority, even if that authority was in this instance Dez and Gustaf. And that's just me trying to excuse them, when in fact the disagreeable were often but an intelligence that wanted only to be seen as cleverer than everyone else. To sneer at others while seeming not to sneer. Snobs.

What did impress me was that Dez and Gustaf were as patient in their explanations to these clever-clever snobs as they were with the mentally handicapped. My temptation was to tell the sneerers to fuck off. Which, of course, this one-time café proprietor wouldn't: I made my escape from them, as in the café, with some noncommittal remark.

Whatever the subtext to the woodland talks this was so

different to café conversations, which by the time I left hadn't progressed much beyond the price of petrol, the day's weather and last night's telly. But what I didn't get about the snobs – anywhere – was why they felt they had to sneer. I have known so many people who know things I don't, who can do things I can't, that even to measure myself against them, let alone for me to become another sneerer, seems such a ludicrous thing to attempt to do.

Comparisons with café life however were already receding. What mostly brought home that distance from my recent past was the continual retelling – to a tidy-minded public – that deadwood left to rot is part of the natural process; and having to explain the paradox of coppicing, that all woodlands benefit from being cut down.

As well as volunteers we had, in their yellow and orange high-visibility tabards, first time offenders and white collar criminals doing their 'community service'. But even they weren't as difficult to deal with as some café customers. If anything easier. For a start they were overseen, didn't want even the slightest misbehaviour reported back and their sentence extended; and some had never looked at a wood as a wood before, were school failures, became fascinated by what was new to them. Even those who had arrived with the swagger of small town hustlers, knowing nothing of Dez's woodland crafts, they became so taken with his basket making, lathe-turning, that more than a few came back as local volunteers when their community service sentence had finished.

Dez's introduction to the woodland would set some back on their twenty first century heels.

"Before coal. Before oil. Wood was all that we had to cook on, to heat our homes. Wood, trees, were a resource to be nourished…"

But that was only Dez's prepared speech, most of his woodland talk was easy. I've yet to hear anything that would constitute deliberate provocation issuing from Dez's lips. Gustaf on the other hand used his loud laugh to offset his often cutting observations. Although that was not him seeking to hurt, more that his quick tongue ran away with him, and he did so like to be naughty.

* * *

I watched my Hazel in among all these different human beings, chatting to them, laughing with them, encouraging them, and I'd never seen her so happy. Which made me happy. Gone too was her office pallor. I hadn't seen her look quite so healthy since a child.

I tried not to look at the future. Instead I quizzed Dez about his past, how he had come to work in the woods with Gustaf.

The story came out slowly, in bits and pieces. When with groups he was occupied answering their questions, smiling away the middle-aged flirts, swapping backchat with teenage schoolgirls...

"You're such a tease," Hazel wagged her finger at him.

"Me?" he gave her a look of wide-eyed innocence.

"I'll tell Jay," Hazel said.

I had yet to meet girlfriend Jay and toddler son Ben. Hazel had much earlier, when they had been working close to 'their' wood.

The history came my way partly through Dez, on those days when it was just us engaged in ditch clearing, path repair; or the tale came secondhand through what Hazel had picked up.

* * *

In their left-home-and-living-together bedsit Dez and Jay had decided that they hadn't much liked the twenty first century and they had determined to live a self-sufficient life without recourse to 'civilised' society. The bedsit was exchanged for a woodland bender.

"We both loathed consumerism," Dez told me. "The instant gratification that comes with mass markets. Ownership is not planned for, is not considered. Things are sampled and rejected. No pleasure is invested in the prize."

Statements such as this had me realise why he and Gustaf argued so fiercely. They were so alike. I'd already heard Gustaf say, "Class is nowadays closely allied to consumerism. You shall know my status by what I own, by what I wear."

Which got me to wondering how much like them I was. In the café I'd often had the thought, waiting on women with new purchases bagged around their feet, that consumerism made them the privileged class – those who can afford to buy expecting to be served and being critical of all who serve. The Great British Public for instance who think that as soon as they've got money in their pocket, at least sufficient credit, that someone else should clean up after them. The Great British Public who, as soon as they've got the price of a cup of tea, think themselves superior to the person preparing the tea.

Where I wasn't like Dez and Gustaf was that trees to them were already a religion, reforestation the paradise to be attained. Tactics and strategies were the sole disagreement between these two zealots. Dez, for instance, wanted to reintroduce wolves to keep herbivores such as deer down. Which was mostly, it seemed to me, because he loathed the weekend huntin' shootin' crew. So did Gustaf, but who saw the wealthy hunters as a necessary evil. Much like wolves.

* * *

While still within civilisation – I've never found out precisely where: a suburb of a suburb? – Dez and Jay both read up on woodland crafts, survivalist books and, choosing a large neglected wood, they built themselves their 'bender' – saplings pulled over and tied to the base of other saplings. When I said, testing him, "So you had twenty first century rope," Dez showed me how to make 'string' by running two stones along a bramble to rid it of its thorns, the shredded remains being as strong and pliable as sisal. He did however confess, not then having been in flint country, to their both having had a knife and an axe. That and a large saucepan.

Once the bent saplings had been secured he and Jay had woven branches through them, had finished off the roof with lapped turfs.

"What, young trees like these?" I pulled an ash sapling to me.

"Bigger than that. But yes, like that. And fundamentally no different to how houses are built now. The wooden frame goes up first. Then the insulation. Then the brickwork or blocks. And so on. Timber first though."

For bedding they'd used bracken.

"The living accommodation was OK. Food was the problem. It would probably have been OK if we'd been meat-eaters, could've supplemented the nuts, berries and fungi with a rabbit or a pheasant. Squirrel even. And we'd been OK through the summer and autumn." Which had been when Gustaf, looking over Prospectus's latest acquisition, had found them.

Gustaf introduced himself as their wood's new owner. Dez and Jay had always expected discovery, of being told to move on. To meet that eventuality they had a makeshift trolley in which to convey their few possessions – saucepan, knives, axe, and a second set of clothes each – and off they'd go in search of a new wood. Gustaf though surprised them by being impressed by their bender's construction, by asking how they'd made their few bits of greenstick furniture, what they did for drinking water, for a lavatory…

They asked if they could stay. Gustaf said, "Yes." He thought the way of life they were attempting wonderful. He examined their stash of wool – gathered from hedgerow snags – and considered with them their plans for spinning it, asked about cooking, how they cooked when it rained…

What Gustaf didn't ask that first visit was what they did for contraception. Answer, as winter set in, became apparent.

On his second visit Gustaf saw the swedes that Dez had

lifted from a frost-weighted field on the wood's edge, the failed acorn bread that Jay had tried to bake in a self-made clay pit, and beneath the woollen layers the swelling of her belly.

"I could do with some permanent help," Gustaf confided in them, while sharing his cheese sandwiches. He proceeded to tell them what Prospectus was attempting – the treeing of England; and how, on his own, he couldn't manage. He had tried employing permanent staff; but, although at interview every prospective employee had said they believed in what he was attempting, all had turned out to have a nine-to-five mindset.

"Maybe it's me," he said. "But I seem to scare them off. In one of the woods I've got a couple of old caravans and some polytunnels. No trees growing in the tunnels. There were, but the last lot of staff let them dry out. The caravans could easily be made habitable. I know it's not what you wanted, but I'll give you a wage."

Gustaf left them to ponder the offer. A week of swede breath, rumbling stomachs and one swelling belly had them agree to take up his offer. When Gustaf arrived back at their bender they told him yes.

"I forgot to tell you about the horses," Gustaf said.

Thirty-five

It's not the meshed bark that makes the ash, *fraxinus excelsior*, distinctive. Rather it's the coal-black buds on its twig ends. Which twigs themselves curl up like beckoning fingers. Skeletal fingers at that, knuckle bones and all.

However, come spring, when those pointed buds – not one-sided enough to be fingernails – but when those soot-black buds split, what looks like so many small feathery palms erupt from the twig ends.

Give it a few months and those same ash trees in autumn will be hung on their every side with golden 'keys', as if with Christmas decorations. Individual seeds from these bunches of 'keys' will be one-bladed propellers. Small wonder then that in hedgerow and woodland, with each ash tree a self-pollinating hermaphrodite, ash has been one of, if not the commonest English tree.

And it was probably the commonest because it was a beneficent woodland tree. Not only does ash leaf late, and then with thin fernlike leaves, it also drops early, allowing plenty of light through for lower growth.

Ash has been useful in other ways too. In olden days the rims of cartwheels were made of ash, as were the handles of spades, chisels, hammers and pickaxes. Because not only is ash strong, it doesn't easily splinter. Which is why it has been favoured by some sports – for hockey sticks, oars, skis and tennis rackets. And because ash can be so easily bent it continues to be used in the making of furniture.

Widespread throughout Europe ash has been here a long time, takes its name from the Anglo-Saxon *aesc* and from the Scandinavian *ask*. Indeed the ancient Scandinavians, a superstitious crew, believed that it was a giant ash that was the Tree of the World, *Yggdrasil*, whose topmost branches reached right up to heaven, its roots going down to hell.

All of the above would have been valid for centuries, right up until a few years back, when the fungal infection, *chalara fraxinea*, wiped out 90% of the ash trees in Denmark before reaching these shores. Every ash tree we come across now we look first for die-back, then reach for the aerosol, consider the chainsaw...

* * *

    eroded coal nut
    black ash bud about to split
    and spray feathery green

Thirty-six

I think that, to begin with, I fell in love. If not love I was certainly attracted to them both, was happy in their presence. Toddler Ben, like any bonny two-year-old, was of course a pleasure to have around. But I used to find myself just watching Dez and Jay, and having to snap out of my trance-like state and hope – having caught myself in it – that I hadn't blushed at being so caught.

Because Jay I discovered, when finally we met, was as tall, as dreadlocked, and as outdoors slim as Dez.

That day of our first meeting Hazel and I had, to begin with, gone to the woodland where we'd been supposed to help with a workshop. Only to discover that the school had got the day wrong and had cancelled. Gustaf and Dez were not surprised. Neither had a high opinion of the organisational abilities of schoolteachers.

But that woodland being not that far from where Dez and Jay had their caravans Dez suggested that Hazel and I go there to help plant out, I seem to remember, some holly seedlings. Although I don't think we did that day. While I was being shown around Hazel was off playing with little Ben.

* * *

A short track through their wood led to the two long brown and beige caravans parked side by side on the wide floor of an old quarry. The polytunnels were in the most open part of the quarry, stable and paddock for the two horses at an angle to them. The two heavy horses, Titan and Herbert, were Jay's responsibility and love.

The horses weren't in the paddock when we arrived. After introductory mugs of tea and thick home-made biscuits my part of the tour included a meander down to the horses' woodside field. And they were huge magnificent creatures, straightaway came wandering over to greet Jay, herself a magnificent creature.

If that makes me sound like a lesbian, then maybe a repressed lesbian is what I am. But I just loved watching Jay move. She had the unconscious elegance that some tall big-boned women have. As she reached up to smooth Titan's dark shivering flank I watched her bra-less breasts move within her cotton top, glanced over the line of her back as she turned with the horse, her long lumbar muscles curving down into the rise of her buttocks as she reached further up into Titan's mane to extract a burr, murmuring to him, "Where you been big boy? Where you been?"

I suppose I shouldn't but I used to imagine her and Dez making love, one perfect physical form meeting another perfect physical form. In actuality their sex was probably nothing like my slow-mo candlelit versions, was probably as clumsy and grunting and as fumbling about in the dark as the rest of us. Although just watching their daylit selves, their easy natural grace, the tilt of Jay's neck, Dez's lean hands and forearms, Jay's long fingers, the rounded knuckles, each uninhibited movement, the tapering haunches, the inviting valley of their buttocks... Hard to believe that their sexual congress could be as that of we chubby mortals.

"Aren't they both lovely," Hazel said at the end of that first day.

"Yes," I said, though I doubted that Hazel found them 'lovely' in quite the same way I did. Though one never knows; and one doesn't like to speculate on the sex lives of one's children.

* * *

Where does aesthetic appeal end and sexual attraction begin? I knew only that I felt privileged every time I found myself in Dez and Jay's company. Their quiet way of speaking, their every casual gesture... I felt that I had embarked, when with them, on a new, more elevated way of being.

Aware of my fascination, of my near-infatuation with the pair, I tried looking at them through a cynical lens. But try as I might I couldn't find a category for them among the Great British Consuming Public. Jay and Dez were almost of another species. A wood-dwelling genus?

Nor was it as if they made a show of themselves, didn't appear that different from other weekend hippies. Aside from the shoulder-length dreadlocks and their clothes a tad on the workaday scruffy side, and of course only of natural fibres – dark cotton trousers, stained T-shirts and un-darned woollen jumpers – outwardly they were no different to anyone else. Of a type the dreadlocks only meant that shampooing wasn't required, had been carried over from their bender days into caravans with no mains water. Dez and Gustaf had rigged up guttering to collect rainwater into barrels, with a solar-powered pump to take it up to a cistern on wooden scaffolding. Waste from the caravans went to a cesspit.

Nor did Jay and Dez make a show of their sexual partnership, were companionable rather than affectionate. That is they didn't display their affection for one another with endearments or by gestures such as hand-holding or hugs. Confident of one another they had no need? The most that I've seen pass between them, and it was so rare that it almost came as a shock, was a light kiss on parting once when I collected Dez for a trip.

* * *

If the above makes my lurking presence seem all very intense it's wrong. Dez and Jay were simply good company, their very enthusiasm for their way of life a part of their attractiveness. That first day at the caravans for instance Dez had been keen to show me the charcoal stove he had recently cobbled together to heat the caravans, and his tree seedbeds, the planting on, the extension he was making to the arboretum... And he told me how they were able to reside there, the site having once been a timber mill, old machinery rusting away at the back of what was now a corrugated log shed.

Jay's enthusiasm, aside from little Ben – not yet dreadlocked: "Hair washing still a part of bathtimes," Jay said – her enthusiasm was for Titan and Herbert.

"Why Herbert?" I asked: it seemed a small name for such a large beast.

"Came to us as Herbert. Poor Herbert," she leant against his face. "Poor Herbert is a gelding. Aren't you Herbert?"

Every evening Jay fetched both horses from the field, and took them from the paddock back to the field in the mornings. Such a routine didn't fit with the image I had of their easygoing life. At least in the café I'd been able to organise days off for myself.

"Isn't that a chore?" I asked her. "All weathers?"

Jay said not: "And it's essential the horses are used to being regularly handled."

She told me this while leading both horses on halters behind her. I was stumbling and staggering along beside her, very aware of the horses' huge plate-size feet being planted a metre or so from my heels.

"These two beauties are worth thousands each. Too much of a risk leaving them unattended in the field at night. And with this daily handling it makes it that much easier to get them into boxes." Jay meant the horse transporter truck that she drove.

She groomed both horses regularly too, plaited their manes and their tails when she took them to county shows. Although Titan nor Herbert had yet won a rosette Gustaf encouraged Jay in showing them. The show visitors who came up to stroke and ask about the horses were told that they were genuine working horses, which implicitly accounted for their not being fancy enough to win rosettes. Jay described what work the horses did best in the woods, and which gave her the chance to tell of Prospectus.

Truth be told, despite Dez always suggesting to Gustaf

that they fetch the horses – the big feet of Titan and Herbert didn't compact the soil like tractors and other heavy logging machinery – Prospectus didn't make use of the horses but once a year. The two horses were more often rented out, with Jay as their handler, to those woodlands where the owners were concerned about ecological damage, designated ancient woodlands or Sites of Special Scientific Interest.

I still have the photo I took of Ben grinning down at me from the broad back of Titan. The light made a halo of Ben's hair.

Hard to say from this distance if it was Dez and Jay's enthusiasm, their sense of mission that infected me; or if it was simply their being two attractive people whose company I enjoyed; but I measure my increasing interest in matters woodland from my meeting with them both.

Thirty-seven

I can't pin down quite when I came to enjoy the woods for their own sake, but one day does stick in my mind.

"This is exactly like my school projects," Hazel laughed at me.

We were walking back along a new-made path. I had just pointed out an old beech tree that was splitting from the crown – "Tendency of beech" – a dark stain seeping down its pewter-smooth trunk.

"You're going to end up knowing ten times as much as me. Again," she said. "Remember that history project I did? On Elizabethan England? Could have been your Mastermind specialist subject."

"It got me interested," I defended my once enthusiasm, smiled as if at a fond memory. Because I had known at the time – Thomas Tamworth, Walsingham's brother-in-law, leading me to an Italian holiday – that the engrossing research had been a welcome distraction from the rut of my marriage, rut of my working life. As was this woodland volunteering – such a big project, an escape from my small-scale life.

I listened again to Hazel laughing at me. Had she resented me taking over her homework? Had I unwittingly stolen a part of her life? Her now shortening life? Ask her, I told myself.

"Did you mind me muscling in on your homework?

"The opposite. Only too grateful. And I thought it funny. You were my secret resource."

Conversations in woodland go at a steady pace. A few yards on I said, "What about now? My being here?"

"Don't be silly. This is lovely." And she linked her arm through mine.

* * *

Without Dez to so often tap me on the shoulder, grab my elbow, say, "See this…" I do wonder if I would have become quite so enthusiastic a woodswoman. But they were educators both. Gustaf for instance one day asking Hazel and I how we would know this wasn't ancient woodland.

We were thinning saplings in a Prospectus new addition and a stiff-backed dog walker had just paused to knowledgeably tell Hazel and I, with our long-handled secateurs and curved pruning saw, to proceed with care, warned us, "This is ancient woodland."

"It isn't," Gustaf said when the man was further down the track. "Not going to argue the toss with that know-all twat though. Throws his purple dog-crap bags in the ditch. Be better off not bagging it. Had a run-in with him once before…"

"Why isn't it ancient?" I said. "Old parts look ancient to me." Huge gnarly trunks whiskered with lichen.

"Because broadleaf here is predominantly sycamore, and sycamores weren't introduced into this country until the fifteenth century."

All such snippets of information, lunch break debates, sun-doped in a woodland glade philosophising, all point of departure disagreements between Dez and Gustaf got me going online later, occasionally ordering books to check if what I had been told, had overheard, could be the truth; and what I discovered by-the-by in the books leading me to reconcile that with what I had seen on my recent travels with Hazel

Much of what I was learning had me feel that I was waking to a world new to me, yet which – disconcertingly – had been there all the time, unrecognised.

"Magicians depend on it," Gustaf lectured a shuffling, inattentive school group. "The eye sees only what the mind tells it to see."

And this was more than my getting carried away with one of Hazel's old school projects. What I was learning in among the trees seemed to marry up with my one other lasting enthusiasm – for antiques.

"Look at the height of this," Dez said of a scabbing pine (he often paused to count the branch stumps circling ladder-like a pine's trunk). "Got to be fifty to sixty years old."

His awe of a tree's age chimed with my love of antiques, with the idea that this artefact had existed before my time, that other hands had traced the wood's contours, that this table, this chair, this dresser was only temporarily in my keeping. There was comfort in knowing that someone else's dishes would be placed on this dresser. I hated the throwaway one-use-one-owner culture, could sympathise with Dez standing before an ancient oak and asking, "Wonder who else has stood here and looked up like us."

For my part I was looking at the living trees from which my furniture had come, all those household smoothed and polished grains…

When first the realisation had come home to me that wood had once been trees I had been ashamed of my disjunction, my disconnect, between furniture and trees. Oh I had known the name of the wood before ever Hazel had found Gustaf, and I could have identified the more obvious trees, but they had been separate areas of knowing. Now I looked at the red lustre of my rosewood dressing table, at the subtle tones of my walnut escritoire, the white of my beech-top kitchen table, my Dutch stained-dark oak dresser, my cross-grained elm coffee table, even my pine dining table and wheel-back chairs; and I saw beyond the furniture to the history and the future of the trees. How they grew, where they grew best, how they were felled, their timber sawn and seasoned… That is aside from my one greenwood beech carver. Dez said that he'd get me along to one of the greenwood furniture workshops.

Couldn't deny it, I was enjoying myself. I even took acquisitive delight in the logs Gustaf let us drop into the boot of my hatchback. Out by the bins we were steadily amassing a stack for winter; and Hazel and I did so enjoy sitting either side of the wood burner with our books, and our mugs of hot chocolate keeping warm on the wood burner's iron top.

I had known so much as theory – oil, petrol, pollution – only now was I starting to connect it with my every action, every thought.

"What we're looking at here," Dez stood in a beech wood among a group of 'volunteers', "is CO_2 storage."

To another group – could have been the Women's Institute: I seem to remember being within the whispers of a crowd of women – Gustaf said, "Because there is more CO_2 in the atmosphere trees are now growing faster than before."

So caught up was I with this new outlook on the world there were times when I almost forgot how I came to be there. And I felt, given the reason for my being there, that I should hide my pleasure, my excitement at being there. Yet, just driving Hazel to and from the various woodland sites, that driving had changed.

* * *

My home has been suburbia. I travelled through the countryside to get from one set of streets to another. Some countryside beyond the car windows was choc-box prettier than others, looked as the posters and the films said that it should look. My thoughts had been taken up with where I had come from, where I had been bound. Oh we might have stopped at tea rooms, even at a picnic spot. But it was not until I stepped off the paths with Hazel that I started to take notice, met with concepts and connections new to me, with words previously unconsidered. 'Bole' for instance was a word I could now identify with, round and heavy-seated, like me.

It was almost with shame that I recalled my pre-Hazel trips out with Ian. Then the agricultural countryside had just been what we had passed through in our passage from town to town. Some of it had been hilly scenic, cottage picturesque, but most of it hedgerows, fences and flat fields; plain countryside followed, if not by more countryside, then village and town outskirts, countryside again…

Now I was naming tree species as I recognised them; and, already indoctrinated by Prospectus, looking to sites where more trees could be planted. Or, seeing a tree I didn't recognise, I searched for its likeness that evening in one of my new books, which told of the soil that type of tree preferred, and which led me to buy books on geology, to frown over underlying soil structures and to relay to Hazel what I had just learnt.

"Yes Mum," she'd say out of her own book.

Nodding the new information into my head I'd read again my latest discovery, make sure I had it right.

Already – thinking I'd known so much I'd known so little – I looked back on my life, at the characterless suburbs I'd lived in, the lookalike High Streets I'd shopped in, driven through. Now I set off daily looking forward to woodlands known for their difference.

"Know why being in woods is psychologically comforting?" Dez asked me. "We own the collective unconscious of an arboreal species."

Whatever the reason, he was right. What I loved most

about the woods was their quiet. After all the noise of the morning's work, even if we'd used no machines there would still have been the thud of an axe, scrape of a spade, I would wander a little way off from the post-lunch murmur, fill myself with the woodland's leaf-whispering quietness, its slow-growing distance from the world's busyness.

* * *

I at last received a definite offer for the café premises lease. An auction house collected up the café contents, the display cabinet, crockery, tables, chairs and Bakelite.

Finis.

Thirty-eight

Hard to believe now, so naturalised, so self-regenerating have its helicopter seeds made of it, that the sycamore, *acer pseudoplatanus*, wasn't introduced into this country until early in the fifteenth century.

Before that the sycamore, or Great Maple as it is also known, grew naturally in middle Europe as far north as Paris. Which makes its late introduction into the British Isles a puzzle, given that by the fifteenth century travel between France and England had been happening for ages. An even bigger puzzle is why silviculturalists should have initially assumed that the sycamore was of the same family as the mulberry and/or the plane tree. Especially as the plane tree's buds are set alternately and the sycamore's opposite. Nonetheless the misnaming persists: sycamore timber is still known in Scotland as 'plane'.

Sycamore, despite being deciduous – its hand-shaped and heavily veined leaves fall in October – is as hardy as evergreen spruce, and like spruce often gets planted as windbreaks, especially in coastal areas and around upland farmsteads. Left to itself – no sheep, no deer or rabbits – sycamore would readily reforest the entire country. Sycamore seeds like that of the ash are one blade aerodynamic, although in the sycamore's case even more so, the blade being curved and wider than that of the ash, the seed rounder and heavier and thus more likely to travel further.

Given that we do have sheep, deer and rabbits, no introduced tree gets to be so widespread as just a windbreak, sycamore's timber also has to have been of use. Fast-growing sycamore can soon reach as high as thirty-eight metres: once felled its ripple-grained wood is the preferred wood for the backs, sides and stocks of violins and guitars. Sycamore's other one-time specialist use was as the boards for sprung dance floors. Nowadays the lathe turners' love making sycamore into bowls, kitchen spoons and rolling pins.

Of occasional concern to the lay person are the black spots on sycamore leaves. This is the tar-spot fungus, *rhytisma acorium*. Fortunately the fungus doesn't damage the leaves, and will anyway only be seen in the countryside. As with roses these black spots won't be seen on the leaves of city trees because of the pollution there. City aesthetes might suppose this to be a good thing.

Aesthetes might also be disappointed by the sycamore's being known as The Great Maple. Because, come autumn, sycamore's leaf drop lacks the russet glory of other maples. Sycamore leaves tend to wrinkle to a dead brown before seesawing heavily to the ground.

So far as legend goes the sycamore is also known as The Martyrs' Tree. It was under a large sycamore in Tolpuddle, Dorset, that the first trade unionists met to campaign against starvation wages. For their trouble the leaders were transported as criminals to Australia. …and at mention of The Martyrs' Tree here come our singalong choirmasters Gustaf and Dez: "All together now! It's the rich wot gets the pleasure, it's the poor wot gets the blame. It's the same the whole world over, ain't it all a bleedin' shame…"

*　*　*

Despite the many varieties of maple in gardens and parks only one maple is native to the British Isles, and that is the field maple, *acer campestre*. Not really a timber tree this lesser version of the sycamore is found nowadays mostly on the lime rich soil of the south and then mostly in hedgerows and on scrap ground.

Although small, rarely getting above eighteen metres, with a couple metres girth, a field maple is unlikely to be mistaken for a young sycamore. Not only are its leaves and seeds smaller but a field maple tends to a twiggy growth around its trunk.

Field maple's timber, when it does get to a size worth felling, can be used for turning, keeps its shape. Indeed the Welsh name for maple being *masara* led to the name 'mazer' for a particular maple bowl ornamented with silver. But field maple, being a hedgerow tree and thus annually clipped, rarely now reaches any size at all.

* * *

Mulberry, both *morus nigra* and *morus alba*, came here from Japan and China to be grown in gardens and plantations – the black mulberry in walled gardens for its raspberry-like fruit, the white mulberry in plantations as food for the silkworm. As a fully grown tree mulberry resembles the hawthorn.

* * *

The London plane tree, *platinus acrifolia*, is an accidental hybridisation of *platinus orientalis* and *platinus occidentalis*. When this hybrid's resistance to pollution became evident was when it became known as the London plane.

Being a hybrid, although each tree carries both male and female catkin-like flower heads (green versions of alder's bobbles), the resultant seeds are mostly infertile, rarely set. So London plane is mostly spread by cuttings and is therefore rarely found in broadleaf woodland.

In parkland London plane can be readily identified by

what looks like military camouflage on its trunk and larger boughs – hand size areas of cream through to green. This 'camouflage' is caused by the tree's serial shedding of flakes of bark. Which is precisely how London plane survives pollution so well, this continuous refreshing of its bark keeps its pores unblocked, allows the tree to breathe.

Plane's timber is similar to that of beech, and like beech does not last long when used out of doors.

* * *

When the blackbird shriek-
shriek-shrieks rabbit and red wing
pause to look around

Thirty-nine

Having been Dez's teaching aid all morning, or just fancying a break away from all the chatter, lunchtimes I often took myself off for a woodland wander. No-one usually followed me, assuming I suppose that I'd gone off for a bracken-hidden pee.

Given my scurrying hither-thither way of life then, those lunchtime walks felt a pure indulgence, a going-nowhere-in-particular traipsing along tracks moss-soft, pine needle quiet, leaf-scuffed. And here it was that I became aware of my own love for forests, of my own affinity with trees.

I would find myself stopped, say, by sight of one old tree, something about its lumps and scars, its age and immensity that demanded my respect if not reverence. Also, given my own years/experience on this unreliable planet, knowing how delicately held was all life, and I felt a longing kinship, a wistful solidarity with the trees' wooden solidity. Albeit as bogus as Hazel's robust health.

Or I'd find myself paused over a fern-deep gully, the day's heat held there, one or two brown butterflies trying to move the green air, the white, tree-filtered light splashing back up off the flat leaves of hart's tongue ferns. Or I'd bend to peer into the small soft caves formed by eroded roots, the black insides of hollowed out trunks: a whole other life could be happening in there... Or, head back, I'd gaze up into the world of tree. Or, as if in a sculpture park, I'd study the naked end-on stacks of lumber, a collection of almost circles; and I'd breathe in the scent of unhealed sap: no smell quite so clean as fresh-hewn wood.

* * *

Actually I was altogether more relaxed during this period. To cut down on the driving Hazel and I had been finding cheap hotels in order to stop over. Those tall hotels just off motorways, rooms near identical, just the view out the window marginally different. Evenings we'd find somewhere local to eat, wander back to the hotel, take turn and turn about having the double bed or the pull-out/fold-out single. We would read and chat, giggle often, into the night. Mornings, having stocked up on the breakfast buffet, we would stop off at a garage shop for a couple of sandwich packs before returning to the wood, often being the first there.

* * *

In a beech wood one day – no bracken there, no volunteer group either, just Dez, Gustaf, Hazel and I – we were possibly ditch clearing. Memory has a somewhat confused chronology, one wood one time overlaying another. We could have been thinning new shoots, or I could have been in another wood helping Dez demonstrate wood-turning. No, we weren't, it was definitely a beech wood and just us four that day.

As per my usual come lunchtime I'd wandered off, was stood daydreaming, not looking at anything in particular, sight drawn on by the lessening perspective between grey pillars of beech, when I became aware of Gustaf approaching from behind me.

I could tell it was Gustaf by his heavy tread through the

leaf litter. Dez and Hazel picked their way over the ground, if not quite gazelle-like they definitely made as little contact with the woodland floor as they could. Gustaf walked as if he wanted to leave his impression on it. His footprints were always the deepest. Truly he was more bulldozer than statuesque Viking.

Anyway he arrived beside me.

"You sure we never..?" he nodded to the beech tree just to my right which had a healed split in its stem, could have been said to resemble a young girl's vulva.

"Never." I was certain.

He and I had already chit-chatting compared the whens and wheres of our past and, although of almost the same age – he was younger by a few years – our paths, and most assuredly our genitals, had never crossed.

"Will we?"

Without looking I could tell just by the tone of his voice that he was smiling, that this wasn't meant to be taken seriously. Although if I were to...?

Gustaf often flirted with volunteer women, just as I used to flirt with those café customers who had seemed to invite it. That said I hadn't been seriously approached by any man for years, not since I'd first opened the café and had been in receipt of those 'accidental' touches across my backside as I moved between tables, or there had been fingertips tickling my palm as I had reached out for change. All quite pathetic.

Gustaf Eriksson's intentions, however, even if smiling and with one eyebrow raised, weren't open to misinterpretation.

"Will we?" he had said. And I could pass it off as a joke or take it in earnest. I was tempted, just to see how he would respond, to pretend to take it seriously. Decided it wasn't worth the possible complications.

"Never," I straightfaced said.

* * *

I knew that Gustaf had a couple of 'lady friends.' Or so I had learnt from Hazel via Jay, and that he often stayed overnight with one or the other, depending where he was in the country. (No change there then.) Or one or the other came to stay at his place.

Hazel and I had thus far stayed at his place the once – an old farmhouse which had been a roofless ruin when Prospectus had earlier on acquired it along with that bit of neglected woodland.

When I had first been told that Gustaf had restored the building I had imagined a characterful farmhouse of mellow stone. His farmhouse though had been but a part of a working farm, was of brick cement-rendered and its dull grey made darker by being within the woodland grown up around it. Nor had Gustaf made the least attempt to lighten it. Any treeless spaces around the house had been filled with bits of idle forestry equipment – a log loader, a flat bed trailer with one deflated tyre, an old battered tractor, various of its chain-hung attachments parked higgledy-piggledy in a partially collapsed outbuilding, probably one of the original farm's barns.

Inside the house was as much a mess, leaning piles of books everywhere, even on the half-landing. Hazel and I had slept in the one spare double bed, more piles of books in there. The bedroom that is, not the bed. The rest of the house had at least one sagging sofa in each room and trestle after trestle stacked with loose piles of papers, a stone on each pile holding it in place. Thankfully kitchen and one of the bathrooms was functional.

The evening and morning that we had stayed Gustaf had played the very proper and solicitous host. There had been no sexual overtures at all then.

But that had been when Gustaf had been less sure of us, uncertain what he could say to us. To me especially.

I think that to begin with Gustaf had seen Ian and I as the respectable couple who had adopted his accidental (incidental?) daughter. Respectable as opposed to his unconventional haiku-writing, tree-hugging, pop-promoting self. And he had probably been right. Ian and I had been, to all outward appearances, your conventional suburban couple. 'To all outward appearances' being what had mattered to the both of us.

Now however I was acting in a decidedly unconventional manner – carting my adopted daughter all over the country for her to spend time helping her recently discovered biological father. While Gustaf had still been, behind his pleased-to-see-her face, unsure of Hazel's motives; and he hadn't known quite how to pitch his approach to me. Especially as I often play the world with an unresponsive face.

* * *

As was my face kept blank that day in the beech woods in response to his, if jocular, still a sexual overture. Because I'm sure that had I shown the least positive interest Gustaf would have been happy to take me to his untidy bed, make me his number three 'lady friend.' And which would have made us all one big happy family, and which I had sometimes – just lately – seen us as. Gustaf, me, Hazel, Dez, Jay, Ben and the two horses, one big woodland family. Already like a family we had built up our own private history, ongoing jibes and jokes.

For instance, I'd got used to jollying some of our volunteers along. To encourage one wife-led man I had winked at him behind her back. Then got worried when he had come back alone and had followed me around. The family, Hazel included, still teased me over that.

And in an odd way I had become proud of Gustaf. For all his 'be realistic' arguments with 'utopianist' Dez, with Gustaf keep saying that Prospectus 'had to live in the real world', still he didn't moderate his views to suit his company, was nobody's lickspittle. I had come to expect him to speak his mind.

"When Thatcher said that there was no such thing as

society," he boomed, "she was telling us what a callous, self-centred, selfish cow she was."

Those white-haired volunteers who had assumed a wealthy man like Gustaf Eriksson to be kindred to their middle-class selves, themselves obviously one time supporters of Thatcher, were stunned into, if not shock, then mumblings of outrage. Although the outcome of the mumblings was, because they did so enjoy coming to the woods, that Gustaf got made acceptable as 'a character'.

Margaret Thatcher was one of Gustaf's obsessions. Which was a bit of a puzzle to all below forty who knew of her, if at all, only by reputation. Maybe it was that persisting reputation – of Thatcher said to be a 'conviction politician' – that bothered Gustaf so much.

Another time, a quieter delivery, part of a tree stump lunch debate – "When Thatcher said that there was no such thing as society, only individuals, she was committing the greatest heresy of civilisation. Because we are, each and every one of us, from nomads to tree-dwelling tribespeople to metropolitan commuters, our society."

Mind you I had started out wanting to show him how unimpressed I was by his wealth, his reputation. Silly. He was but a man. One not in the least like Ian, true. Gustaf didn't have Ian's social timidity, lack of ambition. Ian had been too shy to network, had scoffed at golf – too pedestrian a sport for him. Ian had wanted the instant gratification of adrenaline. Even his garden games with little Hazel had been over-exuberant. And safe.

Gustaf it was who had taken the life risks, even to fathering Hazel. Ian had been quietly careful not to openly disagree, even with racists. Gustaf voiced, and when I say voiced I mean he barrelled out his opinions regardless: "All politicians become apologists for atrocities."

I laughed out loud one day when we got lumbered with a couple of macho-competitors on a workgang. Men who didn't so much want to debate as to score the point, win the argument. Albeit that they were all more or less in agreement, Gustaf suddenly roared,

"I'm self-made like a volcano!" And he beat his chest gorilla-like.

* * *

So, yes, the idea of belonging to Gustaf's made 'family' was passing attractive. However I'd only need to look over to my big-eyed daughter to know that any such membership couldn't last.

Her condition, it's true, was not continuously at the forefront of my mind, rather it loitered ugly and thuglike in the background, but was there all the time, like an unwanted jingle that keeps bursting through.

With the 'family' I'd look at her, especially when she was visibly tired, see the effort it was taking her to get through the day, and I wondered if she was only persisting with Gustaf just so I'd have another interest when she was gone...

Then there were those times on our own – asleep beside me in the car, or sprawled on the sofa across from me – and I looked at her and all my insides screamed "No!"

"You that sure?" Gustaf was grinning now at my determined rejection.

"Not even when hell freezes over," I said. To which he gave one of his large laughs and, chuckling to himself, he made his way back to Hazel and Dez.

Listening to his rumbling chuckle I smiled. There hadn't been any real heat to my rejection of his maybe-joking-maybe-not advance, it was just a dance we had at some point had to make. But say I'd leapt at the chance... I wondered what the tabloids would have made of such a relationship: Errant Father Forces Sex On Adopting Mother?

Gustaf though wasn't that big a celebrity, was never on telly, would have been unlikely to attract that amount of interest.

* * *

    crossing meadow bridge
    my mortal shadow draws
    rays of golden light

Forty

I have to explain why I was so adamant that I would never have sex with Gustaf Eriksson. Too important not to explain. The reason after all is what has determined the whole of my adult life. Until this point that is, until this sea change in the woods with Hazel, Gustaf, Dez and Jay.

I have a short vaginal canal, which makes having conventional sex, in the missionary position especially, uncomfortable. Not in itself physically painful – there are few if no nerve ends in the cervix – but with my sexual partners pushing and pushing and not understanding why their regular-sized erections wouldn't go fully in, I used to find myself inching further and further up the bed...

Of course my very first attempt to lose my fifteen-year-old's virgin status – the loss carefully planned to take place in my own single bed, the virgin's blood on my sheets to be explained to my out-for-the-day parents – was as I had expected painful. That the next time, in his single bed, it was as uncomfortable; and the next; and the next... I didn't understand. This was not how my fifteen-year-old self had supposed sex to be.

My A-stream schoolfriends used the euphemisms current for sex at that time. They enjoyed 'cuddles', smiled secretively when said. Any direct mention of physical parts, however, led to grimaces of distaste. Unless it was a dirty laugh and a "Waugh!" when hinting, but only hinting mind, at an exceptionally large penis.

Still fifteen I had known only the one penis. As I didn't any longer much like the boy the penis was attached to – I especially resented his post-sex presumed ownership of me

– and I assumed his erection to be of the larger Waugh! variety. So I tried one of his friends. If anything his erection was larger and he took longer to come, prolonging – no pun – the discomfort.

None of my schoolfriends so much as hinted at a similar problem. I'd even overheard coarser girls remarking on the inadequate size of tampons; and that when a normal tampon had caused a sore on my cervix the year before. That young doctor – waiting to spare a young girl's embarrassment? – having examined my cervix hadn't passed mention on the shortness of my vaginal canal, had simply prescribed a course of antibiotics and suggested that in future I use only sanitary towels.

The only doctor who did comment on my short vaginal canal, and it was when I went for my first cervical smear, asked if 'sexual congress' wasn't uncomfortable, and if I had considered corrective surgery? But by then Ian and I had already adopted Hazel and my marriage had been set in its sexual ways.

* * *

Although it had been my mother who had dragged my cervical sore along to the doctor – she had seen the sore's discharge on my knickers – I hadn't confided my fifteen-year-old sexual troubles to her. The less than perfect sister having to admit to another imperfection?

And by that time an elemental distrust had become mine. Not knowing what to do to please, who to please, doubt at the core of myself proceeding hand in hand with a need not to be seen as a freak but as almost like everyone else meant that there was no way I could risk confiding in her. Even if having confided it turned out to be a family trait and my mother too had, as well as a truncated imagination, an abbreviated vaginal canal.

My mother was very much a woman with a peculiar sense of what was proper, what was said and more definitely what was not said. While at the same time, should she not have such a family trait, and seeing no contradiction, she was the kind of woman – her idea of distinctiveness – who boasted of family quirks. I had already been told that I was odd, didn't want to become odder.

Possibly I had inherited this shortened vaginal canal from my father's side. He wouldn't know. My grandmother was said to have been miserable. An unsatisfactory sex life could have explained that.

When I tried another boy, with the same result; then another... Young and inexperienced themselves they assumed that my sudden Ohs! and Ahs! were the surprised sounds of orgasm and not exclamations of discomfort; and some told of them... Thus was my schoolgirl slag status established for the remainder of my schooldays, which in turn led to the growing distance between me and my nice A-stream girlfriends. All reasons contributing to my not taking my A-levels and signing up to a secretarial course in another town, getting myself away from home and into a bedsit.

My life to that date already decided by a shortened vaginal canal.

* * *

In coded references my parents warned me what young men might like to do to me alone in my bedsit. I had the sense though that, aside from a hidden approval of such antics, theirs was a going through the motions, that they didn't really care, were glad to be shot of the lingering parental responsibility which was me. Lorna had left for university the year before. Without her easy chatter a whole year of awkward silences had been sitting with me in the family home. I left knowing there had been no way I could have confided to either of them my anxieties over my sexual experiences.

The bedsit – basin, electric kettle and microwave – allowed me to experiment more, to try different positions. There was at that time a fear of AIDS, young people being encouraged to try non-penetrative sex. It was Hazel's generation who got lumbered with concerns about chlamydia. From a mother's distance I advocated the use of condoms. To which she pulled a face. And I watched her become excited by her own new sexuality, exploring the many aspects of it. Without intruding into her sex life I impotently hoped that she didn't turn out like me. She ended up with Kevin and an inherited terminal condition.

But back in my day, and thanks to the laboratory of my bedsit, although I had soon become quite adept at oral sex, had come to quite like the taste of semen, connie lingus was altogether a revelation. A slippery male tongue pressing on my clitoris gave me my first orgasm, other that is than via my fingers. Which fingers had got me thinking that I might be a lesbian. Except that I wasn't in the least attracted to women, didn't even have any close female friends.

* * *

I knew what he meant when one boyfriend said that he much preferred oral sex. So did I, both as giver and receiver. What I most liked about giving blowjobs was the way the curl of my tongue could be made to fit under the dented head of the penis. If I disliked anything about blowjobs it wasn't the taste of the penis, like a warm savoury lolly, it was my hair getting electrostatically caught – first in their jaw stubble, then in their pubic hairs. It got so I wouldn't even start to have sex, let alone slide down under the covers, or drop to my knees, until or unless I had my hair tied back.

I didn't have any women friends, preferred the company of men, but who for their company expected sex. My sex life became a routine of my giving them a blowjob first, then saying, "Your turn," and guiding them towards my crotch. Only after I had cum, and if they were still capable, did I allow their resurrected erections near my vagina. Even then I manoeuvred them into entering my labia from behind, with me either lying down, where maximum vaginal penetration of a woman flat on her belly is an almost physical impossibility, or in good old doggy fashion. I could then better control their depth of entry. (In the missionary position, expected discomfort aside, I had come to see myself as no more than a tortoise stuck on my back, pale underside open to the light and vulnerable to every hook-beaked predator.)

Because it was their sloppy seconds – this vocabulary I had picked up from my new and older partners – it took them longer to cum. My experience with blowjobs, however, had long since had me discover that it is the speckled base of the penis that stimulates ejaculation. So when doggy fashion I'd reach back between my legs, as if to cup his scrotum, and I stroked the base of his penis and the perineum behind the scrotum, my fingertips almost touching his anus. They came quickly then.

Talking of anus what did puzzle me was why some of these men – of all ages – would suppose that as I did not have an overreaching desire for vaginal sex that I'd be OK with anal sex. I wouldn't even let them try.

With my older men I was grateful, to start with, for their lack of a young man's urgency. But still there came a time when they too wanted to stuff it home up to the hilt. And the hilt I knew was what mattered. The swollen head of the penis was all sensation, it was a firm grip on the nubbly base that triggered their pumping ejaculations.

Such knowledge had a couple of men telling me that I was the only woman they knew who was good at wanking. I did not take it as a compliment.

To find out what men wanted I had read sex manuals, theories of sex, and every magazine article that made mention of sex. I had also questioned those of my sexual partners who liked to talk, and so had learnt that what men found sexy was nowhere near the same as what women then presumed made them sexy.

I came to think of the mermaid as symbol of that division. Imagine, not the fish scale version, but a fancy dress mermaid in her green paper tail and fin, wig taped over her nipples. So peculiarly unerotic. As one of my men put it,

"How to fuck her? Without tearing the tail apart? Would feel like rape."

It was only then that I realised that it was little girls, pre-sexual girls, who liked the idea of mermaids, and who carried that idea over into adulthood.

Another man told me the male version of Erica Jong's zipless fuck. Most teenage boys' fantasy is that, in just going around the block, they'll meet a girl who wants to be fucked there and then. Be ever ready my angel…

* * *

Despite my expertise in matters sexual my partners didn't last. I was no social asset, no long-legged blonde hanging off their arm and onto their every word. I was a dumpy, big-chested thing with a long history of scepticism.

Although ready for sex at the sound of a zip I assumed that, their being unable to fully penetrate, and despite coming, my men felt in some way cheated, the act incomplete. And if after all that activity their orgasm had been unsatisfactory my own orgasm had often been non-existent.

I started to describe myself as an unfinished woman. But what are fingers for?

At first, latest man gone, being single again was always a relief. No more pretence. And being an otherwise healthy young woman, with healthy appetites, I gave in to consecutive nights uninhibitedly pleasuring myself.

Gradually though loneliness would close in on me, and I'd find myself craving company.

Was there love? Certainly I made attempts at it. And discovered that love is one thing – selfish. To be satisfied, to not be alone.

And love is unselfish. To satisfy, to accompany.

I failed on the satisfaction level. Add to that the desire

to be thought normal, and therefore acceptable, that desire being as powerful as the longing for love, and at that most fundamental, vaginal level, I knew myself to be not normal, and therefore unlovable.

* * *

By my early twenties I saw a long spinsterhood ahead of me; and in my early twenties such a prospect did not in the least appeal. The remedy I believed was that I had somehow to take a man beyond the *a priori* of sex; spent and gone, move on. Because always after sex, breathing up into the dark, there were other things to consider. What to wear to work in the morning... And it was there, through work, that I began flirting with Ian. Ian – so quiet, head down, so part of the background as to be almost invisible.

It was Ian's softness, his malleability that appealed. Here, I realised, was the man who could save me from singledom. One such as Gustaf Eriksson would have been too wilful a husband. In a word uncontrollable. Ian though...

On Ian's visits to my by then tiny flat I apologised of its smallness, for its having only a shower and no bath, for the cooking smells from the open plan kitchenette, for the narrowness of the bed... Ian suggested that I move in with him.

Ian was just so suggestible. Very early on I persuaded him that he preferred sex doggy fashion. Wanting a different outcome with him I hadn't encouraged quid pro quo fellatio, had suspected that he might have found that too high a price to pay for his cumming. Instead I had 'let myself' be turned onto my front: "If you must / insist." And once in that position I had been able to control the depth of his penetration by keeping my back straight and my buttocks tensed; and by reaching lovingly back to his scrotum I could hasten his ejaculation.

Since Ian's death I have found myself hoping that one of

those cycling ladies had let Ian go deep within her. He hadn't been a mean man, had deserved better in bed than me.

* * *

Before Ian some of my bedfriends had had me watch porn movies with them. I suppose it was because of my proficiency with blowjobs they made the assumption that I must have learnt the art of fellatio via dodgy videos. Consequently by the time I was training Ian I had known that when in the doggy position the woman has to let her saddle back sink in order to present the flat of her vagina to her rear-mounted partner. By doing the opposite, by keeping my back straight, I had seen that I could limit his access.

Except for rare occasions that was our marital sex life. A whole life down to one shallow vaginal canal. And probably the reason why I never conceived, and why we had to adopt Hazel.

Although we did try for a baby. Even to packing two pillows under my bum and, with me ignoring the discomfort, and him manfully perched up there plugging away. And when he was done, dismounted, the pillows stayed under my bum and not a single drop of semen slid out. To no avail; and it was Ian who suggested, unbidden, we give up and return to doing it doggy fashion.

* * *

Once Hazel had left home, and there was no longer the need to keep the domestic peace, sex with Ian became even more of a chore, something to be put off by whatever ploy, and whose absence made even Ian scratchy. Nonetheless we both continued to manage our marriage.

Wanting peace, still believing the sustaining of this worn-out marriage to be for Hazel's benefit, we fitted together like ill-matched puzzle blocks. And I'm sure that good-natured Ian made as many accommodations as me. A marriage can only survive on such lies and omissions. These truths, told here, would not have helped our marriage.

Ian was not a bad man. That he was boring, that even sex with him was boring, was my own choice, of my own design, my own making. I'm so glad that I never told him any of this.

* * *

That's how our marriage went on through Hazel's twenties. Until I found myself looking forward, with increasing sexual excitement, to Ian's cycling weekends away. A long bath, scented oils, an early night in clean sheets, and then that first, pleasant, expectant, fingertip touch nodule of my clitoris... And in doing this I had by now the comfort of knowing that I was not alone. You can even see women demonstrating it on the telly, if unconsciously in their advertising of tables, and of kitchen worktops in particular – that lengthy, one finger, clitoral stroke.

When I found myself sighing in anticipation of his weekends away I knew that the marriage had to be brought to an end. Although, since its end, I don't seem to have bothered that much with my kind of sex. To even thinking about it. Because it wasn't just an unsatisfactory sex life that saw the end of our marriage.

Week on week I'd been a cold-eyed witness to his timidity. And there he'd been looking back at my, not misery, but at my miserableness. We, neither of us, had wanted to be us.

Who holds the power in any pairing at any one time? The one who is most prepared to leave it? The one least dependant on the other?

No way was Ian, worked in the same firm for over thirty years, going to leave. The decision had had to be mine.

Like the majority of young people I'd begun by wanting to be normal, while at the same time wanting to be the star of my own life, to not be the younger overlooked sister. And I had in a way achieved both with my marriage to Ian and with my daughter Hazel. I was me, important to them both.

Then, and so gradual was the process that I hadn't noticed, but listening to the café customers' tales I ended up with no certainty of what was normal anymore. Finally I decided to hell with normality and to be just me. Whoever me turned out to be.

But no sooner separated from Ian than Hazel had been diagnosed, Ian had died... and here I was faced by a beech labia on the end of a twinkling proposition.

The one thing I was sure of in that uncertain time though was that I was no longer prepared to pay the price of bad sex for a man's company. Sex with Gustaf, or with Dez, or with any other flirtatious old man of the woods was most definitely not going to be on my cards.

A decision created out of my life's experience, itself created by my having been born with a shallow vaginal canal. (It's only recently that I've discovered that my vaginal depth is not in fact abnormal. What that smear doctor must have seen was, possibly, the absence of, or the atrophy of the muscles necessary to lift the cervix out of the way during sex. As I understand it a sort of female erectile dysfunction. Not short, nothing to do with my height at all. Not though that this knowledge now makes any difference; and had I known what he meant at the time I would still probably have refused corrective surgery.)

* * *

The biological processes of life – eating, digestion, pissing, shitting, sex – I have always found slightly ludicrous. Even more so now that I am older and, in the latter, am not so driven to partake.

So whenever I saw Hazel smiling fondly across at us, at Gustaf and I as we shared a joke, or as we chatted of the past, I thought, 'Whatever your plan is darling, it ain't going to happen.'

Not that I disliked Gustaf. I was actually starting to quite like him, certainly hadn't taken umbrage at his 'advance'.

Every approach man to woman has to be made somehow. And the answer to Gustaf had had to be no. Aside from my having to embarrassingly expose my now drooping nakedness to someone new, why ever would I submit myself to the humiliation of sex with another again?

Forty-one

Dez and Hazel may have led me to appreciate, nay love, being among trees. It was Gustaf though who sought to recruit me to the cause. Once, that is, the air between us had been cleared of sexual considerations. That removal of the prospect of sex, of the possibility even, had paradoxically enabled Gustaf and I to become closer, less inhibited in what passed between us.

There was still the getting to know one another. What we had to remove, on both sides, was distrust. His distrust of my being a self-righteous, do-gooder adopter; mine of his being a careless coupler. Gustaf though could hardly be said to have ever been half a couple.

Seemingly ready to hold forth on most subjects, getting information out of him about his personal life was by no means easy. Got easier that time we ended up in some woods near his house. That was when he had invited Hazel and I to stay the night.

"All this driving back and forth is doing the environment, and your purse, no good."

* * *

The house, as I have already said, was as ramshackle, as higgledy-piggledy as Dez and Jay's caravans. If anything their caravans and polytunnels were the more orderly, had fewer bits of machines parked up and forgotten.

What I passed comment on first though, because we'd had it on one of our houses, was the flaking stems of a climbing hydrangea partially covering the algae-streaked cement rendering. Then I saw that neither the tiled entrance nor the stone-flagged kitchen, nor the ground floor's bare boards had seen much of a hoover. One could clearly make out Gustaf's regular paths through the house.

Upstairs was less used and therefor cleaner. Even so the landing carpet showed Gustaf's regular route between bathroom and bedroom. Not many paths led to the three spare bedrooms. Hazel and I were allotted one apiece.

"I've spare bedding somewhere." Gustaf was less at ease in his own house than he was in the woods. "It'll need airing. I'll crank up the heating."

* * *

That was the first time. Difficult though to recall all of my first impressions as I've been there so often now, and so much has changed. One immediate decision I made, while he went searching for bedding and while Hazel swept the kitchen floor, was that I was not going to become Gustaf Eriksson's cleaner.

What I did become, but long after he had shown us around the house – trestle tables piled high with papers in two of the ground floor rooms, as well as stacks and towers of folders in his office – was not, most definitely not, his personal assistant. During that period I was more an occasional office colleague.

"Hazel said you ran your own business," he had winced out his proposal. "Don't suppose you'd help me make sense of all this?" A deepening grimace. "It piles up and up. My accountant's not the only one really pissed off with me."

If this approach to our developing relationship appears tentative then it mirrors our still cautious dealings with one another. The big step for Gustaf – because we'd been this close to his house a couple of times before – had been his inviting us to stay. The rest followed from there. He even became confident enough to tell Hazel that she was getting too thin.

* * *

As to the paperwork... what should have been easily compartmentalised – a pile for this, receipts and invoices belonging to that – had been complicated and confused in order – although 'order' is the last word one should use in this context – to hide his money from any treasure-hunting seed of his loins. It seemed though that Hazel and I, being asked to make sense of these paper mounds, we had been taken partially into his confidence. Which back then was my prime reason for agreeing to help.

Not that I was any paper-sorting expert. The most I'd had to deal with, and then Ian had done the lion's share, had been the café accounts. And here was the accumulated dross not only from The Tree Prospectus – run by various trustees, their meetings minuted by not always the same person – but one of two associated companies responsible for the spruce and larch plantations; another trust fund, with some of the same trustees, that had shares in the timber company; Jay's horses' earnings from being hired out, vet bills, feed and bedding receipts; leasehold agreements for some of the woodlands, old grant applications, unfulfilled funding promises, et cetera and et cetera.

In different of the heaps, accumulated sometimes by date and sometimes by category, I started coming across lease agreements for mobile phone masts that had been erected on the edge of Prospectus woodlands.

"Quite the little earner," I said to Gustaf.

"Dez of course disapproves. He just doesn't get that Prospectus has to have an income stream or we stop."

I even came across an old record company contract from his band management days. A letter from one of his bands, when he was in negotiation with EMI, told him that by releasing all his rights he would be selling himself into obscurity.

"Which had been what I more or less wanted. I'd already realised that fame, that fame-seeking, had not been an end in itself but had to be a step to other things. Fame sold the records and the more records we sold the more famous we became, which meant that we sold even more records – sold them to pop fans with their T-shirts and their imitation hairstyles. No different to religious cults. Idols are idols are idols.

"The money I'd made had been what had been exercising me then. Musicians could carry on being famous and making music. Me? I couldn't wait to offload Yellow Black and go back to being a private citizen. What I hadn't worked out then was my next step. What to do with all my accidentally-gotten gains."

"Accidentally?"

"I hadn't thought of it as money. More as numbers, as besting deals."

"So when did you realise you were rich?"

"Shoes. Just shoes. Poor people own one pair of shoes at a time. When that pair gets worn out they have them repaired or they buy a replacement pair. You know you're better off when you get yourself a spare pair of shoes. Beyond work shoes. Then to be on the safe side, you get yourself another pair. I had four pairs of best shoes! Wealth beyond compare."

He was that rich? I looked at my latest stack I was working on slewing towards an older pile, said, "Can we get hold of some filing cabinets?"

* * *

Once the cabinets arrived that became our wet day work. Some dry days too, there being so much sorting to do. I didn't then though want to be stuck indoors sneezing over old paper but out in the woods with Hazel. Which was where Gustaf wanted to be too. Not necessarily with Hazel, but certainly outdoors doing.

That indoor sorting however became my own challenge. I next got Gustaf to buy and assemble some ceiling high racks and to supply me with some deep document boxes. Then I started to archive those woodlands purchased a while back and long established in Prospectus ownership.

Within a month of occasional sorting there were fewer papers spread in collapsing piles on sagging trestle tables. Now we had – Gustaf had to get more racks – print-labelled boxes neatly stacked in rows.

I uncovered papers from other of his enterprises too – a haulage company wound up, a publishers, even a café/restaurant.

"Why all these?"

"Unsatiable ambition."

"Couldn't make up your mind?"

"Having had one big break one gets hungry for the next. The bigger break."

"That how you let this get in such a mess?"

"Never where I was. Always in the next place, in pursuit of the new, the next big thing. To possess, to have. Cash or flesh." A wink. "The next."

* * *

Hazel and I only went home now at weekends. A couple of times I even went home on my own, Hazel staying over with Jay, Dez and Ben. For the rest of the time I was more or less in Gustaf's company, if not in the woods then in the house. And over a tea and biscuits break, or the three of us sharing a bottle of wine in the evenings – in the one comfortable room: sofas, armchairs, thick rugs and a log fire – Hazel and I gradually winkled more out of Gustaf.

Not that Gustaf Eriksson was a total enigma to me. He wasn't, well no more than any man shut off behind his public persona and standing in front of his past.

"Was your mother Scandinavian?" I asked Gustaf.

That evening we were all leaning back in our chairs around his kitchen table, wine glasses at various levels of emptiness.

"My alleged father was."

"Don't tell me," Hazel said, "he was a Norwegian sailor."

"A Danish dairy engineer. Came to England to install

equipment in a milk factory. My mother was a small town girl, got pregnant and was hastily shipped off to distant relatives. All hush hush. Oh the shame. By the time I was born the dairy engineer had long left the country. My mother – she was still only fifteen – guessed at his name and gave it to me. My foster mum and I one time tried to trace him. As you've traced me. But we became pretty sure that – even if it was him, or she was covering up for some local lad, because that's who she married soon as she was sixteen – anyway, she got the spelling wrong."

"What was your foster mum like?" I asked.

"I had three. At least. The last one it was who got me to trace my father."

"You ever contact your mother?"

"She didn't want to know."

"God I've been so lucky," Hazel said, and eyes a'glisten she reached across to me.

I had been concerned that all the attention Gustaf had been giving me of late might have put Hazel's nose out of joint. Apparently not. I looked from her to Gustaf, and I smiled at our little grouping, at what had led us there.

* * *

With just Gustaf and I on our own there seemed no limit to what we could talk about. We even got around one tea break to broaching his unabashed promiscuity.

"But sex is fun," Gustaf pretended to give me the lounge lizard once-over.

"For both at the same time?" I grimaced back at him.

"Oh come on. Sex has to be the best fun two naked people can have together. But you're right, when it stops being fun, when it becomes an obligation, then it's time to go. That what happened to you?"

"Sort of."

It was his turn to be right. Not so much about my reasons for kicking Ian out, but certainly about the sex. Even given how anxious I might have been during the act, once it was over, in those between times of rolling naked around one another, friendly warm skin against warm skin... Mind you that had been when I had been younger, flesh firmer, skin tauter...

"Know what perfection is?" Gustaf asked: we had been naming favourite books. "It's to sit in the warm shade of a big tree, especially after a night of hectic sex, and to look up out of the pages of a good book and watch birds, mindless of yourself, going about their business."

"Good book and a comfortable tree maybe. As for the night before..."

* * *

What was strange was that I felt easier talking to Gustaf about sexual matters – Gustaf with whom I'd never had sex and who I was determined never to have sex with – than I ever had with Ian. Because I'd had to hide so much from Ian? Or was it simply my age? My having gone beyond caring? Beyond having to sexually prove anything?

Nonetheless, woods or house, in the pickup going from or to, I often had to banter back at Gustaf about the sex.

"So it's all one-night stands with you, no relationships. Frightened of commitment?"

"Nope. Just like to keep my distance. In a society where we're all victims the pseudo-feminists have decided to give men a good kicking."

"Pseudo-feminists?"

"Married shoppers."

"Married... what?"

"They buy into the wedding and give up their names, let themselves be consumer-fodder thereafter."

"You're a misogynist."

"Not at all. I just want people to see beyond the status quo, not play by its rules, not make virtues out of necessity."

"Pseudo-feminists?"

"Pseudo-feminists confuse the woman with her present

social function and they defend the function rather than the woman."

Which had me accusing him, "Now you're being political." Politics, along with religion, was a subject to be steered clear of in café conversations.

"As if politics is a bad thing? Of course I'm political. How else Prospectus? This is our contribution to trying to save the world. The world, not society. With society we no longer believe in the politically possible: always we end up with leaders as reactionary and as alien to us as this lot."

"There are moral values as well as political."

"Nah. Those who prescribe morals presume a physical constancy – that people will be housed, fed, and have sufficient funds for both; and all that will change is the weather. We're dealing here with more than a change in the weather, we're trying to change the weather. Which is why, despite our many differences, I have more in common with Dez and Jay than I do with anyone else."

"Not Hazel and I?" I had thought I was pretending to take offence.

He grunted, but not dismissively more as if he was following his own train of thought. Which had him say, "Parentage is a conceit of the born wealthy. The rest of us are one-generation orphans. Or bastards. Take your pick."

"Both?"

He returned my smile, said, "One of my foster mums was like you. Could never tell what she was thinking either."

"You still in touch?"

"She passed on in my early twenties. They were getting on when they fostered me. Had started, unofficially, years before. Looked after a neighbour's daughter who'd got in trouble…"

Wherever we were our conversations meandered on. Gustaf though still kept a degree of physical reserve with me, was even careful to avoid touching my fingers in the passing round of plate or glass. Whereas with Hazel he had become very easy.

"Odd your mother should have named you after a tree." He enclosed her in a one-armed hug and smiled across at me.

* * *

"Why The Tree Prospectus?" I waved a document at Gustaf.

"Initial plan was simply to grow more trees wherever I could rent land. I wanted to call that plan Tree Tenure. Tree Tenure, I thought, would get across the transient nature of woodland, and that all woodland needs caring for, needs management. Calling us Tree Tenure though would have got us confused with carbon storage scams. Like those in Ghana."

The next day I came across a solicitor's letter confirming a court injunction taken out against someone called Lungren Swift-Eriksson, barring him from this house and other properties, from contacting – 'by whatsoever means' – Gustaf Eriksson.

Wanting to know where to file the letter I showed it to Dez. Gustaf was away that day at a meeting.

"Under personal I suppose," Dez said. "He's Gustaf's son."

* * *

grey rainlight darkens the rooms:
the smell of never-dried clothes

Forty-two

"It's the one time," Gustaf pushed the letter back to me, "I did try to be a father."

We were sitting either side of his kitchen table a couple of days later, having a break from this wet day's paper-sorting. Hazel had taken my car over to Jay and Dez.

"Oh?" I said.

"Not with Hazel. Though might've been better all round if I had."

"Very much doubt it," I told him.

He frowned disagreement with that, but let it pass. "I'm talking about my son," he said.

Gustaf's face was screwed up: he was almost having to fight words out of himself.

"I know." I let him off the hook. "Dez and Jay told me about him."

* * *

"Lungren is," Dez had told me when Gustaf had been away at the meeting, "one truly horrible man."

"Worse than horrid," Jay had added. She and Ben had also been at the house. Hazel too. "Lungren is evil incarnate. D'you know one time he got a dog, called it…" she looked around for Ben, lowered her voice, "…called it Cunt. That was its name, Cunt. Just so he could let it loose in the park, shout Cunt after it. Got him into fights. Which is all that he wanted."

"And he is…?"

"Gustaf's son."

My initial reaction on hearing that had been to suck my lips back against my teeth. Gustaf, curse him, this reckless giver of life. How many others had his wanton dick sired?

One of Nyrene's favourite mutterings, on seeing yet another pregnant teenager come into the café, was, "A child's for life not just conception." Hard on the heels of Thought One Thought Two told me that I was being unreasonable. Only two children that I knew of. Hardly reckless.

Thought Three, expanding on Thoughts One and Two, told me that all life must be reckless in its spawning, in its seeding. Fish lay thousands of eggs, have to know that only a few will survive. Trees send out on the wind thousands of seeds. Of which maybe one will germinate and grow to adulthood, and it too will send out its thousand upon thousand seeds. Gustaf had given me Hazel: who was I to carp?

"So where's this son now?"

"Well," Dez indicated the letter in my hand, "that'll tell you. And it's not the only one. There's a load of injunctions stopping him coming near this place."

"And near his mother's."

"Was Gustaf married?"

He hadn't been.

But as the story unfolded that day, Dez and Jay each chipping in, I wondered how much Hazel having been adopted had figured in Gustaf's staying to be Lungren's father.

Gustaf had already been living with Lungren's mother when she had become pregnant. Despite, according to Jay, her increasing promiscuity Gustaf had stayed with her for the first few years of Lungren's life. Gustaf had finally moved out when Lungren was five.

"I was unlucky enough to meet her once," Jay said. "Hysterical vindictive cow."

"Being Lungren's mother'd make anyone hysterical," Dez said.

"Lungren was her creation." Jay really didn't like her.

According to Jay the mother had filled Lungren's head with hatred for his father. At one time Gustaf had had to make repeated court visits just to gain access to his son. Gustaf had hoped that his steadfast presence would somehow counter the bizarre accusations that Lungren's mother had been making against him.

The once-a-month access didn't work. By the time Lungren started secondary school he had had so much contempt for his father stuffed into him that he refused to see Gustaf. Gustaf conceded that his was a losing battle. He accepted Lungren's refusal, and continued to pay maintenance.

Then, when Lungren was fifteen, Gustaf got a call from the police. Lungren had beaten his mother unconscious.

"More than unconscious. She had a fractured skull, smashed up hand and broken ribs where he'd given her a kicking. And she refused to press charges."

At fifteen Lungren was still legally a minor. Social Workers got involved. But the mother remained unreasonable, had seemed still to want only to win out against Gustaf. Even when Lungren's violence against her had been triggered by Lungren's discovering that Gustaf had, contrary to his mother's many claims, all through his childhood been paying maintenance. The real cause of Lungren's anger had been not so much at the deception, but that she had denied Lungren spending money while not stinting on herself.

Rather than go into Care Lungren had been persuaded to come and live with his father.

But this fifteen-year-old Lungren was very different to the skinny boy Gustaf had last seen. Lungren had started bodybuilding, taking steroids, was proficient in martial arts, had a shaved head as well as, although illegal, a couple of ornate tattoos. He didn't look fifteen. And he had already become a sexually active homosexual.

"A predatory homosexual," Dez said. "Not your sweet gay guy loving all the glitter and gush of showbiz. No, Lungren's the kind who likes a bit of violence with his sex. Heard he'd been charged with rape back awhile. Male rape. Case never made it to court."

All that this new-found son wanted from Gustaf was a residential address – for the benefit of the Social Workers and the court – and spending money. Lungren told Gustaf that he hated him – for having left him all those years with his stupid mother.

Back then Gustaf had just finished renovating this house. Lungren stayed but a couple of nights a week in the house, was off out the rest of the time, came back only for more cash. Gustaf, wanting to make up for the last years, kept him supplied with the wherewithal; but he did question, tentatively question, the way of life that saw – in just that one year – Lungren come home with bloodied fists, black eyes and gonorrhoea.

Gustaf did once try to reason, in stern fatherly fashion, with Lungren. Lungren held Gustaf off the floor by his throat.

That time, wanting money, Lungren let him down and apologised. The next time Gustaf dared confront him Lungren broke Gustaf's jaw, his nose, and ruptured his spleen. By which time Lungren was sixteen and Gustaf told him to leave. When, a few weeks later, Lungren came back and Gustaf refused to let him in Lungren went around the house methodically breaking every window.

"That was the first injunction," Jay added to Dez's telling of the tale.

My sympathies were with Gustaf. From what I already knew of the man I could see that, although in pursuit of his ambitions he might be overbearing, Gustaf was no bully. He had only had Hazel in tears the once, and then he hadn't known it. He had asked her one day, a reasonable question, "What are you doing here with me? Why aren't you getting on with your own life?"

"I am getting on with my own life," she had said; and at the first opportunity she had wandered away from him. It was only later that she had wept to me.

"I am getting on with life," she mumbled to me through her tears. "All of life. I'm still a part of it. The whole of it. That's what he's shown me. Part of the whole. Subject to it, a moving part of it. Whether I want to be or not."

As for Lungren... After Gustaf's refusal Lungren went to his mother for money. When she didn't have any in the house he marched her to a cashpoint. When what she gave him, cashpoint limit, wasn't enough he there and then smacked her head against the wall.

This time there were witnesses and he was charged. In court he asked to be sent to prison, said he'd enjoy himself there.

"Did he go?"

"Not sure," Jay looked to Dez.

"One of the ex-offenders told me," one woodland workgroup was of supervised ex-offenders, one of whom had added the two Erikssons together, "that Lungren now goes in for outdoors sex. Where they watch others having sex. Said he's notorious for always joining in."

"No wonder," I said, "Gustaf was so chary about meeting Hazel."

* * *

All those conversations were in my head that day in the kitchen, looking across the table at the man, his bewilderment at what had befallen him unconsciously on display; and now nodding slowly at the news that I already knew.

There's a stillness, a quietness to any indoors when it's raining out, creates an inertia that's hard to move against. I heard myself tritely say, "We always hurt the ones we love."

"Not so," Gustaf said. "We do not hurt those, only those we love. We hurt those we can, those we have the power to hurt."

One of those near palpable silences followed, neither of us knowing where to take the tea break talk from there; but both knowing that on this subject there was more needed to be said.

I had never seen hurt in Gustaf's face before. I'd seen his twinkle of amusement, had seen him eyes-part-closed shrewd, or a long frown at a there-and-then problem; but not this face of bewildered despair. It was so unlike the man that I thought I'd come to know.

"Not much cop at picking partners were you?" I tried to lighten our tea break. Gustaf though was determined to see the moment miserably through.

"My personal life has been one long mess. Milieu I mixed in maybe. But you're right, my early choice of sexual partners was not sensible."

"Think that could be," I wanted to move him away from

the subject of Lungren, "because you never knew your real parents?" This was a subject I'd given much thought to. "Role models? Loving partnerships?"

"Don't think so. I'm not alone in not having known my biological parents. All theory anyway. Even within monogamous relationships the mother often strays. The moralists used to, for instance, hold up birds as models of monogamy, of lifelong fidelity. Until DNA testing came along and they discovered that the hen bird often strayed. In species terms the scientists saw this as healthy, added variety to the gene pool. So parent unknown, unknowing, how we are created really doesn't matter." Gustaf had obviously given the subject as much thought as I. "Nurture it is that's important. Primacy of the child. Look at the difference between Lungren and Hazel."

"That was down to stability, consistency, rather than us having a 'loving relationship'. We were estranged when Ian died."

"I wasn't thinking of marriage as a universal norm. We all reach accommodations, even within marriage. Especially within marriage? No, I was thinking more of the children. You know that children are our responsibility, not our possession. Lungren's mother wanted to own him, have him all to herself. He had to fight to be free. Come the end physically fight to be free. By which time fighting, unfortunately, had become his default response."

While the past was open this wet day for tea break dissection I thought I'd probe a little about Moira. Until then all I'd heard of Gustaf's side had been via Hazel.

"Had you known of the pregnancy would you have stayed with Moira?"

"Doubt it. Not only was I young myself, but she was already flaky. And, though I mixed with them, I'm no airy-fairy artist. With my musicians I was the manager, the diary-keeper, the money-maker. And when I did meet up with Moira later, way after the adoption, a couple of kids later I think, she was an addict. But she was way beyond a simple addict. Moira's need, though expressed by then as an addict's craving, had always been for more. Great for a young lusty man. But it was her wanting more, all the time more, that took her beyond your junkies' burglaries. She undertook ridiculous, attention-seeking robberies. A knitting wool shop once. Straight society had to see her, to notice her addiction, save her."

"How much do you think Lungren's sexuality created his behaviour?"

"The martial arts and bodybuilding probably began as denial. Then came defence. Offensive defence. All mixed up, adding in side-effect aggression from the steroids, plus his mother's input... And I've come to see, from other homosexuals I've known, that at the core of a certain homosexuality is a desire for decadence."

Unsure where this conversation might have taken us, "Paper awaits," I said and pushed myself up off my chair.

* * *

Grass from the same root,
 blade upon blade, each grows
  away from the last.

Forty-three

She is dead. My Hazel is dead. She died. My Hazel died.

That is what I said to myself – to try and make myself believe. To try and make myself accept. Which I did. And I didn't. I didn't want to. Had to. So I told myself again. She is dead. My Hazel is dead. She died. My Hazel died.

Then out of nowhere, as I was writing that, I remembered how I came to a standstill once. In the time before.

I'd been on some errand around the house, and I found her asleep on the sofa, her limbs all curled up around her torso, wrapped in herself. Even her fingers were slotted together, like a piece of folded cloth. And looking down on her I had felt this huge expanding ache in my chest. This was years before she became ill. And I knew then, with what was like a growing vacuum in my chest, that to look at someone and to know you love them can be as painful as it is fulfilling.

* * *

All words here. Just words.

I see her in those last weeks. I notice how thin she's got, realise she's been taking herself to bed earlier.

And she was so thin, gone beyond the fined down fitness that summer had given her. Suddenly there she was sunken and skeletal. And she said, "I don't think I'll be going in tomorrow. I'm seeing the nurse. I've told Gustaf and Dez." And all I could say from the depths of my armchair that evening, head inside a book, book inside my head, was, "OK love. Sleep well."

"'Night," she took her time saying. And again I heard my faraway self say, "Sleep well."

The book was by Anthony Howell, and I'd just read him saying that poplars shake like misplaced souls. They don't, I was silently disagreeing with him, irritated with him for interrupting the flow of the narrative with such a silly description. Poplars twinkle like themselves.

Poplars!

"Sleep well," I had said. Nothing more profound. No words of sympathy, of understanding. Just, "Sleep well."

* * *

Later than evening, book in lap forgotten, looking into the space where Hazel had stood, all I could think was that Gustaf and Dez knew. Something in Hazel's manner, something in their attitude (a watchful reserve?) said that she had told them.

I hadn't. Whenever they or Jay had mentioned anything even slightly connected with Hazel's health, voicing concerns over her weight loss, or her pallor, I had ignored them as if they hadn't spoken, had walked away or had begun blithely talking of other matters.

But Hazel had told them. They knew. And, having followed Hazel's instructions, I felt betrayed. By Hazel.

This wasn't theirs. It belonged to Hazel and I, to our life together. Not theirs. Ours. But she had gone and told them, had told them the most private of our family secrets. And they didn't deserve to know, were just her latest acquaintances. Hazel was mine. How could they know her like I did? All those years of knowing. Of worrying.

And now that they knew how would I speak to them of it? That was my concern that evening, book in my lap looking into the space where Hazel had been.

Looking into the space where Hazel had been... I was to do a lot of that. Hazel left a lot of spaces.

* * *

Those last weeks, before that evening, were odd. Odd too that I can only now see the accelerated pace of her decline.

Whatever path we had been on she had started stumbling, falling sideways. Tried to laugh it off. And there she was one moment playing a chasing game in and out of the stables with Ben, straw being thrown, and she looked so full of life and happy, and days later I glanced across to her in the car, skin pulled tight to her back teeth, her neck so thin I feared that if she nodded forward her head would fall off. Braking carefully I pulled over to the hard shoulder and slowly eased her seat back. She hadn't woken.

* * *

She hadn't woken. So easy to say. She hadn't woken.

Three days after that evening, because that wasn't the night she died. Three days after that evening she had an appointment with the nurse. I went with her, waited again looking out to the half-dead leylandii and the cabbage tree palm.

The illness itself was of no interest to me, had been of

no interest to me. It had no personality, was but a slow bullet. Was part of my denial. My unhelpful denial. Hazel might die, gasping for breath, frightened, and I'd be of no help, no comfort to her.

One part of me, even accepting her recent decline, was still ridiculously proud, and mocking myself for it, that Hazel had lasted longer than the 'six months to a year' that all these doctors and text books had predicted.

That afternoon Hazel took herself off to bed: "New painkillers make me sleepy."

She hadn't woken.

I went in with a cup of tea about five and she was just so small in the bed that I straightaway knew. As if she wasn't there in the bed. Strands of her hair seemed to drop lifeless into the pillow's creases and the duvet was almost flat, no breathing body under it.

My Hazel had gone.

I dropped the tea, splashing across the carpet, and out of my body came this big yell. And I just stood in front of the tea splash with this big yell coming out of me.

My Hazel was dead, and I was undone. Came apart. A sound blaring out of me. Hazel had been my life.

* * *

Knowledge can come unbidden to you in such extreme moments. There and then I knew that parents are as much a consequence of their children as their children are of them. And my Hazel had gone, my life undone.

Of course I must have eventually stopped my shout and moved. I called the doctor. Although why I had to call the doctor I don't know. What could he do for Hazel? But Hazel; had told me, had made me listen, that was what I had to do when… "OK, OK," I'd said. And there I was dutifully doing it.

He came and set in process what is done with bodies left behind by their owners. I glimpsed the arrival of the black ambulance as the doctor was telling me of Hazel's detailed instructions to him and the nurse, told me what a lovely, thoughtful daughter Hazel had been.

Already had been.

In his made-kind voice the doctor, all pink hands and going bald young, told me that in Hazel's medical notes was a yellow highlighted directive to contact the nurse, who had her own list of things to do, first of which was to contact Jay, who was to inform the funeral director, who had another list from Hazel. The black ambulance was theirs.

The body was taken out on a stretcher. Not that Hazel was any longer ill, I found myself thinking, but that was probably the easiest way to carry a body.

"What happens now?" I asked the doctor. According to his notes Hazel had arranged for her friend Jay to visit me.

"Somebody to be with you."

"I don't need that. Tell her to stop."

"Already set in train. You can tell her when she gets here."

After a pause, black ambulance quietly driven off, he asked if I wanted something to help me sleep. I shook my head.

"I expect you've long been prepared for this," he said.

I nodded.

I knew that I hadn't been in the least prepared.

Forty-four

I don't know what I did between the doctor leaving and the yellow pickup arriving. I think I just wandered around the house. I may have hand-washed a few dishes.

Jay didn't come on her own in the yellow pickup. She had a woman with her. The woman had on flat shoes and a dress and cardigan of dark wool, the wools all browns and blues. Jay, reaching to take hold of my hand, told me that this other woman was the funeral director, that Hazel had arranged everything with her.

"Hazel wanted a woodland burial. Has picked the spot." Jay's chin puckered: "She knew you wouldn't be able to cope."

I must have grunted a denial: whole of my life, hers too, I'd coped. Jay put her arm around me, "Hazel didn't want you to have to cope."

Since coming into the house, home of the departed, the woollen woman had worn a professional smile, one that was supposed to say that she understood, was in sympathy with the bereaved, but was a smile that was so pulled-across-her-chops artificial that I there and then hated her.

"Just when will this all-arranged funeral be?" I asked Jay.

"On Thursday." It was the woman who answered – in a professionally softened voice.

Two days.

Too soon.

Jay told me that she had picked up Woollen – can't remember her name – on the way through, would drop her home and come back, stay with me until Thursday.

"No need," I told her: she couldn't sleep in Hazel's bed, and I wasn't going to make up the spare. "Who's looking after Ben?"

"Dez."

"I'll be OK. Just come back Thursday. And you can come with me then to... To wherever it is we're going."

Woollen started to tell me, giving me her funeral director's spiel. I couldn't bear to hear it. I actually wanted to, and looking at her I saw myself, throw a bucket of water over her, watch her woollen cardigan shrink up her arms, her woollen dress tighten around her tubby belly, squashing her massive tits...

I hated her, went and made a pot of tea, laid out some biscuits on a plate... And when I came back into the dining room that was when lovely Jay folded like a collapsing piece of cardboard into Hazel's chair, and she sobbed.

"I couldn't while I drove..." she gulped and spluttered.

And while I stood beside Jay and patted the lumpy bones of her shoulder woollen woman dunked biscuit after biscuit. I hated her.

* * *

Jay must have pulled herself back together, and the yellow pickup must eventually have left.

And I have no idea what I did for the next two days and nights. I must have eaten, must have slept, got dressed, undressed, gone upstairs, come downstairs, slept and ate and showered. Must have. Because there I was ready and waiting when the yellow pickup returned on the Thursday.

Dez, Jay and Gustaf slowly emerged from the pickup's cab, Dez and Gustaf pausing to look around the Close before Jay herded them towards my front door. Once inside, moving around one another, I found three large people looking kindly down on me.

Until that moment, their being in a house used to just Hazel and I, I hadn't realised quite how short, comparatively, Hazel and I were. Gustaf was nowhere near as tall as Dez and Jay but he was still a good head taller than me, double my breadth too, blocked up a doorway.

This was out of all our ordinary, uncomfortable for the four of us. Dez and Gustaf weren't wearing ties, but they'd both been made to put on proper shirts and their best jackets and trousers. Jay, having straightaway said she'd make the tea, was definitely in charge.

On their best behaviour both men tentatively reached out to touch me, say how sorry they were. I nodded, stepped away from contact and, Jay's having started it, I followed her into the kitchen and busied myself with tea and biscuits. Tea and biscuits. Tea and biscuits became a mantra that day. Deep, dredged up sighs; and tea and biscuits.

* * *

When finally we went to set off they all three objected when I picked up my car keys.

"Don't be ridiculous," I said: no-one had told me what to do since I had broken with my parents. "I'm perfectly capable of driving."

"And on the way back?" Jay said. "No, we'll drop you back. Hazel's instructions."

"Where's Ben?" I said. "You'll need to get back for Ben."

"He's at my mum's."

So Jay and Dez squeezed their long legs into the back seat of the pickup, and I sat in front with Gustaf. Who, if he was in company had to talk, and must have found my silence unbearable. After a couple of miles, once Jay had directed him out of the estate, he said,

"I couldn't figure out, at first, why she was sticking around. You know? Your Hazel? I was coming up with all sorts of theories. Once, that is, the money consideration was out of the way. Thought she might be pregnant."

"She wasn't."

"Yea, I know. But that's what I thought. And I thought she might have come looking to see what her baby might be like."

The motorway fed itself under me: speech didn't belong in my head.

"Once pregnancy was obviously not the case," Gustaf continued, "I thought she was maybe compensating for her father being dead. Your Ian. But there was no hint even of my being seen as a replacement father."

Although his pause expected a response no words found their way to my mouth.

"So then I figured that maybe she had got hooked into this ancestor research that everyone's doing these days. Got a past, no future. But I'm a cul-de-sac, a fostered kid. So why was she hanging around? Why did she keep coming back?"

"She enjoyed being in the woods?"

"That did occur to me. Even so… She…"

"Hazel."

"Hazel, yes. Hazel was a thirty-year-old woman. Should've had her own life. Should have had a job. A career. What was she doing becoming a full-time tree-hugger?" This time his pause wasn't waiting on me. "Then I thought that maybe, with you dropping her off every day and hanging around out of sight in the carparks, she was maybe a spoilt brat. Mother indulging the every whim of her only child. She didn't, though, act like a spoilt little rich girl. Then I met you, saw your relationship, so that theory went out the window too."

Relationship? I pondered that for the next mile or so. Relationship sounded static, fixed, was a word that didn't seem to apply to Hazel and I. Mother-daughter, daughter-mother: what was between us had seemed natural to me, to have grown with us, from her childhood to my menopause.

"So when did you find out?" I asked Gustaf. "Hazel tell you?" Hazel had arranged even this, their collecting me. Had kept it from me.

"Didn't have to tell me. I saw the energy slip from her a couple of times. Like someone pulled the plug on her. And, you know, sometimes she'd just go yellow. And, without articulating it to myself, I sort of suspected she had something wrong. Why you were in attendance. And I could see that you, a practical-minded woman, concerned mother, just wanted the best for your poorly girl. And if she wanted to mess about in the woods, then why not? And I decided that if she wanted to tell me, then she would."

"When was it you reached that conclusion?"

"Few months back. For absolute certain when she started arranging all this with Jay. It was Jay told me it was terminal."

"It's not," Jay said, leaning forward from the back seat, "that Hazel wanted to shut you out. Her one objective was to spare you the worry."

"I'm sorry," Gustaf said beside me. "Just so sorry. Don't know what else to say. I just thought I should explain…"

"Don't worry," I said. "Helping you with Prospectus gave

meaning to this last year. That's what Hazel wanted. You provided. So thank you."

Gustaf took several deep breaths before saying, "Think I'll let Dez drive you back."

Forty-five

I had expected the woodland burial site to be in a forest-deep glade. The pickup instead pulled into a grey carpark on the side of a bare hill. Bare that is bar a low rustic fence and a few well-spaced saplings, each stick-thin tree attached by a black band to its as-thin stake.

In the carpark was a blue soft top BMW and a builder's van, brush's bristle end sticking up behind the cab like a misplaced moustache. No other cars. Kevin had left a voicemail, said that he couldn't make it, had started a new job just that week.

Below and beyond the hill a spread of green and yellow fields disappeared into a blue haze.

"This it?" I said to Jay, who had come around the pickup to take my arm.

"Hazel chose it," Jay said. "We researched it on the net."

They must have done that at Gustaf's: I tried to picture when.

"Hazel came here?"

But Jay had turned away, seemed to be waiting. Gustaf and Dez were standing on the other side of the pickup, low murmurs now and then passing between them.

I could see Wool Woman down by some fresh earth, a sapling its roots sack-wrapped beside her. And away over to the right, trying to hide themselves and their shovels behind a group of too thin trees, were a couple of workmen.

"She talked everything over with..." Jay signified Wool Woman. "Willow casket. Everything."

I could hear traffic passing along the hilltop road.

"Not what I thought she'd have liked," I said.

"The tree she's chosen for herself," Jay told me as the

conventionally black hearse turned into the carpark, "is a poplar."

The hearse came to a stop. Quietly. Even its tyres were quiet. Some yellow and red chrysanths were laid beside the woven coffin in the hearse's long window.

Six men in dark suits emerged from the hearse. Quietly. Their professional stealth though offset by the buzz and snarl of the traffic along the hilltop road.

The six darksuited men pulled out the beribboned coffin. A basket case, was my thought. My little Hazel a basket case.

* * *

As we followed the six men solemnly carrying the coffin down the still new path Jay, clinging onto and seeming to be leaning on me, said, "Her poplar's one of those with big flat leaves. Go almost black in the autumn? Have a silver underside?"

I nodded, and thought on the tree growing, the rings of growth that that long twig would thicken into, reaching an age my Hazel never had.

Jay said, "Hazel likes the way the wind ripples up the leaves, shows the silver. Like a flamenco skirt, she said. Wants to think of the people down there looking up to the ripple of silver."

"Hazel said that?"

I remembered Hazel age six or seven dancing in our old stone-tiled kitchen, her pretending to be clacking castanets, kicking up her heels, flouncing one of my old skirts from her dressing up box, stamping her feet and going, "Olé! Yes! Olé!" The "Yes!" had made me laugh.

And thinking of laughing released the tears. My lovely lovely girl. The rest of the day was lost to me.

Forty-six

The poplar chosen to mark Hazel's grave was a *populus serotina*, the hybrid Italian black poplar, one of several cultivars of poplar. Had hers been the native black poplar that would have been too ironic for words, one of its characteristics being its short life span.

Populus comes not from the many varieties of poplar and their being so widespread, being popular that is, but from the Greek *papaillo*, meaning flutter. Probably where the French *papillon*, butterfly, also comes from.

This fluttering on the poplar is a combination of the length of the leaf stalk and the comparative expanse of each leaf. And with the poplar leaf having a much paler underside the slightest movement of air causes each leaf to move and thus the whole tree to seemingly tremble.

Towards autumn this trembling is accentuated by the upper side of the leaf becoming, as Jay said, almost black with the underside silver. When fallen to the ground these leaves form black and silver mosaics. Prior to that, and in any breeze, the leaf-turning rustle of big poplars can be remarkable only when it stops.

If Hazel's sole intent had been to twinkle on her hillside I'd have thought her first choice would have been *populus tremula*, the aspen. Maybe it was her first choice and she got talked out of it. As with so many of the other poplars aspen is prone to the bacterial canker, *pseudomona syringae*. I suspected Gustaf and Dez's hand in her choosing the very ordinary hybrid *serotina*. Which doesn't, I have to say, diminish in any way its attractiveness when planted singly.

As a tree on its own, *Serotina*, the Italian black poplar is beautiful, especially in its changes. Coming into leaf late in spring its first colour is a seaweedy olive-brown, opening fully to mid-green, each leaf the same shape as a Dover sole, though smaller.

Very few poplars however are grown solely as ornaments. These days poplars are especially useful in their ability to fix carbon dioxide. Not that their timber is of much use for either furniture or firewood. This is due to the tree's rapid uptake of water and equally rapid exhalation. What poplar timber has been used for, when sawn into thin strips, was for the making of matches and for those thin stapled boxes that fruit and veg used to arrive in at the grocers.

Growing on its own, as Hazel's poplar will, especially given its hillside situation (because of their thirst and rapid growth poplars normally favour a wetland setting), her poplar will no doubt succumb to poplar's other habit – of irregular branching. A lopsided tree for a lopsided life.

Even so… Even so, for Hazel it is still not the most representative of trees, Italian black poplars all being male.

Forty-seven

Grief, such a small round word. Read and noted. Knew what it meant.

Grief: sadness over the death of a loved one. Move on.

I thought I knew what it meant.

Not so.

* * *

I was lost, didn't know what to do.

Days, nights, were vacant.

I was a vacancy. Empty, I was filled with an emptiness bigger than myself.

I told myself that I should have been prepared for Hazel's going. Had told myself that I'd been prepared for her going.

Now that she was gone I knew that I hadn't been in the least prepared for her going. All the time I had secreted away the notion that the medicos might have got the diagnosis wrong. Hazel had, after all, lasted longer than any had predicted.

Every extra month of her being alive had abetted my denial.

* * *

She had gone, had left me alone.

I looked around me, physically turned my head to look around me. How could one person contain, exist among, so much emptiness?

What did I do now? What point was there in my doing anything?

Café was closed and sold. There was no point, no purpose to my day. Time was suddenly featureless. Days slipped into nights. Mealtimes seemed arbitrary. There was only me to cook for. Only me. Which thought had me quietly repeating the two words into the emptiness, "Only me. Only me."

And I disliked that self-pity, despised myself for it. Yet here was that huge emptiness, bigger than me, but inside me. And all around me.

Hazel had been the best of me, my one clean deed in this dirty confusing world. Without her I was nothing, undone.

Only as a child with a skipping rope had I been unquestionably me. Counting counting counting, and laughing when I tripped. Untwirling my rope, and starting again… Counting counting counting… Since then it has all felt, if not an act, then contrived.

* * *

When does that start? That sense of not being your true self?

When as a child you are first mocked for telling the truth? And thereafter you learn to guess the answers people want? And by age eight candour has become a childhood trait. All is pretence and you no longer know who you really are.

* * *

Even in my fifties I'd still been waiting, like a chick inside an egg, for the time when I'd break out, become me. Whoever that me would be. In the meantime I'd been Hazel's mother.

But that too had been a sham, a camouflage, a self-given title to cover my uncertainty. Because as an adult I'd still been guessing at what was wanted of me, had still been expecting to be told what to do; or, more likely, to be told off for what I had assumed I should be doing, to be scolded for what I had unthinkingly done.

I didn't know. Didn't know. Didn't know.

I did know that I was ill, physically ill, with grief.

* * *

I hurt, had a stone at the base of my chest, an indigestible lump sitting in my stomach. My bladder and my arse sent icicle shafts of pain up through me.

Was it hunger? Maybe. But I did eat, must have eaten.

I must have got up out of chairs and walked out of one room and into the next. I must have filled the kettle, must have switched it on, made myself a mug of tea. I must have gone to the freezer and taken out food for a meal. I must have forgotten to cook, forgotten to go to the freezer, because I lost weight. I must have gone to the lavatory. I must have had a bath. I must have gone to bed. Because I woke up in bed, woke out of a dream of Hazel. Because she was there, was in a room somewhere, said, "Come on Mum. You said we could. You did." And she was not asleep in the next room, and she was not in the bathroom, her noises were not downstairs; and the grief came out of me in one long exhalation and I again soaked my bedsheets sobbing.

* * *

I must have washed and changed bed-sheet and duvet cover. But slowly.

I can remember finding myself stopped on the stairs, or in the hall, at the living room window, and wondering what I was doing there. Then wandering on through the empty house, empty days.

One time waking my brain was stone, let no thought in.

Another my head was so empty that light and air came drifting through.

Know what grief is? It's nothing. Nothing, a concept – as young Ian would have said – a mathematical concept. Nothing cannot exist. Yet, by naming it, nothing exists. A paradox.

Grief is a paradoxical nothingness. Is what you are. Nothing. Of no worth. What gave you value is gone. And everything around this worthless you is equally of no worth.

* * *

The assumption can be made that the time a clock stops, battery run out, spring wound down, it must mean something. Reality is that it doesn't mean a thing, except that the battery has run out, clock needs rewinding. Same for when a life stops. Doesn't mean a thing. Is meaningless.

Yet with every death, not just Hazel's, for someone left living life will have lost its meaning. The life lived with that person close to you, their having died, makes your life left behind meaningless. The small expectations of that remaining everyday life – something that day seen to be told them – gone!

So what's the point?

Tell it to yourself?

Yourself who's already seen it?

Meaningless. Without meaning. Like stopping by a house where you once lived. Sitting in the car outside you look at the curtains, different to what you had, windowsill ornaments different to what you had, and the house now has nothing to do with you. Although in some of your dreams you walk through its rooms. This real house you're outside however... a nothing much house, as befitted an up-and-coming accountant's family, rooms conventionally decorated, conventionally furnished, conventionally clean... A house in which nothing much happened, except cleanliness and cooking and the virtual ticking of battery clocks.

* * *

I stopped to talk to a silver-framed photo of Hazel.

"I loved you so much. So much." And the cry came up my throat again and bounced back off the walls.

I hid all the photos. But that felt like a betrayal, a death doubled. So out the photos came again. And looking so very young Hazel seemed that much further away, of a time other than this, gone, dated, not of me, not of here...

I wept. Found myself squashed in a corner of the sofa, sodden balls of tissue all around.

I wept. Found myself staring down at a half-moon reflected in the frying pan's oil, a wringing wet tea-towel in my hand.

From out of my own mind, or harkening to a similar voice in the Close outside, I heard Hazel's words, her clarity of speaking, the way she growled the end of some words... And then I see again that small lozenge shape in that big bed, and my Hazel is dead, dead all over again, and again I lock myself around my grief.

* * *

In centuries past the death of a child, three out of every five, was to be expected. And with death so commonplace parents knew how, had examples to follow, to deal with their grief. A wailing, a sentimental verse or two, wear black for a year, then move on.

My Hazel was dead and I was empty inside, was hollow, yet still I displaced air as I moved from room to room. Fraud, I accused myself.

Worthless fool.

The body practical – food, lavatory, sleeping – took care of itself; and felt like a betrayal. Because she wasn't alive to do any of it.

So does self-hatred continue to grow. I loathed myself, admitted to the fundamental falsity of my life – a pretend mother, the fake sex, the denial of her illness.

* * *

Did I think? Yes, tadpole thoughts, black and wriggling and going in no particular direction. Thoughts circling about thoughts, memories of small events that had grown into Hazel's life…

More a dwelling on than thoughts. An image – Hazel fallen oopsadaisy on the garden step, four years old, brown skirt up over head, frilly knickers fully on display. On a ward, myself arranging two separate bunches of tulips – one red, one yellow – on her Formica bed table. The knee-scraping fall she had running to meet Ian, the languid sofa-bound teenage phone calls, just me and her playing charades last Christmas, the tracery of veins on her temples as a baby… The time when, showing off to her friends, she burnt her nose on her birthday candles, called the blister her 'beginning-rhinocerousness'. She and her giggly college friends blowing bubbles in the kitchen when I wasn't there and next day all the café cakes tasting of soap…

Image accentuating absence was all that my mixed bag of memories were. They were not comforting ghosts. These memories came to flaunt, to taunt. Because in the empty finality of grief there are no external spectres, no resurrection, no living-on spirits. That was all shit. The shit forced out by the past. Squatting and straining to deliver one huge turdish lie. Nothing lived on. My Hazel was gone.

* * *

I saw myself passing from room to room – slowly – like an invalid carrying her pains inside her, afraid of sudden movement. One stumble, one jerk having the throb awake.

My Hazel had been buried without fuss. We were a no-fuss people.

My Hazel had been buried on a to-be-wooded hillside under a to-be-twinkling poplar.

I hated that tree: and I wanted now, I needed now, to make a fuss. My body spent hours just howling.

* * *

Nothing, zero, exists; and it was inside me. How could one short woman contain so much emptiness?

To have something other than empty me in the empty house, to have some other sound, other movement, I put on the TV. But the voices were so banal, so intrusive they were soon muted. My emptiness then had the accompaniment of meaningless images – faces, mouths, dusty streets, dead bodies, deodorants, a pretty girl, a silver car, redshirted players on a green pitch, a meal steaming on a square plate, a pianist's pink fingers spidering across black and white keys...

* * *

I woke in the armchair, my neck cricked.

Like a tortoise peering out of its shell I looked sideways left and right. Where had she gone? She was there. Or had we been in a wood somewhere? And slowly the realisation came – I'd been talking to the dream ghost again.

That had been in the day. In the dark it was uncertainty that ruled. Not sure if I was asleep, not sure if I, that is my body, existed. Was all this breathing mass below me a lightless hologram, black pixels undifferentiated from the pixels of the equally black duvet. Was I about to disperse, was I about to float away?

Even awake, upright, lost in a daze, I saw myself this little woman in her little house, her little hutch-house on its hutch-house estate. And beyond her hutch-house walls and throughout the world of hutches people busy as insects going about their lives. And I hated them all: they were alive and my Hazel wasn't.

I hated myself. And not just for being alive. I had always thought, had prided myself even, that to myself I'd been totally honest. I hadn't.

I'd had no idea that this howling, this wet and wailing woman had been in there, inside me.

I was as much a fake, as self-deceived as the rest of the Great British Public. By my simple physical inability to enjoy straightforward sex with men I had believed myself beyond entrapping emotion, undeluded about sentiment. Why then this howling, this flat-out weeping?

* * *

I felt most at ease indoors those days it rained. When I could stand and stare out at the wet-shined garden. If it hadn't been for the double-glazing there'd have been the drip of rain all around enclosing my silence.

Wet days I could waste hours watching raindrops gather and roll down the conservatory windows, dozily look on the pattering pocks on the patio slabs. A day when I couldn't do anything other than be where I was, no half-felt guilt to be elsewhere doing something else.

Other days there was an uncomfortable silence to being indoors alone. One cloud-dark day – or had it been dusk anyway? – I'd lit a candle. For quasi-religious comfort? To have something moving in the house beside myself? And I spent hours feeding the soft spilt candlewax back under the flame.

Another day, stalled in the bathroom, I leant over the basin watching a bar of white soap melt and, finger-stirred, disperse.

* * *

I must have gone to the supermarket. Must have driven to get there. Must have taken the emptiness with me. Must have filled my trolley. Must have carried my 'For Life' bags back indoors. Must have emptied them.

My emptiness was visible. I looked up from my pillow at my open reading glasses – me minus my face. I was ceasing to exist.

Forty-eight

If the landline rang – its artificial bell shattering the house's enclosed air like brittle aspic – holding myself rigid I waited until the answering service cut in.

My mobile was switched off.

When I returned to movement, the drift of my thoughts dispersed by the phones clatter, I'd try to piece those thoughts back together. Or memories, if I'd been working back through them.

* * *

After the funeral Gustaf had tried to be comforting. But life had ended there for me. While for them, despite their all showing concern for me, I knew that the funeral had just been one part of their day. They were going on to do other things. Jay had to get back for Ben. Dez had said something about having to meet up later with an old woodsman. Just another part of another day. The end of my Hazel existence.

Memory doesn't tell me how I got home from the funeral. I had to have been brought home. Think I maybe stayed the night at Gustaf's. Have a sort of memory of it, sleeping in my bra and pants.

* * *

Within grief is no time to philosophise. But there I was alone in my hutch-house asking the purpose of life. Born to die? My Hazel born to prematurely die?

My part in life had ceased to make any sense whatsoever. Why was I going on going on?

Nor was this questioning anything new. I had already been questioning my life, way before Hazel's diagnosis, way before Ian's crash. That questioning had been what had me kick Ian out.

What had I done with my life? What had I done with all that time given me? I'd raised Hazel – to prematurely die – and I'd run a café and made Ian unhappy. I certainly hadn't made Ian happy. And I found myself missing him. In that I wished him back in the house to tell him some of these thoughts.

Realising just what I was wishing I became angry at myself: how dare I miss him now that he was dead and not when I was glad that he had at last left the marital home? And it would have taken but one of his oh-so-predictable responses to my heartfelt outpourings for me to want shot of him all over again.

My thoughts weren't only taken up with Ian. I looked at all those others connected with me and I questioned their purpose in life, their contribution to mine. My parents – why had they had me just to be dissatisfied with me? Kevin – who hadn't known what he had wanted until Hazel had removed herself from him.

* * *

At Kevin's age I had been no better. My life entire back then had seemed to be about getting and having. Getting married, getting pregnant, getting a home, having a car, getting a divorce...

Hazel had been more concerned with being. Even before leaving Kevin Hazel's life had seemed to have had bigger concerns. She had joined Amnesty International, had taken out a direct debit to War on Want.

Hazel had been a better woman than me. She hadn't indulged the comfort of self-delusion, had had an open ruthlessness about her relationships. All mine had been sneaky, underhand, hidden even from myself.

Once diagnosed Hazel had looked back through her life, accepting what had gone before, and had acknowledged what was to come. In that acceptance she had been more like Gustaf than Ian or I.

Maybe Hazel had taken more after Gustaf than she had learnt from Ian and I. Ian had been all about self-gratification, focus on himself, not through himself. Same for me. Hazel and Gustaf though looked out at the whole wide world through the lens of themselves; Gustaf planting his trees, Hazel with her charities.

Want and get. In my life previous I had been nothing if not single-minded. Want and get, be it child for adoption or café for distraction.

I despised myself. And I despaired of all those wasted years, saw all my café days only as me moving sideways between chairs and tables, bum against the back of one chair, tummy rubbing across the back of another and looking to the order to be made up…

* * *

Circular thinking seems to be the lot of those grieving, the one bereavement bringing to life other deaths. What part, for instance, did I have in Ian's crash?

One moment I felt unutterably guilty – over Ian, over Hazel. Should I have done this, should I have done that different? Guilty over ditching my parents, guilty even for needlessly closing the café.

I tried to defend myself. I had done what I'd thought right at the time. But the very next moment I wanted to feel guilty, to make it all my fault and so savour the guilt.

So did I come back again and inexorably to Hazel's death.

Death. Dead. Gone.

All deaths leave an absence, a vacancy. Turn around and there's no-one there. A thought untold. A purposelessness, a pointlessness to the next movement, the next hour.

The circularity of grief, snake feeding on its own tail. I grew impatient with it, angry at my own grieving.

* * *

A lassitude of the soul is not the only prerequisite to despair, at trying to make sense of this death-filled existence. I've spent most of my life feeling lost, trying to make sense of where I was.

Instinct for survival does however eventually have to

kick in. Alone in that house there had to come a point where I stopped staring into the past. I only know that it felt a long time coming.

The decision came to me that I had to get out of that gloom-ridden house.

I showered, dressed in all clean clothes, and managed to walk around the garden. Before the sky grew enormous, the world beyond its fences formless, empty without her. And I hurried, crouching, back indoors, turned the locks.

Wore me out. Took two more days to build myself up to get into the car and drive to the supermarket. And all the while under the supermarket's white light I felt as if I was holding my breath, so terrified was I of physical contact with another human being. I couldn't even make eye contact with the chatty checkout girl. As for the prospect of bumping into anyone I might know from the café: I could feel the sweat forming vertical puddles in the small of my back.

No sooner was I back indoors than I had a shower.

At least the kitchen cupboards were restocked. I was ashamed of myself though.

"This won't do," I told myself, wandering again from room to room. "This won't do."

* * *

Finding myself in the bathroom holding a saucepan I asked myself, "What have I been doing?" Louder: "What have I been doing?"

I came to standing with my back against the front door. "What about me?" I heard myself shout. "What about me?"

That time I left my parents' house, having quietly decided never to see them again, I had felt as if a physical burden had been removed, a weight lifted from me, the future freed up. They had been a consideration that no longer had to be made. Same when I had decided that I'd had enough of Ian. I had felt that I had become more me, solidified.

But with Hazel gone... I was less of me. Without edges.

If Hazel had had an obituary it would have said, '... survived by her adopted mother.' How though was I to survive? Just me? I didn't want an incomplete life.

Mrs Oak Tree Café, Mrs Bakelite, Mrs Hazel's mum, Mrs Ian's Wife... We've all done it, have trapped ourselves behind facades that were only ever meant to be of the moment. Who was I now to other people? What would they say? What would I say? The idea of talking to anyone, of sharing words about Hazel... Only to meet up with misconceptions, wrongful assumptions uncorrected... The very idea was unbearable.

At the same time I knew that I had to – if I was to survive my daughter's death (survived by her adopted mother and recently discovered birth father) – I had to, I must go among people again.

The best I could manage though was to go out at night, wandering the estate streets, sneaking glances in telly-flicker windows – at the mindless day-to-day existences of most people. There had to be more.

I was alone, had less.

* * *

A hatred grew in me of the lit uncurtained windows, theatre glimpses of families. I hated them all. Pitied them too. Like them I had known the comfort, the security of rituals. Now I knew though that to lose oneself in day-to-day tasks is how one becomes lost to one's self.

I looked in lit windows at people with futures being planned; and I, whose thoughts of a future were all in the past, I wondered what it must be like to think they knew what was ahead, each member of that aquarium family each having their thousand fantasy futures. No disappointments.

* * *

This was my life now, I told myself. I was no longer beholden to Hazel, could do whatever I wanted to do.

I didn't know what I wanted to do. My future as blank as a tide-out beach.

One night I stood for hours at a junction watching a bat flickering its leathery black wings in and around an orange streetlight as it fed on the insects drawn to the light. I felt that the all-but-blind bat and the insects attracted to the lethal light should stand for something. The metaphor was beyond me.

* * *

I had to go again to the supermarket. Halfway round I realised that, although I was dressed (I'd glanced down to check), I'd forgotten to brush my hair, caught a glimpse of myself in a chill cabinet's glass door – a mad tangle.

Another time I couldn't recall having brushed my teeth, pushed the trolley head down, tongue circling upper and lower sets.

* * *

Even when out and about I was alone, removed from all warm flesh. I watched myself shying away even from accidental touch. This then was to be a self-perpetuating loneliness.

I was alone; but I had to tell, tell of all that Hazel had meant to me. But to tell it without a voice giving back to me a misinterpretation, without some known stranger talking back to this other name ghost of myself and confusing their story with mine; and without me then being provoked, in challenge of their emphases, into creating a false past, and finding myself defending that created past.

My love for Hazel had been nothing exceptional, had been ordinary, had been real. I had to tell of that.

But where to begin? How to begin? When I had a fractured stone for a brain? So scattered, so many were my thoughts.

I woke at 02:17 one night having decided to write down what thoughts I could, scribble them each on a separate sheet of paper. Next morning was when I began jotting down the inconsequential bits'n'bobs that have become these thousand upon thousands of words.

* * *

I had a ream of copy paper left over from Hazel's ancestry research, a stock of cheap biros – café crosswords – so I sat myself at the dining table (pine), and arranged paper and pens before me. I took a look into the past and began, 'I told the doctor I was her adopted mother. Made it sound as if baby Hazel had adopted me.'

The landline rang. I ignored it, pulled another sheet towards me. 'Hazel was always surprising me. The way she looked directly at everything… '

When I could think of nothing else that moment to write I took a wander about the house, maybe made myself a cup of tea or coffee, came back to the table and changed what I had written.

From then on I kept a couple of sheets by the bed, and out of my wakefulness jotted down more memories, a few times the words indecipherable. I spent the following days puzzling over the scrawl.

I woke from dreams of hiding in a room, in fear of being found, and as discovery loomed barricading the door against… who? Always an unseen threat, a bully from my own school days perhaps and nothing to do with Hazel. Nothing therefore to form into words.

* * *

At the table (pine) I smiled over a written memory of young Hazel. Frowned at the sideboard (oak), asked aloud.

"That what I'm doing? Bringing her back to life?"

"The past is all I have," Hazel had said.

"Same here," had been my rejoinder, back then not wanting her to sink into self-pity. "And I can't," I'd carried on, "remember the half of it." Less than half. A lot less I was coming to realise now that I was trying to write it all down.

Time had passed, years merging one into the other; and there I was, stuck thoughtless with pen (biro) in hand.

When next the landline rang I had half a ream of written-on paper. I decided to put those sheets into some kind of order. The answer service cut in. My mobile was still switched off.

* * *

One memory prompted another, which required an explanation. Days wove into weeks. Weeks slid under weeks, and another month was gone.

Forty-nine

I thought the high-sided lorry darkening the windows was a removal van. But there'd not been any For Sale signs in the Close, which was why I was at the window, looking to see which house the van was going to. Which meant that Jay, in the horse truck, saw me.

I had to answer the door.

Jay left the truck blocking my drive and next door's. That at least meant that she wouldn't be stopping long. I took some small relief from that as I opened the front door.

"You been away?" Jay asked as she came towards me. "We've been ringing and ringing." And she closed me in a hug.

Usually when hugged by taller people either my face is squashed into their chest or it is only our shoulders touching, their backside being stuck out way behind them like a stand-up piano player. For once though, Jay being a step down on the path, ours was a face over each other's shoulder hug.

The hug seeming to go on and on I jerked myself free, got the front door closed behind her.

"You look awful," Jay said. "You been in hospital?"

"No," I said as I hurried to push together the scattered papers on the dining table. Jay stood awkwardly, and big, behind me. I pressed the written-on sheets into a sideboard drawer, made the usual noises about cups of tea, saw Jay looking at all the framed photos face down.

"Couldn't bear it." I heard myself almost shout. Repeated it quieter, "Couldn't bear it."

Jay made a sympathetic sound somewhere between a sigh and a growl of exasperation, and she went to enclose short me in another hug.

"No," I said, and made for the kitchen.

"You seen a doctor?" Jay followed me.

"Why would I?"

"Look at the state of you."

I grunted a dismissive response. But Jay said, "No. Just look at you. Come with me." And she grabbed hold of my arm, led me out to the mirror by the front door.

As I was stumbling along beside her the thought came to me that this was a woman who regularly handled two massive horses. And I found myself held beside her in the mirror.

One moment a two-ton horse, next a naughty child. A child with unkempt hair, a blue-tinged indoor skin, sagging jowls and black bags under her eyes. Beside and above me, hair pulled back into dreads, the smooth brow gleaming with good health, an out of doors active life beaming out of her every pore, brown bright eyes glaring down at me. At me – ivory skin pale and greasy, a wax model of a deranged self.

"You been eating?" Jay almost shook my arm.

"Of course." I pulled away as if to free myself. Jay didn't let go.

"Not enough," she said; and I was thrust ahead of her back into the dining room.

Although I did continue to mildly protest, say there was no need, I was at that moment happy to be passive, happy to let myself be sat down, to be given a cup of tea; and I agreed to Jay making a doctor's appointment for me (I could unmake it later, or not go), ate the toasted sandwich she made from bread out of the freezer, watched as she stood all the photo frames back up.

"Hazel was a lovely girl," she said. "And it's so sad. So sad. But do you think she's the only one we care about? Do you? Dez and Gustaf been taking turns to call you. We've been so worried. Don't you dare not answer your phone again."

* * *

When Jay had quietened down, got promises out of me – about the doctor and the phone – she asked, "You given up on Prospectus?"

I shrugged, hadn't give it a thought.

"Dez and Gustaf would like you back."

They probably would, could always use another volunteer. It would be odd though without Hazel there. I managed to say as much.

"What else you going to do?"

And that was the thought Jay left me with.

* * *

Dez phoned that night, said that Jay had got home all right, regaled me with a tale about Ben 'helping' him and Gustaf all that day.

Jay's visit had got me thinking back to the last time I had been in their company, at Hazel's funeral. I knew that Jay had organised it, but who had paid for it? Is that why they'd been calling?

"Hazel paid for everything," Dez told me. "All Jay had to do was follow her instructions. Very detailed instructions. Which Jay did to the letter, got all the notifications and invitations sent out. The reason there was only us there was its being a weekday. And I don't think Hazel had taken into account the site's being so far away for everyone."

* * *

Jay phoned the next evening to make sure that I'd been to the doctor. A promise kept.

The doctor had been the same one Hazel had seen when she had forsworn all further treatments. I told him that since the death of my daughter – I had wanted to shock him with it, blame him – I had been feeling increasingly unwell and a friend had insisted that I make this appointment.

I looked at the word 'friend'. Was Jay now my friend?

The doctor asked the usual – other symptoms, was I having difficulty sleeping? I said none, that I was falling asleep all the time, except at night. He took my blood pressure, advised me to keep awake during the day, and told of seeing Hazel the week before she died: "A very brave and loving young woman." And when I there and then sank into a heap of tears he offered me grief counselling.

Back home, counselling declined, I thought – promises kept – that was that and I pulled the written-on papers out of the sideboard drawer, thought a moment on this latest visit to the doctor, found myself writing about another.

* * *

I was writing again the next day when the phone went. Dez this time: "You OK?"

"Course I'm OK. No need for you to keep phoning."

But they did. And next day it was Jay's turn, then Gustaf's deep voice: "When you coming back to Prospectus?"

"I dunno…" What I wanted that moment was to get back to my pile of papers.

I was beginning to resent these interruptions.

* * *

Writing, I had discovered, was nowhere near as easy as reading. I have had to worry these words onto paper. Words that, once there, didn't tell me that was exactly what I had been thinking, exactly what I had felt, didn't help my understanding of my own part in all that had happened. Or show me that I'd had no part at all.

Pen in hand I even had to ask myself who I was trying

to explain all this to? The naive woman I once was? Fool, I called her. Or was it to myself now, wise with unwanted experience? And not so wise. Or was this being written for the woman I wanted to be? The woman I would have liked to have been?

This is, was, my confession. This was my – another contemporary usage – disclosure. And disclosure frightened me. Disclosure I knew to be akin to suicide. Tell all and there can be no going back to denial. To exhume, to examine all those of-so-carefully constructed previous identities; and to admit that each was based on falsehoods, on outright lies, and that person I was, and still am to some extent, that person is all lies...

Disclosure has to be as destructive as it can be apparently constructive. Certainly no way back from it.

* * *

No phone call the next day. Instead the yellow pickup pulled up outside, Dez driving.

My first thought on seeing him was to be pleased that since Jay's visit, and since going to the doctor, I'd got back into the habit of showering each morning and of having breakfast before coming to this growing stack of paper. I had also cooked myself evening meals, if only a pre-packed jobby in the microwave. I had also completely cleared out one of the sideboard drawers so that I could, in case of a visit such as this, drop the papers in.

"Checking up on me?" I greeted Dez. "No need you know."

"Yes there is." He grinned at me as he came up around the two cars.

Once indoors, tea and cake before him, Dez told of a group he'd had the day before, a pre-release prisoner group, and the jokes that the prisoners had told. The prison officer too. One long joke-telling session.

"Come the end of the day my ribs were aching from laughing so much."

Come the end of his visit my cheeks were aching from smiling at Dez being unable to finish any of the jokes for laughing.

* * *

Odd what provokes one to action. Every time I'd glanced out the window to the Close I'd been looking past Hazel's car; and not seeing it. Dez not being able to bring the pickup into our short drive was what got me next day ringing around garages to find someone to buy Hazel's car.

"You need closure," Jay had lectured me. At which I'd snorted. Another latter-day cliché easily said; and I didn't know what it meant. Doubt that Jay did. And I was certainly in no hurry to close off what had been the one good thing in my life.

With all these comings and goings though (due to all these comings and goings?) something was happening to me. Was I in the process of recovering from Hazel's death? The ache for her was still there; and the thought that she had badgered the three of them into looking out for me could have me again in tears.

I had been loved. That was the hardest part to understand, to come to terms with. I had been loved and I wasn't worthy of love. Yet my daughter had loved me, had even sought to care for me beyond her death.

In every way Hazel was a better woman than me. I have never thought of myself as a nice person. The best, insofar as self-esteem goes, is that I've held myself to not have the certain faults of certain others.

Hazel was my daughter: I'd never been unkind to her, so why shouldn't she have loved me? What was now puzzling was why Jay, Dez and Gustaf should persist with the pretence of wanting me to return to Prospectus, and going way out of their way to do it. Hazel had gone. Why me?

A puzzle, but of greater importance at that time was did I want to let those three large people back through the doors of my life? I saw them as giants with gigantic boots about to tread down the carefully nurtured garden of my past.

Was a return to Prospectus what I wanted?

Why did they want me?

Jay on the phone told me that I should get out more because I was looking so peaky. I think that's what she said, but all I heard was the word 'should' and I have always responded badly to the word 'should'. 'You really should… ' 'You should… ' My mother and sister's, "With your build you should…", "You really should try something different with your hair…" My mother: "If you want to keep a man you should lose some of that weight for a start. Look at your sister…" People coming into the cafe: "You should serve…", "You should try…"

* * *

Dez stopped by again, still parking across the end of the drive. Again he regaled me with tales of the woodland, the jobs they were doing. Unlike Jay he put me under no direct pressure. But there is a stubborn softness to Dez, a principled resilience that both adds to his attractiveness and, depending on one's own position, can exasperate beyond measure.

The next time the yellow pickup came, Gustaf driving, it could park behind my car. Engrossed in my writing, loath to leave a sentence unfinished, I'd been slow to the phone the last couple of days and the answering service had cut in before I'd reached the receiver. No messages had been left.

Where Dez had been all easygoing smiles, Gustaf like Jay wore a concerned frown. He even directly asked, "You OK?"

There were lots of sighs too over his tea and cake. Finally he got to say his piece: "You do realise we're following Hazel's orders? Which were quite explicit. And we're going to keep on doing it. She said that we had to bring you back to the woods. Her words, 'Don't let her rot at home.' Only now it's not so much that you need to come back to us. It's got that we need you." And like Jay he said, "What else you going to do?"

I didn't, couldn't then, it was all so new and untested, tell him about the writing.

Fifty

The phone calls continued; Jay or Dez offering to stop by and pick me up – did I want to visit? – or wanting me to help with some 'light' pruning, or assist a group I'd previously worked with, got on well with…

The very thought of having to explain to any group about Hazel, or worse their embarrassed knowing and so not mentioning her… I invented some other activity for that day, took myself back to my scribbling.

It was Gustaf who finally got me out of the house. Not with one phone call, took several. He wanted me to accompany him and Dez to look over a brownfield site. Had been a coke works, then a breaker's yard, then toxic waste had been stored illegally there.

The toxic waste had all been removed; "And Dez and I are more or less OK with the tree planting. But you wouldn't believe the amount of admin this requires. And you know very well my admin skills. Dez's are non-existent. And I want to match up the specs they've given us with the site itself. I don't know who else to ask…"

I hummed and hawed, asked why he couldn't get one of the trustees along. They had at least one accountant and solicitor in their number.

"Can't spare the time," Gustaf said. "Being this badly toxic it's new to us. Different types of grants, from different bodies. Different subsidies… Please…"

As it wouldn't mean my meeting anyone other than Gustaf and Dez, eventually I said yes.

The yellow pickup was outside my door next morning, even though I'd said I was perfectly capable of driving myself. Found out later that his driving me had all been part of Gustaf's plan: if I'd had my own car I could at any time have driven home. Instead he took Dez and I back to his house after the vast black-puddled site.

Jay and Ben joined us at the house that evening. Ostensibly for the three of them to discuss the acquisition of the site, and to draw up a plan of action.

Aside from Ben all was businesslike, no overt shows of affection, no sentimental references to Hazel. And Ben only said what Jay had led him to say: "Hazel gone. Sad." And he pulled what he thought was a sad face, before chattering on about something else. Which that evening was the Poundshop glasses on the end of my nose. I'd got them when I realised that I couldn't always read my own writing, especially when it was a small and squeezed in afterthought.

* * *

Gustaf was right: the bureaucracy involved in this reclamation site was by no means straightforward. His worry was, it being such a big site, should just one of the grants or subsidies not materialise Prospectus could easily overreach itself and put all its other projects into jeopardy.

"We're good at juggling lots of balls," Gustaf said. "Balancing this one big ball on the tip of our nose though could prove calamitous."

Ben picked up on that, pretending to juggle, balance a ball, then returned to lowering his head and looking at me like me over the top of my glasses.

With some of their other derelict sites Prospectus had relied on natural regeneration; and here again Dez spouted his let-it-be mantra, "Alder and birch always grow first."

But would alder and birch readily take on land left so toxic? And with no nearby woodland to disperse the seed? And would reliance on self-regeneration alone satisfy the grant-givers?

Prevailing wind was discussed, plus Gustaf's idea of planting yew, itself toxic. When Gustaf added that they could sell the yew trimmings for conversion to a breast cancer drug Dez audibly sighed. Dez had never liked commercial considerations. This time however Gustaf didn't rise to the sigh... And I was drawn back in – on Gustaf's side.

* * *

Gustaf claimed that he was too tired to drive me back that night, would I mind stopping over? Jay suggested that I return with them to the caravans, but I didn't fancy being squeezed up in the truck with Dez going on about Gustaf's yew proposition. I said that, apart from having no clean knickers, I'd be fine in Gustaf's spare bed. One of Gustaf's lady friends had left some clothes there. Apparently she wouldn't be back for a couple of weeks, and next day I managed to squeeze into a pair of her for-show panties.

Gustaf wanted to make another visit to the site: a survey had said there was a stream piped under the land. We couldn't find the pipe. With neither of us credulous enough to believe a diviner could, we discussed it nonetheless, map held open between us.

With other diversions and digressions I didn't get delivered back home for three days. I knew I'd been kidnapped, and by the time I got home I was happy, and relieved, to have been kidnapped, to have something in my head other than dredged memories of Hazel slipping from mind's grasp.

Fifty-one

The evergreen yew, *taxus baccata*, is most definitely toxic. Left alone very little will grow under the spread of its branches. Like most poisons however the yew has been found to possess medicinal properties. These days even yew hedge trimmings get mulched, and treatments for breast cancer get extracted.

One of England's three indigenous conifers – Scots pine and juniper being the other two – yew can be found forming groves in otherwise broadleaf woodland. Most English people though will have first encountered yew in graveyards, cultivated there to deter owners of livestock letting their animals wander among and soil the graves.

Legend of course holds otherwise. Christians would have us believe that the yew is in the graveyard, now the churchyard, because that is where the earliest preachers stood – due to the yew's dense cover – to deliver the gospel. Pagan legend on the other hand has it that the yew's longevity had already made of it a fetish tree. Superstition still holds that if one walks backwards seven times around one of these ancient graveyard yews while making wishes, then those wishes will come true.

It is claimed that some graveyard yews, their aged boughs prop-supported, are over 1,500 years old. But no matter how ancient – and no menopause for the yew – come the autumn the female tree will put out seed.

Whether the mother tree is young or old these seeds will be a pinkish red and look for all the world like sweetshop candies. The outer casing, the soft pinkish red, is loved by song thrushes and clucking fieldfares. It is the hard black seed within the pink fleshy casing that is highly poisonous. These black seeds pass through the birds' digestive tracts whole, leaving the bird unharmed, with the seed being deposited in its own circle of bird-donated fertiliser.

Being slow-growing yew timber doesn't often come to market. When it does its orangey-red heartwood is usually snapped up by high-class furniture makers. Most of the timber is exported to Europe for veneer production.

In the pre-industrial past of course it was staves cut from the outer white of the yew trunk, the sapwood, that was used to make the famed English longbows.

* * *

Juniper, *juniperus communis*, just about survives in England, and then only in the wild uplands, clinging onto mountainsides, shaping itself to rockfaces and just about weathering the predation of nimble-footed sheep. Juniper is a victim of both intensive farming and the increase in, dare I say, broadleaf woodland.

Being low-growing juniper is often overlooked as a tree, at a distance can easily be mistaken for gorse. If conditions allow, however, juniper can grow to a straggly thirty feet. That is if it doesn't encounter heathland fires, its waxy needles being readily flammable.

When crushed the needles' scent triggers a hard-to-pin-down collective memory. I know and don't know it, suspect that memory's roots might lie in juniper's once having been held sacred. The burning of juniper branches was believed to have kept evil at bay.

All things considered the memory smell is more likely due to juniper's dusk-purple berries having more recently been harvested for the one-time flavouring of gin. Those berries nowadays much appreciated by migrating birds.

* * *

The two distinct varieties of birch to be seen in England are the silver and the hairy birch, with all sorts of crossover hybrids in between. Like most everyone else I see the glimmering white trunk of a birch and I call it silver, *betula pendula*, be it pure pendula or not. If it is pure its bark will be white and its delicate branch ends will droop, although not to the ground-sweeping extent of the weeping willow.

The older a silver birch gets the more black patches, algae-filled cracks, will appear on its bark. Birch of whatever variety, however, doesn't get very old. Seventy years if lucky. So birch woodlands are mostly of slim trunks. Which grants them their own beauty, and not just their being tall and slender. I especially love the purple haze of their pre-spring buds.

Hairy birch, *betula pubescens*, is the tree that makes up the Siberian taiga, miles upon thousands of miles of it. Here, in our mixed woodlands, hairy birch can be distinguished at distance by its lack of drooping habit. Although, as said previously, there's been so much cross fertilisation that any self-sown tree is unlikely to be of pure genus.

While both trees are mostly self-pollinating, carry male and female catkins, hairy birch – so-called because of its downy twigs – usually has more discoloration on its bark, acquiring dark horizontal bands the older it gets.

The bark is what birch is most useful for. Its easily peeled bark being waterproof native Americans used the bark for the outer skin of their canoes. Dez and Jay used lapped birch bark to make their benders rainproof. The difficulty, Dez said, was in finding bark not fungal-damaged.

All varieties of birch are prey to fungal infections, in particular the bracket fungus *polyporus betulinus*. Wherever they are grown birch and fungus seem to go hand in hand. The most famous fungus associated with birch probably being the scarlet flycap, *amanita muscaria*, the red toadstool beloved of children's book illustrators.

Birch timber itself is of little real use except for firewood. Foresters mostly use birch as a pioneer/nursery tree. Slower growing trees such as oak can be planted in their shelter.

Fifty-two

My return to the realm of the living didn't come about through just that one, welcome if clumsy, intervention. My recuperation took place over months, one or other of them collecting or calling me to one woodland site or another.

Many of those first visits back took in the toxic site, if only to see how work was progressing. But to be among trees was really, each time, where I wanted to be taken. Trees don't care who of us bipeds lives, who dies. The forest weeds don't care. What were Hazel and I to them?

* * *

Some part of me saw my being among trees as probably the best way of dealing with Hazel's death. Although trees are basically large vegetables that we can spend our lives looking at and often not seeing, they do have their own characters and a much longer life span than our own. Even then trees do not have a simple beginning-to-end narrative. Trees can be cropped, and come again. Fully grown though, or growing still, they do offer quietude.

Although I probably never said as much to them I was grateful to Gustaf, Dez and Jay; and I did go wherever invited. Ostensibly to help, if only to keep Jay company, or to mind Ben as she delivered Titan and Herbert to a show or to a wood – the five of us on a chill morning walking into clouds of our own breath.

Or I again acted as fumble-fingered foil in one of Dez's woodland workshops. Or I met up with just Gustaf for some ditch clearing. When, as soon as I was decently able, I wandered off – to feel myself enclosed by trees, threading myself through the pale slim trunks of an overcrowded wood, to chance upon the ivy floor of an ancient dell like so many points of light, smile at the round shelves of bracket fungus ascending a birch trunk...

Or I'd find myself stopped, looking in admiration at the way just one tree had designed itself, each and every leaf a mini solar panel converting light to substance. Dual purpose too, each leaf directing rainwater to the runnels on each twig, twig to branch, then along to the trunk and down to the roots, also dual purpose – taking nutrients from the soil as well as sending out suckers to replicate itself, a fail-safe mechanism should its blooms fail to get pollinated...

Just one tree in a forest of trees, tree sheltering behind tree sheltering behind tree sheltering behind... The taller the tree the more shelter it gave, the more light its leaves took...

* * *

Despite my eagerness to be on my own in the woods I only slowly came to realise how much I had missed the forest's embrace, the quiet comfort and companionship of trees.

I will leave airy-fairy notions of woodland's spiritually

enhancing properties to the likes of Gustaf and Dez. I simply liked, preferred being in woodland, whether I was just wandering through it or even if I was felling and sorting timber. I was still a part of the woodland's long-term processes.

When young, time on my hands in between male company, and again wandering distant hospital towns when Hazel was first diagnosed, was undergoing tests, my feet, my despair of ever making sense of this life, often took me into empty churches. But they were just lofty ceilings and old varnished wood. Trees alone have offered me the salve of timelessness. Trees are the high church of my dreams. Among trees is where I am uplifted. Alone among trees is where I spread my arms and raise my face to the laced sky.

And to be there at the very beginning of a woodland is such a privilege. As with the big site, where we undertook some major landscaping, opened up the stream, dug a pond, made some hillocks, planted Scots pine, a grove of yew, and with mixed woodland for the rest. Won an eco prize.

Though that was years later.

* * *

Some of the people in Dez's workgroups had known Hazel, and there was that awkwardness when nothing at all was said, the absence of both the words and Hazel larger than any ghost.

In the woods themselves I didn't expect her to come from behind every tree. That wasn't how we'd been in the woods. While I had gone a'wandering Hazel had stayed nattering to whoever we'd been working with that day.

Of course there were moments of almost unbearable sadness. Curiously what seemed to provoke them was – in every wood – my catching sight of a wren. Such a small flesh and blood creature to be independently alive. And Hazel wasn't.

Hazel wasn't. I've always felt incomplete, a part of me missing. That part now had a name – Hazel.

* * *

One time in a hillside wood – I'd gone a'wandering – and so dozy was I that day that inertia took over.

A concerned Gustaf came looking for me, found me sitting on a mossy mound, my back to the nobbled bole of an ancient oak.

"Sorry," I started to struggle up. "Didn't realise the time."

"No need to apologise," Gustaf said. "Great and sensible discoveries have been made sitting under trees."

"Possibly," I said, "but wasn't Newton…" I had been about to say something clever about oak apples not being so weighty as eating apples but Gustaf cut in,

"I was thinking more of Buddha."

Pondering on semi-conversations such as that gave me the sensation of slowly waking. Or as if I'd been half alive and a new half of me was being born. It was not a going back. Not a renewal. What is organically old cannot be renewed. Cannot become as-good-as-new. No, the past is the past, dead is dead. Gone.

* * *

At every turn I seemed to come back to death. My family gone I had doubt of my own existence. Awake nights it seemed that only the dead had known me alive. Substance of course returned with the mornings. Even so for my own sake, my own sanity, I needed still to make some kind of sense of death.

Although the shock of a death can linger what comes next has to be new. New as if the past never was. And I wanted to be among the new, the growing, the never-been-before. So did trees begin to fill my emptiness. I found comfort in knowing that the oak seedlings we were planting that day had been acorns two years ago, and that in a hundred years a full-grown oak would be standing where my hand was now pressing down the damp soil.

Is it by such small shifts in perception that we reconcile

ourselves to the death of a beloved?

Within some woods were old lines of moss-coated rocks, the part-squared-off base of a once-building, cottage or barn. Lives once lived there. Other lives, long gone, unknowable and because unknown somehow reassuring.

I noticed too that, before I left the house in the mornings, I put the radio on for the weather forecast. And it was by way of many such small acts that I again started looking, not just ahead, but outside myself.

* * *

tree to tree to tree
the watching forest is joined
by single strand webs

Fifty-three

Although I had Dez to chat to most lunchbreaks, and if it was just us two ditch clearing or thinning we'd have on-off conversations stop-starting throughout the day, I still had no-one I could confide in, who might be able to explain me to me. Only I knew all about me. Ergo, I had to do the explaining.

How, for instance, had I ended up scrabbling about in various woodlands with the 'fostered son', Dez, of the genetic father, Gustaf, of my adopted daughter, Hazel?

Maternal was probably the last thing I felt for Dez. And how did Dez explain himself? He told me of his parents living in South Africa within a gated community. They cared, Dez said, only about themselves, about their own standard of living, what their money could buy them. So had Dez come to abhor consumerism/capitalism and the rest of his life had followed from that.

"Deforestation here was caused by the wool trade, by unchecked, unregulated capitalism."

That was Dez explained. Me? I went back to the stacks of notes I'd made after Hazel's funeral. But my handwriting, much of it illegible, was of no help in reaching an understanding. Even prescription glasses were of no help in deciphering the smaller notes I'd squeezed in among others. So when I was back at home I started entering all the more or less decipherable notes into my laptop.

* * *

First attempt at giving the printed-off notes some kind of order, at sorting them under various headings, only led me to dashing off more scribbled notes. Many of which required new headings.

In the woods, Dez momentarily elsewhere, I fumbled the small notebook out of my pants pocket, muddily scribbled with its thin pencil, 'Title of today's paper – An Imaginary Psychologist Explains Me To Me.'

An imaginary bereavement counsellor tried to explain the emptiness still within me. An imaginary marriage counsellor tried to analyse mine and Ian's marriage...

I tried to recreate my many states of mind within that marriage, from its beginning to its end... But all of me had changed, was changing. The only constant was my memories, which – I had to admit – were also changing.

I want this here to be right. I want to use words that tell exactly how it was. Not use words to disguise how it really was. I see my sole task now as getting it down right. Not to simplify the past to the point of inaccuracy. The present neither. But not to complicate it either to the point of obscurity. At which point I have to ask – Why am I explaining this to me? When the bottom line has to be that my life has only ever been important in how it has affected the lives of others?

What I really want to write here is that I don't know, I don't know, and to keep on writing that I don't know. And what I don't know is what I don't know. A formless blank that I find myself staring into, while feeling all the time that I should know what it is that I don't know. I keep hoping that this pen will tell me what it is that I don't know. It doesn't. It just tells me about my not knowing.

"All we leave are footprints," Gustaf said. He was talking about, was justifying the brevity of his haiku. I had even wondered back then, these thousands of words ago, if we left even footprints.

* * *

It was not always just Dez and I bending to our work, or smile-dealing with woodland work groups, Gustaf was often there to join in our debates. Although debate is to give our frequently voiced disagreements, this-versus-that, too grand a title.

And I have to confess that Dez's default position of lauding every practice of yesteryear did irritate. Yes, intensively produced natural fibres would keep people in work. But look also on the overall effect of new technologies – on human health, on sociological health, no more children labouring dangerously in the cotton mills. At least not in this country. I wanted to say to him, "Don't dismiss something just because it's new and technological." But I held my tongue back then.

Gustaf was more ready to speak his mind.

"I want this country to be covered in trees," he said.

Now, when it was just the three of us, it seemed to be me who was most in opposition to Gustaf, with Dez the onlooker. Or it was Dez joining forces with Gustaf against novice me. (Small wonder I ended up writing this.)

"If the country's covered in trees," I said, "what will people eat?"

"Let cattle forage in among the trees."

"What about the vegetarians? Where will the field crops be grown?"

"Where trees won't."

"No such place," Dez chipped in. "If an edible crop will grow there then so too will a tree."

Which would have Dez seeming that time to side with Gustaf.

Still the two of them disagreed over Prospectus's commercial plantations – Dez sighing his disapproval of the clear-felling of thirty-year-old trees for pulpwood – and I sensed that Gustaf, just by his terse responses, had himself become tired of those arguments. And because I one time agreed with Gustaf over the use of a herbicide to clear some ground, whenever I found myself at odds with Dez in the months thereafter he would look for the opportunity to say, "And what does the chemo-forester think?"

Not that we three were at loggerheads non-stop. Some sponsored runners passed through a wood one day, followed by the do-gooders with their charity collecting buckets. Not one of us three had any change in our working clobber, were left feeling guilty.

"It has to sit uneasy," Gustaf spoke for us all, "having a good standard of living while millions starve. Yet what little sacrifice I might make, even if I turned over all my holdings, would have minimal effect on the world's starving. Maybe stave off death a day or two for a few thousand. But then, being penniless, I'd be thrown on the charity of others. So what to do?"

"As the world is arranged at the moment," Dez said, "as voters, as opinion-changers, as citizens we have been rendered ineffectual. Politically, insofar as changing governments goes, we have all been disenfranchised by those prepared to bend their principles to the system. So we campaign uneasily outside the system. Planting trees."

"Woodland increases soil depth year on year," I contributed a snippet recently acquired. "Best investment anyone can make."

* * *

Some days my woodland life was one long reminder of Hazel. Even those days I was enjoying Gustaf's company could lead me to wonder how Hazel's life would have differed had she searched for and found Gustaf earlier. Would she not have then, for instance, sunk into the telly-watching lassitude of life with Kevin?

I wondered too if having known Gustaf earlier would have given Hazel some small advantages. Returning, as I often did when in the vicinity, to the hillside grave I one time met the manager of the burial ground. He told me that the woman in wool was no longer with the company. I hid my pleasure behind my face.

By this time some poorly looking conifers had been planted by the fence. The majority of the latest grave trees were oaks, one weeping willow.

In discovering who I was the manager also told me that, solely because of Hazel's association with Prospectus, special allowance had been made for the planting of the unsuitable poplar. Thanks to Gustaf.

What I also learnt from another chat with that manager was that Gustaf had been excited to learn that once someone had been buried in a field then that field automatically became a protected site and more trees could be planted there.

"More trees eh?" Gustaf had apparently gone off smile-muttering to himself.

I wondered then at my reaction that, rather than taking offence at Gustaf seeming to exploit Hazel's burial wish, his eagerness to plant trees whatever the opportunity had me too smiling to myself.

* * *

Not all reminders of Hazel passed so easily.

Dreading the emotional impact I asked Jay to come and help me sort through all Hazel's clothes. The older, like her favourite green jacket, had been shaped to her.

Jay took Hazel's almost new work jacket and a couple of scarves for herself. The rest we stuffed into black plastic sacks and left them at a charity shop.

After all my putting off doing it, come the end they were just three more soft plastic sacks left in a High Street doorway.

* * *

When I was put in charge of a group for coppicing – thinning out oak saplings, keeping the straightest – I listened to words coming from my mouth and wondered that I should ever have spoken thus: "Coppicing," I corrected the group leader, "actually comes from the French 'couper', to cut."

Another time planting out I heard myself tell a school party, "Here, cursed with rabbits, we use protective tubes."

Wet days saw me at Gustaf's house catching up on admin, and discovering that his Public Liability insurance was two months out of date. I was angered too to discover that Prospectus had to have Employers Liability insurance for Dez and Jay, even though they received little by way of cash.

Gustaf sent me for chainsaw training with a very serious man in a flat cap. I came back with my certificate and wood chips in my cleavage.

"In every wood we leave some fallen trees lying, and some standing deadwood," I told a party of tidy-minded pensioners. "Deadwood acts as homes for the smaller animals, for insect life and birds such as nuthatches and woodpeckers. You will notice that we also leave deadwood in streams. Helps keep the water clear."

* * *

As they had my daughter the woods had begun to give meaning to my life. Here the harmony of a self-sustaining existence, one seasonal task flowing into the next. My daughter had made this life for me: I determined to throw myself into it.

"We always plant close to begin with," I told a questioning volunteer. "Leaf cover cuts down weed growth. And we can always thin the trees later. Meanwhile being planted close encourages straight stems."

"The best way of discouraging bracken," I told a party of schoolgirls, "is to walk round and round a tree, squashing down every frond. Dez's little boy loves doing this. He gets a long bit of string, like this, loops it around the trunk and then goes round and round the tree, letting out the string as he goes. Here's your string. Pick your tree."

What I didn't tell them, not wanting a chorus of squeals, was that the trampled bracken would provide open areas for basking snakes and lizards.

The talk none of us liked to give was having to explain, to justify, grey squirrel culls. To save us being met with outrage Gustaf had a handout printed. When I asked why he'd spelled cull with a K he said that he wanted it to look like kill so that no-one could have any illusions about what was intended.

With some of the regular groups – be they a workshop making green furniture, lathe-turning, willow weaving or charcoal smoking in a neglected copse – I still found myself, and was irritated with myself for doing it – was a reversal to type, Missus Tubby Café Proprietor, and I had outgrown her – but there I was taking along and handing out home-baked cakes and pastries.

If the cakes were pleasantly received not all of the work could equally be called pleasant. Some days, after bank holidays especially, we'd go rubbish collecting in some of the more popular woods. Broken glass, carrier bags, lager cans, takeaway cartons, plastic bottles, foil crisp packets, used dog poo bags, farmers' windblown plastic, food wrappers... With sacks full and heaped in the back of the pickup to be taken to the nearest tip, we all of us ended those days disgusted with the GBP. Also not so pleasant, were the occasional odd-hat men, independent thinkers who wanted to be thought of as characters; and who are unfortunately to be found in most volunteer groups. At least to begin with. Because in those days they were very soon out-charactered by a hatless Gustaf, who didn't even seem to compete.

"We are all victims of the past," Gustaf asserted as only he could assert, "not products of it. We have to become doctors, cure ourselves and cure our planet. Grab a shovel."

Gustaf once met the odd-hat wearers rarely returned.

"According to the Stoics," Gustaf declared on some newly acquired heathland, "the universe dies in fire and is reborn in fire. Likewise gorse. Who brought the matches?"

* * *

a pleasing image
can distort the truth – clouds
are stored in the forest

Fifty-four

Writing of time is odd, bears no relation to the space on the page. A decade can be a short paragraph, an eventful hour can take five pages. Not that I'm about to write of either. Suffice to say that these developments took place over a longer stretch.

* * *

Whenever I went to a Prospectus woodland Dez, Jay and Gustaf pressed me to stay with one or other of them. Although I appreciated their concern for me, with neither was it the most comfortable of arrangements.

Gustaf for instance was every inch the considerate host. But his domestic skills were, at best, imprecise. Always an ingredient missing in the kitchen, or something so basic as his having forgotten to bring logs in for the fire; and the memory lapse seeming always to have preceded a wet winter's evening when he was occupied with something else.

He wasn't always there. If he had a gig with his band he might stop over near there. (Shades of Hazel's conception?) I asked if his performing haiku with a band, the middle-aged poet wandering about the stage, about the room too apparently, spouting even three line haiku wasn't a bit weird.

"Been done before. Years ago. Zoot Sims and Kerouac

even made a record of their efforts."

Then there were the times when he approached me, always pulling the strangest of faces – lips twisted to one side, eyebrows up, eyebrows down, whole mouth getting sucked back to the other side – to tell me that my stopping over that night wouldn't be convenient as he had a 'guest.'

"Female variety?"

"Well... yes. D'you mind? Bit awkward tonight."

If being turned away was in itself discomfiting, a mounting cause of discomfort in my stopping over with him was that I saw Gustaf and I getting to be like an old married couple – comfortable with our little habits and long silences – and I didn't want to be part of an old married couple.

We tended to sit around most evenings with our books, have the occasional light-hearted dispute over whose turn it was to make a cup of tea; with later him or I saying, "Mind if I put on the news?"

Maybe if we'd had sex this domesticity wouldn't have felt so strange, contrived almost. An act. Then again if we'd been having sex he'd probably want me to stop over on just the odd night here and there, like his 'lady friends.' Who we didn't mention.

Although so seemingly familiar Gustaf and I were still careful in what we said to one another. Our evening conversations were mostly run-of-the-mill stuff carried over from the day's work, reservations about a new piece of woodland... But occasionally, prompted by a passage in a book, or the kitchen radio news, we broached the emotionally perilous.

"I'm guessing," Gustaf said one evening, having laid aside his book, "but I'm pretty sure that neither of us were unconditionally loved as children. Which could be why we both tried so hard with our own children. I certainly did my best to love Lungren, and failed. You succeeded with Hazel, but lost her." Piece said he picked up his book. "Now all we have left are trees."

"Trees!" I shouted, and almost wept laughing.

Another time I think one of us had just read, or had been reading, a survivor's woe-is-me book. Gustaf had no sympathy.

"These authors want to be different solely by virtue of the damage done them. When they realise however that they're not that much different they chafe at their ordinariness. When we're all of us ordinary in our freakishness. I'm a freak. I'm not like other people. Any other people. You're a freak." (More than he knew.) "You accept it." (Less than he knew.) "And while you and I try to achieve something all that they do is look for ways to get through another day."

My stopping over at Dez and Jay's was as awkward. But for entirely, almost entirely, physical reasons.

Even with the two caravans space was at a premium. My staying over therefore required stuff to be cleared, a bed to be made up. And because they didn't have mains sewage Dez had taken out both caravan's lavatories. The compost lavatory he'd made outside, and despite Jay's best efforts, wasn't at all comfortable to use. And while little Ben was my constant enthusiastic companion, I couldn't help but be aware that I was gooseberry to the couple.

Living so cheek by jowl I have one abiding memory of my staying there, of waiting my turn mornings and watching Jay bend to wash her face and underarms.

Naked I'm all rolls, folds and creases. Jay is stretched muscle, smooth like a barkless tree's twisted grain. No bra straps ever squared off her long strong back; and there was something almost joyously religious about her uninhibited half-nudity. Her smile was certainly beatific when she turned to find me waiting there, dressing gown wrapped, toilet bag in hand.

Although my near breathless attraction for Jay was a puzzling concern, what I did unreservedly enjoy was walking the horses back to the field with Jay, was disappointed if Dez and I had to leave before she took them. And, as I said, Ben was just fun to be around.

This may sound silly, but fruit was a problem with my staying there. Not fruit itself, but their tea bags. We had served fruity tea bags on request in the café, and Hazel occasionally had one at home. But, milkless, that fruit-flavoured tea felt bodiless to me. While Hazel, being of that fruit tea generation, had taken stopping over with Dez and Jay in her stride, indeed had preferred staying there than with Gustaf.

* * *

When Jay became pregnant I more or less stopped staying with them. With Gustaf too. And it was then that Dez started expressing concern over my production of carbon dioxide in driving back and forth from my house. Although the expression of his displeasure became often no more than his frown at my saying that I was off home, it did get to me.

Dez didn't even like Jay using the horsebox as a run-around. While his sole objection to Prospectus taking on new woodland any distance away was often that management would involve yet more 'petro-chemical travel'.

Although Dez and Gustaf's arguments were often on the merits of horses versus tractors, sweat versus petrol, CO^2 versus methane, prior to Prospectus I had shrugged off most eco-concerns. Or rather I had been put off by the people expressing eco-concerns. I'd seen them as self-righteous bombasts, scruffy waste-of-spacers spouting impractical, hard-to-pin-down cares for the world. "You really should recycle your coffee grounds separately," I was told by a customer, the week before she was flown halfway round the world for her eco-holiday.

While driving back and forth across the country, staying in hotels, hadn't seem to matter when Hazel had been alive. Alone I had begun to count the cost, and not only in money. Living out of bags in the back of the car, fitting myself in with others' bedtimes, I never felt that I got enough sleep.

Eating smuggled-in pizzas straight from the cardboard

in my hotel room, or sitting among the couples in the café-cum-restaurants had me looking continually at my single self. And at them. At men who, when young, would probably have greeted each other loudly in bars, were now sitting quietly across from their wives, a tablecloth between them, and both turning to look at me – sitting alone. And staring back

I didn't belong anywhere. I came back to my house and more than a few times I stayed sitting in my car – looking at the front door and the windows and thinking it so strange that those windows and door should be 'my home', the address on my driving licence and passport. Sitting in my car I knew that inside that front door would be a pile of envelopes, mostly junk mail, but some to me by name. Whoever I was.

I didn't belong anywhere. But then I never had, felt as if I had spent my life moving from one period of dissatisfaction to the next. I had almost come to believe that there was no cure.

Buying a campervan changed my life.

* * *

My first was by no measure a big campervan, could fit easily into most parking bays. But I could stand up in it and walk from front to back; and it had a cooker, water tank and sink.

Research for the campervan hadn't been as thorough as I'd have liked. Attempting online research had brought too much to mind when Hazel and I had been googling every mention of her condition. 'The condition, inherited...' 'The condition, a genetic dysfunction affecting the distaff...' 'The condition requires palliative care only, although symptoms can be alleviated by...' That condition had almost come to obscure my daughter. I had closed my laptop, went to a campervan specialist, plumped for the most popular type seen in carparks, and got part-exchange on my car.

What that first, and not entirely satisfactory, campervan did mean was that I could park up in whichever woodland we were working and stay there the night. The bed of course folded out, and if I needed heat winters I could leave the engine running for a bit.

To begin with, as I had when waiting in woodland carparks for Hazel, I left evidence of my overnight stays in part-buried tissues. Then I bought a small portable lavatory, a square plastic contraption with its own flush and only the height of a footstool. Which was perfect except that when driving the portapotti would distractedly slide back and forth along the campervan floor. Until, while velcroing a cushion to its lid – for disguise – I hit on the idea of also velcroing it to the side of a floor cabinet.

Inordinately pleased with my innovation, I have to say that that secondhand campervan changed my life. From its windows I had all sorts of sylvan views. Opening the side door quietly I stepped out early mornings, and I mean before sunrise, and took myself off for woodland wanders, always in the hope of glimpsing a deer or a fox slipping away. Or the animal and I both stopped head on, one as surprised as the other to find ourselves there, that heart-leap moment of here-and-now exaltation. Alive!

Not always peaceful. A weekend afternoon's slumber could be disturbed by the flap and clatter of two treetop pigeons having sex. But, once parked up, what I went looking for was more of those moments here-and-gone. And sometimes I didn't even have to leave the van. As when a flock of longtailed tits appeared in the carpark trees. I became aware of their squeaking, their chittering to one another as they worked their way through the trees, upside down, one replacing another, suddenly close, entrancing, and gone.

Wildlife wasn't all there was to look forward to. There was the stillness in my warm indoors on a wet day waiting out the rain, glancing up at the thud of an occasional heavy drop landing on the roof. Or, work for the day finished, picking ramson leaves from the wood to garlic-flavour my stir-fry, or blackberries for a crumble. Or there was autumn's soft bounce of wax-bead berries from a drooping yew dropping all around the van. Or on a winter's day watching the air freeze in spikes just the other side of the glass.

I very soon came to expect being woken most days by birdsong and rook caw. One dawn, looking out at the cool greys – I was parked field one side, wood the other – the mist-made muscle of a white charollay bull made his slow walk into the day straight towards me. Mine was the deep sigh privilege of being witness to such beauty.

When my food stores needed replenishing I drove to the nearest town, found a public lavatory to empty my portapotti tank. If any of the other cubicles were occupied when I went in they very soon weren't. Probably because I was expecting the pong the stench never once made me retch. (I couldn't empty the tank at Gustaf's as the odour-killing chemicals added to the portapotti would have had an adverse effect on the breakdown bacteria in his septic tank.)

For personal hygiene I made do with strip washes. Shampooing was the most difficult. I did briefly consider resorting to dreads like Jay and Dez, but persevered with my hair in a bun and jug rinses once a week.

Dez and Jay of course initially approved of my new 'traveller' status. Dez now told me that he'd been aghast at mine and Hazel's carbon footprint but, liking Hazel, had figured early on that Hazel must have had good reason for being driven all those miles every day and that, for once, it hadn't been his place to say.

After the police had interrupted my carpark slumbers a couple of times, and they called Gustaf who told them that I was allowed to stop over, I had printed an 'authorisation' on Prospectus headed notepaper and signed by Gustaf. Laminated, and slid onto the dashboard, this said that as an essential worker I was permitted to remain overnight in all woodland carparks managed or owned by The Tree Prospectus.

I was no longer anyone's guest. I was always home.

***

I think it was when I came to see the campervan more as my home than my house that I considered moving – moving what I had come to think of as my base.

There were of course other influences.

It's funny how of all the words spoken to you some stick – stick like chewing gum to your shoe. And it was only an off-the-cuff remark of Gustaf's. For some reason he called at my house one day, after getting lost in the estates.

"They're all the same," he complained. "Some roads curve. Some are straight. Take a right, come round a corner and you find yourself in another near identical Crescent or Close. All uniformly horrible. Why do people live in these places?"

"Where else do we live?" I said defensively.

"Point taken," he was quick to say, not wanting me upset. "But they're all so damn rabbit hutch soulless."

I couldn't even then disagree: dormitory town, commuter land suburbia, but "What real choice do people have?" I asked Gustaf.

"Always choice," he said. "Needs to be a will for change and those in power will, eventually, make the changes. No-one should have to live like this."

Easy enough for Gustaf to say; and no-one except property developers can like the countryside getting covered in bricks and mortar. How else though did all these people get housed? Gustaf could only go about planting trees because of the money he'd made selling his record company, that record company only so successful because its records had been bought by people living in houses like mine. All human life, I had at the time concluded, although that had come from arguing with Dez, has to be fundamentally artificial, fundamentally contrived.

As dissatisfied as my neighbours, all of us wanting something other, I hadn't then seen the need to change. It was parking the campervan in the drive and noticing how its extra height darkened the indoors that made me realise how rarely I had looked out the windows before. What had there been to look at? The answer was – nothing. Or rather I had looked to see only who was coming to my door, or not, no further than my own miserable little rut. At what needed doing next, at who I was angry at. And he had been indoors.

So did I come to question my living alone in that four bedroom, two reception, conservatory, garage and garden all alone, my only winter companion the fire to be fed. A log fire that fulfilled a visual void, that wasn't a functional necessity.

* * *

The word 'alone' carries so much emotional weight. I use it here solely to describe.

I've never much questioned my being alone. Granted my circumstances of late may have verged on the extreme, but mine were by no means unusual. In an increasingly crowded world there are – as a result of the crowding? fearing contact? – so many of us now unattached and living alone.

Even though externally my house differed only slightly from the hundreds of others around, still its small differences carried too many accusing memories, every other indoors corner springing guilt. In the few framed photos of Hazel the garden shrubs were already bigger now than then.

My house wasn't precious, was just somewhere I was. Aside from my antique sticks and the kitchen I'd put minimum thought into the house. What had mattered to me had been Hazel and the café. That's where I'd invested my thoughts.

Now both were gone. And when I came to move house, steeled myself to throw out the last of Hazel's odds and ends, I was afraid that it might send me back into despair.

I was almost ashamed when it didn't.

How often in our lives though do we force ourselves to make serious choices – the jobs we go for, the places we live, who we love? This choice made itself, was more a progression, a consideration of the available options than a heart-searching choice.

Took me a year or so to find what I was looking for, which was a third floor two bedroom flat in a four storey block with its own fenced-off parking lot around the back. Although I had to sell off some of my larger furniture – the beech kitchen table – the removal men managed to get the oak sideboard up the stairs and into the small sitting room. I also kept my walnut escritoire and the rosewood dressing table. But the Dutch dresser and the dining room pine table had to go. So too the cross-grained elm coffee table, fond as I was of it, it was too awkward a shape for the small flat.

Losing possessions isn't like losing people. As to my one valued possession now, I could look down from my third floor window and be reassured by sight of the campervan's roof. I could even look out over the nearest estate roofs, some slate, some tiled, and take some pleasure from birds grouped on power lines, the soft green humps of occasional trees.

Gustaf's view wasn't improved.

"Just posh slums," he said. "Packed together, covering ground."

* * *

In my campervan I had a radio, books, laptop, and time on my hands. I was even writing this, my first attempt at stitching together all the notes I'd made, and making more. The listening, the reading, the writing and the rewriting all went together.

Time on my hands it was in my campervan that I began to see that in all the books, in all the stories, no matter how they dressed it up, the authors were, like me, trying to explain themselves to themselves. How did they get to be this way? What way were they? Who was this mysterious self? How came it to exist?

And that is what I've been attempting to do here – here in the campervan and in my empty hours back in the flat.

Instead of woe-is-me crying about it, or looking for others to blame, I've been trying to come to an understanding.

To justify going day on day to the woods Hazel had told me that she had to do something that gave meaning to her life, to what little life she had left. So did I have to explain to myself all that I had done. And not done?

'We become what we are,' A S Byatt wrote in 'The Game', 'by a series of involuntary half-choices.' The choices not made wholly for us, not made wholly by us.

In writing down my history I have seemed to be always in the process of contradicting myself, and of then having to reconcile the two aspects. Much paper has got thrown away. Which would be when I'd look up from paper or laptop and out of the window – at a wall of summer leaves or through winter's dwindling perspective of rain-black trunks.

The campervan had most definitely become my home. Which was not to say that I didn't enjoy an occasional return to the flat. Something very comforting about hot water coming out of a tap.

* * *

motorway noise
confused with the soughing
of a hilltop copse

Fifty-five

It was Jay's mother, Emma, who asked me to be around, by which she meant close by, for the birth. Emma had missed Ben's birth.

Although they had "...never actually had a big falling out..." and that according to Emma, they had become distant when Jay and Dez had first started living in the woods.

Almost as tall as Jay, and as slim, Emma was one of those women who, since puberty, had been aware of the power of her looks and had dressed accordingly. She told me – talked a lot did Emma, mostly when out of Jay's hearing – she'd hoped that Jay "...with her figure..." would have become a model. "Instead she went to university and met," a sideways nod of the head, "him."

Where Jay's face was open, often wide-eyed with excitement and enthusiasm, Emma's had hardened long before ageing. Emma's accent was harder too, as if she had once sought to make herself streetwise, "...nobody's fool me." Emma followed fashion, went with the crowd. Jay, more than Dez sometimes, would spend days trying to determine the worth of a new proposal. Once decided she wouldn't budge.

Emma was a shopper, hadn't understood Jay's attraction to radical politics, demos and sit-ins. Divorced, separated, and with several house moves and step-dads behind them, Jay and Emma had become distant long before Jay had left for university.

By her own lights Emma had wanted what was best for Jay: "Nice lad Dez, I said to her. But like I told her, he ain't going to change the world, and he certainly ain't going to get a mortgage."

That had been back when Dez and Jay had been active over 'green issues', chaining themselves to power station fences, sitting on railway tracks, invading petrol refineries. It was only when they came to realise that their sloganeering wasn't going to bring about change in the way the world was run that they decided to change their own lives by setting up house in what was to become one of Prospectus's woodlands.

Being always disapproved of in her adult life Jay had long before stopped telling Emma of her and Dez's plans. Consequently Emma had no idea of their going to live in the woods, or of the subsequent change Gustaf had brought to their lives – the caravans, the horses, Dez off working in different woodlands, and Jay being pregnant.

"First I knew about Ben he was a year old. I got a grandmother card. Home-made of course."

Emma was not an unkind woman; but she would voice such stereotypical opinions, values courtesy of the advertisers and newspapers, that it was hard to warm to her. She did though have genuine affection for Jay, Ben, and even for Dez, drove up to see them almost every other weekend.

Of Hazel's death Emma said to me, "I can't think how you must feel. What it must be like. I just can't imagine it. When Jay went off into the woods I was beside myself. She didn't mean harm by it. I had no idea though where she was, didn't know what to do with myself. Sorry, it's not about me…"

* * *

Emma talked to me more than to Jay, who could silence her with a glance.

Jay had decided, for the sake of her own children, to suffer her mother's love and had reluctantly agreed to let Emma be present for this 'home birth'. My part in it was to be close by when the contractions started so that I could phone Emma and take care of Ben.

All went according to plan. First contractions came in the middle of the night. Campervan was parked the other side of the stables. At daybreak Dez wandered over to tiredly tell me that Jay had started, and he left Ben with me. We phoned his Nan.

That part of the mission accomplished I told Ben that he could watch a DVD on my laptop while we waited. The caravans had no telly: it was only with Emma and I that Ben got telly treats. But first he had to help me take Titan and Herbert to their paddock. Ben had less fear of the horses than I.

* * *

Ben was well into his cartoon, looked up blank from the screen when his Nan arrived. I walked with her over to the caravans where she straightaway took charge, put in another call to the midwife, who was already on her way.

"Stop worrying," the midwife told Emma after she'd examined Jay. "Good healthy girl yours." A young woman the midwife had the same estuarine glottal stops as Emma.

"She missed so many appointments," Emma said.

"Not all necessary." The midwife, thick blonde hair knotted back, nursed her mug of flowery tea. "Makes a good strong brew does Dez."

Emma didn't want to hear anything positive about him.

"Wouldn't have a scan," she turned to me. "What she think technology's for?"

"Had to dredge up a few old-fashioned skills," the midwife said. "Made easy by your daughter being such a healthy young woman."

The midwife smiled at me as Emma went striding off looking for a mobile signal to call her work. I returned to my campervan to see if Ben had tired of DVDs yet.

* * *

Jay gave birth to a girl just after lunch. Ben wasn't impressed when Dez came across to fetch him. I told Ben that he could watch the end of his fourth DVD after he had said hello to his new sister.

"What's she like?" I asked him when he came running back.

"Purply-pink," he said, resuming his position, belly down on the van sofa, laptop before him. "Bit squashed. They said you can go see her now."

I pressed play and left the little square eyes to it.

* * *

Even basted in sweat Jay was still beautiful. And the blanket-wrapped baby purply-pink.

"Tell her," Emma, uncomfortably squashed up against Dez in the caravan's small bedroom, told Jay. "Go on, tell her."

By Jay's frown this wasn't the time and place of her

choosing to tell me anything. But she said, "We were thinking of maybe calling her Hazel. If you don't mind?"

Strangely the suggestion didn't strike a chord of any kind, neither had me in sentimental tears nor even mildly affronted. Rather I felt sorry for Jay being put on the spot by her clumsy mother.

"Kind of you," I heard myself say. "Don't want to lumber the poor little mite though. Wouldn't it be better, if she's got to have a tree's name, and given your height and Dez's, and your mum's, wouldn't Willow be more suitable? Then you could have Hazel as a second name if you still want."

By Jay's smile up at me, babe hefted in her arms, I knew I'd said the right thing. Then the midwife tried to squeeze back into the bedroom and, pleased with myself, I left.

As I wandered back to my campervan I mulled over what had just happened, my emotional remove from it, and decided that it had to be because I was getting old, life's dramas all behind me, never again to betray or be betrayed by love. Because – and I can remember thinking this as I looked down one of Dez's polytunnels between the neat rows of holly seedlings – I had failed at love. I hadn't been able to save the one person I had unconditionally loved.

"Done with, finished," were the three words I dispassionately said to myself. "Done with, finished." I was now what I was. No more battles to be what I guessed – and it had only ever been a guess – what I wanted to be. "Done with, finished."

Time to send Ben to bother his Nan.

The baby girl got called Jennifer Hazel.

* * *

bullfinch, white rump,
turns among naked branches
pink breast like a blush

Fifty-six

I can mark my increased involvement with Prospectus from when Gustaf won a haiku prize and wanted to go to Japan to receive it. Until that point mine had been a semi-formal role; as a favour I helped out with Gustaf's admin and volunteered for those work groups I enjoyed. Or, if asked, I went along to assist Dez or Gustaf with their groups, even babysitting for Jay if Emma couldn't make it.

Although a lot happened in those years, and I did a lot, in retrospect I hadn't seemed to be involved. Numb years. And I am talking years. The work, if it can be called that, was what one does with and for friends, and was what allowed me to stop overnight in woodland carparks.

That changed with Gustaf's plans to go to Japan.

To go all that way solely for the prize-giving ceremony seemed an extravagance: Gustaf wanted to see the country and to sample the culture as well. Prospectus was already such a part of my life that it took no persuasion on his part for me to agree to become a Prospectus trustee.

I was taken to meet some of my fellow trustees – a retired solicitor, a charity consultant, a one-time forester... They were told that I would have Gustaf's executive powers while he was in Japan. And of course once I'd agreed, once Gustaf had sensible me to sign cheques and deal with Forestry bureaucrats, his Japanese plans grew. Next thing we knew his band was going with him, gigs booked from Hokkaido to Osaka.

* * *

"Why a band?" I asked him once. He said that haiku alone had a limited audience. At one time he had thought to widen their appeal by having photos accompany his haiku, "...the instant twice captured. Except it didn't. The photo was just a photo. Point of focus singular. Image distinct from the onlooker. Incorporating haiku with the band though –

music, place, audience – brings something else to haiku altogether."

The kind of conversations I had with Gustaf I couldn't have with anyone else.

"Still don't get why haiku?" I said.

"Capture the universal in the particular. Where the particular meets the universal it becomes more than itself. But only so many times in a life one can manage that. So it's back to work."

We were thinning ash saplings that day. Which made it a non-specific woodland conversation. Not the kind we had when I accompanied Gustaf to meetings with council officials – sometimes to put our case for a grant, sometimes seeking permission for a change of land use, which would depend on how the proposed woodland, or possibly already conservation woodland, fitted with the council's local plans, budget predictions.

Also as part of the preparation for when I was to deputise for Gustaf I only had to ask and I got sent on a course – on woodland management, on silviculture. More often though I was dispatched to look up Forestry regulations, to investigate grants...

Even before the trip to Japan had been mooted Gustaf had had me undertake all Prospectus dealings with the Swedish manufacturer of a board cutter.

"Whoever they send always assumes I'm Scandinavian, if not Swedish. And I have to explain, every time, in slow English, that I'm not. It gets tedious."

* * *

His trust in me seemingly proven Gustaf sent me off on my own to investigate three separate strands of sycamore, large *bifurcal* sycamores in some hillside woods. Without, so far as I know going to check himself, Gustaf accepted my recommendation that Prospectus purchase the two strips of land between so that we could amalgamate the three stands.

He also sent me to research the use of large grazing animals in some woodland ecologies. Long-horned English cattle seemed favourite. Picturesque too.

And before leaving for Japan Gustaf took me to inspect the square plantations of spruce on the plain. He gave me the names, contact details of the contractors used for the planting and the felling, told me which nurseries to use and to take Dez with me to assess the health of any nursery-bought trees.

Our last outing together before he left was to look over a gale-damaged larch plantation. We both remarked on the amount and density of the pale green lichen.

* * *

While Gustaf was gone I stayed in the house, even got to drive the yellow pickup. Depending that is on where Dez and I were working. Most days I left the pickup with Dez. And all went well.

Gustaf was so appreciative that on his return he, or rather his accountant, suggested that I keep my executive powers.

It seemed a natural progression: even before the Japan trip had been proposed I had been brought into discussions on the purchase of new machinery, or whether Prospectus should take on a new project. And I had listened to Ian enough to know that in business one should always hearken unto one's accountants. The Prospectus accountants, trustees too, had been badgering Gustaf for years to formalise Dez and Jay's standing with Prospectus beyond their grace and favour caravans.

Because of Lungren Gustaf had got in the habit of not telling anyone where all his money was held. I suspected even back then that that included his accountants. This near paranoid secretiveness had almost become a character trait. However, and albeit with Gustaf's frowning blessing, and resisting pressure from our retired solicitor, my first executive act was to make Dez and Jay tenants of

Prospectus. I got them a ninety nine year lease, with the expectation that Ben and Jen could take over the tenancy if they so wished.

Before that I had asked Gustaf why he hadn't offered the wage he proposed for me – with Ian's pension I had no need of it – to Dez. Given only the state of their clothes Dez and Jay could certainly have done with the money.

"They were both adamant that they wanted to live without money. And they still, you've heard them, boast of the years they've spent managing without money. That is until Ben arrived. Amazing the stuff a baby needs these days that only money can buy. Even so I had to force the minimum wage on them. And they never, on principle still, put in a timesheet. And do you think I could persuade Dez to undertake the admin? He hates admin more than me."

Gustaf had told me some of that in Dez's presence. Just to me Gustaf said, "Dez knows his trees, but he has little business sense. Can't see the wood for the..?"

And Gustaf was right. Before one really got to know the pair of them one might readily assume, based on Gustaf's outspokenness on oh-so-many topics, that Dez was the down-to-earth, the sensible one. Until Dez came out with something in all seriousness like, "We could have acorn bread. Sliced and unsliced. Healthier than all those chemically-treated fields of wheat and barley."

A proposal easily destroyed by asking just how many oak trees would be needed to supply the whole nation with acorn bread? Our formal trust meetings – local worthies in attendance, me the minute-taker – occasionally verged on farce. The time, for instance, when we were deciding to do away with some spruce plantations.

There had been two big fires that summer. Gustaf proposed that we go over entirely to larch – larch being less likely to combust in a lightning strike. Dez, who regardless of the topography always favoured natural regeneration, started going on about Prospectus becoming 'control mad'.

"Control?" Gustaf said. "It's not control. We're in league

with vegetable anarchy. Conifers were here before the dinosaurs…"

What followed was an un-minuted and heated debate on conifers-versus-ferns: "Define conifers."

* * *

Dez and Jay's idealism however was attractive to the local groups who sought Prospectus out. Those concerned local residents banding together to save a green space from a developer saw Dez and Jay as a most welcome change from profit-driven businessmen and their pushy representatives.

As those early days of Prospectus were also those of carbon storage the new woodlanders often found themselves pushing at open doors. Providing, that is, Prospectus had sufficient in the coffers. Because in that pre-bust property boom, developers rampant, Prospectus was asked to take on far more than just Gustaf and Dez could manage. Even by the time of my arrival most new acquisitions were either scrub gone mad, seedling or old root runners regenerated, or if a one-time deliberately started woodland nothing might have been planted for centuries. Which I was to discover was at that time most of England's unofficial recreational woodland, either untended coppice with a mix of big and small trees; or mature plantations, conifer or deciduous, high forest with its straight stems.

Whatever new land we took on, no matter how Prospectus had acquired the acreage, what we straightaway set in motion was to place it under a covenant, one that contained within it the words 'in perpetuity'.

The words offered no guarantee against future exploitation. But as Gustaf said, "Though a covenant can always be argued against, point is it'll need to be argued against. And that'll take time, and time to them is always money."

* * *

Dez, I came to realise, was reluctant to interfere in any natural process, preferred to let be. So he often objected to Prospectus doing anything, anything at all, and he would seek reasons to justify his objection. Which led to my minutes on occasion bearing near philosophical statements. This, lifted from my minutes, is one of Gustaf's.

'Prospectus is not offering a viable alternative way of life. We all know that this is our one planet and that it needs looking after. We also know that we can't grow enough food in England to feed everyone in England. 75% of arable land in England is given over to farming, 12% to woodland. Throughout the world there's already too many of us and too little arable land. Land misused. The poor, the uneducated, have too many children. If we were to raise their standard of living, if we were to educate them, their birth rate would fall. We also know that the world's power-educated politicians won't do that. So we plant trees.'

* * *

Gustaf had got the contract for some roadside planting – along both sides of a new bypass. Which had upset Dez. He had refused to have anything to do with it.

"We're encouraging them. Well... not encouraging, but being a part of their seeing more roads as a solution to the traffic problems they create – by having more roads."

We hadn't had the resources, the trees to fulfil any future roadside contracts. And, truth be told, although it had been a profitable business venture, neither Gustaf nor I had relished working either side of a four-lane bypass planting token trees as screening for the unwelcome road.

* * *

Many of the trees we planted at this time were cherry. Because, and it amused me, Gustaf had returned from Japan more taken with their variety of cherry trees than with any Zen poetic enthusiasm for their blossom festivals.

* * *

path through cherry wood
chunks of nougat quartz
laid as hardcore

Fifty-seven

The edible cherry, *prunus avium*, has been with us in England a long time. But best to begin by not confusing *prunus avium* with *prunus padus*. *Padus*, despite is non-avian name, is the bird cherry, its fruit small and dark, its bark smooth. *Prunus avium* is the edible cherry, and that is the cherry that we celebrate.

Called *guina* in Italy, *gaen* in Scotland, *mazard* throughout the rest of Europe, in England the fat red fruit of *prunus avium* was traditionally looked forward to and harvested by the poor and, back then, made into tarts and jams. While nowadays cherries are more likely to be converted to cough syrups.

One-time landed gentry planted cherry within their estates solely for its delicate white blossom. The birds appreciated the summer fruit and further spread the seeds. Now, although preferring chalk, cherry grows pretty much anywhere in England.

Favoured for both fruit and blossom many varieties of cherry have been developed. A good fruiter is *prunus sargentii*, brought here from the Japanese mountains. *Sargentii* though is the exception: most Japanese varieties are grown for their blossom. And most common of these, the one to be seen in many pubs and gardens, is the excessively pink *prunus kanzan*. *Kanzan* is grown in England mostly by grafting onto wild cherry rootstock.

Varieties of Japanese cherry have had whole books written about them. I'm with Gustaf in preferring the later white flowering strains, *shirofugen* and *shiritae, Fuji* too.

With or without fruit or blossom, cherry's copper-coloured trunk can be readily identified by its cork circles, like perforations, rising one above the other. These are known as *lenticels*, breathing pores,

A wholly beneficial tree the cherry supplies us not only with pretty blossom and edible fruit; its timber is also prized by furniture makers. Being both hard and strong, cherry wood – lustrous brown with hints of gold and green – gets sliced thinly for veneers.

Fifty-eight

Although I continued to stay on and off at Gustaf's house, whether he was there or not, I still preferred my campervan stays in woodland carparks.

I kept meaning to, still mean to, come by a compass so that I can know straightaway where to park so that the rising sun will shine in through the back window and the later sun will be on my sliding side door.

I aired my frustration at so often getting my 'feng shui' parking wrong to Dez. He told me that all I had to do was walk into the wood and see what side of the trunks the moss and the lichen was on.

"Should mostly be on the south side." And if no lichen, no moss, he said, say it is a well-drained beech wood, then I should look for sun-scorch. Sun-scorch too will predominately be on the south side.

So, south-facing having been established, picture me on a fine morning sitting on my fold-up chair beside the van's slid-open side door (to let out the sleep smells), mug of tea cooling on the step and me closing my book as that day's work group start to drive in. I will pass the time of day with the first arrivals and, once the group seems complete, I will launch into that day's spiel. Be it on ditch clearing, pruning, path making/repairing, pruning, thinning, or measuring trees prior to thinning.

"For timber we want straight trunks. So not too much

thinning or we'll find growths starting on the side of trunks. These are called epicormic shoots, stimulated by light." I do so relish saying epicormic.

And on I'll go, the spiel by now emerging from its own neural channels: "What we're after is continuous cover. Not to make the woodland dark like in a spruce plantation, but just so there are no gaps in the summer canopy. To decide which trees to fell we're going to measure the tree's diameter at breast height. That's your breast height," a smile here, "not mine." And I show them a Hoppus tape.

There are other methods of measuring, of assessing the volume of timber in a tree, even in a whole woodland, but the Hoppus tape is enough to get and keep most groups interested.

* * *

Day's work done we will troop back to the carpark, them making plans for the evening, and I will open up the campervan, be aware of their cars leaving, and – if not already decided – consider what to cook for myself later. I might make myself a mug of tea, switch on the radio, glance out to any post-work dog-walkers arriving.

More often the radio stays off and, once alone, I will again sit outside and listen to the wood's noises – the whisper-whisper of a crow's wings, the bursting song of the blackbird, a distant woodpecker's yaffle, the creaking call of finches…

Once dark has settled in I will close up the van and take myself to bed knowing that I will wake to dawn breaking apart the eastern sky, and with who knows what wild creature looking in at me. Fingers crossed not a grey squirrel, arch enemy of silviculture.

* * *

At Prospectus meetings Dez often found some way of questioning my travelling about the country. The minutes of one meeting say that Gustaf will try to persuade local groups to take 'total management responsibility' for their woodland. Dez's proposal being that all we would then have to do would be to keep a watching brief.

The minutes say that I volunteered to keep the watching brief.

We each had our pet causes.

Despite Dez's carbon footprint misgivings, Prospectus's scattered holdings meant that we had no option but to travel. For instance one February I made a cross-country trip with Jay to pull up fences that had been weighted down with snow, letting deer into that plantation. Jay would rather that she and I make that slippery winter journey and have Prospectus go to the expense of high deer fences than slaughter Bambi.

It's no good: I have to confess to my having become increasingly exasperated with Jay and, in particular, Dez. Even to loud sighs down my nose whenever Dez came up with yet another half-baked objection at our meetings.

Has to be said that, like many good-looking people, Dez and Jay saw themselves in romantic roles. Whatever each their good-looking idea of romance is. I had known from the beginning that if Jay and Dez hadn't had the confidence that comes from having good looks they wouldn't have taken to living in the woods. And when Gustaf came across them, if they hadn't been such a good-looking pair would he have offered them the caravan alternative to their 'alternative' way of life?

There was however no heat in my occasional exasperation with their idealistic naivety. That the good-looking start with an advantage was something I'd long known. The confidence it gives them – to be different, to be whatever they want to be. Would Dez and Jay have tried dreadlocks if both hadn't known they could carry them off? Such unconscious self-confidence meant that they could be whatever they imagined themselves to be.

And this is something I have known all my short dumpy life, have just never felt the need to put it into words before.

I do wonder though how deep the self-knowledge of the beautiful people goes?

And let's be clear, theirs is not vanity. Life has taught them that they're good-looking – from bonny babyhood through to being the one sought as schoolfriend. Not the seeker. They are the one who turns heads, not the one sneakily turning to look. The good-looking, the attractive, from infancy onwards accept their status, are not forced to question. Consequence being that they take up causes, adopt creeds like clothes knowing that they'll look good in them.

Like most good-looking people Dez and Jay believed in love. In being in love, in love renewed. While to me love had been but a sexual habit. But there were those two, once at home, forever touching and kissing. And yes, it was something I liked to see, but it hardly applied to me. Their romantic reality was so different to mine. To Gustaf's too. We worked at what we saw, external to ourselves, at other than ourselves, had to suss our part in it. If any.

* * *

thanks to an evening sun
fresh oak galls are being
pinked into fat quinces

Fifty-nine

When I did occasionally stay with Gustaf we were still like an old married couple. Except that we probably didn't bicker as much as an old married couple and, with more of ourselves to tell – exactly why we had done such and such, had believed so-and-so – we probably talked more than such a pair. Once Hazel had left home Ian and I could go a whole weekend on just nods and grunts.

Possibly the reason Gustaf and I talked quite so much, aside from our still working out each other's bottom line values, was that very human desire to explain ourselves to those closest to us. Or, as here on this page, to our own selves.

So did Gustaf read this to me from a book one evening. (I've since looked for the quote, can't find it, think I've remembered it aright.)

"Dulled is the mind that accepts, that does not investigate physical phenomena. Thus do the sciences and the arts spring from the same curiosity."

Not that he had been pressing a particular point on me, more likely that on the page his own thoughts had been spoken, or it had neatly encapsulated some science-v-art argument he'd been having that day with one of the volunteers. Could even have been a couple days prior: he did tend to dwell did Gustaf. And suspicious of all group thought, of easy argument, Gustaf's was an instinct, an impulse for counterconformity.

For instance, and as I've said before, he loathed Margaret Thatcher, cursed her whenever her name cropped up – whether in woodland conversations, on the telly or the radio. I asked him why he hated her quite so much.

"She was a fraud. Presented herself as principled, as business-friendly. She was neither. Hers was political egotism pure and simple. Just one more party politician, much like our current leader, another devaluer of democracy."

Once started on her Gustaf couldn't stop, a brief pause, and off he'd go again: "She had no business brain, a poor understanding of science, did solely what the multinationals and her shopkeeper prejudices told her."

That was always his starting point with Thatcher: "No business brain. She didn't get what drives business. Like all Westminster politicians she was pro-shareholder, not pro-business. Probably because she was born privileged. While we, that is individuals from the underclass, from the underclass and not prepared to be the underclass, we have always had to battle against the well-connected elite."

Thatcher was by no means the only party politician

Gustaf despised: "We who keep a weather eye on politics have to listen to the old farts, repetition by unchallenged repetition, building themselves into legend."

I had some sympathy with those views. Gustaf did though have some odd ideas, views I was suspicious of, wondering at their origins, his 'pseudo-feminists' for instance.

Now I'm no wanting-to-be-as-a-man feminist ready and eager to take offence. I just won't be treated as a lesser being – by anyone, be they male or female, officialdom or any other snotty individual. And it wasn't that Gustaf had that male ego that doesn't believe a woman's life complete until she has him in it.

Although I did overhear him once saying, "A man knows he is beyond old when girls no longer preen before him."

Ah diddums.

* * *

Gustaf said that he had to talk to me as he never knew what I was thinking. Which is why I'm writing this, because I didn't know what Hazel was thinking. Or, even, what I was thinking.

Both Hazel and I met the world with an unexpressive face. No actorish grimaces from us. Having no knowledge back then of her biological physiognomy I had to assume that Hazel had based her straightfacedness on Ian and I. Ian's one other facial expression, as if he had spent his life waiting to be told what to do, was a pair of lifted eyebrows.

Gustaf and I had no agenda: most of our evening conversations were built on something overheard, or said, that day. Gustaf for instance explaining to someone how the topography decides how land is to be used. That day he'd been comparing South and North America. South America's topography, he had claimed, required a collective, a co-operative approach, an environment to be lived with rather than, as was happening in North America, imposed upon.

"In fact," he elaborated that evening, "being exploited

to extinction for the benefit of a few wealthy corporations."

No subject was out of bounds. One evening I asked why he hadn't gone looking for Moira when he had learnt that baby Hazel was to be put up for adoption.

"I liked Moira. She was fun, happily unconventional. Her being not that intelligent though meant I couldn't stand her company for more than a couple of days at a time."

One day we were in the yellow pickup, stuck at some traffic lights. Gustaf nodded to a concrete lavatory on a patch of green, hornbeam and verbena shielding its male and female entrances. I thought Gustaf was going to say something about the trees.

"One of Lungren's cottages," he said.

"How d'you know?"

"He beat somebody up in there. Police were called."

So open was Gustaf with me that I got to wondering if he knew that, when tucked away in my campervan and flat, I was writing this. He certainly seemed to talk to me at times as if to a fellow writer. Or was it because in my writing this that my questions had become pertinent? I now knew the struggle required to find the right description and so he, sensing sympathy, felt at ease in talking at length about his writing?

"A poem, like a tree, is a growth," he said. "It will happen, needs no stimulus other than itself, than the desire for it to come into being."

Another time: "I want my poems to take to themselves a life of their own. Where my authorship is almost overlooked. Almost."

"There are poems, whole novels even, by those who only have language, who are capable only of verbal trickery."

"Literature cannot be about a whole life. The absolute best it can achieve is to give instances of that life."

Hazel would have liked to hear him talk about his poems. It even got me doing a search for the rules of Japanese poetry. Then discovering what other languages had made of haiku made me aware that, among the peoples of this world, there were no absolutes. Some peoples read from left to right, some from right to left, some from top to bottom. Consequently the many updates and contradictions surrounding haiku in the end seemed to come down to just one rule – 'make the ordinary amazing.'

"What's your ambition with your poetry now?" I asked Gustaf.

"What it's always been – to resonate in another's mind, create a sympathetic lodging for my words there. Possibly to clarify their thoughts for them. Which is a big ask for a little haiku."

Gustaf was by no measure self-aggrandising. For instance he later stopped me on the stairs to say, "There's a fundamental falsity to every writer. They know that everything they do is artificial, that everything about them therefore inevitably becomes artificial."

A couple days of his thinking later had him pause by me, his chainsaw on idle. Pushing his visor up he said, "The sense of what is being said is of more importance to me than how it is being said."

"Oh," I said, logs weighting my arms. "Right you are."

* * *

Although I told myself that we were friends I nevertheless found that friendship hard to accept. What, I asked myself, is friendship? It couldn't be only timeworn familiarity. I had been familiar with Ian and that had driven me nuts. Whereas even Gustaf's irritating habits, his occasional bombastic delivery, I accepted as part and parcel of the man. Was it gratitude? Because he'd brought me out of desolation? Or was it his zero expectations of me? Gustaf's was certainly the more enlivening company.

In an odd way, things he said, through knowing Gustaf I started to make sense of myself. But if at any time I got tired of his blathering then, like an old married couple, I took myself off. If we'd been married it would've been to another room; in my case it was back to my campervan and to a woodland carpark, possibly even back to my flat – to get myself thoroughly clean, laundering all my clothes. Even doing some baking. For old times' sake.

After a few days in the flat however – shopping done, campervan stores replete – a physical craving would come over me. To be out of doors again, unconfined, to feel air moving past me. So see me draw up in a woodland carpark and sit there a moment, after all the forwards motion of the drive there letting the stillness settle around me. Then I open the van door, step down and take deep lungfulls of oxygen-rich air.

First task usually was to replenish the carpark birdfeeders. Some woods I might just wander about bagging up litter. Any fly-tipped metal I'd make a note for Gustaf or Dez to collect. Even then I'd be aware of my wearing an incipient smile: I had come home.

* * *

When close by I called in at the burial ground. Although the burial ground was the only place I was drawn back to it wasn't the only place I revisited. The others I happened to find myself at. As with Ian's crash site.

The road had been resurfaced, hedge regrown. I didn't bother stopping and going into the field. And as I drove on I wondered why I'd made that first visit. Had it been to try and feel something? Grief? Despair? Something?

But I had looked at the ordinariness of it all – broken down hedge, tracks, bashed Scots pine, wilted bouquet – and I had felt, if anything, and as usual with Ian, irritation verging on exasperation. Which hadn't been enough to justify my having gone there.

My return to the rhodie carpark had an altogether different effect. Actually I hadn't first realised, because the rhodies were no more, that it was the rhodie carpark. Now there were vistas off between the trees.

To justify my staying there a couple of nights I set about putting up some bat boxes. And I wrote quite a bit of this there, found myself sitting back from the page and wondering if these chaffinches squabbling about the feeders were the offspring of those I'd so long ago thrown crumbs to while waiting for Hazel.

* * *

woodsmoke, saw-buzz, scent of sap
infiltrating the furthest glade

Sixty

Hornbeam, *carpinus betulus*, takes its name from Olde English, 'horn' meaning hard and 'beam' meaning tree.

Where hornbeam grew naturally in the South of England its toleration of pollarding meant that in pre-industrial times it kept the then much smaller population supplied with firewood. Their cattle also browsed on its new shoots.

As durable as iron hornbeam was then used as mill cogs, and for the hammers in old-fashioned, that is mechanical, pianos. Those olde time uses of hornbeam have however long been superseded. These days wire fencing has pretty much replaced hornbeam hedges – I've been told there might yet be a few in the South-East – and plastic and metal are now preferred to hornbeam tool handles. Even butcher's blocks, where hornbeam was once the only wood hard enough to bear a cleaver's daily bashing, now those blocks are made of a dense polyurethane.

A fully grown hornbeam can easily be mistaken for beech, its trunk being a silvery-grey and its leaves a similar shape. Except that hornbeam's trunk doesn't have the round smoothness of beech but tends to coiling ribs, commonly called flutes. Most hornbeam though can nowadays be found gracing those roadside verges where a fat candle-flame-type tree is required.

* * *

Viburnum lantana, the Wayfaring Tree, despite its common name is not actually classed as a tree. More a shrub. Although, given its circumstances, a deep hedgerow say, if left untrimmed viburnum can grow up to four metres.

Viburnum leaves are pale green, soft and fleshy. The flowers are a flat plate of white florets, in autumn becoming red-going-black berries.

More often found in hedgerows than woodland, and these days as often planted as occurring naturally; but so common and widespread is viburnum that it is also known as Twistwood and the Mealy Tree. Despite this latter name one would be advised not to make a meal of either its soft leaves or its berries as both can cause vomiting and diarrhoea.

A reason for viburnum having so many names and being so widespread is that its stems pre-gunpowder were used for arrow shafts. While these days, as with that concrete public lavatory, fleshy-leafed viburnum is more often than not used to screen that which is deemed unsightly.

Sixty-one

It was Jay had to phone me. Dez did sometimes use his mobile, but reluctantly, mobiles being too twenty-first century for him. Even though the far-flung nature of our work made mobiles a necessity.

I'd been parked up in one of our northern woods, mostly because I liked the wood's carpark. Well hidden from the closest roads it had a view down the valley through the treetops. I'd been tapping away on my laptop – versions of this – and watching jays fetching and burying acorns, great tits chiselling open cob nuts.

"Not heard the news?" Jay asked.

"What news?"

I didn't usually turn the van radio on until lunchtime, and then not always. Although I did make a point of catching the telly news at ten. Not that I needed to: going online for emails I'd half-note headlines being bannered across.

But wanting that morning to get on with this book I'd given myself a rest from emails. And it had been one of those sharp clear autumn mornings, hint of frosts to come. I'd taken a pre-breakfast stroll part way down the valley, had stopped to poke about in one of the jay's acorn hoards, to lift flat-topped fungi, see if they were edible. Dez would've known: I was never certain, never confident enough to add them to the pan.

"There's been an accident," Jay said. "Well... not an accident. It's been on all the news. There was a fire..."

At mention of an accident I'd thought of Ian, and then when Jay had said 'not an accident, a fire' my assumption had been that one of our plantations had caught fire. Which, in Jay's pause, had me more puzzled than concerned: woodland fires belonged to summer droughts, not wet autumns.

"It's Gustaf," Jay said. "He was in the club. You haven't heard?"

"No."

"A cellar club."

I picked back through my memory, recalled possible mention of Gustaf's upcoming gigs. Hadn't been a clash of dates so I hadn't paid much attention.

"Survivors say he was instrumental in getting everyone out. Without panic. As the place was filling with smoke. He stayed on the mike... Gustaf didn't get out."

* * *

Jay didn't now know what to do, who needed to be told, wanted me back in the fold.

As I packed up, got everything safely stowed, searched for roads south, I had on the news channels.

'Gustaf Eriksson, performance poet and one-time pop promoter of the band Yellow Black... as the cellar club began to fill with smoke he stayed on the mike telling club members to make for the green light at the far end of the club. Not to push, not to shove, not to panic... he and two of the other band members got cut off by the explosion. One band member got through the flames... Five people died including... One of the surviving band members is in hospital with 60% burns...'

The irony that Gustaf's most important work, Prospectus, hadn't so far rated a mention in one news report would have had Gustaf – I can see him now – wearily, wryly, accepting his media fate.

That he had died a hero almost had me smile. Was the kind of death he might have imagined for himself. Although straightaway I hear him saying, with that big man's loud confidence, that he would rather have stayed alive a coward.

* * *

By the time I pulled up at chez Gustaf the radio pundits had pretty much decided that a faulty air-conditioning unit had been the cause of the fire, and that a lamentable lack of regard for the emergency exits was responsible for the five deaths. 'An inquest will determine the exact causes.'

"Eventually," I added, recalling how long it had taken for Ian's inquest to be held.

Sixty-two

For hospitals a death is just another event in their busy day. Was Gustaf's death going to be just another death in my life? No. Gustaf's was a life incomplete, so many tasks left undone, projects unfinished, unbegun. Unlike Hazel Gustaf hadn't known that he was about to die. There was another kind of poignancy to Gustaf's passing.

But, and though Gustaf's was to have as much if not more of an effect on my life than Hazel's or Ian's, I did feel distant from Gustaf's death, not emotionally connected to it.

Even though I had far more to do with the post-death processes.

This time, Jay being wrapped up with the baby, it was me who had to deal with the many bureaucratic ramifications of Gustaf's death. For instance, because the death was deemed newsworthy, it was me, the Prospectus trustee at the house, the stand-in manager, who had to fend off reporters. I even got to stand in front of a camera and stutter out, "Gustaf Eriksson has devoted this latter part of his life and his fortune to the reforestation of England."

Gustaf's death was made the more newsworthy by there having initially been a suspicion of terrorism, the fire having taken so quickly and there having been an explosion. To those questions, "Did Gustaf Eriksson have any enemies?" the Prospectus solicitor had me repeat, "Not that any of us here are aware of."

The post mortem established that Gustaf had died from smoke inhalation. Or so I was quietly told by our trustee doctor, retired, who had it from a friend of a friend. The inquest, like Ian's first, was opened and immediately adjourned to await further reports; and Gustaf's body was released for burial.

An emergency Annual General Meeting of The Tree Prospectus was called. Because I had so successfully held the fort while Gustaf had been in Japan, but mostly because I knew more about Gustaf's peculiar concept of admin, I was there and then voted chairwoman of the trustees, with my becoming managing director already being mooted. So, although I continued to feel emotionally distant from Gustaf's death – "Poor Gustaf" would be all that I would manage to say at his funeral, not one tear – the effect of his death on my life was to be huge.

* * *

I had stayed at, had more or less moved into, Gustaf's house – just to answer the never-stopped ringing phone. With everything happening so fast, decisions being asked of me,

I had at best a few quiet moments for reflection. By end of each day I was so exhausted that sleep came like a shutter closing. To be woken at daybreak by the ringing phone.

Over a coffee on my own, however, waiting for someone to call back, I'd think, tell myself, "Gustaf is dead." And I'd find myself naming the other dead I'd known, including café regulars, Franny too; and if there seemed too many important deaths in my life I told myself that every life has to contain some deaths. Is bound to. Not everyone can be born at the same time to die in one's own old age. And there's bound to be accidents like Ian's, misfortunes like Hazel's, and tragedies like Gustaf's.

Even accepting that every life must have its share of death, with Gustaf now getting killed I did feel particularly hard done by. That Ian had gone and got himself killed in a car smash was, because so predictable, almost readily acceptable, if not deserved. While Hazel's dying had been the sum of so many fears. But I had still been getting to know Gustaf, hadn't even imagined his dying.

Here too, trying to explain all these deaths, I tell myself that I truly am not morbidly inclined. I certainly don't want to inflict on you my death. Better to simply disappear, I have decided, to one day just not be here.

I started writing this, that has become this book, as an attempt to come to terms with the deaths of two loved ones. And, having spent a couple of decades caring what happened to him, I do count Ian as a loved one, even occasionally used the word love to him. Hazel I loved. Gustaf though…

When I started to write this Gustaf's was a death I hadn't anticipated. His was a life I couldn't with any confidence say that I knew, so different was it to mine. His death – the death of a man who, if I had not at times disliked him I was certainly wary of him – his death has left no sense of absence, only of discontinuance.

"Poor Gustaf."

* * *

Dez and Jay were stunned. And, with Gustaf gone, concerned for their future too.

"We crave a fundamental order to our lives," Gustaf had said, "no less than the predictability of the seasons. About which we change our routines. The small plans with which we order our days. Because, free as we might like to think ourselves, we are all trapped in habits, have expectations of continuity. Death is a rude surprise. An illness we can recover from, can at best be an irritation. Death is a stepchange. Can disorder everything."

He had been arguing with Dez, way before Hazel had died, when he couldn't have known about her condition. I remembered because I had tried to fit his words to our situation.

In this new step-changed present I put Dez and Jay's concerns to one side and I tried to get hold of Lungren, tell him about the funeral. I figured that if he was anywhere in the country he would have heard of his father's death. With the court injunctions stopping him coming anywhere near Gustaf's house, near Gustaf, I wanted to let him know that as Gustaf's only son none of those injunctions now applied.

"Why you bothering?" Dez asked me. "Man's a total shit."

"Who knows," I knew what it was to be opposed to one's parents, "he might've changed."

"Not him."

"Deserves a chance."

"Not him."

So miserable, so hangdog was Dez that I sent him off on an errand, got on with dispatching funeral invites. 'No flowers by request: donations to The Tree Prospectus'.

And the funeral? That had to be a woodland affair, and where else but the same hillside plot as Hazel? And his tree? Given the haiku that he'd been enthusiastically writing since his return from Japan, that had to be an English cherry.

Lungren didn't make it. I wondered if he'd left the

country. The walking wounded from the band turned up, so too two of Gustaf's occasional lady loves, both taller and better packaged than I, and seeming to be old friends. Both looked at me curiously.

I hadn't been able to get back to the flat for something smarter, had managed only to launder one of my tops and pop into town for a skirt (too small) and some black tights and heels.

I wobbled about between Dez and Jay, with Jay lurching to the left trying to restrain Ben. As the service (humanitarian) went on I managed to hide behind baby Jennifer. And I lost myself looking over to Hazel's poplar and wondering at her and Gustaf's life journeys that had ended with them both being buried on the same bleak hillside.

* * *

At the house after the funeral the blonde-streaked lady love came up to me and said that Gustaf had told her all about me, about my having lost Hazel, and of all the work I'd done for Prospectus. Which surprised me: I'd assumed that Gustaf, at Jay's behest, had just put up with me, had maybe grown to like having me around. I hadn't thought of myself as actively contributing to Prospectus, rather as having been allowed to help.

Jay and I had made sandwiches, had put out wine glasses and one of those tall press-on-the-top coffee flasks that Gustaf had got for trustee meetings. Gustaf's obituaries were mentioned, one even got read out.

That obituary must have been written while there had still been a suspicion that the fire and explosion might have been a terrorist attack. Gustaf himself was quoted: 'Terrorism itself undoes the justification for terrorism. All that the onlooker responds to is the damage and the deaths that the terrorist act has caused. No-one seems the least interested in why the terrorists claim to have committed the act, only with horror that they have chosen to act so.'

With coffee cup in hand, stood behind a chatting pair, other of Gustaf's words came to me: "Your obituary's the only free publicity you'll get." I forget where or why he said that.

* * *

Myself, Dez, Jay and four of the other trustees – retired accountant, solicitor, teacher and retired doctor – were taken into Gustaf's office for the reading of the will.

"Straightforward," our trustee solicitor interpreted for us. "Everything, lock stock and barrels if any, goes to Prospectus. That's it. Simplicity itself."

"That's what you think," I said, and indicated Gustaf's still piled high office. "It's me going to have to dig out all the lock, stock and barrels."

* * *

Heat haze wavers:
home pasture calf lies curled
in her mother's shade.

Sixty-three

A relief to be away from yet another meeting and back in my flat. Especially for my long soaks in the bath.

Those long soaks are the closest I've come to blanking out time. And if I did happen to be taking stock while soaking I wasn't actually aware of thinking.

Other than occasionally lifting my big toe to let in a little more hot water, once I'd shampooed my hair I didn't have anything else to do in the bath. I had years before, following Jay's example, stopped shaving my legs.

When I had first given up shaving the hairs had seemed luxuriantly black. Now they were only black when wet, and they seemed fewer.

I wondered if Hazel had spent more time with Jay then she too would have stopped shaving her legs. I doubted it.

Hazel hadn't been able to bear even a bristle, used to spend evenings smoothing lotions up and down her shins.

The one bath thought that I was aware of, my one fear that I kept returning to, was to wonder what, with Gustaf gone, I had let myself in for. Was Prospectus to become another of my life's ruts?

Lying in the bath, cooling water up to my chin, Prospectus didn't feel to have the makings of a rut. Three days at the flat so far and the phone hadn't rung. I'd even picked up the landline handset to see if it was connected, had checked my mobile to see if I had a signal.

The Prospectus solicitor had taken me aside to suggest that we needed, now that Gustaf was not there, to clarify the trust's constitution: would I seriously consider becoming managing director of the charity The Tree Prospectus? He could think of no-one else, he had said. But no-one was chasing me for a decision to be made. So I carried on pottering about the flat, going down with buckets of bleach to give the van a good clean.

And when that was done I was back indoors alone, as I had been after Hazel's death. My being alone this time though wasn't so telling. Rather I was aware of it as a peculiar absence. I have the feeling still. As if a rival has fallen at the first fence and I'm running on on my own. I still have the race to win; but where is everyone?

By day four I did think of phoning Dez to see what he was up to. But something held me back. I asked myself if my reluctance was simply that I needed a few more days holiday from Prospectus.

The money had all been sorted. That is so far as the accountant and I could tell. Because what Gustaf had told Hazel and I about his wealth hadn't been wholly true. He had had an extensive stock portfolio, which he left to Prospectus, whose funds had leapt. Nor were the stock portfolios all: he'd had funds secreted away under all manner of names and limited companies – inactive companies. Hidden away from Lungren if not from the taxman.

* * *

Doing nothing doesn't suit me. Seemed my brain had need of another project; and as none were presenting themselves the project my brain plumped for was to make a book of Gustaf's cherry haiku.

"I'd rather my works outlived me than me my works," Gustaf had said. The least I could do.

After his Japan trip Gustaf had written a whole haiku series on cherry trees. Not on cherry blossom as was, apparently, usual. I'd already looked into getting a booklet of them printed. But the one publisher I'd found in his address book had told me that the examples I'd sent weren't 'worked enough'. The publisher of his previous collection, the one Hazel and I had first seen, had gone out of business.

Not all the haiku were about cherry trees. That was just how I thought of them. A haiku enthusiast had, too soon after Gustaf's death, pestered me for permission to publish some of Gustaf's haiku. I'd been curt with him: his timing and his manner hadn't helped his cause. Now my dismissal of him had seemed to make me, by default, Gustaf's literary executor. Maybe, I told myself, that was what had been bubbling away during my daily bath soaks.

Even so I wasn't sure that I was the person best equipped to do it. I am too unlike Gustaf Eriksson. Gustaf took centre stage, whatever the stage. I prefer to be behind the scenes, if not sitting in the dark with the audience. Such timidity though wouldn't stop me putting a book together in his name.

When I had asked him why he persisted with the band he had said that he needed the recurrent reassurance necessary to fame. "Albeit my small fame. The applause, that pat on the back that tells me that I, Gustaf Eriksson, still exist."

I can remember thinking when I read somewhere that

'...Gustaf Eriksson has been numbered among the dead...' he would not have been pleased to find himself numbered among, not when most of his life had been give over to raising himself above a number.

"Gustaf Eriksson...?" a middle-aged Commissioner of Oaths said to me. "Wasn't he something to do with...?"

Words, sayings... All I had to do was look out of the flat windows, out over all the rain-glistened rooftops, to hear Gustaf say, "Without trees we have deserts." So I also wanted to include in the haiku book various other of his sayings, along with part-notes of his that I'd come across in my financial diggings. "I ally myself with trees. Trees will always win."

* * *

The idea of the book, my homage to Gustaf Eriksson, was what got me refreshing the water in the van, replenishing my supplies, and heading back up the motorway to Gustaf's house.

I only had a few of his haiku on my laptop, those I'd taken a fancy to, and I knew that he had more dotted about in various files on the Prospectus PC. And I'd come across some on scraps of paper, easily lost.

"Fire and fungus, a writer's nightmare," Gustaf had said.

* * *

among the aconites
one cherry blossom stuck
to a black beetle's back

Sixty-four

I may have allowed myself to become managing director but I was determined that I was not going to live in Gustaf's house. I didn't want his life, enjoyed my own, tootling from wood to wood in my campervan, occasionally popping back to my flat for rest and relaxation.

Although I'm not by any measure tall I always feel that I can stretch out in my flat, open my arms in a big yawn, lay starlike in the flat's double bed. Not overlooked, wholly private, hot water, wandering naked room to room I can indulge the every comfort of home.

Until my muscles feel soft, my lungs underused, and I am overcome with the need to get back to some physical work. Or just a change of scenery. I see myself setting out from the van, spade or saw in hand; or carrying hammer and nails to put up bird or bat boxes in some newish woodland... So off to a wood somewhere go the van and I.

To be greeted by early year sunlight travelling through woodland and touching amber to the sides of trunks, to some hanging catkins, newly uncurled beech leaves; all soaking up the post-rain sunlight.

It is by no means all work. I relish those days when it is too wet or windy to work. Then I make a point of taking myself off among the trees. Which is when I chance upon the wild creatures of the wood – a fox glancing my way and holding my gaze just long enough to determine my intent, prior to slipping away. Or I stand breath-held statue-still while a small herd of deer tread delicately by. I can even find myself smiling to see a grey squirrel floating S's across the ground, from winter store to the safety of the nearest trunk. Or, come dusk, I might just about catch sight of a grey badger rustling by.

And after each encounter I become aware that my face is wearing an inane grin.

That grin, however, was pretty rare back then. I kept having to pack up and go back to Gustaf's – if only to deal with phone enquiries and to use the Prospectus PC. There was no-one else to do it. All the other trustees had day jobs or, publicly spirited, they had other retirement commitments. So it fell to me.

For instance I had just set myself up in the middle of a Prospectus spruce plantations, near a grove of firebreak larch, where I had determined to crack on with Gustaf's cherry tree haiku.

I had hardly got started before I got called back to the house.

* * *

In case my complaints make it seem that I wasn't upset over Gustaf's death let me make it abundantly clear that I was. Even so Gustaf's death did not leave the ache of Hazel's. I was more angry on his behalf. His dying had been just so unnecessary. And I was puzzled as to where his death had led me, all these responsibilities I had been landed with.

* * *

I was at Dez and Jay's caravans one morning about to collect Dez – the yellow pickup having failed its MOT was in for repairs – when my mobile went, a patched-through call from Gustaf's landline, a forgotten form needing to be signed, which meant my having to go back to Gustaf's.

My exasperation all too evident it was Jay, watched by Dez, who asked, "You going to stick with Prospectus?"

"Not at this rate," I said. "Can never get away from the bloody place. No sooner do I get settled, think I can spend a few days here or there, than something else crops up. Always something."

What I didn't say was that it wasn't just the upset of my little plans, being MD meant my having to be around lawyers and accountants on the board of trustees. At breaks in meetings I'd hear all those dry little chuckles and think I was back living with Ian. When what I really wanted was to be back in a wood somewhere, parked up and clothed in birdsong.

This misanthropy, my estrangement, was nothing new. I have always, even in the café of my own creation, felt out of place, out of time. It has only been among trees that I have felt that I belonged. The moment that I'm under arching branches with on all sides tree beyond tree trunk beyond tree... feels like I've come home.

Through Hazel and Gustaf I have come to recognise my own kin, trees; and with that recognition the realisation that I probably always have been happier within woods, with their perspective of shrinking, narrowing verticals. Big views – gazing out over squared fields or unpeopled heathland – have never moved me.

My wanting to be off on my own makes it sound as if I was being wholly self-centred, maybe even ungrateful for all that Prospectus has done for me. Often though I was being interrupted while doing Prospectus work.

I'd made it part of my managerial brief to visit possible new sites, check out neighbouring land usages, find out who was responsible for boundaries and if us what clearance would be needed for neighbouring machines, for arable farmland's combine harvesters and the like. And it was surprising how much more I learnt about a place just by sleeping a couple of nights there. Although, truth be told, there was an element of selfishness: I'm never happier than when I'm striking out on my own.

One phone call though and back I'd have to come.

"Dez and I," Jay glanced to him, "been talking. Why don't we move over there? Crowded here now with the four of us. And Ben having to travel miles to school..."

I didn't have to think.

"Good idea," I said.

* * *

Of course it didn't happen just like that. Although we kept one downstairs room as the Prospectus office we had to clear out all the boxed files. We archived them into one of those lockable metal boxes, an obnoxious blue, like a half-size shipping container. We also had to get a stable ready for Titan and Herbert and rent a nearby field for them.

The stable came in kit form. Dez put it together while

Jay made ready a room each for Ben and Jen.

Finally they moved across, and for weeks Ben and Jen were taken with the novelty of flushing lavatories. While Dez, stable paddock cleared and completed, began wondering what he could make of the old, roof-collapsed outbuildings.

* * *

With Dez and Jay removed we had to get someone else into the caravans. At Jay's suggestion we didn't advertise the vacancy as a job but as a life choice. Of all the interviewees it was a pair of women, Robyn and Marie, who chose us and took up residence.

Both tree evangelists, both women the same height as me, stocky with short fat arms; both had piercings and came with a couple of Labradors. Robyn and Marie however didn't have Dez and Jay's self-mocking charm. Or had I become used to Dez and Jay's tree earnestness, took it as a given?

Then out of the blue, to us at least, Robyn and Marie had a falling out, lots of tears and self-agonising; and the caravans were again left empty. Until a Polish couple, Frederic and Sylvia, happened along. Can't quite remember how: friends of a friend of one of the trustees? Not that it matters because Frederic and Sylvia have become our mainstays.

"Ah yes, forest," Sylvia said. "Sylvia means wood."

In the years that have followed the sound of Frederic's motorbike negotiating potholes on the approach to my carpark will have me look to the windows of my van with a smile, expecting any moment to see their two shining helmets bobbing hellos to me.

Meanwhile back at the house I had Jay made a trustee, a signer of cheques and forms, and she soon proved herself a proficient fender-off of phone calls, kept in touch with me by email, and I was at last free. Or as free as I wanted to be.

* * *

badger and fox go
sniffing among leaf litter
for fallen cherries

Sixty-five

The last few years have seen so many changes. I even upgraded the campervan. Which is as nothing compared to what Dez has done at Gustaf's. He's become quite the builder.

It all started with Dez and Jay adapting Gustaf's house to themselves. That was when I was still using Gustaf's old office as Prospectus's headquarters. We none of us liked the blue iron archive box, sat outside like an alien artefact. So we were discussing various types of alternative outbuildings, none agreed on, when Prospectus was contacted by a university wanting to use Prospectus as a resource centre.

One of their basic requirements was for a meeting space with room enough for tables and chairs. Even though that initial approach came to nothing the idea grew. I investigated planning restrictions, and we have ended up with Dez building a series of wooden outbuildings that have now almost encircled the house.

To make space Dez had to demolish the still standing walls of the old farm buildings, orange sparks spraying out like fireworks as he cut through the rusted ironworks. No iron in the new. For the new all the timber has come from Prospectus woodlands; and I have to say here that has been done with 100% support from all at Prospectus.

Dez has fitted each new building with a ceramic woodburning stove, wired them not only for electricity but with powerpoints too – for the visiting professors of silviculture and their student entourages. The end result being that we are now held in such esteem that more than few professors have come seeking, if not research space or Prospectus funds, then our blessing for use in their funding applications.

Dez's enthusiasm for building has grown with each new construction, all subsequently linked. Always now some students spending their holidays as his helpers, one of the old bits of barn having been converted to a bunk house with sleeping platforms.

And with Dez locked into his various projects I'm more often out in the woods on my own with Sylvia and Frederic. Neither of whom are big talkers, which suits me.

Talk in Dez's workshop – self-built – is of lumber, timber, milling, going against or with the grain... "...less carbon is released when wood is used exclusively in building." Dez now makes all our footpath bridges. His woven bridge got a must-see mention in a tourist guide. The last of his bridges I saw under construction was an arched affair in the Chinese style.

To go to the house now is to be among excited young people. While their rapidity – of speech and movement – can have me flustered, I can say with confidence that Gustaf would have loved it. So many knowledgeable people to argue with. He might even have found himself back at his musical roots: just the other day I came upon a young woman sitting on a step and picking out a tune on a guitar.

Nor is it any surprise to come upon Dez with a couple of students experimentally shaping a trunk with an adze, or holding a conversation on either end of a double-handed saw. Though I must say I did flinch the day I came upon young Ben cleaving logs. Not that I needed to be overly concerned. Ben was by then already quite the woodsman. And he has both his parents' height and good looks, if no dreadlocks. I now see schoolgirls nudging one another towards him. Even some of the older students flutter around him.

* * *

As well as creating the resource centre Dez seems to have shed many of his reservations over Prospectus's moneymaking ventures. (Hmmmm... how people change.) For instance he jumped at my suggestion that we hire out our portable mill – he was after funding to wire one of his new buildings at the time – and when coppicing now we always make some charcoal, sell barbecue bags of it back at the centre.

Frederic and Sylvia, being more often in the woods, are partners to Dez and Jay in this enterprise.

Frederic and Sylvia are more homemakers than ever were Jay and Dez. Both caravans now have a pergola covering them, with honeysuckle, clematis and briars trained up over both roofs. And within the quarry Sylvia and Frederic have also made a large vegetable patch, a small lawn, flowerbeds, even a shrubbery.

* * *

Planning permission for all Dez's buildings hasn't been easy to come by. But I am nothing if not persistent. Dez and Jay now call me the juggernaut. In that I really do seem to have replaced Gustaf. Once my mind is set on a project, Look Out! they say.

Not that I have Gustaf and Dez's evangelical certainty. What drives me, and I suppose it is the same, is that it seems obvious to me that wherever there's been desertification and famine it's because all the trees have been cut down. Solution? Plant more trees. A job of work more than a mission.

One result of my juggernauting and Dez's building means that we now have the space where we can host conferences with other foresters. And, though I was initially nervous, the wonderful thing is that there is no competition. So long as more trees are being planted who they're being planted by is of little concern to us.

And having our own conference centre saves me having to go to meetings in the overheated botanical gardens. I remember trying to stay awake in one meeting, technicalities important to someone being droned on about while I stared out through glass at an ornamental willow – last to lose its golden leaves that were lying about the paths and lawns like so many stranded fish – my fear being that if I did fall asleep I might snore.

Another benefit of our being able to host meetings is that I don't have to go so often into city offices. I hate seeing myself in the crowds of towns, my one round head among all those other round heads. Singular me, not even a molecule, just one more atom adrift.

It's not that I'm like those romantics Dez and Jay, once Gustaf too, who place themselves in starring roles. If only in the theatre of their own minds. On their own all three are still less than one molecule. For me it is that in any crowd I feel less, and for reassurance at such times I tell my shrunken ego that what we are doing at Prospectus matters. No matter how apparently ineffectual and unending the doing.

Indeed the most frequently voiced concern at those conferences is frustration in living in a world so far beyond our control, of such slippage that we can realistically take no responsibility for it. We have to acknowledge that the best we can do is make amends. Slight amends.

For myself I know that I have no real stake in this civilised present. A few of us individuals may consider ourselves wise, but as a group we are still the clever and foolish apes who will destroy their environment and themselves. All our cities will become rubble. Eventually.

Allow the passing of one generation, however, and the forest will have begun to reclaim the land. Because trees persist. Seeds can lie dormant for decades if not centuries. Trees will even defy disease. Eventually. We have woods with elm suckers sending up new shoots metres away from the dead stalks of the parent elms. Trees persist.

We woodspeople at Prospectus are on the side of time. Granted in this country we have almost run out of defunct railway lines, slag heaps, opencast mining and the like to turn into woodland. Albeit that one of our latest projects is the planting out of an old and no longer viable airfield. Our thinking caps are occupied with what we can make of the moss-grown airstrips.

* * *

As a virgin site the airfield is the exception these days. Most of my summers now seem to be spent considering invitations for Prospectus to take over, or to become involved in, other people's woodland enterprises. All as different as the topography. So do we find ourselves working in tandem with other tree trusts, as well as with charities such as the RSPB and the Council of Lepidopterists.

Carbon Storage planting has long tailed off. The latest fad is for woodland pasture, catering to those who can still afford meat. One consequence of the global food shortage is that more and more of England's open fields are being given over to arable crops.

For the sake of the food shortage I'm in favour of the re-introduction of cattle into woods. Some cattle. Some woods. Dez is pleased to see pannage coming back into vogue.

His nostalgic harking back however does continue to irritate. I've taken every opportunity of late to say that the mission of Prospectus is to reverse Neolithic deforestation. Emphasis on the 'Neolithic'.

Equally of late Dez and one of his students have become more excited about growing fungi than forestry as such. They've bought inoculation kits and are in the process of setting up a business to sell to metropolitan delicatessens.

They have also been experimenting with making wine and shampoo from birch sap, along with insect repellent from the oil in birch bark. The tree has to have more uses other than 'good for logs'. As yet the enterprise hasn't made sufficient quantities to generate a realistic income, but it's fun for all involved, including Ben and Jen, who have made it a school marketing project.

***

Still though Dez has a moan about many of the uses I find for our woodlands. I remind him of what Gustaf used to say, "I bridle at 'Private' signs anywhere. Prospectus must encourage open access."

And being Gustaf he had a lot more of course to say on the subject, the gist of which was that there being no sense of community in England open access to woodland takes on increased importance. 'Opposing 'their' woodland's exploitation can unite people in a cause.' And he was always going on about 'the downward spiral of distrust that comes from ownership.'

Gustaf reckoned that owners who were frightened of all outsiders put up ever higher fences. The outsiders, the non-owners, to then get onto the land broke down fences and deliberately – an act of vengeful spite – left gates open. So, to protect their unpeopled property, the owners added barbed wire to the tops of the fences and padlocked the gates. The outsiders, even more resentful at being kept out of this unoccupied land, when they did manage to breach the fortifications, contemptuous now of the private property, left their mark by damaging it. Followed by bigger fences, more padlocks. "The more open access, however, the more people use the woodland the greater the chance of it being self-policed."

Gustaf also said, "We have become a people so far removed from the natural that we no longer know our place in it."

Following Gustaf's example I now actively welcome all sorts of activities in woodland – from paintballing, off-roading, survival camps, orienteering, rope treetop adventure trails and ranger-led walks to fishing (where there are ponds as part of and rivers passing through the wood) and even mountain-biking.

I took real pleasure in collaborating with some hell-for-leather mountain-bikers in laying out their tracks through a hillside wood. I even, recalling Ian having to sleep in the back of his estate, arranged for a standpipe and a portaloo to be sited by the carpark.

"We have to offer more than shelterbelt-cum-wildlife corridors," I tell Dez. But the man's a reactionary purist. I now realise why he used to exasperate Gustaf so.

* * *

Before ever I step a working foot in new woodland I will have checked to see if the local council's strategic plan includes the woodland. I will also have done a search for local covenants, rights of way and commoners' rights – their being allowed to take firewood for instance. Shooting rights, even mining rights – as in the Forest of Dean. (In what was only a small wood, and because he hadn't thought them likely to exercise their rights, Gustaf had ended up in a three-year legal tussle with a mining company.) I will also have checked out the 'wayleaves and easements' of the utility companies, that is their rights of access and passage for overground cables and underground pipes.

We avoid anywhere that has an historical/archaeological interest, which would necessitate even more consideration/consultation than the topical and geological. Even then, though there may be nothing of known historical note in the few hectares, that's not to say that the past will not have breathed over the terrain. Often there will be a few broken bricks, one gatepost, odd-shaped stones, a corner too obviously squared... Events beyond recall, requiring an educated guess, but one that might result in a recategorisation of the land. So a guess best kept to ourselves.

Then, once I've used the GPS to map out the boundaries of the newly acquired woodland, Frederic, Sylvia and I will go about digging soil pits to assess what type of soil where.

We're wary most of all of coming across ironpans, that thin impermeable layer of minerals that will restrict root development and water flow. If we even so decide to go ahead with planting such a virgin site Frederic will come back with the digger and break up the layer with ditches.

I then make regular visits to the new site to ascertain what's growing there, and round and about, and in which season. I've gone way beyond identifying hedgerow trees by leaf, bud and bark, now I reel off their Latin names in time with my stride.

What is always a worry, when I go back to check on a new site in autumn, is to discover a rising water table. A winter spent in water will kill off any roots developed over summer.

As well as the geology I look to any existing trees for the prevailing wind, and have learnt to keep an eye out for honey fungus and butt rot.

Once we're satisfied with the acquisition we have to decide what nurse species to use... Which is where the real debates begin, every professional having their own preference. Mine is always for silver birch, such an all round pretty tree from its white bark to the massed purple of its twig ends, its twinkling heart-shaped leaves.

By this time I will also have been in touch with any local woodland campaigners, future volunteers, to see what they want of any woodland, chary always of any tendency to over-management, a too tidy woodland leading to a lack of bio-diversity.

Most of our debates will have taken place not in the woods, but back at headquarters. With us having to decide what demonstrable 'public benefit' is likely to get us a Forestry grant – the most exhausting and nerve-wracking part of the whole process.

* * *

What I most like to do these days is make tours around our present woods. To simply pull up in the van and take a walk, on and off the beaten track, find myself again enclosed by the scents and colours of spring, or the cool green light of summer, or the comfortable rustling of autumn. Even to be among the dark naked bones of woodland's winter, wet-shined trunks like so many onyx pillars, fat drops thudding onto the van's roof.

A participant in the calendar rituals of country life every season brings its tasks and its joys. What, for instance, could be better than to be in oak woodland, full summer, with small gobbets of sunlight disappearing into lakes of bowed-over bracken and a slim green frog going by leaps ahead of me to my work? My work... I am now the one stood in shallow summer streams and building bridge piers with a new volunteer passing me rocks.

What could be better in summer? Unless it's to be wandering among tall hillside pines and pausing to breathe in the resin-scent sweated-in white streaks from their rough-patterned bark. I can even find myself smiling to find, having shouldered aside close-packed prickly spruce, a single oak, its mosspainted boughs lapping up the light. As sensually pleasing is the occasionally shimmering birch. Or, a conifer/deciduous reversal, my delight in seeing as if for the first time the pink glow of a stand of Scots pines within an oak wood.

High summer I can easily spend a hapless hour contemplating the patchwork of lichens on an ash's grey trunk, marvelling at the way a blob of sage green laps up against an almost garish lemon yellow beside ribbons and spots of black.

I returned one summer to where we'd felled some old spruce and replanted with silver birch. The small green leaves of the young birch were hardly visible among the purple upon purple acre of head high foxgloves. And the whole of one September evening, until the blue of dusk drove me back to my van, I watched humming bird moths sipping nectar from some late honeysuckle trumpets.

* * *

Autumn often sees me assessing gale damage, chainsaw clearing paths of fallen boughs, on occasion whole trees.

Some visual satisfaction even in the post-storm damage,

the ground having been torn up, tilted root-held slabs of earth; or in the peculiar geometries made by trees snapped over at head height and lying one across the other.

Satisfaction too in sniffing the fungal rot of autumn, knowing that mycological symbiosis is busy at work underfoot, while I myself am as busy at work thinning ash saplings for all the world like small palm trees. And being autumn I glance up to see mist stealing in through the trees.

Walking back to the van, mist now closed in, I might stop in amazement at the sudden bright red of berry-laden mountain ash. And then again at a thin twisted bough sleeved in lurid green moss.

* * *

Most of our heavy work is done in the winter. Keeps us warm. That is when I'm not snow-dreaming out of my campervan windows. Though that's a rare few days. More often, fingers fat with cold clawed around the rubber of a secateur's handles and working on my own, I look up from my thinning/trimming to a single crow. And in winter it always seems to be a single crow, to be snow's more-than-black crow, and hunched in the white branches of a crooked ash. We two will have a conversation. Leastwise I will talk to the crow, while he will cast his harsh judgements elsewhere.

As well as pruning we will be coppicing and pollarding; and winter is when we fell those broadleaved trees that need to be brought down.

Here I find myself agreeing with Gustaf: the felling of old trees is both exciting and sad. The slow crash, the sudden increase in light, and with the ground icy we will have the horses in attendance. The weighty tread and chink-clink of their harness, the peppery smell and heat of them, along with the scent of fresh-cut wood and whiffs of chainsaw petrol exhaust.

And if the horses are there Jay's there, and probably the children too. Makes of the felling an event. Our breaths all asteam, a gathering of our woodland clan. With timber lorries manoeuvring in the carpark, because beech, cherry and sycamore have to be taken straight to the mill and storage. All will soon rot if left.

And thoughts of Gustaf are never that far away from any winter gathering:

> one bare oak among spruce
> an inverted cone of light

Then comes the lifting of spirits in even the coldest of Februaries; and I won't even have noticed that the dark will have dragged me down when I chance upon the first buds preparing to break into leaf.

> among snowdrops – white
> light flickers on ivy's dark
> geometric leaves

Springtimes I don't need to be led to delight in sycamore's sticky buds, or in the delicate whiskers of new larch and the green dappling of beech. I've even fed a workgroup a salad of tender beech leaves.

Although, with birds nesting, we don't do that much on the land in spring. Spring is when I get stuck into admin and, for a break, stock-taking the many board-storing depots that Gustaf had dotted about the country.

Spring is also when I usually first check out new sites.

We try not to take Grade 1 arable land. Although we'd rather Prospectus got it than some property developer. Generally though if we discover anyone else is interested in the purchase we let them have it, avoid bidding wars. We have woodland enough to manage and conscientious Prospectus trustees to answer to.

Springtime isn't all paper and spreadsheet drudgery. Some newish sites cry out for planting. Which will find me in another neglected corner of England and pausing, easing my back.

* * *

Our workgroups nowadays by and large require only direction and praise. Although we do still get among the helpers the GBP type, and they can be male or female, who are never so pleased as when they've got something to complain about. I used to watch them come into the café miserable and leave disappointed because everything was, if not perfect, OK.

The one recent discord that does come to mind though, and probably because of my own intemperate reaction, was with a sprightly Daily Mail reader who kept on saying, "Health and Safety," in a mock-resigned tone every time I reminded him to put his goggles back on, to stand behind the person using the chainsaw. "Health and Safety." I got so exasperated with his sneers I ended up shouting at him that the entrepreneur he so admired, Gustaf Eriksson, had been killed in a cellar bar precisely because of an absence of "…Health and Fucking Safety!"

In workgroups he was an exception. The only real awkward customers I regularly get to deal with these days are some of those who own land alongside Prospectus woodland. And persistent hunters.

The hunters are mostly those farm boys who like to shoot small things that move and who, when confronted with their trespass, say nothing but tote their guns and lift a lip at me country sly.

Can't say I'm a lover of farmer's surly sons and their guns, but am even less so of the Executive Weekend Country Sports Break and those landowners who make money from the year on year on shooting of pheasants.

When investigating new sites the minute I see blue feed barrels tied to trees I begin negotiating the removal of shooting rights. Where it was already allowed Gustaf had been ambivalent about hunting in Prospectus woodlands. Dez and I, and Jay especially, are against hunting for its own sake. So it is Dez and I who now, distasteful as it is to the both of us, who oversee the trapping and culling of grey squirrels. For this management task we try to take turn and turn about.

Even when Gustaf was leading the charge the public-conscience trustees had begun a policy of actively discouraging hunting. The occasional culling of deer and grey squirrel they see as a regretful necessity. Not, however, some Saturday shooter polishing his hired Purley and slaughtering hand-reared pheasants. This, however, looks to be an ongoing battle.

I've had to turn down offers that would have substantially added to Prospectus's coffers – providing we kept the wood fenced-off so no walkers would disturb the rearing of their pheasants. We declined the offer on no other, non-contentious, grounds than the Prospectus constitution has it that public access is a must in any woodland owned or managed by Prospectus.

The other side of this argument is that we get grief from anti-hunting groups over our deer and squirrel culls. Although even there, with Jay pressing all the time, Prospectus has become known for its preference for deer fences. Or "Prevention rather than cull," as Jay has it.

Fences not always being feasible, "Show us another way," is ever my negotiating stance. "If you want woodlands, and if you want Prospectus to manage those woodlands for public benefit, show us another way."

* * *

I'm not always so diplomatic. Sometimes it is only head-on confrontation that has any effect. One that requires me putting myself in harm's way. Unauthorised off-roaders for instance.

See me standing in a rutted track, mobile in hand calling the police, with trail bikes, 4x4s and silly jeeps ploughing to a halt in front of me, their face-bloated drivers railing at me that they're legally entitled to drive there, to play there. While I, representing Prospectus, know stubbornly different.

It is not pleasant being shouted at, being sworn at and

being threatened. In the autumn silence that followed the latest set-to, the engines all gone, I wandered along the chewed-up track breathing deep to slow my racing heart, and I hung a step to listen to the graceless dropping, the rattling down fall of curl-edged sycamore leaves.

* * *

Finally, and as sly as the farm boys but who don't seek confrontation, although they still have to be seen off, are the lathe turners and furniture makers quietly scouting our woodlands for fallen oak.

I have some sympathy with them: their objective is to produce something. Trees though are our crop and need paying for. As I point out to those who, having been caught red-handed still try to wheedle some wood out of me, theft is theft.

* * *

With both children in full-time education, and Dez now involved with the Centre, Jay has taken on a bigger role. It's Jay and I now who give talks, who induct putative tree-huggers. Sylvia and Frederic can answer follow-up questions, but their English isn't yet up to delivery of our woodland spiel.

When delivering that spiel I've got in the way of quoting Gustaf. Just as often I make up the quotations. Which can have Jay looking at me sideways.

Jay and I get on well though, both of us concerned this last couple of years for Titan, who is pretty much on his last legs but somehow keeps going. Jay's not sure how Herbert will take to a third horse, so is waiting for Titan to go, in the meantime keeping a weather eye open for a likely replacement.

* * *

preoccupations, perils and compensations of -century forester. I should say pleasures as well, because it pleases me no end when we acquire a pocket of land next to another, unite them, and carry paths through. And with the government always looking to sell off a responsibility, and Prospectus eager to take it on, we're happily busy.

I'm not making a political point, just saying that's how it is these days. I've never had any interest in politics, in the politics of our bullshitting politicians that is. Theirs is a world which most of us know is corrupt, but a world beyond our reach. So we get on with our own lives best we can, not believing the politicians but voting when we get the chance.

I suppose I am political now. In that I join each and every campaign that will allow more trees to be planted... Me campaigning... I grew up wanting something beyond myself that I could believe in. Here I've found it.

"The trees will always win," Gustaf used to say. "When humankind has done its worse, has wiped itself out, has left nothing but desert and swamp, then slowly, very slowly, the planet will correct itself. Where trees have hung on in hedgerows and marshland, or their roots were twisted into rock cracks on crags and have stayed out of reach of our sheep and goats, then once we're gone, taking our husbanded sheep and goats with us, then the trees will begin to spread out over the barren moor and heath. Berries of juniper, rowan and yew will repopulate mountainsides. Wind will blow willow and birch seed from out the swamps. Elsewhere seeds that have lain dormant for centuries will sprout. And trees will gradually re-colonise the land, creating each their own microclimate, and extending it. While we, the damaging species, will be long gone. The trees will win."

* * *

A hedgerow beech,
fagus sylvatica, sun-scarred
on its southern flank.

Sixty-six

Rowan, *sorbus aucuparia*, also known as mountain ash, is a robust and prolific species of small tree requiring little encouragement from the woodsman. This self-seeding pioneer species, overlooked for most of the year, come early autumn, and be it among the dark green of spruce or the white pillars of birch, a berry-laden rowan will positively glow. (Every year that I've known her Jay takes rowan's orange-to-red berries, mixes them with hawthorne and hips, and she makes an excellent jam, which is on the tart side but perfect on breakfast toast.)

Not a big tree, but persistent and thus often the only tree growing on upland heaths, the mountain ash has been misnamed 'ash' I believe because of the similarity to the compound leaf of the ash. Although there any likeness ends. Actually rowan's are not so much leaves as the slim tree's green plumage, delicate-fern-like fronds.

Others hold that rowan takes its name from the Norse 'røn' or the Gaelic 'ruadhan', the latter meaning 'the red one'. Some books suggest that the Norse 'røn' may have become confused with 'rune', Norsemen having carved their runic alphabet into the only wood then available to them – rowan.

It was these runic symbols that probably led to the many superstitions associated with the rowan. Of no real practical value this small tree got planted next to houses – to protect the inhabitants from witchcraft. And on May Days it was the tradition to hang sprays of rowan leaves over doors and around wells to thwart evil. While in some parts of Britain rowan twigs tied with red thread into equal-armed crosses were supposedly talismanic. Druids used both bark and berries of the rowan to dye their robes black – those being the robes used during their lunar ceremonies.

Another Gaelic name for rowan is 'caorunn', the Welsh 'cerddin'. That rowan grows easily on any soil and has these superstitions attached must also contribute to its having become so widespread. Because rowan wood isn't of much use. Only in the harshest of environments, the remote Highlands of Scotland for instance, will rowan wood get made into tool handles and wooden spoons. And where yew was unavailable the longbows were made of rowan.

Sixty-seven

Most human activities are predicated on the assumption that life goes on.
Haruki Murakami

I have a lot to thank Gustaf Eriksson for. Not only did he give me Hazel, and a love of woodland, but it was one of his casual remarks that got me writing this. Not long after we first met he'd been talking to someone – don't think it was Hazel – and he said that when he had a knotty problem he tried to untangle it on paper.

That was the start. One of the starts. Because the writing of this has been an ongoing education in itself. For instance I've discovered that I think differently with a pen in my hand. I've become convinced that the holding of a pen actually changes my thought processes. I may well start off knowing what I'm going to write; but once that bit is written the pen takes over... and I'm left frowning at words, at concepts new to me.

The self-education doesn't stop there. Because when it comes to gathering up my notes – my life one long *memento mori* – and tapping them into my laptop, I might come across something that in writing I took for granted but which could be easily lost on a reader, may even have been lost on my forgetful self. I then educate myself by adding an example, a for instance, which of itself may require another explanation.

A for instance could depend on where I was when the note was first made, what train of thought led to it, what event led to that train of thought... And where I happened later to be parked up, what was beyond the van windows when fitting that note into this laptop story of a life...

What was written/typed for instance when I stopped over in a Dorset wood, left a van window cracked open and suffered a plague of crawling flies? Or when I'd made a friend of a carpark crow: the twist of his head, black eye looking to see if there was to be another crust lobbed his way; or was this thrower of crusts to embark on yet another telling titbit tapped into her laptop?

And what was written in a lay-by I impulsively pulled into, somewhere between there and there, under a long hump of a hill, spruce plantation thrown over it like a velvet green tablecloth; and I stayed there for two days, the wash of cars' wet tyres whooshing by, while I tapped and tapped and tapped...

Another carpark. Well a turning space for timber lorries in a larch plantation. I looked up at a sudden cackling from several magpies...

An unleashed Labrador had cornered a fledgling crow. The fledgling was hissing up at the dog, who was uncertain what to do with this unexpected find. Parent crows were swooping down, even the magpies dropping lower and lower to chatter furiously at the dog. The desperate parent crows dipped so low that they even hit the dog's back and head, finally driving him off. A parent crow persuaded the fledgling up into a tree.

I returned to my tap-tap-tap.

And back at the flat – printed sheets laid out over the bed, carpet and living room floor – came the reordering, rewriting parts to make some kind of sense. For instance the very first couple of pieces I wrote – from Hazel and the doctor's point of view, wrote as Ian leading up to his crash – were solely an attempt to put myself in their shoes. First attempts didn't work. I wrote them again. And again, fighting against what the rhythms in the sentence wanted me to say, and which took me away from what I was trying to describe. So I wrote them again, each time becoming aware of my bias, going back and changing bits.

I must have written the whole of Ian's crash at the very least eight times. Each one a vastly different version.

Book or no book the past doesn't leave me alone. For instance I had been parked up there for two days before I belatedly recognised the one-time rhododendron carpark. The noticeboard was a little worse for wear, the laminate yellow and cracked and there was some washed-away graffiti. I stood looking down at it; and for all that has followed I thanked Hazel.

Then I had a month of passing by the regrown hedge where Ian had crashed.

* * *

I began all this writing wanting to know more of my Hazel, and so keep more, what I could, of my Hazel. I've ended up knowing more of myself. Which is no bad thing. That is if what Anne Enright said in *The Gathering* is true: "The truth. The dead want nothing else. It is the only thing they require."

And that is what I've tried to give my Hazel, the truth. But I'm no Anne Enright and I feel that I've failed at most every turn.

Have all these thousands of words brought me to an understanding of my only daughter? No. Not in the sense that they have got me closer to her. Nor has that understanding brought her back to life in any way. Which was the magical result I think I wanted.

It is you, reader of my imagining, that I have made more use of – in learning what my own life has been about – because I have only been able to look through you at my own life. Like you I am here between nothing and nothing, in this brief space of our knowing.

* * *

This, now a book, has been one long argument with myself. Of discovery too, sudden realisations having me look up from the page, from the laptop screen – right now at a weed-grown clearing marked off with the red lumps of tree stumps.

But with my eyes wide open now at the illusions we all pursue – love affairs, careers, fashions, diversions – and which become a whole life, a life of seeming substance, yet all came from accidents of meeting, from misadventures, decisions often based on misinformation, at best on what we didn't know at the time but we justified back then by our own creative rationales…

And one realisation follows another – that I must have spent the first half of my life conjuring up various scenarios of what it must be like to be old. All based on my then circumstances. While this latter part has had me trying to recall what it was like to be young. We truly are never where we are.

Life's many absurdities. Just lately I've been thinking a lot about my sister. The bright one. Shining bright. Her future held out as a promise. Always to be favoured. Only it didn't happen. She ended up with an unfaithful, bulldozer of a husband, was pressured to stay in the marriage by her parents. (Leastwise I presume so. My mother anyway.) And I think how lucky this dull sister was to have been given zilch expectations. Consequence being that I was able to judge everything on its there-and-then merits, not by how it met with my promise.

Even so I have spent much of my adult life in one long reaction against my childhood (adult complicating factor vaginal). Only now, at this late stage, do I do what I do for its own sake. Am at last my own woman.

Awake I tell myself that. My dreams though are still haunted by that childhood, its unaged people and its unchanged rooms. Which isn't unique to me. According to other people my age, and older, it seems that one's childhood is something that one never completely escapes. Good or bad it will chase us through our dreams.

I might wonder about my sister, but my own past has come to seem less and less real. Memories disappear like sounds. Which makes it strange that I, with so much death in my life, should now be noting the effects of longevity.

* * *

This book has become a recording, a reordering, a replaying of a life. A life that was once locked to kitchen ritual and café routine. I had thought to free myself, once Hazel had left home, by ditching Ian. What I'd been looking for though had not been freedom as such but to bring meaning to my life. And that is the life that I've been trying to explain here. Not Hazel's.

Although I can quote her infant mispronunciations, her amusing childish misapprehensions, can cite silly things she did in her growing up – in my company that is – I didn't know my daughter. Always she was an enigma to me. I never felt truly close to her, and the bigger she grew the further she grew from me. Although, another mystery, she didn't seem to think so.

Mystery upon mystery. As her mother I had to know her better than anyone, and hardly at all. Always she surprised me. And I loved her for it.

She has left nothing written for me. In everything I've had to guess at her intent. If she had one – other than the obvious.

Was Hazel that complex that she defies understanding? I don't think so. My Hazel was simply a good woman, a woman who would rather think well of someone than ill. But by no means a prig. She certainly laughed out loud at my more scabrous judgements.

Or could it be Gustaf that all my writing has been trying to get to the bottom of?

In a Sussex wood I recently came across a handpainted board beside one of the informal paths. It said, 'Please listen to the trees'. And I smiled thinking that Gustaf would have loved that. He would probably not have approved of the board being nailed to a living tree; but the sentiment would certainly have appealed.

Many conversations with him, overheard, actual and memory-embellished replay in my head.

"Trees are a truth repeated," he said, "in a thousand forms."

Much of what he said to Hazel too, and she related to me, in writing it down made more sense than when first heard. Kinds of sense.

I think of Gustaf at times as an ex-lover of mine. He wasn't. Ours was another kind of intimacy, of a kind probably never known by his actual lovers, from whom secrets had to be kept.

No, Gustaf too was who he was, was what he did. No mystery.

* * *

Life at times can be one mess of contradictions. Especially when one struggles to make sense of it.

For instance I was tempted to say that it is harder to write about those still alive than those dead and neatly parcelled into the past. I was thinking of Dez, who still has the capacity to surprise me by acting out of the character I have given him. But no-one dead or alive can be packaged that neatly: Hazel continues to live in me, her past there to be continually reappraised.

What has surprised me is just how many people have gone to make up just this one life. I've had to leave out many, met and unmet (fantasy friends) because it would have all become too confusing, would have been to obscure rather than to enlighten. At one stage I even considered going back over the text to enter details of individual trees, characters in their own right, such as today's grizzled birch hung with a ragged curtain of jade green lichen. And for the reason above I decided against.

Now I've reached the point where I no longer know quite why I'm writing this. Nor do I now know why it once seemed quite so important to collect all these self-agonised scribblings together into book form. It doesn't now feel as if it has been for my benefit. But if not for mine, whose?

In my mind justifications for writing and planting have become confused. Picking over this garbage planet for places to plant trees' picking over this heap of old jottings in search of a complete sentence worth saving here, a part-phrase there, a brown field site, a boggy corner of a field...

What I still want to do, if not change the world, is to at least explain it. If I'd realised, however, that when I began writing, so long ago now, that this book would get this big and take so long to complete I'd have called it 'The Book of the Coming Dead'. Which would have been inaccurate: mine has never been a morbid wish-fulfilment. Rather I have happened to find myself an habitué of death.

Which by no means makes me an authority on death. I simply now know what it is to be around death, some deaths. And sadness still does overwhelm me sometimes. Then, part of a work group say, I hear myself laughing and I wonder how. But, and I hope I'm not stating the obvious, I do not know what it is to die.

Life is what I know and it seems that is what I have tried to tell. And in any life work has to figure. Work defines us, the work we choose, how that work occupies our days and thoughts. I ran a café and latterly a woodland charity.

Latterly... it was coming among oaks centuries old that put mine and Hazel's life into perspective. Picking one's way through forests and jungles has to create self-awareness; and once working here I could see why Hazel had taken such comfort from the stubborn age of trees.

Being within woodland brings home to one how very strange this human life is. In any wood now I know that I am being watched – by any number of creatures, most of whom are afraid of giant me. So do I watch myself; and I tread carefully.

* * *

This last decade and more I've had two lots of work to occupy me, the writing of this and Prospectus. And the important thing for me has always been having something to do, not belonging.

Belonging is so transient. One grows into a family, out of it. I belonged to Hazel as she briefly belonged to me. Dez and Jay are their own unit. For the time being.

Prospectus though has offered me more than just work. When all those closest to you, those who shared a part of your life, have died it truly is a comfort to be among trees older than you will ever be. And like you, however, I am of no great consequence. I only have to stand on the edge of mixed woodland for the twig ends, the hooked fingers of an aged ash to beckon me in; and to know that when wandering those woodland paths one tree will stand out from all the others. Walk on, look back, and that tree will be as all the others.

* * *

Prospectus continues to take me all over the country. I had the new campervan painted a drab green – to avoid shining out like a beacon and attracting the curious and those officious guardians of public spaces. This green van has now become as well known as Gustaf's yellow pickup had once been. Houses I've lived in have been characterless, but one drab green campervan has become me, the container of one smelly old woman carting about the puzzle of herself.

In my own odd way I do belong to people again, as once I did in that other life to the café, Hazel and Ian. Ben and Jen call me Granny Two. Both decided independently that I would not be Nan Two. Another puzzle. They themselves probably don't know why. Probably can't remember. They used to call my other van, Gran's Van, would beg to be allowed to come away with me. Until Nan Emma had a jealous weep. Ben's a young man now. Jen has left puberty behind but has yet to co-ordinate her arms, legs and torso into a coherent whole.

Nowadays I only stop at the Centre out of necessity, prefer my out of the way places.

I've come to love the way the pale greys of early morning filter through the trees, streak themselves across the skies. And as I slowly rouse myself – that early there's no hurry – I watch the small birds, the finches and robins, start their day. They have no expectations that it will be as the day before. Food sources will be according to season. A gale may have blown down a tree. All will change. As it does for humans. Except that I foolishly wasted all those years with Ian wanting my world to be unchanging, to be safe; and blamed him for it being the same old same old. Now no more do I seek security, just an occasional point of rest.

* * *

For company I sometimes give people lifts. A man with red number plates on his way back from delivering a car. He talked about cars and driving. A stranded salesman recently made redundant tried to talk me into giving him a job. A soldier's mother, lost, talked with wonder about her teenage son, not sure what she knew about him.

Interesting encounters, nothing more. I don't seek relationships now. My heart stopped being a heart in the sentimental sense decades ago. At least so far love goes, sensual love that is. The bodily organ I'm happy to report still goes on beating, counting down the years.

* * *

I can go weeks now without physical contact with another human being. Not like when I was in the café. There people were forever accidentally/incidentally touching me – giving me their money, bumping against me as they, as I passed... Now it's a notable event when a worker taps my shoulder, a newcomer shakes my hand...

I don't miss it; have decided that I don't need human

touch. I can put my hand flat to an aged sycamore, smile a hello. Which is not to say, fond as I am of certain old trees, that I have a sentimental attachment to trees as a whole. Be like a farmer becoming attached to his beef herd.

Nonetheless, where the only people I will have seen for weeks on end will have been country strollers or a well-meaning work group, it's still a shock for me to come out of the woodlands to do some shopping among the litter-dropping Great British Public. Or, a similar shock, I arrive at a site to find fly-tipping – fridges, cookers, tyres, builder's rubble... (Fly-tipped because the local council has made rubbish disposal too complicated/expensive for the simpler/poorer/meaner minds of the Great British Public?)

In such cases I put in a call to the Centre and, depending on the amount, Jay will come with Ben and the horse wagon or Frederic and Sylvia will bring the new pickup, and we will cart the rubbish along to the nearest tip. On a couple of the new sites Frederic has dug pits and we have buried all the rubbish.

* * *

Since Gustaf's death, and the extra money that came subsequent to it, Prospectus has expanded too quickly. Our holdings have become too widespread. We're now considering setting up permanent outposts and having them staffed by rangers. Instead of this one old woman – this smelly old woman gone weeks without a bath – infrequently turning up in her travelling home to tell the local volunteers they're doing it all wrong.

Although mine was a long induction into silviculture, being a recent convert I have become the keener – keener and less flexible than even Dez on some aspects of forestry.

My being zealous is not to say that I'm of the temperament than can unselfconsciously take up causes as Gustaf did. I have no public persona that can parade behind banners. But I can plant trees. And be in no doubt, I am 100% behind Prospectus.

I am just so grateful. Through Prospectus the world has opened to me. The very – I hesitate to say it – root and branch basics of this world. What trees grow where depends not only on the geology, but on the altitude and the local climate. How close the sea...? So much I had to learn, still so much I have to learn, always something new. So much undone, so much to do. Our aim now is that wherever bracken grows there we will plant trees. Trees and bracken in England are natural companions, bracken without trees like cream without peaches.

It is because of Prospectus that my brain now has me think globally, as in sphere, as in orb. I actually see where we are on this planet when the northern hemisphere's low winter sun places shadows and stretches its yellow light across a woodland's copper-crusted floor...

Thinking globally, and despite our present difficulties in overseeing all our woodlands, I'm determined not to confine Prospectus to the treeing of England. If genuine opportunities should arise in other countries then we will go there too. On a personal level why confine ourselves to this cold and wet country? Why not doze away an afternoon to the buzz of cicadas?

Considerations of comfort aside we really do need to tree the world. We need to plant trees along the edges of the deserts that mankind has made and, hectare by hectare, tree back towards the desert's centre. A world reforested, healed.

Trees are the corrective the planet needs. Not only for the absorption of CO^2, not only for the production of O^2, not only for improving the soil, but because the rate of a tree's growth makes us human beings look beyond our own life-spans. Among trees we are more likely to look beyond our own time to what came before and what may come after.

* * *

I'm not that zealous that I actually tell the locals they're doing it all wrong. A bit short with them sometimes. I'm just so tired. I know why I'm planting more trees. I know why I want more trees planted. So obvious to me, why isn't it to everyone?

The future is daily becoming more perilous, dirty, tainted – tainted by all that once were just oddball's forecasts, weirdoes' predictions – carbon dioxide pollution, rising sea levels, erratic climate, pesticide misuse, nuclear waste, not thought-through genetic modifications... Science in the hands of politicians is coming up with no answers only complications. So what can Prospectus do but single-mindedly continue to plant trees?

Like people some of those trees will die. fifty years and more since Dutch elm disease wiped out England's mature elms. I say 'mature' because elm roots still send up suckers and elms continue to grow here, if not yet to any great height. One day... one day elm will beat the disease. This I know. Only for the individual is death an end; life in general and as a process goes on. And the space occupied by every once-life will be filled.

In any woodland each tree fills its space right up to the edge of the next tree, and the next fills its space, each tree filling its space right up to the edge of the next tree, and the next, each filling its space...

Trees... my base measure.

Midway through a morning amble I often find myself crouching to study, forgetting the age in my hips and knees, a seedling pushing up through the fresh soil of a mole hill, or the shoot and root together emerging from a split conker that has forced itself up out of the leaf mould.

Groaning upright, almost upright, I will nonetheless give a grunt of approbation at this persistence of life. Myself included in that approval, that I am still here to witness this persistence. And I will go shuffling on, happily repeating to myself,

"Life. Life. Life. Life. Life."